Victoria

By

A. A. von Dessauer.

Victoria

Cover by Kndesign www.kndesign.net

Edited by Angel Editing www.angelediting.com

www.edgeoftheweb.net

Victoria is dedicated to,

Marisa.

Without whom Vicky may have never set sail.

Prologue

There was a time when things weren't looking too good for humanity. A brief moment in the annals of history where it could have gone either way, where each man, woman, and child was asked a simple question. Can you adapt? In those times there were a million tales of triumph and tragedy. But I think none illustrate the times so eloquently as the story of Victoria, the little tug that could.

The test of humanity began with The Good Samaritans' Message. A broadcast sent to all who were listening from a people long since extinct. The message came in sections, each approximately seventy-two minutes long, that where repeated hours later. After a few days, the next section would arrive. It continued like that for four and a half years. The broadcasts were so strong that they disrupted communications on Earth until engineers adapted to them. The message was designed to be understood; the first few sections were a primer meant to teach the recipient the language of the message. After that, the heart of the communication began. The messengers described themselves in this way – as best as could be translated.

"We are good Samaritans who wish to provide all with our wisdom." They described their world and their people. They offered their philosophy and spiritual beliefs. They passed on information about technologies and sciences. They described other worlds and other worldly people they had met. Most importantly, they sent a warning – a warning about the species that was the catalyst for the broadcast. A ravenous species of raiders called the Talc.

The Samaritans described the Talc as a predatory species which had a lust for the kill. They would ravage dead worlds for resources and steal technology, but they attacked primarily for the pleasure of it – for the sport. The Samaritans system was being invaded by the Talc. They were being overcome and hoped to find allies before their demise.

This message was not lost on the people of Earth. A people that often times define themselves most clearly in the light of adversity.

A war that spanned the entirety of the globe had just come to an end. Often referred to as 'The Armageddon', it was the last and bloodiest war fought on Earth. It almost overcame the world. Several hundred million people died, and the aftermath was political turmoil that nearly cast the world to war again. It was then that the message arrived. Leaders from around the world conceded in ways never thought possible. A peace unlike the human world had ever known came to be. No person could ignore the information presented by the Samaritans. No person could be coy about its final sentence.

"They will come."

Chapter One
It's About Time

Sometimes in life there are moments of clarity which bind together the indecisive chaos of change; moments that illuminate purpose where none seems to be. Thorbin was having such a moment.

He had lost himself completely in its design. Sitting comfortably in the cockpit, he was having his moment. The filtered air was clean and cool, infusing him with a feeling of vitality in every breath. The stainless consoles felt smooth and refined, seamless and efficient as he ran his fingers across them. The seat held him firm by molding itself comfortably around him, giving him a sense of safety and freedom. Everything in the pit had been placed in exact accordance with his piloting style. One finely crafted weapon designed solely for him to wield so that the enemies of humanity could know their wrath. Years of sacrifice, pain, discipline, and resolve had led to this prize. He was the best of the best, better than one in a thousand, a pilot that the elite called great. It was the first time he had acknowledged his success on a spiritual level, and he was lost in its design.

Minutes passed before he was interrupted by Charles gently knocking on the canopy. He swayed his head out of his euphoria and looked at his friend through the glass. Charles was smiling, enraptured with enthusiasm and bantering on with glee despite Thorbin not being able to hear a word he was saying. Thorbin hit the canopy release, and the glass slid back with a soft *whoosh*, caressing his cheeks with a gentle breeze.

The outside environment quickly shattered the remaining euphoria. Frightening it away with the warning buzzers from taxies towing fighters into position, signal lights blurring past as birds were catapulted from the deck, that being closely followed by the roar of the turbines. All this was accompanied by an army of jet mechanics and ballistics engineers married by cadence as marines beat their feet in perfect unison as they drilled. All this and Charles was still going on in vain.

Thorbin looked purposely at his friend, pointed to his ears and smirked. Charles smiled again and helped Thorbin out of the cockpit.

They waded their way through the choreographed havoc to a hatch that led off the carrier's main flight deck. Once there, Charles could finally be heard.

"That was amazing!"

"Perfect," Thorbin answered with subtle delight.

"She's a killer. Modified missile systems, advanced NAV and controls, including the new neural interface. All you have to do is think and she'll move!"

"Yeah, she's a killer, Charles. I'll see you at the brief."

"OK, don't be late, T."

Thorbin's heart thrust blood wildly through his veins. He walked slowly back to his quarters, pacing himself to allow the adrenaline to settle. He entered his Spartan bunk and sat on his bed. He allowed his head to fall back then guide his body to the mattress. He stared at the ceiling until an old picture he had tacked to the wall caught his eye. His father stared back at him with a contented smile surrounded by his squad mates in front of a proud F-32.

"I did it, Dad," he said to the picture.

He reflected a bit longer then spoke aloud, being sure to enunciate clearly.

"Open com link."

An inoffensive female voice responded, "Com link open."

Thorbin cleared his throat.

"I'm sorry, I don't know who that is. Could you repeat the name of the person you wish to call?" the automated system responded.

Thorbin's itchy throat croaked.

"Mika."

"I'm sorry I don't know who that is. Please hold while I transfer you to a com link specialist," the automaton responded again.

"My wife, damn it!" he said as he tried one last time before he was transferred.

"Thank you for calling com link. This is Yahanoss, how can I help you today?"

"Hello, I'm just trying to call my wife."

"Mika Monroe, sir?" the man asked.

"Yes," Thorbin confirmed.

"I'm connecting you now, sir. Have a nice day."

Thorbin watched the video screen, waiting for Mika to answer. The monitor turned on and displayed the words 'No video'.

"Hey, sweetie," Mika answered.

"Are you at home?" Thorbin asked, curious to know why there wasn't video.

"Oh, I couldn't get to the phone. What's going on, hun?"

"We just finished a run. What are you doing that you can't get to the phone?"

"Mmm," Mika teased. "You caught me. I was taking a bubble bath all naked and soapy, thinking about you."

"Wow," Thorbin gulped. "Really?"

"No," she giggled. "I just finished taking Agies for a walk."

"Tease."

"It's not my fault you're not here."

"Two more days and this week's tour is over."

"I'll keep the bubbles warm," Mika said, then her tone changed to frustration. "Oh no!"

"What's going on?" Thorbin asked.

"Agies is in the cat liter again. Agies, no!"

"How's she been doing?"

"The vet said it'll take her a while to adjust, otherwise still all cute and puppyish."

"OK," Thorbin said, taking note of the time. "I should go. I just called to say I love you."

"Love you too, sweetie. Agies, no! Don't eat that! I gotta go, love you!"

"Love you." And then the call abruptly ended. Thorbin collected himself and headed to the briefing room.

He made his way back towards the main flight deck until he came to a door that read 'Alpha, The beginning of the end.' He entered and was greeted by Charles, who led him to a table where he had already started going over the schematics and data from the last flight.

He had spread out papers on the table and was bombarding Thorbin with techni-speak. Thorbin was paying just enough attention so as not to be rude. As Charles prattled on, Thorbin's vision was drawn to two pictures hung in opposite corners of a whiteboard. The picture on the far left was of a DC F-41 Peregrine, so named because it was the fastest fighter Earth had ever produced.

"They really haven't changed much, have they?" he asked right in the middle of Charles's reporting.

"What? I realize the change wasn't noticeable, but the new NI is a great addition."

"No, not that," Thorbin said, then nodded to the pictures. "Our birds aren't really all that different from the ones our fathers flew." Charles looked up at the pictures.

"Are you kidding? Are you seriously comparing our Peregrines to the old Super Raptors? They're turn of the century technology – last century. Don't get me wrong, they ruled the skies and all, but it's a far cry from ruling orbit. The original design was fuelled by liquids," Charles said with a laugh. "Not the ones our fathers flew in the war, but still."

"The design I mean. The overall style. The spirit."

Charles took a hard look at the picture. "Yeah, I suppose they look a lot alike, but the insides…completely different."

"Still a human pilot," Thorbin pointed out.

Charles agreed in silence, and their common gaze drifted to the second picture – a popular artist rendition of what a Talc fighter looked like.

Unlike the streamlined Euro-American designs of Earth fighters, the Talc vessels had an eerie organic presence. Instead of being shinny black or silver, they were dull grays and greens and had no sense of symmetry. They were a jumble of rounded, unbalanced, natural shapes. Apparently no two were the same according to Mosot accounts. Their design looked confused, even straining to the eye. In comparison to Earth aircraft they looked very inferior; an odd contrast to the apparent reality that they were the backbone of a navy that destroyed worlds.

Destroyed worlds, Thorbin thought. Certainly they destroyed the Good Samaritans. Their home world had over one and a half million different species on it according to the last message, all of them extinct now. If not for the message, no one would have ever known of their existence. He wondered how many other planets had been destroyed and were now completely lost, even to history.

Thorbin's mind wandered still as Charles turned back to his original analysis. The thought 'lost to history' was still with him as he took notice of Tom as he entered. Tom was different. He was a small man in comparison to the other pilots. In fact, he was a small man in comparison to other men his size. To be clear, Tom was male but not a man, or a least not human. Tom wasn't even his given name. His true name was unpronounceable for the human tongue, just as the name 'Tom' couldn't be spoken in his natural state. Tom's people, however, the Mosot, had two distinct and fortunate abilities that allowed them to endure, despite losing their home world to the Talc. They had the fascinating ability to increase or decrease the whole, or a part, of their body mass by a fraction. This attribute allowed the Mosot to change their verbal abilities and enabled them to speak human languages. The second ability was a mild form of empathy; most useful when first introduced to an alien species.

These combined natural talents helped them survive and adapt when they came into contact with other inhabited worlds. If they encountered a species that was threatening, they could sense the threat and change their appearance to seem intimidating to that species. If they encountered a species that was friendly, they could change their appearance to be pleasing in order to encourage hospitality.

Humanity being a diverse species, both physically and mentally, made Earth a comfortable place for the Mosot to hang their extraterrestrial hats. Most Mosot enjoyed social lives on Earth with prosperous careers in the fields of civics and humanities due to their inhuman ability to communicate.

Social lives, however, were key to their survival. Mild empathy comes at a cost. The ability of the Mosot to sense and express emotional states with each other creates a biological need to be social. If isolated, a Mosot could die from the stress of loneliness long before the ravages of hunger or thirst. Luckily, humans, while not empathic, are compassionate and capable of providing a Mosot more than enough social sustenance.

Tom had come to Earth almost eighty years ago when his vessel made contact with an exploratory ship. He was near death when his name's sake, a geologist named Thomas, found him and nursed him back to health. Tom then learned how to speak English and assisted the team for years until his adopted human father passed away. After that he came to Earth specifically to join the Defense Core.

Thorbin felt an intense kinship with Tom. Tom was a patriot. For the past few decades, humanity had been wholly dedicated to the impending fight with the Talc – the species that had destroyed Tom's ancestral home and threatened to destroy his adopted home as well. Their fight was the same, and Tom's soul was committed to the defense of that which he had come to love, and that which he loved but had never known. Like Thorbin, Tom was motivated by that which was greater than himself, which made this little man a big presence in the squad.

Thorbin smiled and his heart warmed with camaraderie amidst a backdrop of Charles's chattering, that was until a large man entered the room and sat next to them.

"Hey, Tank," Charles said, breaking away from his analysis.

The large man nodded then listened intently. Thorbin and Charles had only just met Tank, and they both agreed never to cross him. To say he was a large man didn't do his physical stature justice. He was massive, stood over seven feet tall and was as tough as he looked. His short graying hair was high and tight and blended downward into his constant five o'clock shadow. Often times he was loud and rowdy, but on occasion he was quiet. The kind of quiet only a true predator knows. His body was scarred from years of unknown peril; the most notable mark being the scar that ran up from his left check, disappeared under his left eye, and then continued above it. When he closed his eye or blinked, the scar completed itself. It was rumored that he had served time for murder, but it was just that, a rumor without foundation. No felon could ever be a test pilot. Still, the thought never left the realm of believability. Tank was a beast of a man.

Thorbin again caught himself losing focus on Charles and his analysis, so he re-centered his attention on what was being said. Charles, like most people, was very different to Tank and Tom. He was tall but not a giant. He was all muscle but not large. His gregarious attitude had been the key to their long friendship. Thorbin was quiet and not inclined to speak if there was nothing to be said. Charles, on the other hand, was not inclined to allow Thorbin the luxury of silence. They had become friends during their studies at Annapolis, then served as partners in the Constable Division of the Defense Core. Their friendship grew into brotherhood while pursuing pirates at the risk of life and limb. Charles had introduced Thorbin to Mika, and he had been the best man at their wedding. He even insisted on being the godfather of Thorbin's firstborn as soon as he and Mika accommodated.

"The Talc don't stand a chance," Charles concluded with his patented charismatic smile.

"Yup," Tank replied, nearly cracking a smile and with a glint in eye as if the fight had already occurred and he was reminiscing.

"Charles, have you ever really thought what it will be like when the invasion begins?" Thorbin asked.

"Well, they send an exploratory party. Then they move a fleet to the outer planets of the system. Then…."

"That's not what I mean," Thorbin interrupted.

"Have you ever thought about how…" He paused. His browed wrinkle as he was thinking carefully about how to express his meaning. "How the whole system will be dependent on us. If we fail, no more Earth. Not as we know it at least. Everything we care about will not only be gone, but won't even be remembered. It will just be a moment in an image that some Talc had behind his sights before he fired. Maybe not even that. We'll just be another destroyed species. While if we succeed, we will be the first to turn the tide. We'll be delivering vengeance for dozens of species – hell, millions if you count the wildlife in the systems too. We may even push them back to their system, and one day invade them, ridding everything from the threat of their existence."

Tank turned and looked Thorbin right in the eye. He placed his right hand on his shoulder, stood there for a brief moment, then laughed.

"You damn rookies are just piss and vinegar," he said in between uncountable laughter. "Shit, man." He turned away, taking notice of the other pilots who had entered the meeting room. "Everything we care about," he mocked. "We'll be delivin' vennnngaaance." He laughed some more then got up to join another table.

Charles tried not to smile at Thorbin, who obviously didn't appreciate Tank's response.

"What?" Thorbin asked as he attempted to hide his embarrassment.

"A little dramatic," Charles said, trying not to add to Thorbin's discontent.

"When are they going to stop referring to us as rookies? We were in the Constable Division for seven years." Agitation was setting in.

"Relax, you'll be back in the bird tomorrow and everything will be just fine."

One by one all of pilots arrived and mingled as they waited for the debrief to begin. The squad's commander arrived with a handful of documents and immediately grabbed the attention of all the pilots. He continued on to the front of the room, set the paperwork on a folding table and conversations concluded while he organized the data he had set down. The commander furrowed his brow then lifted his gaze towards Tom.

"How long until I Day, Tom?"

"Four years three hundred and twelve days, sir."

"You ready for 'em, pilot?"

"Born ready, sir," Tom said with fire.

His commander smiled and gently replied, "Clear," which inspired an enthusiastic reply from the rest of the pilots.

"Clear!" they all affirmed in unison.

Commander Zellart then continued with the brief.

"Anyone notice anything unusual with the flight data?"

Charles, the only one who had actually looked over the data, responded. "No difference from the previous flight, sir."

"That's right, Jackson. Not bad," Zellart said, eyeing the rest of the room. "The firmware for the NI didn't upload properly. The last test didn't produce the desired results."

A young pilot from the back of the room spoke up. "We're going out again aren't we, Commander?"

"That's right, Chin, double shift today. We've got to get these results. The NI tuning is grossly behind schedule."

"When are we going back out?"

The commander looked at a clock on the wall.

"Thirteen hundred now, Engineering should have the firmware straightened out by fourteen. That gives you a short break, be suited up by fifteen thirty. Are we clear?"

"Clear!' the squad answered then headed out on a break.

True enough, Charles was right, when Thorbin strapped himself back into the cockpit, he felt fine. Better than fine, he was getting that feeling again – that sense that he was only complete when he was strapped into to a pair of wings. He grasped the controls, rolling his fingers into position and focusing ahead. The taxi released its rigging, and he was ready.

"You are clear to launch, Lieutenant Monroe," a voice from the traffic control announced.

"Affirmative, Five, four, three..." Thorbin counted and the anticipation mounted, "...two, one." He initiated the launch. His senses collided with the sudden burst of speed. One moment in the bosom of the carrier, kept warm by the glow of the industrious DC Navy, the next moment in the cold eternity of space.

Sam, a few days prior

Samantha Han was exhausted by the time she reached her studio high atop the Palameres Heights tower number one. It was about nine a.m. on Friday. The BART ride from San Francisco to her little place in Castro Valley was the perfect crappy ending to a crappy day. She generally enjoyed the ride home and had been looking forward to it. The daily train ride always felt like victory. But on this day she happened to be seated next to some rude teenage girls. She had caught the train that the high school kids in Oakland took to school in the morning, which was a perfect reflection of how long her Thursday had been. She wasn't certain, but she thought a twenty-four-hour workday was against the law. She must have been wrong.

She practically kicked her door down when it resisted her attempts to open it, then tossed her bag on the table in her studio and nearly tore her clothes off, letting them fall wherever they wished. She opened the only door inside her studio, which led to the bathroom, and stared into it. She really wanted to take a shower, but she wasn't sure if she wanted it more than sleep. She considered it for a moment.

If I take a shower, I could cry while I wash, she thought. *Two birds with one stone. I suppose I could shower and cry in the morning.*

Then from somewhere below her, a meow disturbed her train of thought, soon followed by a fury body flinging itself against her bare ankle. She looked down and smiled. It was one of her beloved kitties, Fat Boy. She inhaled with a sniffle and addressed the love of her life.

"You love me, don't you, Fat Ass?" But as she bent over to pick him up he bolted to the other side of the studio (which was only a few good-sized paces) and sat next to his food bowl looking at her. And that was it, the last straw. She decided she was going to take a shower and cry, so she went over to her futon, collapsed on the top of her blankets…and went to sleep.

Twelve hours later, a sound woke Samantha from her slumber – a terrible horrible sound that never failed to fill her soul with fear and anxiety, the phone. She tired to roll over and see who it was, but she was startled when Pickles (one of the other fury little beasts she resided with) complained about being rolled on. So instead, she sat up, said, "Hello?" and held her breath for the answer.

"Sammy?" asked her mother from the other side of the phone with a thick Korean accent. "Why you home? Friday night? I just leaving message."

"Mom, I'm always home on Friday nights, you know that."

"I know," her mother answered sharply. "That's why you don't have man. Man for making fat grandchildren."

"Mom, please," Samantha said, starting to cry. "Not today."

"Oh, honey," her mother said, changing her tone in accordance with Samantha's stress. "I'm sorry. What the matter?"

"You know how I finally got the project management position. I've been working really hard on it. I was at work all night Thursday until this morning, and everything hates me."

"Everything don't hate you," her mother consoled.

"Yes, it does. They didn't give me a raise. How can you get promoted without a raise? I'm never going to get out of this crappy studio."

"Yes, studio is crappy," her mother agreed tactfully.

"Then Karim over in marketing hit on me."

"Oh that good," her mother said enthusiastically. "What kind of name Karim?"

"He's married."

"Oh, that bad, but see, you very pretty girl."

"And Fat Boy won't stop being hungry."

"That because you feed him too much," her mother admonished, to which Sam smiled and looked over to the begging cat at the bowl. Then she mimicked her mother.

"You eat too much." And then she laughed.

"Good," her mother said. "You feel better?"

"A little bit," Sam answered.

"Now tell me good things."

"The project I'm working on is almost done. And it's not due for another month. That should impress Mr. Harris."

"Then you get raise," her mother interjected. "Burn crappy studio to ground."

"Yeah," Sam agreed. "To the ground!" she said with righteous indignation. "Is there any reason in particular that you called?"

"No, Sammy," the older woman answered. "Just calling to see if you found man for fat grandchildren."

"Sorry, Mom. No fat grandchildren machine yet."

"OK. Magnum PI on, talk later."

"Bye, Mom. Love you."

"Love you too, honey, go find man." Then she hung up.

Sam sat up and one by one her kitties accosted her for attention. There was Fat Boy, the first cat she brought home to the studio, and the largest; Pickles, the cat she got to keep Fat Boy company; and Kevin, the cat she got to keep Pickles company because Fat Boy wanted to be alone. They followed their fearless pride leader to the other side of the studio, where she fed them so they would shut up and leave her alone. Then she took a tear-free shower, put on some comfy clothes, warmed up some leftovers and tried not to think about work.

She got about halfway through her meal when the phone rang again. She picked it up with her mouth half full of nan and refried beans.

"Hewo?"

"Hey, Sam, this is Mr. Harris. Sorry to bother you at home on a Friday night."

Sam quickly swallowed and tried not to let the hot food going down come across in her voice.

"Oh, it's not problem, Mr. Harris. What's going on?"

"I'm really glad I caught you. I need to pull you off the ISO project."

"No!" Sam said instinctively, and then wished to God she could take it back.

"Umm," Mr. Harris said, taken aback by her tone. "Sorry, Sam, it's really important."

"Of course, I'm sorry, sir. It's just I'm almost done with ISO project."

"No kidding," Mr. Harris said, sounding impressed. "It's not even due for another month or so."

"I've been working hard on it." She again spoke instinctively, and she really hoped she didn't sound like she was kissing up.

"Evidently, and I really appreciate your hard work."

Not enough to give me a raise, Sam thought.

"Thank you, sir. So what's the new project?" she asked, crossing her fingers.

"It's a Defense Core contract," he said importantly. "This is a big deal, Sam. The company's been waiting to get a foot in the door of the DC for a long time. I really need someone I can count on."

"You can count on me, Mr. Harris," Sam said. *'You can count on me'?* she thought. *God, I am such a dork ass kisser.*

"Good. You'll be leaving for Mars in a few days."

"Mars?" Sam said, trying desperately not to let her concern creep into her voice.

Liz

Oh, how I hate Mars, Elizabeth thought as she sipped a bottle of water while sitting just outside one of the little cafés that dotted Armstrong Blvd. She was patiently waiting for a nervous little man who had entered the Foolish Digger (a tavern of sorts across the way) to exit with her prize. He was taking his time, which left Liz with nothing to do except hate Mars and think about her life.

When Liz was a little girl, she had been different. Not to say that she wasn't cute as a button in a white dress with her golden locks in ribbons and curls. She just had different ideas. When most little girls wanted nothing more than to be a princess or grow up to be a veterinarian, or president, Liz wanted to be a spy. Little Liz thought that was the 'bestest' most exciting job in world, and her heart was set on it. There was, however, a problem, her parents didn't want Liz to work for the government because they were criminals. Not petty criminals mind you; they were Syndicate – cream of the crop bad guys, wealthy, powerful, and evil. It's a shame really how parents can crush a child's dream. In time, however, she accepted her loss with grace and decided to become a thief.

So there, at a table, on one of the most famous streets in Mars she sat, waiting for her mark to exit. She wasn't sure what it was that she was stealing, but she was sure that the money offered for its acquisition caused her not to care. 'No questions asked' was kind of a mantra in her profession. Although, she was a little curious. She was being paid quite a lot, and the nervous little man she was waiting for was stealing it from a person who was also not the original owner.

Could this guy be any slower? she thought as she leaned back in her chair and stared at the city's cavernous roof. Her thoughts continued, *Why anyone would want to live on this shit hole planet is beyond me. Miners dig a hole in the ground and they call it a city.* Then from across the street her nervous little man reappeared. She stood and was about to cross when a deep Slavic voice encouraged her otherwise.

"Good morning, Elizabeth, please, sit."

Liz closed her eyes and felt like a fool. *How did I not see him coming?* she thought.

She then opened her eyes as she sat back down and spoke through false smile. "Dima, what are you doing here?"

Dima, a middle-aged man, who she supposed was Russian, stood confidently at the other side of the table. He wore an expensive gray suit with pockets that must have been very comfortable because his hands almost never came out of them. He was a popular man, never going anywhere without friends, like the two behind him, also looking sharp in their dark grays. He greeted her smile by nodding to one the men, who pulled out a chair a good distance from the table. Dima then, without removing his hands from his pockets, seated himself while the other two stood behind him like good dogs. After making himself comfortable he answered her while staring at the ground.

"Business. And why may I ask are you here, Elizabeth?"

"Just enjoying the sunshine," she answered merrily.

"Yes, Mars is beautiful this time of year." The two men behind him laughed respectfully. "My dear, I think perhaps you are following Rudolph. No?"

"Oh was that Ruddy? I didn't recognize him."

"It is," Dima said then looked at her for the first time, being sure to make very concise eye contact. "He's working for me. Did you know that?" Liz knew it and wasn't sure how to play this one, she had to answer and make sure the answer didn't offend. She took a sip of water.

"I heard that he might be, but I wasn't sure," she answered. Dima turn his gaze aside.

"Life must be treating you well, Earth water is very expensive here."

"Yes," she answered. Liz knew the change in topic meant the conversation was over. And the phrase 'life must be treating you well' wasn't an invitation to talk about how things were going, but a warning, common amongst the Syndicate, and what it meant was 'life *is* treating you well because I'm going to allow you to live, so long as you don't cross me.' Normally Dima didn't pay such respects to people he felt he was in competition with, he gave Liz a little latitude because he felt a small measure of guilt for murdering her parents. It wasn't the murdering that bothered him, he rather enjoyed that sort of thing, it was that he knew Liz knew that he had done it, personally, that and the fact that he had a thing for her. He thought she looked good in ribbons and curls.

Ben and Vicky

"Yes, Captain, this is Ben from Victoria," Ben said into the console, addressing the captain whose ship he was towing towards the lunar dry docks. "Prepare your boat and crew, our ETA is bout two hours from now."

"Thanks, Ben," the captain responded.

"No," Ben responded in his best customer service voice. "Thank you for using Victoria Towing." Then he closed the audio channel and added, "Asshole."

"Ben!" Jessica scolded. "They paid good money."

"I know," he said, feeling admonished. "It's just I missed good work because that damn frigate of his took so long to tow."

"Smuggling isn't good work," Jessica clarified.

"Maybe so, but the money's good." Then he opened the ship's intercom. "Hey, Johnny, come take the helm, I need a break." He closed the com. "Come on, honey, let's go have a break," he said with a smile, hoping to change the subject. They made their way out of the bridge and down past the main deck to the lower deck, where the bedrooms were. Once there he plopped himself on the bed, and Jessica leaned into his arms.

"What am I going to do if you get caught?" she asked with a sincere concern that hurt Ben a little.

"I ain't gonna get caught, Vicky's been towing and smuggling since I was a baby; you know that. My daddy never got caught, and I ain't never gonna get caught neither."

"Your father had to do it, towing didn't pay the bills. It's not the same for you – you do it just for fun."

"Damn, woman," Ben said, frustrated. "What the hell's wrong with that? Besides, it's only weed. Even if I do get caught, they just gonna give me a fine and tell me I'm a bad boy."

Jessica looked up at him and smiled. "A bad boy?"

Ben laughed. "That's right, baby, I'm bad."

Jessica giggled. "OK, bad boy, give me a kiss," she said, and they smooched merrily. It was such a grand kiss it felt like the whole ship was shaking. Eventually their lips parted, and it turned out the whole ship was shaking.

"Ahhh, what the hell?" Ben asked as he reached over and hit the intercom. "Johnny, what's going on up there?"

"Port turbine is acting up again. Don't worry I got it."

"Well damn it, hurry up already, me and the misses is trying to take a break."

"Yes, sir," Johnny replied.

"Johnny, you know better than that, my daddy was the last 'sir' on this boat." Then he closed the com. "OK, baby, where did we leave off?"

"Right here," she said, approaching for a second kiss. This time there was no shaking.

A short while later they lay content in each other's arms. Jessica sighed.

"What's that?" Ben asked.

"Nothing," she answered. "Just happy. That's all."

"Me too," he confirmed.

"Do you think…?" she began then Ben cut her off.

"I knew it, how come you always say nothing when there's something?"

Jessica ignored the question and continued with her own. "Do you think we could go to San Francisco?"

"Oh, honey," Ben said, not wanting to talk about this subject.

"We're going to be in orbit for a few days. You could take me to Disneyland."

"Baby, you don't want to go to Earth. It's horribly crowded. Remember New York, and that time we went to Tokyo?"

"Yes, but none of those are the happiest place on Earth."

Ben didn't know what to tell her, he just hoped something would magically make the conversation go away. Then the intercom snapped on again.

"Ben," Johnny said from the bridge.

"Damn it, Johnny, I told you to handle it."

"It's not that, we're about to be boarded. We got picked for random screening by the port authority."

Ben snapped up in the bed. "Quick, woman! Hide the weed!"

Lorilei

Lorilei sat quietly in her little black dress, combing her long brown hair and staring out the window down on Earth. She smiled prettily at the little blue and green marble and wished desperately that she could be there. She was fairly certain it was a safe place to be. She had been thinking about safety a lot these past few days. Ever since Mr. Moore had told her that he was sorry, but he was gong to have to sell her. She liked Mr. Moore, she had been with him for almost ten years and he had been very kind to her. But now, she would belong to somebody else. That was why she was wearing the little black dress. That was why he had instructed her to no longer appear to be his age and to increase her skin tone to a subtle brown tone. He said the man she was being sold too wanted her to appear youthful and sun kissed. Which she didn't mind, she didn't really like appearing to be an elderly human woman. She did it for Mr. Moore because he wanted her to grow old with him. But now, he was dieing, and he needed the money, so he cried when he told her not to look like that anymore. Lorilei was sad.

Lorilei stood and faced a mirror, trying to find a deeper meaning in the lovely reflection that stared back at her. She shifted her hips uncomfortably under the pressure of a brand that lay beneath the soft black fabric. It had been sent by her new owner with explicit instructions that she was to wear it all times since money had officially changed hands, and she now belonged to him. She pulled the delicate dress up around her waist and thumbed the elastic of the lavender panties in an attempt to align them more comfortably around her natural curves. It didn't help. The discomfort didn't come from their silken caress but from the stylized embroidered 'F' that had been stitch all over her uncertain future.

"You look pretty like that," Mr. Moore said from the door of her room, disturbing her thoughts. She turned and hid her anxiety by beaming a pretty Lorilei smile at him while she readjusted her dress back around her hips.

"Thank you."

He was a grizzled shell of a man. You wouldn't know it looking at him, but he had once been a handsome and powerful Syndicate boss. Now he looked sickly, and while still powerful he didn't command the respect he once did. His men obeyed him because he paid well, not because they feared him. "You look sexy in that robe," she said, standing and walking over to him.

"You flatter me, love," he scoffed, reaching a hand around to pat her on the bottom. "I should have had you appear like this more often," he said, looking into her big blue eyes. Then he remembered. "Oh, he doesn't like blue eyes."

"But you said Caucasian."

"I know, brown, he requested brown."

"OK," she said.

He watched as her eyes turned from light blue to deep brown. Then he turned her around to face the mirror again. "There, how do you like that?"

"It's not what you like?" she asked.

"That's not important," he answered. "But you do look beautiful, I think I do like it."

"I like it too," she said, even though she didn't. She liked her eyes big but preferred lavender. She didn't like being Caucasian one bit; she preferred a soft brown skin tone. She thought the dress was all right, nothing special. She knew it didn't matter; it was only a matter of time before her new owner had it off of her anyway.

"Good," Mr. Moore said. "He's waiting, are you ready?"

"Yes," she answered.

With her arm in his, he led her through the plush estate she had called home for the last decade until they came to the rotunda where her new owner was waiting. He was younger than Mr. Moore, she guessed somewhere in his mid-forties. He wore a typically nice suit that did a fair job hiding an oversized belly.

He eyed her oddly as they approached. It made her uncomfortable, usually the first look a man gave her was full of lust; no matter, she could adjust.

"Mr. Fordess, I present you Lorilei," said Mr. Moore. "I hope you find her to your liking."

"She'll do," Mr. Fordess said with all the condescension he could muster.

Mr. Moore sighed. "She's really quite wonderful, she's made me very happy," he said with a hint of regret.

"Moore, you're a worthless piece of shit. I'd like to say that I don't really care what makes you happy, but that would be a lie. I already have two of these, the only reason I'm buying this one off of you is because I know it bites your ass." Then he approached Lorilei, who smiled at him. He didn't smile as he approached; he just grabbed her firmly by the arm and pulled her towards the door.

"Goodbye, Lorilei," Mr. Moore said with despair as he watched her leave.

"Goodby..." she started to say.

Then Mr. Fordess squeezed her arm painfully and instructed her with a whispered, "Tell him to fuck off."

With tears streaming from her pretty brown eyes she obeyed.

"Fuck off!"

Chapter Two
Times Up

Thorbin

As Alpha cruised back from their test flight, Thorbin allowed himself to relax a little. His bird knew where it was going, and for the time being he was enjoying the view. He watched from the far side of the moon as the Earth set into the horizon. The gentle blues, greens and browns disappearing behind the star-lit lunar plains. In the distance, he spied what looked like an old tugboat towing an injured freighter to port. Thorbin watched as a pilot boat greeted them and released the dusty old tug from its charge, where it then drifted off as a silhouette against the azure glow of home. It was breathtaking. Thorbin smiled to himself.

Never again will anyone think that old hunk of junk is beautiful. Then thoughts of beauty led to thoughts of Mika. He longed for the end of this week, which would release him to her soft embrace. He breathed deep, thinking about how her smile would beam down upon him. How their intimacy would complete him.

In that moment, it suddenly occurred to him that all his dreams had come true. He had a loving wife, a beautiful home, and now he was a test pilot. His purpose had truly been realized. God had given him all his desires, met all his needs. All he had to do now was his duty – his duty to Earth as her defender. He felt purpose. He felt proud.

About an hour later they decreased speed and entered a notable amount of traffic. Thorbin turned his com to the public channel and listened as captains communicated with traffic control. A pair of constable patrollers sped by, and it reminded him of being a patrol pilot.

Go get him guys, he thought to himself. He liked listening to the steady banter of dozens, sometimes hundreds, of voices negotiating the hectic task of the eternal night sky – civilian captains practically begging to be allowed to enter the atmosphere ahead of others.

One conversation was particularly interesting. A senator from Luna was irately arguing with a traffic control officer who was obviously unimpressed with the legislator's tone. The senator should have known better. It didn't matter who you were, or where you came from, when you entered a traffic controller's jurisdiction, you became whatever the controller said you were. Thorbin laughed, knowing that the senator was about to be chastised to the back of the line – and so he was. To add insult to injury the controller requested that the aristocrat have a nice day. The ship held position as ordered and the senator himself was in the middle of an idle threat of retribution when Thorbin heard something else over the public com channel.

"PAN! PAN! PAN!" an unfamiliar voice declared in terror. "We are under fire! Being engaged by Talc fighters! Taking damage! Request back up, HQ!"

That's a constable, Thorbin thought to himself. *Did he just say 'Talc'? That can't be right.* All public chatter went dead as a thousand people were questioning what they had just heard. As if to answer, the DC pilot came back on.

"DCHQ, I repeat PAN! PAN! PAN! We are engaged with Talc fighters and taking heavy damage. Need back up units NOW!"

Zellart broke in. "That's us, Alpha. We are first responders. New orders. Proceed across Luna. Assist constable wing. Wing commanders offence formation, prepare to engage enemy." Alpha slowly began to respond.

"Move it, Alpha! This is not a drill," Zellart concluded. Ten wing commanders responded.

"Clear." The commander of wing 10 was now broadcasting to his charge.

"Let's go, team, stay in formation until we reach objective then follow my lead. Like the commander said, this is not a drill, do not break wing formation. Sync armaments. Tank?"

"Clear, Steve," Tank replied with the clear implication of who was senior.

"Lee?" the commander continued, withholding aggravation.

"Aye, sir," Lee responded.

"Romanov?" he continued.

"Romanov clear," replied the pilot.

"Jackson?"

"Clear, sir," Charles answered.

"Monroe?"

Thorbin pushed the armament initialization switch. He could hear the firing mechanism of his canons shift to the unsafe position, growling as if eager to taste battle. The weapons sight aperture appeared on the cockpit glass and the on-board system chimed.

"Clear, Commander." And fifty experimental DC fighters raced to their destinies on the opposite side of the moon.

Sam

Sam sat as comfortably as she could in her business-class seat aboard Mars flight 36. At least it was an end seat, the one by the aisle. Two seats to the right sat a nice man a few years older then she, and in between them sat his nephew. A cute ten-year-old boy named Rodger that had quickly taken a liking to Sam.

"But Sam is a boy's name," he told her.

"Well that's what my friends call me, my real name is Samantha."

"Oh," he said thoughtfully. "I guess that's kinda like how people call me 'Rod'."

"Yeah," Sam agreed, normally explaining that Sam was short for Samantha really pissed her off, but he had dimples, and she found it hard to be angry at dimples.

"Except at school," Rod continued. "Sometimes they call me 'Ram Rod'. I don't really like that."

Sam laughed. "I know what you mean. I grew up in Hawaii, and the kids at school used to call me Sam Spam."

The little boy broke out in a fit of giggles which got his uncle's attention.

"Leave Sam Spam alone," the man said to his nephew, giving Sam a friendly smile.

"Uncle," the little boy defended. "She doesn't like that, how would you like it if she called you Anthony Panthony?"

The boy's uncle laughed. "I have no idea what that even means."

"Panthony?" Sam smiled.

"Yeah," he said, throwing his hands in the air. "I think the not knowing bothered me the most."

"Uncle, Sam's real pretty, you should marry her," said Rod, and suddenly the conversation went from silly to uncomfortable.

"Um," said the uncle. "Rod, how about you let Uncle Anthony find his own dates."

"But Grandma Jean says you need to find a woman for grandchildren."

Embarrassed, Sam tried her best to disappear into the seat.

"I know, Rod, but you just can't say stuff like that. I think you've made Sam uncomfortable."

Sam popped out of her seat. "No," she said, lying poorly. "It's just kids."

Anthony shot another friendly smile her. "You know, Rod, she is kind of cute when she's lying."

Oh, Sam thought. *Disappear, Sam, disappear.* Then she smiled back at him. He was kind of cute, in a pudgy, big-nosed kind of way. But she was completely unprepared for this sort of thing. *Quick, say something,* she thought. *He's looking at you.*

"Come here often?" she asked. Both the little boy and the man were confused and looked at her accordingly.

"No?" he answered, unsure if that was the correct answer.

"Mars, I mean," she said, recovering.

"Oh. Yes. Rod's father and I work for Mine Core," he said, nodding towards the little boy. "Rod and I were just visiting grandma. How about you?"

"Job relocated me," Sam said, hinting at disappointment.

"Mars isn't all that bad. You'll be fine. What kind of work do you do?"

"I'm an engineer."

"Wow," he said, obviously impressed. "Beautiful and smart."

Sam blushed.

Then they all flinched as their ship jolted violently. Unsecured baggage flailed along with unsecured passengers.

"What was that?" Anthony asked, looking out the window. Sam leaned over to take a look herself. The stars were spinning wildly, and briefly she caught a glimpse of an unfamiliar ship, then she lost it.

"This is your captain speaking," a voice said over the intercom. "Return to your seats and put on your seat belts."

"What the hell is going on?" someone screamed from in front of them.

"There's some kind of ship shooting at us!" another man answered franticly.

"Sam!" the little boy yelled, grabbing her by the arm. "You have to put your head down!"

Liz

As the dust began to settle from the explosion, Liz noticed out of the corner of her eye that everything had not gone well. She hastily placed the small velvet pouch that held her prize in the breast pocket of her shirt then quickly stepped over Rudolph's body to catch Paul before he collapsed to the ground. He had been hit, badly, and she struggled as she lowered the both of them to the ground.

"We've had a lot of fun, kid." He spoke with pain. "Looks like this is the one, huh?"

"Don't talk like that," Liz said as a tear cut a path through the dust on her cheek. Paul raised a bloody hand, and smudged the tear away with a finger.

"You remember the Astor heist?"

"Yes," she said, forcing a smile and hoping to ease his pain. "The necklace with that huge ruby pendant."

"After we stole it, back in the hotel, you put it on." He coughed, struggled for breath, then continued, "It looked so good on you."

"It better have," she said, having trouble keeping the smile. "I wasn't wearing anything else."

A huge smile ran across Paul's face, then he died.

Liz bit her lip as she laid her dear friend on the ground, sending him to the next life with a kiss, then she told herself she had to go, now!

She heard footsteps quickly approaching and leapt upright, dashing towards an exit. As she ran, she heard a door behind her open. She pulled her weapon and fired wildly behind her. She smashed through a door that led into a hallway, and as she sprinted towards the stairwell a Slavic voice could be heard bellowing in anger.

"Kill her!"

She had barely made it to the stairwell door when shots began piercing the walls and ground around her. Making her way down the stairwell, she heard people coming up. Her feet spun her around and quickly lifted her up the steps as she blindly squeezed shots downward to discourage pursuit.

Two flights later she had reached the top of the still-under-construction building that had been chosen for the transaction. A regrettable decision that had cost Paul his life and had now left her with nowhere to go. The only part of the building that existed on this floor was the steel risers and concrete floor. Liz looked franticly for her next move and fired a few more shots down the stairwell, hoping to buy a few more seconds to think. Her shots were answered by the clatter of several fully automatic weapons that apparently didn't like being shot at. After very nearly being hit she leapt back and ran towards the street-facing direction of the building. She smiled as she saw a line of slow-moving cars floating past her floor.

"Rush hour," she said happily for the first time in her life and bolted towards the edge of the building.

God, if you let me live, I'll never do it again, she thought desperately as she fell towards a blue sedan.

The driver of the vehicle received quite a scare as the blonde bombshell hit his hood with a thud. He hadn't been traveling that fast, but nonetheless, when he slammed on his brakes there was enough force to send her sliding off the front of his hood despite her impressive arm flailing and scratching. She watched the underbody of the car fall up and away from her as she descended until she landed hard on top a bus in the lane below.

She thought for sure she had broken every breakable part of her; at least it felt that way. She wasn't sure if she could move until the roof of the bus began to pop and shred from taking fire. She instinctively threw her arms over her head and looked for her next move. It presented itself when the blue sedan from the lane above was struck by gunfire and lost control, plummeting right for her. Her next move was clearly to get off the bus, so she rolled to the side and off the roof, hoping things would just work out.

She landed squarely in the lap of man driving a red sports convertible. He swerved wildly but was able to get the vehicle under control.

"What the…?" he began to ask. "You just fell out of the sky."

Liz, dusty and bruised, still had it. "I'm an angel," she replied. "God wants you to make the next right."

Ben

Ben leaned back at the helm, bored as the port authority inspector reviewed his ship's records. Ben was pretty sure he was screwed. The young man wore his uniform well and searched through Ben's records with a fervent need to catch a criminal. Ben wasn't afraid of being caught; he'd been doing mildly dirty deeds long before this guy was a glint in his father's eye. The thing what worried him was his enthusiasm. This guy would search Victoria in and out before his gut told him 'Sorry, I guess there isn't anything here.' And that was going to take forever. Usually the inspectors would board, walk around the main deck, ask him if he was smuggling anything, then ask him to sign some port document before leaving. This guy seemed like the type who would check the underwear drawer.

"Records indicate you stop at Jacob's Run regularly."

"I suppose they do," Ben answered with as much polite condescension as he could muster.

"That oasis is known as a smugglers' port," the young man added.

"Really. Then maybe you should be looking there," Ben said wryly. He watched as the young man struggled to stay professional.

"Sir, I know you're hiding something from me. And I'm going to find it." Then he stared at Ben as if he were waiting for him to confess. Then another inspector entered the bridge from the spiral staircase that led up from the lower deck.

"D," he said. "Are you finished?"

"There's something here," he told his colleague.

"What?" the man asked, sounding irritated.

"I don't know, but I'm going to find it."

"Damn it, D, you always do this. It's a friggin' tugboat. What do want to do, call in a deep scan? To find what? Maybe some weed?"

Ben tried not to look scared. The hairs on the back of his neck stood up as the inspector continued. "Confiscate it, tell him he's a bad boy, then explain to the chief why we called in a scan for nothing."

"It's our job," the young man responded.

"Right, and our shift is over in thirty minutes. I gotta use the bathroom."

"There's one in the office," Ben said, pointing behind him.

"Thanks," the man said. "Tell you what, D, If you haven't found anything by the time I'm done, we're outta here."

Minutes later, Ben watched from the bridge as the port authority ship drifted away. He was in the process of seeing them off with a one-finger salute when Johnny came rushing in from the office.

"Ben! Turn on the public com channel."

"What?" Ben said, startled by Johnny's urgency. Johnny reached across Ben and swung the console in his direction to turn the channel on himself, where a desperate voice could be heard.

"DCHQ, I repeat PAN! PAN! PAN! We are engaged with Talc fighters and taking heavy damage. Need back up units NOW!" Then the channel went silent.

"Did he say 'Talc'?" Ben asked. Then the channel opened up again. It played a series of three consecutive buzzes, then an announcer spoke.

"This is an announcement from the emergency broadcast system, this is not a test."

"Holy shit!" Johnny interrupted. "I've never actually heard a real one of these before."

"Shut up," Ben instructed so he could hear the rest of the broadcast.

"Not a test," the announcer reported calmly. "Talc fighters have been spotted in the skies of New Tokyo. All civilian vessels are to leave the lunar orbit now. All military, constable and civics personnel are to report to their posts immediately. All other persons on Luna should report to their designated invasion shelters. All other persons on Earth should remain where they are and await further instructions."

"Time to go, Johnny," Ben said, turning the console back in his direction and plotting a course away from the moon. As he came about, far over the lunar horizon he could see a Defense Core carrier racing into action. He had never seen one move so fast. "Good luck, guys," he said. Then Jessica came rushing in from the office hatch behind him.

"Ben, did you hear that?"

"Yeah, baby, I heard," he said, continuing to bring the ship about.

She stood behind him and threw her arms loosely around his shoulders. On the back of his neck, he could feel her heart pounding through her chest.

"Ben, I'm scared."

"Me too, Jessy, we gonna get out of here though."

Suddenly, there was a brilliant blue flash of light that for a moment seemed to wash out all other light, then it was gone. Not long after something struck Victoria hard. Ben struggled for control as her bow dipped forward and she was struck again. The console came to life with warning indicators; Ben struggled to keep up with them. The lower deck, where the living quarters were, had been hit by something. He activated the intercom.

"Johnny, if you're in the lower deck, get out of there and seal the hatches now."

The intercom responded. "Ben there's something down here." Then a flurry of Defense Core fighters soared by. One of them stopped, came about, then hailed.

"Tug class vessel. You are being boarded." Then the fighter approached close enough so that Ben could see the pilot. He was pointing to the bottom of Victoria. Johnny came rushing up the stairs from the deck below. The pilot continued.

"Seal your decks," he said as he brought the fighter about so the two boats were facing bow to bow. "I can shoot him off."

Johnny slammed the hatch leading down while Jessica closed the one into the office behind them.

"Sealed!" Johnny said.

"Sealed!" Jessica confirmed.

"Fighter," Ben hailed, frightened out of his mind. "My bridge is sealed, get 'em off of me."

The fighter's guns blazed and Ben could see foreign-looking pieces of debris shattering from beneath Victoria. Then he winched as he saw pieces of Victoria among the debris. It was most unsettling when his saw his bed float past along with his dresser leaking various items of clothing.

"Oh," Jessica said, taking notice. "I like that shirt."

The fighter pilot came back across the com.

"Target destroyed. Sorry about your lower deck, Captain."

"No problem."

"I'd power down if I were you, makes you look less interesting. And be careful, their ship's gone, but a few of them could have made it on board."

"What do I do if they got on board?" Ben asked, terrified.

"Kill 'em," the pilot responded. "If you can't, secure yourself and send out a distress that you're boarded, the marines will take care of it. I gotta go," he concluded and gave Ben a salute before speeding off.

Ben turned back to the console and tried to assess the damage to Victoria.

"The whole lower deck is destroyed, but the main and upper decks seem OK," he said to the others.

"How do we know if we've been boarded?" Johnny asked.

"I guess we check," Ben answered.

"Oh no," Jessica inserted. "We're just going to stay here until the marines show up."

"The marines aren't coming here," Johnny said. "Not for a while at least, there's thousands of ships out there with more crew than us. We're gonna be last in line."

"OK," Ben said. "I'll check."

Thorbin

Alpha tore across the lunar horizon ready for a fight. As they approached the skies of New Tokyo, an unsettling and unfamiliar flicker of red light illuminated the skyline. Soon after, Alpha engaged the enemy.

They came upon two DC patrollers who were being mercilessly harassed by Talc fighters and were taking damage. The Talc vessels spewed brilliant red bursts of fire from their sickly grayish green vessels. The streamlined silver and black patrollers fluttered franticly as they wrestled to keep control of their birds and avoid further damage. As Alpha approached, a majority of the ill-looking adversary broke from their prey to meet the test squad.

Zellart barked, "Two, Three, blow past these guys and help out those patrollers. Everyone else, let's give 'em a warm welcome."

Wings two and three dove and everyone else let loose a barrage of steel hell that downed six of the oncoming Talc in seconds. The remaining Talc vessels passed right through the squad's ranks, suffering nominal damage.

In an uncontrolled fit of excitement Tank yelped, "Welcome to the neighborhood, you sum bitches."

Then the fighters looped, banked, and dove in order to pursue the remaining enemy, who hadn't gotten far. Wing ten in the rear position was closest. Thorbin and Charles came about, first destroying the rear Talc with tandem fire. Shortly after, craft to craft missiles whizzed by them and finished off the other two.

Wing commander two reported, "Patrollers secure, sir."

"Good job, Alpha," Zellart confirmed. "Reestablish squad formation team. Let's get these pilots home."

Tank piped up. "Hey, Monroe, was vengeance sweet enough for you?"

"It was fine, Tank. Thanks for asking," Thorbin responded, wishing Tank would just go away.

"Hey that wasn't so bad," Charles pontificated.

The wit continued on like this for a few minutes while everyone was coming down and really just wanted to call it a day. Thorbin sank back into his seat in relief. The question on everyone's mind was how had the Talc arrived five years ahead of their projected ETA? What did that mean for Earth and everything else?

"How did they do it?" Thorbin said aloud to himself.

Zelart's distressed voice came over the com. "DCHQ, this is Alpha! More Talc incoming!" he said as the entire surface of the moon was thrust upon by an electric blue wave of light. Thorbin looked over his shoulder to see what had caused the brilliance, and to his shock several hundred Talc fighters had appeared, and with them a carrier." It's a whole damn carrier division," Zellart called out.

"We're headed your way. Try not to engage until we arrive, but you hold that position commander." HQ answered.

"Try not to engage? Hold the position?" it was Chin, and the panic in his voice wasn't exclusive. "Is he serious?"

"Squad, we will hold this position," Zellart commanded with reinforcement. "This is the big day. Stay with your wing and let's give 'em hell!" Those words were the best motivation he could muster.

The next few moments were chaos. Alpha's pilots had no choice but to engage, even though they were outnumbered at least ten to one. Before long almost half the squad had been forced to eject or had been destroyed.

Thorbin and Charles lost their wing commander but were able to stick together. They were being engaged so heavily that the Talc were inflicting damage on each other while trying to hit them.

"Charles!" Thorbin cried out. "They're on me!" he shouted as his aft took fire.

"Hang in there, T!" Charles said as he came from above. Three fighters were laying heavy fire on Thorbin, who was evading well considering the circumstances. He got a lock on the leader.

"Cluster off! Up, T! Now!" and so he did – a perfect maneuver. Thorbin rose as the munitions exploded, destroying the lead and damaging the two behind. More were closing in.

"Charles on my ten!" Thorbin said, letting loose munitions. They hit their target, and for instant the explosion created a visual barrier. Charles fired through the confusion and the oncoming Talc never saw him coming, after which they were no longer a threat. It was another, behind Thorbin, that he should have been concerned about. It decimated Thorbin's tail section and his fighter began to break apart.

"MAYDAY! MAYDAY! MAYDAY!" Thorbin said as his cockpit warning indicators lost their minds. Then in an instant, the cockpit detached and he was launched above his bird before it shattered apart.

The ejection caught Thorbin completely by surprise. "Commander, my bird's down! I've been ejected," he said and waited for a response.

"MAYDAY! MAYDAY! MAYDAY!" he heard; it was Charles. "My starboard turbine is out!"

Thorbin looked around franticly to find his friend until he found a fighter that was in a flat spin.

There, he thought to himself.

Then he saw Charles eject over the explosion of his fighter. Charles' pod spun wildly away from the debris.

"I'm out, I ejec...." Charles began, but before the sentence was complete, a Talc ship collided into the capsule at high speed, reducing the both of them to ruble instantaneously. Thorbin stopped in mid inhale, staring at the wreckage in morbid disbelief.

"This can't be happening," he exhaled. "Charles," he said, pressing his hands firmly against the cockpit glass in shock.

"Where is my Goddamn carrier?" Thorbin heard Tank scream over the com. "Chin's down, I don't know where the hell Zellart is, and I've lost track of my whole damn wing."

Thorbin looked away from where Charles had been killed and saw Tank strike any enemy fighter as he went by before he was out of sight.

"Where is the Goddamn...? Oh shit MAYDAY, MAYDAY, MAYDAY," then Tank was silent.

Thorbin beat against the cockpit glass in frustration and agony.

In the distance he could see two more Alpha fighters fleeing the position with several Talc wings on their tales. They turned and flew across the lunar horizon until he couldn't see them anymore. He stared at the moon, then at Earth. He had failed. Tears were coming, then he heard command.

"Fighters first then the carrier!"

Shortly after, the wings that had pursued the two Alpha fighters around the moon came back in a hurry. A DC carrier division was right behind them. Thorbin looked to Earth, held his breath again, looked back to the carrier, then released. Then he did the only helpful thing he could. He prayed.

The fight was intense, but the Talc were definitely taking the brunt. Hundreds of fighters engaged in what was the largest battle Earth had ever fought in space to date. An hour later the tide truly turned when the second Earth carrier arrived. In that hour Thorbin had cried as he saw unknown comrades fall. Thorbin had rejoiced as he had watched unknown comrades persevere. He had prayed that this day would bring Earth victory, and it looked liked his prayers were going to be answered. The Talc fighters were all but destroyed. The battle was focused on the Talc carrier. It was in retreat, but there would be no escape for it. The new carrier was moving into position while the other was pulling back.

The moon's orbit had grabbed a hold of Thorbin and was slowly pulling him away from the battle. The distance gave him a full view, and he was ready for this long terrible day to end. He looked back at Earth and longed for it. He could see most of Europe through the clouds. They were calm; they didn't appear to be rain clouds, white and dispersed. Then to his horror they flashed electric blue.

He quickly turned back to the battle and his worst fears were realized. A tear in space was opening, framed by an electric storm. And from it another Talc fleet emerged with multiple carriers. Alongside them came another much larger ship.

His heart sank to a place it had never been before. Tens of thousands of Talc fighters spewed forth from their carriers' decks.

For the next two hours, the Earth warriors fought valiantly but were simply outnumbered. Earth threw everything at them. At one point the DC even launched some retrofitted ICBM's. But even these, hundreds of the most powerful and destructive weapons man had ever crafted, couldn't stop the onslaught.

First the fighters were defeated, then the carriers. All the while, the large Talc behemoth slowly circled around to the far side of the moon, opposite Earth. It was colossal – the largest unnatural thing Thorbin had ever seen. He watched in terror as a red glow began to emanate from within its belly. It looked like a weapon, and it looked like it was going to attack the moon. The glow became deeper, more intense, then it let loose. A violent lance of red was launched towards the moon so fiercely that Thorbin's pod shook and lost power. He didn't even notice.

The moon was hit just west of New Tokyo. The shot drilled through the surface and the heavenly body fractured in two; the two halves slowly drifted apart. The blast, however, was not stayed; it penetrated, continuing on to Earth – a direct hit on Northern Africa. A black plum rose from the point of contact. Thorbin watched in horror as a dark cloud devoured the lovely blues and whites of home until the atmosphere was gray and cold. Earth was dead, a lifeless corpse of a planet.

Chapter Three
The New Girl

Thorbin

Thorbin opened his eyes. His head ached harshly from unrelenting grief. The living nightmare was inescapable, and he had nothing to distract himself from it. The physical, emotional, and spiritual strain had caused his body to shut down. The only company he had as he drifted onwards to nowhere was his imagination – his cruel, unrelenting imagination. It tortured him, creating visions of horror on Earth. Imagining in detail how beloved people and places had suffered before their end. The time he spent sleeping was no different. Hours seemed like days, and they might have been. Depressed, he sat in the pod, wishing he could just die.

Then, from the abyss, he yawned. He was hungry. Hunger, a welcome change, though he hardly regarded it. Instinctively, he reached under his seat and searched for his survival rations. The intuitiveness fled when the rations made themselves difficult to find. He found himself focusing on something other than despair. Then he felt thirst. His thoughts were changing. He removed his restraints so he could better reach under the seat. Once removed his body drifted forward, so he placed his left hand on the cockpit glass to leverage himself against the zero gravity.

Soon he had found the containers and the straps used to hold them in place. He pulled the Velcro loose, grasped the containers, secured them to his lap, and then put his restraints back on. The containers were a series of rectangular boxes stacked on top of each other and held together by magnets. He separated the boxes and inspected what was in them through their transparent lids. One was filled completely with toiletries, another with flares and signal beacons. As he continued searching for the rations container, he discovered a survival blanket, a compass, more flares, and a first-aid kit along with many other survival-related items. He then found the food. Five weeks of rations for one person if proper discipline was applied.

Each section of the box had several two-ounce packages of high-calorie flavored bars. He inspected the flavors to see what he was interested in: beef jerky, chicken, cornbread, and a variety of others. He couldn't decide until he came across one labeled 'dessert'. He snapped the lid open and pulled them all out. He shuffled them around, trying to get a more descriptive explanation of the contents. There was none, so he placed all but one back in the box. He reassembled the containers together then let them float off as they pleased.

"OK God," he yearned. "Something good."

As he unwrapped the package, his prayer was answered, a two-ounce piece of Swiss chocolate revealed itself. It gave him an odd sense of security – at least there was chocolate. He bit off a tiny piece and savored it. The sugar sent a sensation straight to his head and his stomach burbled its acceptance. He jammed the rest of the piece into his mouth and reached again for the containers.

This time he opened the one with the flares and signal beacons as he chewed happily on his chocolate. He was looking for his emergency personal journal unit. The personal journal unit (or in true military fashion referred to as 'PJU') was a pilot's only personal effects allowed in a fighter. The emergency PJU was stored with the rest of a pilot's survival gear and updates itself when the fighter is docked. It was a tiny computer, not much bigger than a postcard. The majority of the face was taken up by the screen. What wasn't screen was speaker and microphone. Stored inside the PJU was all the data the pilot kept while serving. All their work data, personal data, and the military data that the pilot was privy to. Emergency PJU's had one more element that others didn't, survival data. It has information on everything from the periodic table of elements to the proper way to rub sticks together to make fire. Any useful piece of information that humanity ever conceived was in the emergency PJU.

Thorbin could care less about elements and sticks, what he wanted was to see if his pictures and videos had been uploaded. He franticly discarded everything not PJU. He was almost enraged with frustration until he found it – at the bottom of course. He gently reached for it then cast aside the now empty container. He touched the screen and it began to boot. The cockpit was illuminated by the screen's glow as it ran its post test and loaded the PJU's operating system. Finally it was up, and he began navigating through his personal files until he came upon the videos. He had them, all of them. Hundreds of home movies collected by his family for generations, including the ones with Mika in them. He selected all the video files that she was in and opened them. One by one, the videos began to play. He watched for a few moments until he paused the playback and minimized the movies. He opened up his music files, searched for a while, decided on Marvin Gaye and then returned to the movies. He held the PJU in his lap and watched Mika in all her loveliness as Marvin took him straight to her arms.

Long after Marvin had sung his last lyric Thorbin was still watching movies. Depression had caused him to change over from clips of Mika, and he was now watching videos of his buddies back in the Defense Core. He had said a prayer for Charles and was wondering if anyone else was still alive like he was. If they were, he wondered if any of them weren't going to be strangers, although a stranger would do.

Then a piece of debris caught his attention as it drifted past his pod. It was a metallic piece, most likely part of some unfortunate ship. The sun's light reflected off of it, and he could feel its warmth. Due to his pod's position he hadn't seen the sun for a long while. He turned his cheek towards it to savor the warmth. He appreciated the way the sunlight shimmered off of it. He thought how pretty it was despite being proof of such terrible events.

Then, disappointing him greatly, the reflected light disappeared.

"Of course," he said to himself. "The only thing out here besides me, and I have to block out its sun. Sorry little guy," he said to the debris, then looked back down at his PJU. He perused through his files a bit more then decided he should make a journal entry for posterity.

"To whoever may find this," he began. "My name is, or was Thorbin. I am…"

He was interrupted by the crash of something large against his pod.

"Damn! A debris field," he said, concluding his journal entry and sitting up to see what was going on outside.

Dozens of pieces of debris ambled slowly by. Some danced as they collided gently with each other. Smaller dust like particles swirled around the pod, caught in its wake. He contemplated that he was no different than the debris. He and they, at this moment in time, shared a common fate. No fate, or really no important fate aside from existing. The number of bits increased. Hundreds, and they began pelting the pod like tender rain on a tin roof. Slowly, the clatter increased and the debris appeared to be moving past faster.

"Why are they moving faster?" he asked himself.

"Or," he thought aloud, "am I moving faster?"

A violent jolt nearly jerked him into the cockpit glass as all the unsecured items flailed about. Defensively, he batted away one of the containers before it could hit him in the head.

"Something's got me?" he said, not sure if he should be excited or panicked. He fumbled open a compartment and from within retrieved a pistol and belt. He decided that he had a bad feeling about this turn of events and frantically put the belt on, holstering the firearm. His eyes darted around the pod, searching for anything else useful. If the Talc were reeling him in, he wasn't going out without a fight. He noticed the container that held the chocolate. He tore it open and grabbed every piece of chocolate, then shoved them into his pockets.

"No chocolate for them," he muttered. "Not, while I'm alive." Then he pulled his pistol, yanked back the slide and felt satisfied as it slid forward, chambering a round.

Whatever fowl thing was dragging him into its clutches was about to reveal itself. A brilliant blinding light flooded in from behind him, and he was being dragged into one of the unknown vessel's orifices.

The light slowly began to dim; he was certain that meant he was inside. He could see shapes but nothing discernable. Then he made out the opening, the one he must have come through, and it was growing distant.

The pod started to vibrate softly, and he could hear the rattle of what sounded like a crank. Then the noise and rattle stopped, and so did the pod. He had been set down.

Thorbin rolled his fingers around the grip of his pistol. The opening he had come through was beginning to close, and the light was dimming to a point where he could more clearly discern his surroundings. The first thing he could make out was a set of cargo containers on his starboard side. The sight gave him an intense feeling of relief. He was in an Earth ship – its cargo hold to be precise. The exterior doors finished closing and a symphony of mechanical clatter slowly started to radiate as air was restored to the hold. He unbuckled himself to get a better view. The interior walls looked more like a rusty cavern than the inside of a ship. There were a few portions of the hull that had large pieces of steel welded to it. This ship hadn't gone unscathed. Thorbin noticed that he had been set amongst a verity of wreckage. Whoever captained this vessel was obviously collecting debris in the hope of repairing his own ship.

Thorbin refocused his search on signs of life. On his port side he spotted a blanket with human-shaped creases in it. He felt a since of remorse for that fallen soul, but took heart in the sight. They would only be covered if there were someone compassionate on board.

Then there was a knock on the starboard side of his pod. Thorbin's head and sidearm swung in the direction of the knock. There, above his sights, a middle-aged man was staring intently through the glass. He had very short curly graying hair and a five o'clock shadow to match. Dried-up blood had set itself under his nose, blending in with his dark complexion. The man quickly shot his hands up in response to Thorbin's pistol and smiled in a way a man smiles when he is asking not to be shot.

Thorbin and Ben

Thorbin lowered then holstered the pistol, and the man mouthed out the words, 'Are you OK?'

Thorbin responded with a thumbs-up. The man then motioned, suggesting that Thorbin open his cockpit. The power was out so he couldn't. Thorbin demonstrated a lever motion with his hands then pointed to the front of the pod. The man walked around to the front, knelt down, and a few seconds later Thorbin heard the release pop. He placed his palms against the glass and slid it towards the rear. The man could be heard finally.

"Are you OK, man? Let me get you a stool."

Thorbin lifted one leg out of the pod, set it on the stool, and then the next. He was glad to be out. He looked at the pod stoically. He had never seen an ejected pod up close before.

"Hey, are you OK?" the man asked again.

Thorbin turned and looked at him. "I'm good, thanks to you, friend," he replied as he stepped down off the stool.

They faced each other and said nothing for a moment. Not just any moment but a good moment. The kind of moment where words failed and two people could come to an understanding that life had been real tough recently, but maybe, hopefully, it was about to get better. The two men stepped towards each other. Their arms and hands rose and fell awkwardly as they tried to negotiate whether they were going to shake hands or hug. They both really wanted a hug and figured the occasion surpassed the manly 'men don't hug other strange men' code, but neither was sure if the other guy agreed. The man finally just took it upon himself and gave Thorbin a full, and manly, hug. They stepped back with smiles and the man offered his hand for shaking.

"The name's Ben," he said as Thorbin received his hand.

"Thorbin," he answered. "It's good to see you."

"It's good to see you too."

"Looks like you've been through hell," Thorbin said, getting a closer look at Ben. He didn't appear to be bleeding now, but the stains on his head-to-toe tatters suggested that not long ago he had been bleeding a lot. "How are things here?"

"Fucked, still fucked. I'm the only one left on board. Well besides you now," he began, then started to walk away and motioned for Thorbin to follow him. "The Talc boarded us," he said as Thorbin followed.

Ben picked up a shotgun that looked like it might have been a hundred years old.

"Any left?" Thorbin asked de-holstering his pistol.

"Yes. Three," Ben responded.

"What kind of weapons?"

"Some kind of blade, real nasty."

"Knives?" Thorbin was perplexed. "They brought knives to a gunfight?"

"No," Ben said with great distress. "They brought swords to a boat whose crew has no weapons. Knives is not a good description. You'll see," Ben said, trying to explain.

"Why does this crew have no weapons?" Thorbin asked as they traveled down a hallway, stepping over rubble on the way.

"No weapons allowed on board. Standing order by the captain," Ben answered.

"What about that relic you've got there?"

"I'm the captain," Ben answered. "There was four that boarded before their ship was destroyed. We was surprised. They got Johnny when he went to check on the lower deck. They jumped me and Jessy when we were checking the cargo bay." His voice strained and hit a pained pitch. "They cut her up real bad before I could even do anything. I shot one, in the head – killed him. The others ran. I trapped 'em in the galley. I got 'em all at least once. But they're still alive in there."

"That may be a relic, but are they bulletproof?"

"Using salt loads. They hurt real bad, but they're only deadly real close. I was hoping you would finish 'em off with that piece you got there."

"My pleasure, Ben," Thorbin said understandingly.

A few steps later and they reached the hatch that led to the galley.

"In there," Ben pointed. The Good Samaritans last message never did describe what the Talc looked like. Thorbin was curious. He peered through a porthole-style window, and there they were, standing in a triangle, unaware they were being watched. They were hideous. They could have easily been any troll you had ever read about in a children's tale. Head to toe they were proportioned like a human but without hair, just fur – a grimy greasy fur that was rusty brown with a silver undertone. It covered the whole of their grotesque form. There were no ears to speak of, although their faces had a canine affectation, broad noses more like snouts and dingy yellow fangs. They drooled and spit as they communicated with each other. Thorbin watched as one defecated as it stood there; none of the others seemed to mind. The conversation was no doubt about their captivity. They conversationally bandied about their afore mentioned weapons. Ben was right; knives were not an accurate description. They were more like machetes that wreathed like a weapon of torture, and these were dressed in human blood.

Thorbin raised his pistol to the glass, steadied himself with a half-step back, and acquired his sight picture. The front sight aperture blurred and his target came into focus. He squeezed. The pistol cracked, the glass shattered, and where there were three, now stood two.

As Thorbin's victim slumped to the ground, his companions hit the deck. One leapt behind an overturned table, the other failed to find suitable cover before the rest of Thorbin's magazine hit it. Still alive, the injured Talc fell forward on the ground, attempting to pull itself forward. It squealed and hissed as its limbs failed to move it. Thorbin released the magazine, pulled it from the pistol and placed it in his pocket before reloading his weapon. He aimed at the injured Talc, watching as it lost traction on the deck slipping in its own blood. Calmly, Thorbin executed a headshot, and it fell limp to the ground. Thorbin then turned his attention to the table. He knew the Talc was hiding behind it, but he couldn't see where. Mentally, he broke the table into sections, and one by one, he fired a round into each. A hiss of agony pronounced the score of the fifth shot. The Talc fled from behind the table holding a wounded arm. Thorbin opened up on it as it ran. He scored a leg shot and three to the midsection before it scrambled out of sight around a corner.

"Damn," Thorbin said as if he had lost a poker hand.

"Did you get 'em?" Ben asked.

"One left. We have to go in," Thorbin answered. "He's not going to be much trouble. He's hit."

Ben began to release the hatch as Thorbin kept his pistol intently aimed through the porthole. Ben signaled that the hatch was unsealed and picked up his shotgun. The hatch squeaked as Thorbin opened it with his free hand. Just a crack at first, then, when he saw it was clear, he swung it all the way open and entered – handgun first. Ben followed, surveying the damage through the sights of his weapon.

"You shot up my table," he said in measured disappointed.

"Sorry," Thorbin responded.

As they approached the second downed Talc, it grunted. The barrel of Ben's shotgun swung wildly towards it, pelting the beast with supersonic rock salt. The sound was impressive. The stainless steel cabinets and cupboards reverberated in the thunderous blast.

They don't make 'em like that anymore. Hundred years old or not, Thorbin thought to himself. Ben furiously cocked his weapon and prepared to season the enemy once more.

"Hold on!" Thorbin said. "I got 'em. Just watch around the corner for the last one," Thorbin said, pointing towards the corner.

"OK," Ben said, slowly moving to the far side of the room, opposite to where the Talc had run off. Thorbin scored another headshot Then another, this time assuring it was dead. Then for good measure he shot the first one again. He cautiously sidestepped towards Ben, who was motioning with his weapon.

"Right there."

The Talc hadn't gotten far past the corner and had propped itself up against the wall. Thorbin reacquired a sight picture, aiming for the head.

"No," Ben said. "Mine."

Thorbin nodded but didn't take his eyes off the target.

The Talc was quivering from fresh wounds. As Ben moved towards it, he could hear the gurgling breaths it was taking as blood filled its lungs. Ben moved closer, only a few steps away. The Talc attempted to flee but could only shift its weight slightly. Ben stepped up to it and firmly placed the barrel of his shotgun against its left eye, taking sadistic pleasure in seeing the fear in its right eye. The Talc started muttering. Ben wondered if it was praying or begging. He hoped it was begging. He jammed the barrel into the Talc's eye socket, and it squealed hideously in anguish. Ben was experiencing true hate and genuine pleasure, knowing that the creature understood that he hated it.

Thorbin knew Ben was trying to extract satisfaction for his loss, but he couldn't allow this to go on.

"Ben, you're giving him a chance to act. Don't assume you're safe. Back up and finish him off." As Thorbin spoke he repositioned himself in case action was needed.

Ben turned his head and looked Thorbin scornfully in the eye, then he squeezed the trigger.

Muffled by the Talc's skull, the blast wasn't as loud as the first. As the salt load entered the beast's left eye, the right eye shot out of its socket, and the beast drooled blood and innards from its maw. Then it slumped to the right. Ben turned his head back to see his handiwork.

"OK, Ben. Let's...ah...let's get rid of them," Thorbin suggested, not because that was what he wanted to do or felt that it was the best course of action, but because Ben was in a whole other place – a bad place.

Ben didn't respond, he just stared at the dead Talc; limply holding his shotgun in disappointment, wishing it was alive so he could kill it again.

"Ben?" Thorbin probed, he was starting to wonder if the man was in there at all.

There was no immediate response, but a few tedious seconds later Ben flinched, let the shotgun fall to the ground, and took a few steps back. Then, like a falling barrier, the darkness collapsed under a deluge of despair. Ben brought his quivering hands to chest.

"They killed her," he said, beginning to fall apart. His hands covered his face, and he began to weep. "They killed my Jessica."

Thorbin holstered his weapon and cautiously approached.

"What I am I gonna do without her?" Ben spurted.

Thorbin didn't say a thing; he just approached softly and put an arm around him.

Ben turned into him and set his forehead on Thorbin's shoulder.

Thorbin was totally lost for words. What would he say? 'It'll be OK?' 'She's in a better place?' Those were the types of things people were supposed to say in these circumstances, but they just didn't seem to fit. Instead he wrapped his arms around Ben and rubbed his back until he didn't feel so bad.

It took a while before Ben started to recover, but the tears did eventually stop. He raised his head from Thorbin's shoulder and looked at him.

"Sorry," he said, trying to wipe the misery from his face.

"No reason to be sorry," Thorbin assured. "My wife was on Earth. I was no different a few hours ago."

"Sorry," Ben said again, this time about Thorbin's wife. "I gotta bury her."

"OK," Thorbin said. "You know we're in space, right?"

"Yeah," Ben answered. "I got an empty cold storage container in the cargo bay if you wouldn't mind helping me."

"Not at all."

Thorbin and Jessica

Stoically they proceeded to the aft of the ship. In the cargo bay they stood quietly next to a cargo container and over two covered bodies. Thorbin waited awhile for Ben to instruct him, but the man kept silent. He decided he would open the container and see what happened. He followed the container to its end and found the latch. A cool air seeped out as he swung the double metal doors ajar. Afterwards, he came back around and Ben was still standing there silently.

"If you want," Thorbin softly suggested, "I can take care of this. If you want."

Ben nodded, sniffled, then turned and walked away towards the hall. Thorbin waited until he was out of sight, then turned his attention to the two bodies. Despite being covered by sheets, it was clear which was Jessica. He started with the other. Struggling, he managed to get the man into the container. He tried his best to be tender as he placed him in. After setting the man down, he arranged him solemnly and made sure the sheet would remain in place.

He then came back to Jessica and found it difficult to simply pick her up and set her into the container. Despite being completely covered, the sheet contoured to a perfect generic feminine form. It could have been any woman under there. It was hard for him not to picture Mika under the shroud.

"Pick her up," he told himself, trying desperately to find the motivation. Slowly he knelt by her side with a pang in his chest and a lump in his throat. He reached a hand around the back of her neck, brushing aside a soft blanket of hair, then he slid an arm under the small of her back, his hand trembled as he cradled her by the waist. Pulling her towards him was physically effortless compared to Johnny. The emotional effort, however, felt crippling. He stood holding her, on the brink of tears, unable to disconnect from his own loss. He shifted her weight in his arms and brought her head up under his chin. The sheet fell from around her face, revealing a deathly pale but lovely face. She was beautiful, but not Mika. The revelation allowed him to breathe again and he inhaled deeply.

Looking at her, he felt sure that she must have been a kind woman. She looked it, or maybe it was just the look of eternal rest.

"No," he said. "I'm sure you were wonderful." Taking another deep breath he held her firmly and walked towards the container.

It wasn't Mika, but still, he felt a sense of intimacy laying her on the cold steel. It felt like the closest thing he would ever have to saying goodbye to his wife. Like the other body, he arranged her compassionately, making sure the blanket covered her completely but stopping at her face. He softly arranged the hair around her head and out of her face. Then spoke he to her.

"It was nice to meet you, Jessica," he told her. Then he pulled the blanket over her head and stood. As he turned to leave he met Ben, who had returned unannounced and was just outside the container looking in. He was a breath away from falling apart. Thorbin didn't say a word to him; he just stepped aside and walked past with a consoling pat on the shoulder. Thorbin stood just out of sight as the moment took Ben. He had made sure to stay close in case the man needed anything. After a while, it was apparent that what Ben really needed was beyond anyone's control.

A few moments after the crying had stopped, Thorbin poked his head around the corner. Ben was holding Jessica's hand. Red eyed, Ben looked at him.

"I'm going to walk around," Thorbin said, really he was asking permission to take his leave. Ben nodded and Thorbin left him.

Thorbin and Victoria

Standing in the cargo bay, Thorbin started to take his first good look at Ben's ship. The bay was the aft most section of the boat, and the largest – two stories tall, twice as wide, and three or four times lengthwise. In each corner of the bay was an old spiral staircase that led to a rickety-looking catwalk that lined both sides from the large door at the aft of the boat to the front of the cargo bay. The entire interior hull of the bay looked as if it would shatter at any moment. A mosaic of silicon-filled cracks were spattered everywhere, broken up by large sections of metal plating that had been welded to the hull where silicon patching wouldn't do. All of it was coated by a thick, reddish gray layer of dust and rust. Above hung a track and rigging, where a large yellow magnetic crane dangled as it waited for its next task. In the bay were a few large shipping containers, one them the cold storage container. On the opposite side sat Thorbin's pod amidst a column of various debris.

Looking forward, towards the bow, there was a single hallway, the one Ben had led Thorbin down to get to the galley, where they had fought the Talc. Right above the hallway the upper deck began. A large pain of glass stretched nearly the width of the ship, allowing people up there to look down into the bay. This was the bay's control room. The spiral staircases at the forward of the bay led up towards this room. Thorbin climbed one of the staircases.

The top led him onto the catwalk, which stretched back towards the aft, and a hatch that led into the control room. The hatch was open and he stepped through it.

The control room was full of stations that controlled everything in the bay from the large exterior doors to the crane. Around each station reflective yellow tape had been laid around the perimeter atop the white tile floor. Brilliant red warning signs were plastered around every station, making clear the safety hazards of each control. Unlike the cargo bay, this room was clean and Spartan – nothing that didn't belong was here. The white tile floor was designed specially to contrast harshly if a single piece of dust landed on it. Opposite the glass wall was the forward facing wall. There was nothing notable there except a hatch with a sign above that read 'Office'.

Thorbin passed through the hatch and into the office. The room was longer than the control room, full of half cubicles nestling desks and workstations. In the center was a large conference table encircled by chairs, a few of which had been knocked over. In the forward left corner was a closet-sized room with a sign that designated it as the office head. Thorbin made his way around the table and across the grayish blue carpet to the other side of the office, where there was another hatch. It led to the bridge.

The bridge was the forward most room in the upper deck. As Thorbin entered he was greeted by the captain's view. The entire forward section of the bridge was a window that looked out over the bow and into the field of debris the boat was drifting amongst. To the left of the entrance was the command chair. A deep seat mounted to the deck and adorned with command consoles. The seat cushions looked well used, patches of duct tape ran in small strips, keeping tears from growing larger, The right armrest had dark spots around a built-in cup holder, the left arm had an attachment sewn onto it to secure a basket to the left of the chair. Thorbin peered into the basket and grinned, it was an ingenious masterpiece of amateur fabrication. Potato chips and sunflower seeds, magazines and water bottles, even a few beers were all arranged in their own little cubbies in the basket.

Thorbin couldn't help himself, and he took a seat. As his butt settled in, the consoles came to life and arranged themselves around him. One came directly over his lap while others pulled around the side, everything came within reach but not so close as to confine him. Thorbin took a look at the center console; it displayed a damage report that didn't look too comforting. As he read it, it informed him that the ship had three decks; the upper, which he was on; the main, which was below him; and the lower, which had been completely destroyed. He also gathered that the port turbine was almost completely incapacitated, which explained why they were adrift. Then somewhat to his surprise, it reported that the ship's spyder was repairing hull fractures on the bow. Thorbin was impressed; he didn't think Ben had the kind of income that could afford an advanced robot like a spyder.

Thorbin minimized the damage assessment and started browsing through the ships files. He soon came upon the ship's registrar information. It read:

Ship designation: Victoria
Class: Commercial Interplanetary Tow/pilot
Make: GMC-Lock
Model: Rig L
Commissioned: May 2091
Port registrant: New Tokyo, Lunar port F-3
Owner registrant: Benjamin Reagan
Registration status: Current

Thorbin laughed.

"Interplanetary tow. I'm on a tug boat?" He leaned back into the seat, the consoles followed, but he wasn't paying attention to them. "Victoria," he said, considering her. "You survived the invasion. I guess you're a lot tougher than you look. Could be worse. Could be better."

Thorbin stood and the consoles swung out of his way, settling in their dismounted positions. In the deck of the bridge, to the far left, was another hatch. It led down onto the observation deck, the room directly below the bridge. He descended.

The observation deck was laid out similarly to the bridge. It was a little larger and had a large dome-like window that looked over the bow. Against the far wall was a couch and coffee table, set on the portside of the room was a pair of armchairs and end tables, and on the starboard, a bar with stools. The room felt like a cozy place where one could kick their feet up and relax. Next to the couch, on the back wall, was the hatch that led to the hallway.

The hallway stretched down the length of the main deck, from the observation deck at the front of Victoria to the cargo bay at her aft. He walked slowly down the narrow hallway, passing first a set of hatches set equally across the hall from each other. One was labeled 'Port turbine room', the other 'Starboard turbine room'. He decided not to explore the engine rooms and continued on. Near the end of the hallway that led out into the cargo bay was another set of matching hatches. On the starboard side was the galley; on the port was the common room. He had had more than enough of the galley for today so he turned and took a peek into the common room.

It was a mess; on the far side was another hatch that looked like it had been welded closed. There was a bookshelf that had fallen over and dumped its contents on the deck, along with what appeared to be the remains of a table. Against one of the walls was a sad-looking couch that had lost all its cushions with a broken end table where they should have been. All in all, the common room best reflected Victoria's overall condition.

Thorbin and Ben

Thorbin stood at the hatch looking in, trying to discern what had happened when Ben approached him from behind. "I closed the container," he said solemnly. "When we get to Mars I can give them a proper burial."

"Of course," Thorbin replied respectfully. "What about the hitchhikers? We just going to leave them in the galley?" he asked facing Ben.

"Sure, don't think they gonna eat much," Ben replied. "All the crew quarters been destroyed. That means this room is the bunk. I don't feel much like cleaning messes up right now."

Ben looked and spoke wearily. "I figured maybe we'd have a sit and get to know each other. Then maybe move a few things. Take it from there."

"Sounds good," Thorbin replied. "Maybe I can take care of the Talc," Thorbin insisted.

"Soon, soon. Really ain't much we can do with 'em anyhow. The spyder'll get rid of 'em. First it needs to take care of the bow. The hairy bastards will be off my ship in an hour or so."

Ben squeezed past Thorbin, who then followed him into the common room. Ben turned back, holding out a hand of caution.

"Watch your step. Don't step on my cards," he said as he fumbled with the shelf, spilling even more of its contents onto the deck.

Thorbin came around to the other side and offered a hand, being sure not step on anything that resembled cards. After leaning the wounded shelf against the wall, Thorbin began to arrange the mess into neater piles. He came upon a loose deck of cards. He squatted and started picking them up – Ben obviously cared about them. Holding one in his hand, he inspected it. The corners were bent and frayed, but otherwise serviceable. It was a traditional poker card on the face it and had the typical number and suit, but on the back it had a picture of Victoria and inscribed in silver ink the words 'Ben's house'.

"Thanks," Ben said. "We can put them over here."

Thorbin stood and handed Ben the cards. In return, Ben handed Thorbin two glasses. "Here, hold on to these for me, they're goin' with us." Thorbin smiled at the glasses, really they were mason jars. "OK, let's go," Ben said, holding a small green corked jar and a large jug.

With glasses, jug and jar in hand, they turned down the hallway and headed to the observation deck in the bow of the ship. Thorbin made himself comfortable on the couch, while Ben climbed the stairs to the bridge and returned with snacks.

"Now," Ben said, seating himself next to Thorbin on the couch. "There might be a little dust on the bottle. Don't let it fool you 'bout what's inside." He smiled as he filled Thorbin's mason jar liberally with the bottle's crimson contents. "Made this myself. It's raspberry wine."

Thorbin wasn't much of a drinker and wasn't sure if he could hold down a full pint of what Ben had poured. But Ben's expectant smile was waiting for him, so Thorbin put the glass to his lips and took a sip. "Nice. It's sweet, almost like juice," he said, pleasantly surprised. Ben snickered as he poured himself a glass.

"Oh yeah, it's good. Make it myself," Ben confirmed with a grin, then he took a deep satisfying swig and sank back into the couch. "So, you a pilot?" Ben asked after a comfortable moment.

"Yup, runs in the family. How about you? How long have you been captain of The Victoria?"

"Vic-to-ria," Ben sounded out. "Oh, Vicky and me go way back. I been her captain for 'bout twenty-five years. Since my father passed. I been working her my whole life. Tug work mostly. Transport work on occasion."

"Transport?" Thorbin considered aloud. "Victoria's cargo bay is big enough to make money?"

"It's not about the volume, it's about the quality and discretion."

Thorbin turned and looked at Ben. "Smuggling you mean."

"Smuggling is such a dirty word. Every now and then I deliver something to someone who really wants it, and values their privacy."

"Like who?"

"Mostly Syndicate."

"You've got to be kidding?"

"The Syndicate's not so bad."

Thorbin's jaw dropped in disbelief at what he heard.

Ben smiled. "OK, they're bad, all I'm saying is we never had a problem with 'em. That's all. All you have to do is keep your end of the bargain and you're fine. A man can work with the Syndicate as long as he only agrees to what he's capable of."

Thorbin picked up his glass. "You're lucky to be alive," he said as he brought the glass up for anther sip and discovered it was empty. Ben poured a second round then continued.

"What do you know about the Syndicate?"

Thorbin scoffed in a friendly way. "I was a constable for seven years before

I joined the DC. Most of that time I was hunting Syndicate. They have a nasty way of terminating business relationships."

"Ah shit, long arm of the law on my ship. The world really has come to an end." Ben took a big sip of wine. "Vicky! What were you thinking picking this guy up?" Thorbin grinned.

"So, what you're saying is you'd rather of picked up a Syndicate."

"Hell no," Ben said, then took another sip. "Shut up and drink your wine." A few seconds passed then Ben started again. "So you hunted Syndicate for seven years?"

"Mostly," Thorbin answered. "Although I did chase pirates for a while."

"Oh, those sons of bitches. You never see me around them types. That I can promise you," Ben declared. "Back when my daddy was Vicky's captain and I was a teenager, we came across a pack of them assholes. They boarded us, took control of the ship and locked us in the mess. Then they musta figured we had nothing they wanted so they came back to kill us. My daddy promised that he wouldn't give up their location if they'd just let us go. They could care less. He had to promise them a shipload of supplies. Beer is what they mostly wanted, but they let us go."

"Don't tell me you dropped off their beer and that was that?" Thorbin asked.

"Hell no," Ben answered emphatically. "We never went back to that sector again," Ben snorted. "It's been thirty-some-odd years and I ain't been to a sector that's adjacent. You can keep your pirates. You shoulda spent seven years chasing those bastards around."

"Right, because chasing Syndicate was bad for business." Ben chuckled some then reached into his pocket and pulled out a small red glass pipe. He then de-corked the green jar, and the intense aroma of cannabis wafted out from within. Ben then plucked out a bud and started packing it into the pipe. Thorbin just sat there and looked at him in amazement.

"First the Syndicate now this?" Thorbin really didn't care that much, but Ben's assumption that he wouldn't mind surprised him a little bit.

"Oh what?" Ben lowered the pipe from near his face and stared back at Thorbin. "Now I can't smoke weed on my own ship?"

Thorbin quickly reconsider giving Ben a hard time. "Hey, give me another glass of that delicious wine and we'll call it even."

"Even! I don't see you contributing to this fine evening. First you board my ship. Then you kill my Talc. Now you want more wine."

"Hey you asked me to kill those Talc."

"I woulda got 'em just fine. I was just working on my strategy."

"What, you were going to season them to death?"

"Oh you think you funny, let's see how funny you are without my delicious raspberry wine." Ben reached across and slid Thorbin's glass from in front of him. They stared at each other, trying not to smile. Then Thorbin remembered something.

"OK, I got something for you."

"Oh, now that I took your glass you got something for me," Ben said as Thorbin reached into his pocket and pulled out two packages labeled 'dessert'.

"Huh," Ben said as he grabbed one of the packages. "What do we have here?"

"Open it up. I think you'll be happy."

"Oh you think I'll be happy," Ben said sarcastically, although thoroughly interested in Thorbin's gift. He tore the wrapper back and was stunned.

"Is this chocolate?"

"No," said Thorbin. "It's Swiss chocolate."

Ben almost leaped out of his seat. "I haven't had *any* chocolate in years. OK, you get your wine privilege back." He slid Thorbin's glass back over to him and filled it to the top, then made a big show of taking a bite of his chocolate. With a single bite, he looked like a child that had never been loved getting his first hug.

"Ah, good job, Vicky, you found us chocolate."

So in the shadow of despair, they ate chocolate and drank raspberry wine, finding joy in each other's company. Hours passed until the last of the jug was being poured into their glasses, despite the both of them already having had more than enough.

"Ben," Thorbin said, making sure his grip around his glass was firm. "It's our first evening together. We should have a toast."

"A toast to what, T," Ben asked.

T, Thorbin's heart smiled. "I don't know."

Ben looked at his glass thoughtfully, placed a hand on one of Victoria's nearby bulkheads, and toasted.

"Here's to the end of the world, and this old girl."

Chapter Four
All Busted Up

Ben

There in the cargo bay sat Ben; smoldering pipe in one hand and a chrome piece of Victoria in his lap. He hadn't slept. After Thorbin passed out, he had tried to rest his eyes, but he was restless. He tried to work on Victoria, and he did, a little, but he couldn't concentrate. So there he sat in the cargo bay, confined in a prison of sorrow and smoke, staring from behind its murky curtain at his beloved's tomb.

He raised the pipe to his lips and futilely tried to inhale the sorrow away. He knew better, but reason was not his companion. His smoky crutch was his habit, it allowed for the perception of control, the inconsistent illusion, mocking cruelly with subtle moments. Victorious moments that lead us to believe we play a role in our destinies. True moments, like the one that Ben was having, that display clearly – something larger affirms or denies us all. He took another hit.

Thorbin

Thorbin awoke on the floor, lying partially under the table. His eyelids felt heavier than most mornings; slowly, they released their blockade on his vision. Wearily, he gazed through the half-dome glass of the observation area. The stars seemed painfully brighter than normal. He turned his head to escape their subtle assault on his pupils. Strenuously he placed his hand on his forehead, letting out a stale groan of a breath. He felt his pulse through his brow, beating its way into his eardrums. A grimace appeared on his face as he took a deep, slow, dry breath and tasted the morning breath of the day after.

He leaned forward, propping himself up on his elbows. A spinning dizziness came and went, leaving him staring out of the dome glass over the bow. The spyder was working tirelessly on the hull, where it had been all night. He stared at it until his vision focused on a single image. He fixated on the faint sensory lights emanating from its torso as its eight robotic legs slowly chittered round the damaged area. It had repaired a considerable amount since last night. He scooted backwards on the floor and out from under the table. He leaned forward, lifted up one knee for leverage then stood.

Standing there he realized he was alone. He rubbed the back of his head as he took a second look around the room and confirmed – no Ben.

Entering the galley Thorbin noticed the faint bloodstains where the Talc bodies had once been on the floor and against the wall, and the table which had been turned upright despite being riddled with bullet holes. He walked over to the sink and opened cupboards until he came across a glass for water. After filling it, he took a sip and felt refreshed, then he took another that he didn't swallow. He swished it around for a few seconds then spit it out into the sink. He then turned around and leaned back on the counter as he began to drink the rest thirstily.

He inspected the floor and walls to survey where the shots had landed. The floor on the far side of the hatch was their final resting place. He walked over and fingered one of the holes in the floor. The damage was minimal. He turned and glanced to the wall where Ben had unleashed his vengeance, a pink stained hole with a rock salt and skull fragment halo. Not far away was a trashcan whose lid was being held open by the pummels of Talc blades.

Thorbin returned to the sink and was refilling his glass when Ben walked in.

"Morning," Ben said, polishing a chrome piece of Victoria. "Know anything about turbine repair?" he asked.

"Yes, sir," Thorbin replied, almost out of his haze. "One year advanced turbine training at Annapolis."

"Good, I could use a little help, and don't call me 'sir'. My daddy was the last 'sir' on this boat."

"Aye-aye, Captain," Thorbin answered with a grin.

"Captain Ben." Ben smiled, evaluating the address. "I like the sound of that. How's the head?"

"How much did we drink?"

"A lot. Come on, scallywag," Ben said, heading back out the hatch.

"Clear," Thorbin said, following. "Is that a thermal intake?"

"It is," Ben answered.

"Chrome? You building a hot rod?"

"Hey, kid, function and beauty," Ben said with an informative tone.

"Nothing wrong with that," Thorbin acknowledged as they stepped through the turbine room hatch.

"Wow!" Thorbin exhaled, seeing one of Victoria's turbines for the first time. "This is amazing."

The turbine rooms ran nearly the length of Victoria, one on each side of the ship. The turbine took up the lion's share of space in each room and was die cast a deep rich blue, almost black. On its belly were the thermal intakes, lined up from front to back on both sides. Function and beauty, essentially they were air filters that sucked in clean air that cooled the magnetic turbine as its inferno raged. On the top were the thermal exhaust pipes, also chrome. Ten of them in total rose from the top then snaked down the side of the turbine and turned aft. The dark blue and chrome marvel was an engineering masterpiece.

"You're not kidding. This thing is actually air cooled?" Thorbin asked with disbelief.

"That's right, it's my daddy's design. Custom," Ben said proudly.

Thorbin reached forward and touched one of the exhaust pipes. It was cool to the touch and smooth in only the way finely crafted metal can be.

"Hey you gonna smudge my chrome! Get your damn hands of that!" Thorbin jerked his hand back, and Ben polished the area he had been fondling. "Everyone's gotta touch," Ben muttered, then barked, "If you want to touch something, go grab my sockets and I'll show you how to put new filters in."

"Yes, sir. Ah, Captain," Thorbin replied, then found the toolbox and grabbed the socket set.

When he returned Ben was under the turbine and motioning for Thorbin to join him. He grabbed an air filter, slid under the massive engine, and handed it to Ben, who then demonstrated how to unbolt the intake and properly place the filter.

"Easy enough," Thorbin said. "This can't be the extent of the damage, can it?" he asked.

"No," Ben answered. "Some of the magnets got warped and the field's all messed up. The starboard turbine is fine, but this one's running at two percent of capacity. I was hoping that replacing some of the older intakes, and all of the filters, would compensate enough to get her going a bit better. That way we don't have to spin all the way to Mars." Ben demonstrated the spinning with his hands and a smile. Thorbin laughed.

"How much do we need to get the job done?"

"Three percent will keep us steady, but we won't be moving too fast."

"I'm guessing Victoria running at a hundred percent would get us to Mars in a month or so. At three percent it could take years."

"Yeah, you're about right. We're gonna have to catch an oasis."

"An oasis? How far is the closest one?"

"At three percent?"

"Yeah."

"About a week, give or take a day excluding any other trouble. Jacob's Run though. Pretty big one. They may have a turbine tech, or with all the recent debris, I'm sure some pirates collected a few turbines we could use until we can get this one fixed."

"Sounds like a decent plan."

"So I just figured we'd head to Mars, you good to tag along?" Ben asked.

"Sure, unless we meet up with some DC."

"DC? You *were* there, weren't you?" Ben looked over at Thorbin in disbelief and disappointment.

"Well, yeah, Ben, it's my duty," Thorbin said, trying to stay his dismay.

"There ain't no DC ships around here. Duty gonna get you killed."

"Well someone's gotta do it," Thorbin continued in a gentle tone.

"Do what? Get killed? Plenty already have."

"I'm a pilot, there's an invasion on, and I'm sworn to protect Earth," Thorbin insisted.

"Earth isn't what it used to be, T. You can't fight for something that's gone."

"We're still here."

"Oh, so you gonna fight for me then?"

"You, me, everyone else."

"Huh," Ben scoffed. "A patriot that won't admit defeat. Quick to run off and get his ass kicked."

"If that's what fortune dictates, at least I gave it a shot."

"Fortune is for fools. You can keep your fortune. Luck too. You know what the problem with fortune is, T? You want a good piece of advice?"

"You ask me as if I could say no," Thorbin smiled.

"Don't make fun of this. I'll tell you, but you listen here." Ben paused. "The problem with being fortunate is that when it's good, it's great. When it's bad, the good don't make up for it. You can keep your fortune. I prefer what I got control over."

"Maybe fortune was the wrong word."

"No, it wasn't. You go find the last stragglers of a defeated navy and hope to fight off the Talc. What you're hoping for is luck. Luck, that's fortune. Don't try for good luck. Work with what you got to make it better."

"Ben, you can't win a battle if you don't fight."

"You're stupid to fight a battle you gonna lose."

"So what...run away?"

"No, not run away, just know when to hold 'em, know when to fold 'em."

"All right," Thorbin said, wanting to change the subject. "Tell me about yourself, Ben."

"I know when to fold 'em."

Thorbin looked over at Ben as he tightened the last bolt on the intake. There was a few seconds of silence. Then they moved to the next intake and prepared to remove it. The silence stayed and the work continued for a while until Ben couldn't take it anymore.

"A DC pilot, a graduate of Annapolis. You were born to fight the Talc."

"That's how I see it," Thorbin responded.

"Well, can't hate you for that. Was your daddy a pilot too?"

"Yes. He fought in The Armageddon."

"No kidding, which side?"

"Allies, he was an American pilot."

"You from America?"

"No. DC brat. My dad never could settle down after Tokyo. That's what Mom used to say at least."

"Tokyo? Was he in the Battle for Liberation?"

"From beginning to end."

"Wow, musta been a tough man. Did he contract the radiation?"

"Yeah, wasn't too bad though."

"Well, that's good," Ben said, tightening the last bolt on the last intake. "Hey, only one bolt left, then we can close up and see what Vicky will do for us."

"Three percent. How much do you usually get when you replace the filters."

"Dirty filters usually knock efficiency down to ninety-four, ninety-five percent when the turbine is in good repair, so this should give us at least one point." Ben applied torque to the last bolt on the last housing, the expression on his face would have you believe he was fastening the only bolt holding the boat together. "OK, got it. If you clean up and put the tools in the hall, I'll start sealing the hatches. We can get some breakfast while we wait for the temp to drop in here."

After breakfast Thorbin sat at the helm and was familiarizing himself with Victoria's controls. It was all very quaint compared to the fighter systems he was accustomed to, but the automated wrap around console was neat. He was weaving his head back and forth, playing with it, amused at how the controls followed him as he swayed. Aside from that, not much had changed in regards to Victoria's general condition, except the bow structure had gone from critical failure to all right as long as nothing happened due to the spyder's tireless effort. After a few moments Ben came up the stairs with several thin boxes about the size of large books.

"Control cards?" Thorbin asked.

"Old ones. I'm not even sure if they'll work." Ben placed the control cards on the floor then knelt down near a panel behind the captain's chair to the left. He placed his hands flush to the wall at shoulder width, then pushed his fingers through the latch covers and pulled the panel with a subtle grunt. Once removed, the panel revealed the server cards for most of the ship's functions.

"I'm just going to pull long range altogether. Watch the console and tell me if short range comes online."

Thorbin pulled up the ship's main status screen and selected short range. Navigation, communications, and sensors were all preceded by an 'Offline' status indicator.

"Short range. Nav, com, and sensors are all offline," Thorbin reported.

"Well I haven't gotten to it yet," Ben said sheepishly. "I'm going to replace the long-range card with a pass." Thorbin heard a snap as Ben pulled one of the cards, then a click as he replaced it. "That was long-range com, any change?"

Thorbin looked at the screen and the short-range communications indicator hadn't changed. "Negative."

"Negative," Ben said with a chuckle.

"Yeah, negative, Captain." Thorbin felt a hint of warmth. "Hey if your sensors were out, how did you pick me up?"

"Self defense," Ben answered without hesitation. "You were headed right for me." Another snap then click. "How 'bout the Nav?"

"Negative," Thorbin responded.

"I've had just about enough of your 'negative', scallywag. Watch the screen – gonna try a cold boot."

Thorbin looked back at the screen and the offline descriptors next to the three systems disappeared then reappeared displaying 'Initializing'.

"It looks like the system sees the cards," Thorbin said, encouraged.

"Are they online?"

"No, still initializing. How long should it take?"

"Should be up."

Thorbin looked back at the screen. The descriptors now read 'Initialization time out offline'. "No good," he reported.

"What's the message?"

"Timed out."

"I was afraid of that. Not surprised though. The forward array is partially attached to the lower deck."

"You only have one?"

"Complete long and short. Yeah, just one. But I have an old secondary short-range array above the office. Let me get a bridge in here, and I'll get back there and power up." Ben pulled the main array card and all the screen messages simply read 'Offline'.

"I'm setting the bridge in port five. Move all short range there." Thorbin fumbled around for the server port controls while Ben installed the bridge card. "The cards should already be in place. I just need to place a bridge card and power up the array. Give me a holler when they go online."

Ben walked through the hatch into the office and went to a desk set against the wall near the center of the room. He set the contents of the desk on a nearby chair and focused his attention on a poster on the wall above the desk – a bikini-clad girl. Taped up, she was partially covering the panel he needed to get to. He neatly pulled the tape off then rolled the poster up, picture inwards, securing the roll with a piece of tape left on the wall, then he placed the poster on the chair with everything else.

He pulled the panel off the wall and set it aside, then brushed a thin layer of dust off the cards inside so he could find the main. It was the one on top. He pulled it from its slot, placed it on the desk, then replaced it with the bridge card.

"OK, I'm 'bout to power!" he yelled towards the bridge as he switched a toggle to the positive position.

In an instant, various LED's and digital displays came to life, casting a layer of green and red shading on Ben's face. He leaned forward and inspected the lights. Everything looked like it was working. He leaned back and turned his head towards the bridge. He was about to speak when a shrieking crackle followed by a demoralizing pop shot silica and dust from one of the cards like a computer hissy-fit. Coughing, he waved a hand in front of his face to dissipate the smoke and try to discern the damage.

"Damn," he said with a sigh, seeing a smoldered hole in one of the cards.

"Short range Nav and sensors are online! Com was for a moment, but now it's off!" Ben heard Thorbin hollering from the bridge.

"Working on it!" Ben yelled back in frustration. "So, not gonna talk to me today Vicky. Fine, bitch." Then he yelled back to Thorbin. "Is there another com card up there?"

"I don't know."

"Can you check?" There was a moment of silence and Ben decided he would have to check for himself.

As he entered the bridge Thorbin informed him, "Sorry, none. You don't have any back ups?"

"That was the back up," Ben answered as he motioned for Thorbin to move so he could sit. "Let's see what we can see," Ben said as the consoles set themselves around him, Thorbin looking over his shoulder.

"What's wrong with the com?"

"Card blew, hopefully we can get one at the oasis." Ben began manipulating the sensor screen. He enlarged, zoomed in and out, minimized and dragged screens around until he came to his conclusion.

"We're at the edge of the debris field. The oasis isn't appearing in short range. If I remember correctly, it's in sector 189,470,312. I don't think we're too far away. Before we lost sensors we were headed in its direction. I think we're around 181,402,401. If we take this heading, short range should pick it up eventually." He was pointing on screen and Thorbin really couldn't tell one way or the other.

"Sounds good," he said anyway. "Has the turbine room cooled down enough?"

Ben navigated the console then responded. "No. But hey, look at that, the spyder's repaired that thruster."

"Any ships in short range?"

"Let me see." Ben initiated a general scan. "No, at least no human ships. Didn't get a look at the Talc signature before we we're attacked." Thorbin leaned over the console and helped himself. Ben gave him a look, which the DC pilot ignored.

"Talc ships give off a lot more heat than our ships. And the magnetic fields are different to ours. I don't think they use EMF propulsion." Thorbin was queuing the sensors to pick up and display heat sources.

"There! Oh shit, what's that, a Talc?" Ben's blood pressure began to rise.

"I doubt it," Thorbin said, unsure. "It's pretty small."

"A small Talc?" Ben insisted. Thorbin selected the object and enlarged the sensor image as he checked various measurements.

"Almost no magnetic field and barely above freezing. It's either a warm rock or a very small disabled ship. One that's taken a good beating. Maybe a large pod."

"Taken a beating? Like us."

"Maybe. It really looks like a pod, maybe from a cruise ship. How long does it take for a full scan?"

"It's an older system, a few minutes."

"Is anything original on this boat?" Thorbin asked rhetorically.

"Um...frame. Oh, the forward sensor array."

"The one that needs to be replaced."

"Still original though," Ben pointed out.

"You know you probably could've bought a new ship with all the money you've poured into Victoria. Maybe two."

"Yeah, but me and Vicky go way back."

"Any weapons aside from your season all?"

"Your pistol." Thorbin grinned at Ben's response. "The scan's done."

Thorbin fingered the screen in order to enlarge the scan diagram. "See, a pod, it's just outside of the debris – above us."

"OK," Ben said, feeling relief, then he stood. "We've only got thrusters. Think you can get us up there while I man the control room?"

"Sure," Thorbin said, taking the seat.

"I have to move your pod out of the way, so just drift under it. Put it right behind us then hold steady," Ben said as he turned towards the office hatch and headed to the control room.

Thorbin minimized the sensor readout and launched the docking thrusters. He could feel Victoria moving forward slow and determined. She started to roll left so he decreased thrust on the starboard side to stabilize.

Thorbin had never flown anything as big and slow as Victoria. Each meter they progressed seemed to take an eternity. The seat quickly became uncomfortable, and the air wasn't filling him with vitality. There was no sensation of grandeur or greater purpose, just the task at hand, slow and steady. His chest wasn't thundering. His nerves weren't fraying. The goose bumps on his arms were there because of the cold, not because of anything resembling excitement. It was all very mundane. However, despite all this, it didn't feel wrong, which was good enough for now. He sat quietly pondering, drifting in the debris of countless untold stories that would mostly remain untold.

Chapter Five
A Bittersweet Voice In The Wilderness

Thorbin

As they left the field behind, Thorbin squinted at the vast emptiness ahead. He hoped to see an object defying the darkness. Only the twinkle of distant stars disturbed the vastness. He turned back to the consoles to verify his heading.

"Right there?" he asked himself then switched back to the navigation screen. It confirmed that he was heading towards the pod. Again, he scanned the eternal night sky, scrutinizing each star until he found one that twinkled different than the others.

"There you are," he said, looking towards it with a sense of satisfaction. He corrected his heading so that he would coast right under it.

He cycled through the various consoles – most of them still offline. He opened up the properties for the com, curious about their settings. There was a myriad of information but most importantly it read 'audio/video offline'. He noticed there was another setting next to the indicator and tapped it with his finger. The message changed to 'video com offline'. He then tapped it again. The message changed again, 'audio com online', then he was instantly bombarded with a mush of digital distortion. A smile came across his face as he pulled up the com application – a small program that lined the top of the consoles, broken up into sections. Thorbin picked the one that read 'Con Rm'.

"Hey, Ben, can you hear me?"

A few seconds later Ben responded. "Yeah, I hear you. How the hell are you doing that?"

"The com card isn't completely blown. How do I scan the audio spectrum?"

"Hit the com button on the far right and hold it."

Thorbin did as instructed and the audio jumped from static-laden frequency to static-laden frequency until a distressed, sweet feminine voice could be heard.

"Can't you hear me? Please let them hear me. Why won't they answer?" Thorbin heard the voice say hopelessly through sobs. Thorbin immediately stopped the scan and engaged the frequency.

"This is Lieutenant Monroe of the Victoria. I can hear you now. Can you hear me?" The sobbing stopped.

"This is Lieu…" she said confused, then she realizing that the voice she heard was not in her head. "Oh! Yes, I hear you! I love you! Are coming to get me?" she said with delight as her dismay morphed into joy.

"Yes, just hold on. We'll be there in a minute."

"OK. Holding on."

"It might get a little bumpy, but that's just us coming about. Are you alone?"

"Yes."

"Are you injured?"

"No. But I'm freezing. Please tell me you have a jacket or something." The suspect star in the distance was now a tiny pod closing fast. Thorbin reduced speed.

"I'm sure we can scrounge up something. What's your name, ma'am?"

"Lorilei," she answered meekly.

"Lorilei, make sure you're seated and strapped in good."

"OK," she said, a little frightened.

"Not much longer," Thorbin consoled as the pod grew larger in the distance. "We're about to pass under you."

Ben broke in through the com. "Hold steady as possible. Nice and slow. The bay is sealed up and the doors are open, I'm ready to fire the tow cable."

Ben

Ben was standing at the cable firing station in the control room waiting anxiously for the pod to pass over. Victoria wasn't really designed to pick up pods. He hoped the new arrival would get on board safely.

"Come on, Vicky, let's catch us an engineer. We could use another good man around here. You did good last time. Don't let me down now."

"Coming about," Thorbin informed over the com. Ben looked down at the sensor grid and the pod was just over the bow. He adjusted the tow cable controls, anticipating the shot.

"OK, hold this position, T," Ben instructed as the pod came into range over Victoria's aft. Ben made some last-second adjustments, held his breath, then fired. The tow cable screamed towards the pod and collided with a shrill clank that reverberated back down the cable. The magnetic hitch was secure – the shot was true.

"OK, move forward just ten or twenty meters."

Victoria crawled forward and the cable slack grew taut. The pod slowly drifted from side to side as Victoria moved forward until the pod was directly behind her.

"Halt," Ben ordered and Victoria came to a stop. The tow cable started to pick up slack as the pod drifted towards the cargo bay doors. Ben started reeling in the pod.

"Are we good?" Thorbin asked over the loudspeaker.

"Good, hold position."

"Clear," Thorbin responded. Ben pulled in the pod like a fish that had given up the fight. He inspected it as it entered the bay. It was big pod, big enough for a few people. It had a few burn scares but was still intact.

Once inside the bay, Ben closed the doors and positioned the magnet hoist above the pod. Using the hoist and tow cable he set the new pod right next to Thorbin's. He released the hoist and pulled it back to the ceiling, then he demagnetized the tow cable, making it fall to the deck with a loud clang.

"Got 'em," Ben informed over the loudspeaker, not knowing that Thorbin was standing behind him.

"Got *her* you mean."

Ben jumped, startled. "You're supposed to be at the helm! Don't scare me like that."

"Sorry."

"Her?" Ben confirmed, sounding a little disappointed.

"Yeah, got *her.*" Then they heard the whish of atmosphere returning to the bay. An indicator above the hatch from the control room to the upper catwalk turned from red to green, indicating it was safe to enter.

"Air's good, let's go meet our girl," Ben said, bucking up slightly. They opened the hatch and proceeded through and down the spiral staircase to the main deck.

"You talked to her?" Ben asked as they approached.

"Yeah."

"She didn't mention that she was an engineer or tech, something like that, did she?"

"Nope."

They approached the pod and looked for a hatch. Unlike Thorbin's pod, there was no glass; it wasn't until they inspected the opposite side that they found anything resembling an entrance. They searched it for a switch or latch but could find none. They looked at each other as if each expected the other to know what to do next. Ben slowly reached a hand forward as Thorbin took a step back, palming his pistol. Ben knocked firmly three times. Nothing happened. Again they looked expectantly at each other. Ben reached his hand out again and before he could complete his second knock the door slid upwards with such force that Ben's knuckles warmed with the friction.

"Oww," he said, pulling his hand away, more in surprise than in pain.

Then, from behind the door, in all her loveliness, came Lorilei. She regarded them with quivering lavender eyes and tear-stained cheeks. Her soft brown hair framed her pretty face save the few long lazy strands that dangled out of place. She placed a hand on each side of the exit and slowly pulled herself out. Her bare feet touched the ground cautiously as they blessed Victoria's cold deck, which chilled them unpleasantly. A shiver stirred from her toes up her bare legs until her soft brown skin yielded to goose bumps. A once snug fitting black dress, now in tatters around her waist, trembled as she held her breath, attempting not to shake apart. A lavender bra and panty set was all she had to stave away the chill of the cargo bay. They were telling undergarments. Not just meant to please the eye, but also to warn the tempted onlooker. A brand of sorts embroidered in the delicate material declared that what lay beneath was claimed.

Eventually she relented to breathlessness and inhaled, which had a stirring effect on her faultless breasts. She crossed her arms under them, holding on to her elbows, trying to coax out any amount of warmth. A brave and inviting smile presented itself as a peace offering while her large lavender eyes shimmered and begged for warmth and acceptance.

The boys stood staring at her, dumbfounded. She was a lovely girl no doubt, well presented even in disarray. Without a word, she called out to their innate maleness. Begging them to reach out to her, but they didn't. As compelling a temptation as it might have been, as easy as it would have been to replace guilt with reason, they stood fast.

Her pretty lavender eyes and intrinsically designed underwear kept them at bay. She wasn't she, she was it. Beyond that, every degree of beauty that she displayed declared loudly that she would not be easily lost, yet here she was, and trouble would soon follow. She wasn't a lost beauty; she was misplaced property, belonging to the sort that murder with less concern than they breathe. A parcel of ill repute most sweet, most bitter, and the boys didn't know how to act.

"Damn," Ben said, exhaling.

Lorilei took this as an invitation and leapt forward gratefully, flinging her arms around his neck. A tear-stained cheek buried itself comfortably in his chest as she savored the warmth of his body. He immediately felt pleased, she had read him like a book and knew he would respond to the whole 'woman in need' angle. Ben began to put his arms around her, searching for some comforting words. Then he came to his senses and pushed her away in disgust.

"None of that," he said, backing her away to arm's length.

"I'm *so* cold and you're *so* warm," she said, playing heavily on the brief nurturing moment she had sensed from him, and she was genuinely cold. Ben pointed a finger at her and was about to speak when Thorbin interrupted.

"Here, Lorilei, you can have my shirt," he said, and he began to unbutton it, revealing a white undershirt. Ben stood there, finger extended, wanting to convey his distrust but not being able to form the words as Lorilei turned her lavenders on Thorbin.

Thorbin nearly melted into a pile of putty-ish chivalry and Eros. He quickly averted his eyes to escape captivity, only to be captivated by her breasts, taking notice of the effect the cold had on them. He slammed his eyes closed, leaving him vulnerable, and he became the next victim of a graciously soft Lorilei hug. The breasts he couldn't look at without losing reason firmly supplanted themselves against his abdomen, while her soft hair tickled pleasantly against his neck and chin. His heart skipped a beat. Like Ben, she held him firmly in her soft embrace. It took all the effort he could muster to set aside the euphoria and counter.

"OK, no problem, miss," he said draping his shirt around her shoulders and gently pulling her away.

"I'm still cold," she begged, falling back into his chest.

"We can make you something warm to eat."

She leaned her head back, making sure her lips were so close to his that he could feel her breath on them. Then she set her eyes back upon him, like deep wells of unavoidable thankfulness.

"I've been alone for almost three days," she said.

Thorbin felt compassion and hugged her. Three days alone is bad, especially for these times, but for a Mosot, it was surprising she wasn't dead.

"You're welcome," he said, and politely broke her advance. "Food?"

"Yes, please. I haven't eaten a thing in days," she said, allowing Thorbin to hold her at arm's length, but still giving him her best lost puppy dog eyes. He pulled his shirt further around her shoulders and fastened the top button – a far more modest covering, but not a degree less fetching.

"Come with me and I'll get you some food."

"OK," she said, taking him by the hand. As they headed back to the galley Ben still had his finger aimed at her.

"The shirt off your back!" he exclaimed. "Now you're going to feed it. That's how it starts." Soon Ben was standing in the bay alone. He looked around at Victoria, furious and frustrated.

"Damn it, Vicky!" Then he rushed down the hall after them.

Lorilei

Lorilei took heart in being led to the kitchen, then in being instructed to sit while the man in the pilot's uniform foraged for something easy and hot for her to eat. Things had gotten off to a rocky start on this ship, but it appeared that the man in the uniform would be the one – her new owner, he was already looking after her and telling her what to do. In her opinion, that was a good sign. Eventually he would tire and she could seal the deal in bed, then everything would be as it should. She wondered what his name was, and she was about to ask when the other man rushed loudly into the kitchen.

"You don't know where she's been! We can't keep her, T!"

"Where she's been?" Thorbin laughed.

"She could be diseased."

"I'm not diseased!" Lorilei objected.

"I'm not talking to you, kitten," Ben said abruptly.

"She's not diseased," Thorbin confirmed.

"How do you know? She's dirty. She could have syphilis."

Lorilei opened her mouth in further objection thoroughly insulted.

"Dirty?" Thorbin said, looking at Ben then noticeably at himself. He was still in his white undershirt and DC khakis that he had been in since he got here, slept in drunk after a battle, then got up in and proceeded with manual labor. While the captain calling the kitten black wasn't wearing a single piece of clothing that wasn't stained with blood or grease and ripped to shreds.

"Ben. I'm just cooking her a meal," Thorbin assured.

"I know! I can't believe you're doing that. You know what she is, right? We have to get rid of her," Ben insisted.

"Ben!" Thorbin said firmly. "I know what I'm dealing with. I know what she is. We're not sleeping together, I'm just cooking her some food. I didn't strip naked; I just gave her my shirt. Any gentleman would do it."

"Any gentleman for a lady, yes, but she ain't no lady," Ben argued. "We don't know who she belongs to. Any moment pirates could be on our ass. Hell, she probably belongs to some Syndicate." The thought terrified him. "We could give her back. We find out who she belongs to, give them a call, give her back, we might even get out of this alive." Then he turned to her and pounded a fist on the table. "Who do you belong to?"

"No one," Lorilei said, startled from the attack on the table.

"Bullshit," Ben said, thrusting a finger at her. "You didn't just appear. You were with someone else before you was here. Who is he? Where's he at?"

"He's dead. The aliens killed him."

Ben stood up. "Does anyone know you're here?"

"What, you think she might have been followed? Ben, try to calm down," Thorbin suggested.

"Calm down!" Ben roared. "We are fucked. I thought for sure things couldn't get worse, but here she is!"

"What do you want to do? Throw her off the ship? You want me to shoot her? Here," Thorbin said, pulling his pistol. "Go ahead, take it, kill her if you want."

Ben stood silently and Lorilei made herself as invisible as possible, things were not at all looking good for her.

"What's she done to us? She's a living breathing person that we just rescued. I appreciate your concern. I know what she is. She's not the devil. She's a frightened girl in the same fubar situation we're in. Relax, buddy. I don't know what else to do. She gave you a hug, not a knife in the back."

Ben had a good thought to go with the finger pointing, so he pointed away and continued his argument. "She most definitely *is* the devil," he said, Lorilei could sense that he was seriously considering taking that pistol and shooting her. "We have to get rid of her now before it's too late."

Ben's sincere tone frightened Lorilei. "I'm not the devil! Please don't kill me!" Lorilei pleaded genuinely. New tears came forth to re-glisten her cheeks. "I didn't do anything! I won't do anything bad! I promise! I swear! I'll be good. I'll do anything you want." She broke down into a sob. "Please don't get rid of me." She pleaded between the weeping. "I'm not the devil. I don't want to be alone anymore, and I don't want to die. I'll be the best whatever you want."

Thorbin gave Ben a 'you're an asshole' look, and Ben softened his presence, turned, and faced the hallway hatch.

"I'll be in cargo bay." Then he was out the hatch and gone.

Thorbin handed Lorilei a napkin, and she wiped her face.

"I know what I am, what I mean, but I'm not bad," she said, looking up at Thorbin and hoping for reassurance. "You believe me, right?"

"I believe you. Look, just don't get in Ben's way. There's nothing you have that he wants."

"OK. T?" she asked, looking up at him as he poured her a glass of water. "Is that your name?"

"Thorbin," he answered.

"That's an interesting name, what does it mean?"

"It means, the bearer of Thor's lightning."

"Thor?"

"Never mind."

"OK, Thorbin. I'm just going to do whatever you say, OK?" Thorbin smiled, and she decided it looked good on him.

"I'm not sure what you mean," he answered, "but that' s fine."

"I mean, whatever you say, I'll do. Whatever you want."

"Like…stand on your head," Thorbin said with a coy smile. He knew full well what she was talking about.

"What?" she answered, she wasn't sure why he would want her to do that. Maybe he was into that?

"How about eat?" he said, placing a bowl of chili in front of her. "Let's start with that."

"OK," she said, accepting a spoon. "Thank you."

"You're welcome. I hope you like chili." He took a seat across the table. "Your ship was attacked by the Talc?" Thorbin asked.

She nodded yes as she spooned some chili into her mouth then swallowed. "I was unchained and we were heading to the pod when the aliens killed him."

"You were chained?"

"Well, ya," she answered as if he were stupid. "By my neck," she said and demonstrated with her hands.

"Like an accessory for your outfit, huh?"

"It wasn't so bad. I've had worse."

"Really?" Thorbin said.

"He was mean, but he didn't do anything bad to me."

"Really?" he said, amazed that the next sentence actually topped the previous one. "He had you chained by the neck, and that wasn't so bad?"

"Better then some of my other owners, one used to..." she began.

"OK," Thorbin interrupted, not really wanting to hear more. "Just so you know, there will be no neck chaining, or whatever it was that you were about to say that was worse. How's that sound?"

She paused from eating, then looked at Thorbin, puzzled. This was all very strange to her, an odd invitation from the man she would serving. Usually when under the care of a new owner she wasn't told what *wasn't* going to happen to her. On the contrary, they usually couldn't stop talking about what they *were* going to do to her. Instead of tearing off her clothes and having at her, Thorbin immediately gave her his shirt. Table activities normally involved being bent over, as opposed to be being seated at with a warm meal and chatting. Ironically, not being immediately twisted up in some uncomfortable position was making her very uncomfortable.

"How's that sound?" Thorbin repeated himself.

Meekly, she answered, "I don't know."

"How do you like the chili?"

"It's different." She took another spoonful. "What's going to happen to me? Where are we going?"

"The end destination is Mars, but we're currently headed to an oasis."

"Chili is good," she decided out loud. "Where's Oasis?"

"Not to Oasis, to *an* oasis. You don't know what an oasis is?"

Lorilei shook her head while still holding on to the spoon sticking out of the corner of her mouth.

"Well it's..." He thought for a moment on how best to explain what an oasis was. "Space is empty so some people got together and made waypoints for travelers to stop at."

"Like a star base?" Lorilei asked, sweet and confused.

"No, more like a floating city." Thorbin could tell he wasn't getting through to her. "A long time ago, there was a Earth program called NASA. They did a lot of the exploration of our solar system when that sort of thing was beginning. On their first manned trip to Mars they left marker buoys along the way. The buoys received data and transmitted it back to Earth. They were just left there, and they transmitted data for decades afterwards. During that time there was a ship called the Ralston. Now this was a while back. It was after NASA but still it took a long time to get to Mars from Earth. Travelers those days really depended on each other in times of need. That hasn't changed much. The Ralston had been damaged and was looking for aid. They picked up a transmit from one of the buoys and thought it was another ship. So they went to it, hoping to get some help. Turned out it was just a buoy and no help was there. They attached themselves to the buoy and transmitted an SOS. No one was around to help and all hands were lost. The ship was derelict. Some time later, another ship was passing the same area and also became distressed. They too picked up the transmit from the buoy and they too thought it was a ship. When they arrived they found the buoy and the Ralston. The derelict Ralston had just what they needed to fix their ship. They took the captain's logs and the dead crew to be brought back to Earth and left everything else. Not only did they leave everything, which was uncommon, but they left the very supplies the Ralston needed when they were wrecked. They regarded it as an act of karma, or something like that. Anyhow, they marked the position on the star charts for everyone else passing through the area. Every so often, a ship would need help and find what they needed there, then leave something in return. It became an *oasis* in space. A place you could go to if you were in trouble. Soon people were traveling there just to see it. Then came an outlaw named Jacob. He was a smuggler and not a very good one until he came up with good plan. He used the oasis for his smuggling operation. It was so successful other smugglers started using it. They called it Jacob's Run. Eventually there was always someone there. It became an incubator for the black market and a travel stop where a weary captain could wet his whistle and get some repairs. And that's where we're going, to get some spare parts that we need to fix Victoria."

Chapter Six
Pirates And Panties

Lorilei

Lorilie stood in the cargo bay inspecting it. There was a line on the wall that stretched all the way around the bay, except for places where large objects were in the way. In those places the line broke from the wall and crossed the object until it found the wall again. Above the line everything was caked with dirt, grim, and rust, but beneath the line was next to godliness. The line was approximately Lorilei high. She nodded victoriously at two weeks worth of work.

"I dare Ben to say I don't do anything around here," she said to herself. "Not like I care."

She picked up a nearby bucket of suds and carried it with her to a folding chair and table. She set the bucket down, unwrapped a sandwich she had made, then made herself comfortable on the gray faded pleather, being sure to sit in such a way that the torn fabric didn't pinch at her cheeks. She had already learned that lesson the hard way. It was one of the drawbacks of running around in nothing but Thorbin's shirt for the last two weeks, which in her opinion looked good on her, she felt sultry, in a bedroom eyes and engine grease kind of way, so long as she didn't sit on anything unpleasantly poky. Everything on Victoria seemed to want to reach out and poke at her, except the men.

As she ate, pieces of the sandwich leapt from her grasp, adding color to the grime on Thorbin's shirt.

"Thanks a lot," she said to the sandwich. "I know I need a new shirt, but you're not helping."

"I ain't the only thing that ain't helping round here," the sandwich said in defense as Lorilei flapped the pieces of bread and impersonated Ben.

"I'm cleaning," Lorilei retorted.

"You can't clean with your britches on?" the sandwich accused.

"I lost them. You got another pair? No? Then I don't want to hear it, Mr. I'm-so-great-cause-I'm-wearing-pants."

"Kitten, you are useless."

"You see," she replied. "That's why you don't get a sandwich."

"I don't want no whore sandwich."

"How come you can't be nice?"

"How come you can't be useful," Lorilei's head began to hurt.

"I am useful," she defended meekly, looking at her cruel turkey Swiss accuser.

Thorbin and Ben

"I'm the captain," Ben complained as he ate a microwaved burrito and stared enviously at Thorbin and his sandwich.

"She'd make you one if you'd give her a break."

"Break from what? Being a whore?"

"Or yelling at her."

"The only thing she's good for is yelling at," Ben pointed out. "Kitten," he added in disgust.

"What exactly does that mean?"

"What…kitten?"

"Yeah, I don't get it."

"It ain't rocket science, all she's got is what I ain't interested in, the kitty. That's all she's good for, and it ain't worth a thing out here."

Thorbin grimaced, deciding that was more information than he wanted.

"I guess it's my fault for wanting an explanation."

"You know I'm right. I can hardly look at her without feeling like I'm betraying Jessica."

"I know what you mean," Thorbin commiserated. "But that's not her fault."

"The hell it's not!" Ben said, throwing up his hands. "She *lost* her britches. Come on, man, she did that shit on purpose, just to fuck with us."

"She's not fucking with us. If you were forced to wear a brand you'd *lose* it too. It's just her way."

"I suppose being a slut is a way."

"She's Mosot, Ben, and not like the ones on Earth."

"They let them on Earth?"

"Well, yeah, they tend to be good people, never met one I didn't like. The ones out in space, they completely revert. I saw it a lot in the Constable Division. It's all about survival, they figure you out and give you what you want, so you'll take care of them."

"Really, well I want her to stop being a slut."

"Right, and how often do you think that's the case?"

"She's fucking with us."

"So what do you plan to do with her?" Thorbin asked.

"Me? You're the one who wanted to rescue her. That's your kitty, and you better clean up after it and make sure it don't ruin the furniture."

"She's cleaned up the cargo bay pretty good."

"A clean cargo bay isn't getting us to Jacob's Run any faster."

"Sure, but that doesn't exactly make her worthless. Once we do get to Jacob's Run, we can get her some clothes, that'll be better."

"What's with this *we* nonsense? Now *we* gotta clothe her."

"You just finished complaining about how that was a problem for you. At least I'm coming up with constructive ideas."

"I got a much better idea."

"What?"

"When we get to the run, we sell her ass to the highest bidder and be rid of the trouble."

"We can't do that and you know it."

Ben was silent. He knew Thorbin was right, but he didn't want to admit it.

"We have to get rid of her, T," Ben said with a pained expression.

"I can't say that I don't understand," Thorbin clarified. "It's not nice, but she's our responsibility. Once we get to Mars they should have a safe place for her. If she doesn't make it to Mars, she's going to end up as some asshole's property. She's an innocent, Ben."

"Yeah," Ben scoffed. "Pure as the yellow driven snow." Then Ben surmised their thoughts. "It's going to be a long trip to Mars."

Thorbin

Thorbin sat at the command console in the bridge scrutinizing the meager amount of information the sensors were able to provide and monitoring Victoria's course as she limped along. He wasn't sure if he should feel satisfied that most of Victoria's critical damage had been repaired, or subsequently band-aided, or concerned that they were doing little more than drifting in the general direction that had been Ben's best guess as to the location of the oasis. He sighed, rubbed his forehead a little, then leaned back into the captain's chair.

"Hey there," Lorilei said as she entered from the office hatch. Thorbin shifted uncomfortably in his seat.

"Hi, Lorilei. How's the cargo bay going?"

"Fine," she said, coming around his right side and leaning up against the arm of his chair. Being in the presence of Lorilei always made Thorbin feel like he was playing some odd game of chess – a variant that he couldn't win because she controlled all the pieces.

"Did you like your sandwich?" she asked innocently.

He smiled politely at her; he knew the question was a trap but wasn't sure what her angle was.

"Yes, thank you very much."

She flashed a pretty Lorilei smile at him, and he couldn't help but soften his defenses. Her smile had an enchanting effect. It was a like a reward she handed out, in this instance for allowing her to make him a sandwich and being appreciative of it. She was rewarding his good behavior, training him to be an appropriate owner.

"You're welcome, I'm glad you liked it," she said, trying to see if there was a way she could sit next to him on the chair. She was thwarted by the automated wrap around consoles. An unintended but decidedly useful feature of the captain's chair as far as Thorbin was concerned.

Lorilei resistant, Thorbin thought. *I wonder if they mention that in the operator's manual.* "Are you taking a break?" he asked.

"Kinda," Lorilei answered. "I've cleaned as far up as I can reach."

"I'll see if we can find a ladder."

"OK," she said, having given up trying to sit next to him she walked over to the bridge glass and stared out. Thorbin turned his attention back to the consoles.

"Maybe I could do something else?" Lorilei asked.

"Maybe," Thorbin said, tapping away at the screen. "There's plenty to do."

"What's going to happen when we get to the oasis?" she asked.

It was a good question, and Thorbin ventured a look away from the computer displays to answer her. And there it was, she had moved the next piece. She stood looking out the window with her back facing him, bent slightly forward, his shirt failing to conceal her rear, which was subtly swaying side to side.

"Knock it off," Thorbin said, frustrated.

"What?" Lorilei said, looking back while keeping her posterior aimed at him.

"Your ass is showing."

"Oh," she said with an impenitent smile then stood up and turned around to face him. "Sorry," she offered, but it was too late, he couldn't get the glimpse out of his head.

"You did that on purpose."

She gave him fetching smile to avoid answering.

"Why do you do that?"

She looked away from him and readjusted his shirt around her hips.

"Lorilei, answer me."

She looked back up at him disappointed. "Sorry, I didn't mean to make you mad."

"I'm not mad," Thorbin said angrily.

"You sound mad," she said softly.

Thorbin took a deep breath. "Can you please stop playing games with me?" he asked. "You're making me crazy."

"I don't mean to make you crazy, I just thought you might like me from behind."

"Why would you think that? Haven't I made myself perfectly clear?"

"You don't mean it, I know I turn you on."

"Of course you do," Thorbin said, that was something he tried to go out of his way not to admit, but at this point it was futile. "But I'm married, Lorilei."

"I know," she said understandingly. "Married men usually like me from behind."

With that statement he gave up trying to come to an understanding with her and just said, "No. OK. Stop." Lorilei stood there, confused and upset.

"I just wanted us to," she began, then Thorbin cut her off.

"To answer your question, when we get to the oasis we're going to get what we need, do what we have to do and leave. It's hard to say what we'll run into there. Chances are there's going to be a lot of people, and possibly pirates."

Lorilei's mood quickly shifted from saddened to concerned. "Pirates?"

"Yes."

"I hope we don't come across anyone like that."

"Me too, kitten," Ben said as he entered the bridge from the office. "Although to be honest, I'm surprised we haven't run into any so far. I thought I told you to stay off the bridge," Ben said, staring her down.

"I…" she began.

"Go!" he commanded.

Lawlessness in Space

When life in space first became a reality, it meant different things to different types of people. Some pursued knowledge, some pursued wealth, and some others sought the deep innocent darkness. Counter cultures finally had a place to go where there was no culture – space.

The most prevalent of these cultures tended to manifest in one of three ways. The first was being part of the Separatist movement. The second was seeking power through the Syndicate. The third through good old-fashioned piracy, rape, pillage, and plunder.

The Separatist movement was founded shortly after space travel between Earth and Mars became a reality. The Separatists were a mix of religious and/or anti-internationalist from around the world who collectively disagreed with the political internationalism that occurred after the Armageddon. The movement had deep generational roots in a variety of society's segments: North American and European, Jewish and Christian organizations that felt divinity and morality had left society, nationalists from around the world that felt the loss of their nation's sovereignty meant the loss of their personal freedoms, and most notably, thousands of expatriated Indian soldiers who felt abandoned by the international community. India had been fighting General Tsung for years before any other nation joined the fight. Millions of India's bravest sacrificed their lives fighting alone in a war that everyone knew they would have to participate in eventually. Once the war ended, many felt that their courage and sacrifice had gone unappreciated and unrewarded, so they were eager to leave an ungrateful world.

Once in space the Separatists became revolutionaries. They adopted a general philosophy that those on Earth were destined to destroy each other through betrayal, and when all was said and done they would return, taking their rightful place as those destined to rule a new Earth. The Good Samaritans last message was a vindication of their philosophy. They were sure that the Talc would cleanse the world of the non-believers. Turns out they were right, in a way.

As opposed to the Syndicate and pirates, they kept mostly to themselves, with the exception of their legendary wrath. If provoked, you may find yourself at the mercy of Separatist warships. While not equal to Defense Core fighters, they were effective against almost everything else. Nearly every ship they built was armed, and their fighter-class ships were flown by fearless warriors that thought of themselves as divine solders. Of all the threats to Earth's established society, the Separatists were the greatest. Only the Defense Core's superiority kept them at bay.

They did, however, become most effective at living in space. They numbered in the hundreds of thousands when they left in exodus. Since then they had developed an entire society in space capable of supporting itself almost independently from Earth. Some of the technology they developed to achieve this feat was superior to Earth's. They were their own human society —the chosen human society according to their beliefs.

The Syndicate, unlike the Separatists, depended wholly on Earth society. They're modern incarnation formed during the Armageddon. Their roots, however, stretched far into the annals of human history – much further than even the Separatists. They were organized crime, gangsters. Prior to the Armageddon they were a loose collective of mafia, yakuza, and triads that spanned the world. They independently became profiteers as the war began. As it continued they became more powerful than they could have imagined. They used this power to recruit or destroy criminal competition. Individually they became the bump in the night that criminals feared.

The prospective governments that they were illegally deifying didn't have the resources to stop them; they were tied up fighting the war of all wars, the Armageddon. Aside from not being able to stop them, localized crime was actually decreasing, so why bother? These organized crime entities didn't involve themselves in petty theft and menial crimes. In many places these empowered organized crime factions actually reduced public crime to nearly nothing. It drew too much attention and risked undoing that which was making them far more money then crimes on the public ever could. The governments became complacent. The drop in spending on their prospective justice systems went straight to the war effort. Often times filtering into the pockets of the new crime bosses.

They had it all figured out, and it was easer than ever to be a gangster. So easy that regional crime families couldn't keep up with the criminal opportunities only they were capable of cashing in on. This caused regional crime factions to unite to meet the regional demand for their particular services. These united crime families created even larger, more powerful crime organizations. It grew like this until each populated continent, with the exception of South America, contained only one organized crime collective.

While the battle for the liberation of Tokyo was being fought, representatives of the various mafia organizations from each continent were signing peace and trade agreements. With the exception of the powerful South American drug cartels, every organized crime member in the world was answering to the same higher power, which called itself the Syndicate. Once this Syndicate was formed, the drug cartels' defiant days were numbered.

The Syndicate was so prevalent that it was profiteering from both sides in the war. History states that the Armageddon ended when the allies liberated Tokyo, forcing General Tsung to fight on three fronts and deal with the anti-communist revolution that was stirring from within. That was what the books said. What they didn't say was that the revolution, a key factor in victory, was entirely controlled, orchestrated, and funded by the Syndicate. It was the Syndicate that decided when the war would end. Calling forth the revolution that was critical to victory. They kept the war going on as long as they could continue to generate revenue from it. Communism was ultimately bad for business, so they ended it. After the fall of General Tsung, the anti-communist revolution spread like wildfire and the allies embraced it. There was peace on Earth. It turns out peace was just a profitable as war.

The last of the three major menaces in space were pirates. Pirates were less of a well-oiled machine and more of an anarchistic collective. As humanity ventured into space, so did petty crime as it was no longer welcome on Earth. Most pirates were born in space or on Mars. They had no loyalty to Earth and no incentive to abide by society's norms. They lived their lives running from the law and picking up the considerable scraps left behind from the Syndicate and the Separatists. They had no moral motivation like the Separatists, and no solid structure like the Syndicate. They were pure opportunists, answering only to those that were more powerful. They regard little that didn't please or serve them. Do what needed to be done, kill who needed to be killed, enjoy whatever was enjoyable. Like animals.

Ben and Thorbin

"I really hope we don't run into pirates," Thorbin said, continuing his train of thought on the possible troubles ahead. "I'll bet we run across some Syndicate, probably won't see any Separatists. That shouldn't be much of a problem though. It's the pirates that concern me. We're lucky we haven't come across any yet. We're exactly what they love to find. A broken unarmed ship, alone and lost in space."

"We're not lost," Ben interjected.

"If they've been reading our erratic course changes, we look lost. Hell, without long range we might be."

"We're not lost," Ben said with a degree of certainty that was surprising but comforting.

"How do you know?"

"Just know. Feels right."

"What's that?" Thorbin asked pointing at the console.

"I dunno," Ben said, pulling it up. Before he could take a good look a stranger's voice came over the com.

"Distressed vessel, hold your position, we are coming about."

"Damn!" Ben said. "You had to go and mention pirates."

Thorbin felt Ben's concern. Then the voice continued.

"Distressed vessel. This is Captain Izo of the Azores Blessing. Please respond."

"Azores Blessing? Doesn't sound like a pirate ship." Thorbin felt relief.

"No it doesn't," Ben affirmed. "Captain Izo, this is the captain of the Victoria, it's nice to hear your voice."

"Hell, it's nice to see you Victoria. You doing OK? Your boat looks pretty banged up."

"We took a beating. Not doing too good."

"All hands accounted for?"

"No," Ben answered.

"Ah shit, sorry as hell to hear that, good buddy. God bless you, man. God bless you. Anyway I can offer a helping hand?" the captain asked with empathy.

"Yes. Are we heading towards Jacob's Run?"

"Well yeah. I was heading there too, but I couldn't find it until we picked up on you guys. You're dead on."

"Our long range is down. Think you could patch over so we can see better?"

"No problem, my com's on it. You should have my long range in a few minutes. So I'm guessing you haven't heard about the Talc movement?"

"No. What are they up too?"

"After Earth, they left the sector and have been heading to Mars. They came up on some ornery Separatists. The Talc kicked the shit out of them, but not before one of them Separatists horticulture ships lost control, or went kamikaze on their asses and knocked out that big gun of theirs. They had to leave it behind, and some Separatists returned and finished that bitch off. The news channels won't shut up about it. Oh yeah, and the second fleet is supposed to be headed this way to meet them in the middle or something. The Syndicate has taken control of Mars. They say it's just a temporary marshal law until Earth government is restored."

"How close are the Talc to Mars?"

"Well they've been headed in that direction for about a week so not that close yet."

"You don't mind staying with us till we get to the oasis, do you?"

"Not at all, good buddy."

Ben set Victoria to cruise alongside the Azores Blessing and they shared their heading towards Jacob's Run.

Chapter Seven
Midnight At The Oasis

Victoria

They moved at a slow but steady pace for another week, and at long last the oasis could be seen in the distance. Its name suited it well for these weary travelers. It offered a sense of relief that many will never know. To see this place was to greet hope and be embraced by it. They all stood in the observation deck gazing longingly at it just to be sure their eyes weren't failing them. They had almost forgotten that humans lived in large settlements. It was alive, thriving in the great emptiness. Light poured out of it, defying the eternal darkness of the never-ending night; it was testament to life.

It was awkwardly beautiful. A sphere mesh made entirely of ships, most of which were connected by enclosed catwalks that led to the center. It was in a constant state of motion, pulling itself apart and reassembling itself together as ships docked and undocked going about their business. In the center were the oldest ships; boats that had been there so long they barely resembled the vessels they once were, and they were long since unfit to set sail. They made up the heart of the oasis, and were referred to as the 'main hall'. They had been remade into market places and lodgings. The exterior of the sphere was where visiting ships of various types and sizes all docked with the catwalks. Cargo and transport freighters sat next to passenger and private crafts. Thorbin scanned for military vessels but could find none.

As they closed in on the oasis they could clearly make out the ships coming and going, Ben mentioned that it was the busiest he had ever seen it. He changed the audio to the controller's channel and sent a docking request hail. An automated response instructed them as to course and speed. Captain Izo said his goodbye and good luck, then followed the course and speed he was given. Soon the oasis was the only thing they could see in front of them. Thorbin pointed out a particularly large ship that was docked on top. Ben was displeased to see it.

It was a Separatist horticulture freighter – one of the largest ships in space. Some of them could be over a two kilometers from bow to stern. These vessels made up the heart of the Separatists fleet and community. There could be a hundred thousand Separatists on it, more than at an oasis on average. The ship was a small city that met the needs of the Separatists in space. It was on these gargantuan vessels that they grew and husbanded food, ran their industrial endeavors, and even buried their dead. No one outside of themselves could know how many of these freighters existed, but there were at least a few dozen. The presence of one here at the oasis was not a good sign. Sharing a sector with a Separatist horticulture vessel usually meant certain death if you weren't a Separatist.

"This isn't going to be good," Ben suggested.

"They're probably just getting supplies, they were attacked too," Thorbin said, consoling himself as much as he was Ben.

"Ben? Is that you?" a Indian accent questioned over the com.

"Raj?" Ben replied.

"Helloo budeee. It is good to hear your voice, old friend. I'm so happy you are alive," said the voice from the com.

"It's good to talk to you too, brother," Ben replied.

"I am putting you at the front for docking. Keep your heading. I am sending a pair of my men your way now. I cannot wait to see Jessica." Ben's heart took a direct hit.

"She didn't make it, Raj."

"Dear God. No. Oh, Ben." Raj was never at a loss for words. "She was good, Ben. She is good. Have you prayed?"

"A little," Ben said.

"I will meet you as soon as you are docked."

"Victoria, this is Iron Man, do you copy?" a voice interrupted and an oasis cowboy could be seen pacing them from the bow. He was in a pressure suit riding a spacecraft commonly referred to as a 'mule'.

A mule was a small means of transportation developed by the Separatists as a way of repairing their larger vessels. The pilot sat on it, not in it. There was, in fact, no inside to be in. It was essentially a turbine with gears and a throttle. It had a pair of handlebars that the rider used to direct his course, and the throttle was attached to the grip. There were wings that served to stabilize the mule's motion, and a few other additions, but not much. The gears were controlled by the opposite grip. They functioned as a means of controlling the power of the turbine; they weren't necessary for the mule to work, they simply provided the rider with a means to control the craft. Without them a rider might accelerate too fast and lose control of their mule and their life if not careful. Each mule was custom-made, and no two were alike.

Cowboys were what the men who rode mules as an occupation were called – a clear reference to frontier America and the dangers inherent to doing work that few were willing to do. Cowboys were a rowdy bunch at times, but necessary if you lived your life in space. They were all adrenaline and testosterone and had a high rate of mortality. After all, the only thing separating them from the cold deadly embrace of space was a quarter-inch-thick layer of protective fiber.

Cowboys weren't the only ones who piloted mules. Pirates were quite fond of them as well. Mules were perfect for finishing off ships whose engines had been compromised. Like cowboys, a pirate's mule was an extension of their personality. Every rider installed saddles and saddlebags that coincided with their fanciful and unique paint jobs. Wing modifications were also common, although they rarely served for functionality.

Victoria followed her cowboy escort until she was instructed to stop a few hundred meters from the exterior of the oasis. The cowboy then pulled his mule about and came within a few feet of the bridge window before stopping. He motioned to another rider that had come about then raced to Victoria's aft.

"Turn your boat around; we're going to back you in."

With Ben's guidance, Victoria did as she was instructed. Once turned around the cowboy, working in conjunction with his partner manning the aft, backed them into their docking location.

"OK, seal then open your bay doors. We're going to insert the catwalk there." Ben had already instructed Thorbin to seal all the hatches going to the bay so he headed to the bay's control room.

When he arrived, Thorbin and Lorilei were already there. Ben opened the bay doors, and moments later the cowboys rode in and parked their mules as far away from the doors as possible. They dismounted, then guided and sealed the catwalk into the open cargo bay. It was a hallway five meters wide and about three meters high. Once it was a few meters inside the bay it stopped, and a large polymer curtain was used to seal the remaining space in the cargo bay door that the catwalk didn't fill. Once sealed the cowboy turned and pointed at Ben, then raised that finger above his head and rotated his arm in a circler motion. It was the signal to restore atmosphere to the bay. Once breathable air was returned, the cowboys mounted their steeds, rode down the catwalk, and were gone.

The three new arrivals left the control room and went to the entrance of the catwalk. The entrance was a room with two doors; one at the end and another down the hall. A figure could be seen coming through the far door and walking towards the bay.

"That should be Raj," Ben said, and when the second door opened a man with a deep brown complexion and of average height with a firm round belly came forward. He stepped into the bay with arms held open towards Ben. In his right hand he held a gold chain with a gold trinket dangling from it.

"Ben, my brother," he said with love in his voice and comfort in his embrace. Raj pulled his head back and kissed Ben on the forehead, then he stepped back, still holding him by the shoulders.

"This is Thorbin and Lorilei. I picked them up on the way here."

"Welcome to Jacob's Run. Please forgive me, but I need to be alone with Ben right now. It is very important."

"We can go to the forward observation deck," Ben said.

"Good," Raj answered as he held out the necklace in a fashion suggesting Ben should bend his head forward. "This Aum was mother's," he said, putting it over Ben's head. "Let it bring you peace. Let's go." Raj led Ben towards the bow. Thorbin and Lorilei looked at each other, waiting for the other to speak.

"He seemed nice," Lorilei spoke up.

"Yeah," Thorbin agreed.

Quite a bit of time passed as they waited for Ben and Raj to return.

"What are they doing in there?" Lorilei asked inquisitively.

"Praying I think."

"What's praying?" she said with a puzzled look on her face.

Thorbin leaned back on the bay wall. He was preparing himself for whatever Lorilei was up to.

"Well, praying is something humans do when they want to connect with…um…" He suddenly felt himself at a loss. How was he going to explain God to a Mosot without sounding crazy? "Um…When they want to connect with their spirituality."

"What's spirituality?" she said then seated herself cross-legged at his feet, staring up at him. She felt substance in his words and was curious, but he didn't seem to understand what he was saying, let alone explain the idea to her well. She stared at him blankly, waiting.

"For humans, spirituality means the part of life that is unexplained. The part that's bigger than we are. A belief that we are all part of one existence or part of one plan."

"What do you do when you pray?"

"Different people do different things."

"What do *you* do when you pray?"

"I talk. I ask for wisdom, or courage. I try to understand if I'm making the right decisions."

"You ask a belief for courage?" she tried to clarify.

"Well, I believe that there is a presence in my life that is controlled by God."

"Oh," she said in an understanding tone. "When you pray you're talking to God. I do that. You made it sound all weird and mysterious. I thought humans didn't believe in God."

"We do, some of us. Maybe not the ones you've known," Thorbin said, he was now the one confused. "Where did you learn about God?"

"God is a human word. We believe in God. I thought humans thought God was a myth. I didn't know that they prayed." It became clear to Thorbin.

"Of course. Your only interaction with humans has been with pirates? There's a lot about humanity that they don't represent. I pray almost every day, and evidently Ben prays too."

"We sing songs too," Lorilei said, excited to talk about herself. "Although I haven't been able to do that for a long time. Not properly at least."

"Why not?"

"I can't make any fire."

"Fire?" Thorbin began before he was interrupted by the subtle clatter of eight robotic feet. Lorilei leapt to her feet and ran over to the spyder.

"There it is! That was outside Vicky, what is it?" she said, not able to contain her excited curiosity.

"That's just the spyder," Thorbin said, smiling at her excitement.

"Spyder? Is that its name?"

"Sypders don't have names, kitten," Ben said indigently from behind her.

"How sad," Lorilei said, more with the expression on her face than with her lips.

"See, Raj, pain in the ass," Ben said with a nod to Raj.

"I see," Raj said, taking in Lorilei's attractive presence. She gave him a liberal dose of her large lavender eyes. "It must be terrible for you," Raj said, returning her smile. "You are quite lovely, Lorilei."

"I know," Lorilei answered then turned her attention back to the spyder and declared. "I name you…Tommy!" Then she sharply nodded her head, accepting her own declaration.

Ben made a point to ignore her and continued with Raj. "Like I said before, this is Thorbin."

Raj extended his hand and Thorbin accepted.

"My name is Raja but my friends call me Raj. Welcome again."

"Thank you," Thorbin said appreciatively.

Ben motioned with his hand. "We got about four tons of hull debris. I picked up the stuff with the most titanium I could find. There's two pods over there, and that's just about it. I need someone to take care of my turbine trouble and a lower deck, or at least a full-sized bathroom. We could use some money for clothes and supplies, and I probably need a new long-range array. Unless your guy can fix the old one."

"I don't think so. I scanned you while you were coming to dock. You do need a new array. It could cost a lot. I don't think there is anyone here who can rebuild your lower deck. Installing a new bathroom we could do. It is hard to say what is needed for the turbine. My guy is going to have to take a look. All the visitors have flooded the market with goods, so there are many deals out there. I will see what I can do. The pods are only good for scrap, and so is the debris. Lucky for you, my friend, that the Separatist ship is purchasing all the titanium they can get their hands on. The price of titanium has tripled because of them." Ben felt irony that he should ever feel fortunate to be in the same vicinity as Separatists. "I can probably get you 15,000 pounds for all the debris and the pods. I may be able to find someone willing to lend you the money if you need more."

"Pounds?" Ben asked. "I need money."

"I am talking about money. The new currency is in weight now that the Earth standards are destroyed."

Ben inhaled deeply. "All right, have your guy give me an estimate, and I'll see if I can scrounge a bit more."

"Of course," Raj said with a nod. "Oh, and if you're planning on heading to the main hall, be careful. Tensions are high, Separatists, Syndicate, and pirates everywhere. There's already been a few...misunderstandings." Then he looked at Lorilei, appreciating her with a smile that stayed just this side of friendly. She accepted and turned on the charm to the fullest extent. "As for this lovely one, under normal circumstances I would suggest leaving her on board. These circumstances are not normal. *Do not* let anyone know she is here. There are many that would regard her as the most valuable commodity at the Run. Market price for a Mosot girl," Raj paused to consider Lorilei's monetary value, "well, more than anything else. That's for sure." Lorilei's charm melted to disappointment.

"That's not fair! I don't want to be stuck here alone."

"You won't be alone, kitten. You'll be with Tommy," Ben said with smug satisfaction. "Now behave while we're gone and maybe I won't sell you to the highest bidder."

"OK," she said meekly, wrapping her arms around Tommy, not wanting to incur anymore Ben wrath.

"I have to go," Raj said. "I will give you 15,000 now, and if I sell it for more I will give you the difference." Then Raj exited Victoria, disappearing down the catwalk.

"So you're Hindu?" Thorbin asked.

"No," Ben answered. "Raj is the closest thing I have to a childhood friend. His mother used to baby-sit me when my parents visited the Run. She'd always make us tea and taught me how to pray and all – I loved her very much. She was like family. Raj is family."

Chapter Eight
Our Girl Sam And The Dark Man

They left Lorilei to her own devices and headed down the catwalk mazes to the main hall. When they arrived Ben pulled out his PJU and confirmed that Raj had deposited the 15,000 pounds to his account. He led Thorbin to a cashier and withdrew 3,000 in cash and gave it to Thorbin.

"This should cover yours and kitten's pods. Don't get yourself into any trouble. Don't pick up any strays. Don't accept any candy from strangers and don't spend it all in one place. I'm gonna see if I can score some more money. I'll meet you back at Vicky later."

"Shouldn't we stick together?" Thorbin asked as Ben was walking away.

"What we should do, and what I want to do don't mix right now. Go get you some breakfast," Ben said pointing to a café and bar.

The main hall consisted of the hollowed-out remains of freighters. The walls and floors had a thin layer of dust that almost hid their worn surface. Commonly walked stretches were lined with litter that marked paths from hatches and doorways. A long thoroughfare stretched from one end to the other with open bazaars lining the walls. There were many people skittering about with intent, being sure not to look each other in the eye.

Thorbin looked to where Ben had pointed and found the entrance to another ship that had been converted into a restaurant. The sign above the double swinging door read 'The Jaded Harpy' and included a painting of a winged woman extinguishing herself with whiskey. On either side of the entrance sat rows of mules, waiting patiently for their drunken masters to return.

The double doors whined for oil as Thorbin pushed through them. The air stank of tobacco and cannabis and had a murky texture that seemed to collect around things. On the far wall was a stage where a band played some good stinky blues while a pretty woman danced slowly in a little black dress. Every so often she would smack a tired note across the room with a well thrusted hip, much to the pleasure of the many patrons. Many were seated at impromptu tables set in a hurry because of the increased clientele. Most of them didn't seem to notice Thorbin enter and appeared to be harmless, but there were exceptions.

It was then that Thorbin was hit with a sudden realization – he looked like a DC pilot, one that had been marooned and hadn't slept properly or shaved in weeks, and he was all alone.

As he looked for a place to seat himself, he knew he *was* being watched. In the far left corner were three Syndicate; easily identifiable by the nice clean suits they were wearing. The three of them had been talking amongst themselves until Thorbin's arrival. The conversation abruptly ended, and a clean-shaven Slavic man eyed the wayward pilot with suspicion. Thorbin made eye contact, and the man nodded respectfully before turning back to his men and restarting where they had left off.

On the far right end of the bar were four Separatists. Three dark-skinned men in turbans and a balding Caucasian, all in Separatist flight suits. They turned away as Thorbin looked in their direction.

Near the stage were a dozen pirates being drunk and belligerent. The ones nearest to the stage were intent on wooing the attention of the lovely dancer with catcalls, and they pawed at her when she stepped too close. In the center of the pack was a man dressed inappropriately well for their kind. He was about Ben's size and was wearing kakis and a dress shirt. A blonde woman that was clearly out of his league sat playfully on his lap, and he appeared to be very pleased about that.

Behind them, a dark man sat alone in the corner. He was clad in what looked like a drab-brown hooded monk's cloak. He was a large man, and although his face was concealed by a black rubber respirator, Thorbin couldn't help but feel like he was watching too.

Thorbin considered leaving, it looked like the pirates were mostly unaware of his presence, but leaving alone right then felt like a bad idea. He looked again at the bar and noticed an open seat between a longhaired woman and a grizzled cowboy. He decided to sit it out and see what would happen.

As he walked towards the seat he noticed a dog lying at the woman's feet. It was a light tan pit bull with a white belly and white patch surrounding his left eye. He thought for a moment that sitting there might disturb the dog, which was smiling at him, tongue a-flop and wagging his tail. He figured that it would probably be OK. Still, he approached cautiously and slid into the seat, keeping an eye on the canine.

The woman noticed his concern and greeted him with a smile.

"He won't bother you," she said. She was an attractive woman with distinct Korean features, wearing a utilitarian green pair of overalls and a light brown T-shirt. Her long brunette hair was pulled back into a ponytail and her smile was friendly. Thorbin was struck by how un-Lorilei-ish she was.

"Hi," he answered. "Just making sure. You don't mind if I sit here, do you?" She shook her head no and returned to her meal. A bartender came and took his order. Corned beef hash and eggs over easy with water and coffee.

Thorbin felt a mild anxiety while waiting for his food and addressed the woman.

"That's a nice-looking dog."

"Are you looking at him?" she said, annoyed that Thorbin was talking to her. "He's mangy all skin and bones."

Thorbin looked down at dog, he had rolled over on his back and was mouthing the metal frame of her barstool. The lady was right, skin and bones.

Soon he had his meal in front of him, and he tried his best not to accidentally look at the woman while he ate. He must have been obvious because she spoke up after a while.

"I'm not going to bite. I'm just a little irritated. I never wanted to go to an oasis, and now I'm here – stuck."

"Me too. Well I'm not stuck, but I'm not where I want to be, that's for sure."

"Where do you have to go that's so great? Where else is there?"

"Well, I'm a fighter pilot."

The woman considered him with a stare.

"If you didn't want to be here, how come you didn't leave with the other soldiers?"

"What other soldiers?"

"The ones that were here the other day."

"I just got here. Where did they go?"

"Off to fight the Talc I guess."

Thorbin tapped his fork against the plate in frustration.

"Great! Showed up late for the counterattack. Guess me and Victoria aren't through yet."

"Victoria?"

"That's the boat that I arrived on."

"Oh, so what are you going to do now?" the woman asked for the sake of polite conversation.

"Keep heading towards Mars."

"Are you taking passengers? I'm trying to get to Mars."

"I don't know if the captain wants to take passengers, we could ask."

"Where's he at?"

"He's around here somewhere. Getting supplies I think. I'm going to catch up to him later after I do a little shopping. If you're interested, you can come. If you don't mind tagging along while I shop."

"Honestly, I got nothing better to do," she answered then turned towards Thorbin. "My name's Sam."

Thorbin looked confused.

"Is that short for Samantha?"

"No, my parents always wanted a little girl named Samuel," she said sarcastically.

"Um…right," Thorbin said, feeling properly chastised. "Nice to meet you, Sam. What's his name?" Thorbin said, looking at the dog.

"I don't know, he wasn't wearing a collar when I found him. I've just been calling him Spot or Rover, sometimes just 'here boy'! Seems to work so far, although he's kind of a dumb shit," she said, pushing his head away from the stool he was still chewing on. "He was on my transport when it was attacked. He followed me into the life pod. I tried to get rid of him when I was dropped off at the oasis, but he just keeps following me."

She tossed him the last piece of pancake from her plate, which he greedily swallowed up, then he looked back up, hoping for more.

"Chew, dummy," she said to the dog then looked at Thorbin. "See? stupid."

"I see," Thorbin said, finishing off his cup of joe. "I'm done, so unless you want something else…."

"No," she said. "Let's go." And she put a few bills on the bar. "Your breakfast is on me."

"Thanks," he said, and they left the Jaded Harpy behind.

Thorbin and Sam

They walked a few minutes down the fairway until they came across a vender selling clothes. Thorbin stopped and quickly found some socks and clean underwear. He then grabbed a few pairs of pants and a variety of shirts. Sam window-shopped as she waited. All the while she had Spot's undivided attention. Thorbin came across an old-style bomber jacket and tried it on. It fit fine so he added it to his purchases. He was ready to go when he saw Sam looking at some skirts, and he remembered Lorilei. She was still wearing his shirt, maybe.

He walked over to where Sam was and began looking to see what he could find for her.

"Are you finished?" Sam asked.

"No," he replied then continued without thinking. "I need some panties." Samantha immediately burst out laughing.

"Well I'm glad you're getting them now cause you can't borrow mine."

"Not for me," he said with a grin. "They're for my…" he paused. *Quick, come up with something,* he thought to himself. "My sister," he said unconvincingly. He was a terrible liar and Sam just looked at him.

"OK," she said, a little creeped out.

"Look," he said quietly. "We picked up a young woman and didn't want her wandering around the oasis. Right now the only piece of clothing she has is my shirt."

Sam considered for a moment, then asked, "Do you know what size she is?"

"No," he said. Then he looked at Sam's figure. "She's about..." he said, holding his hands out towards her and trying to judge. Sam tugged at the folds of her overalls, pulling them tight. Again Thorbin was struck by how pleasant it was to be in the company of a real woman. Thorbin's appreciative stare made Sam uncomfortable.

"Your sizing her up not me fly boy."

Thorbin blinked. "Um...I..."

"Yes, Sam is cute," she said. "We know this, now focus. Is she bigger or smaller?"

"A little bit smaller. And shorter," he said, hoping he was right.

"OK, I'll get them. How old is she?" Thorbin had no idea. Mosot lived considerably longer than humans.

"I don't know, nineteen...twenty."

Sam started with underwear, since it seemed to be an issue. Thorbin watched intently as she selected a variety until she backed him up by suggesting, "These are cute, do you think these will look good on her?"

To which he replied, "Yes." Then he gave her plenty room to proceed. After a few minutes of selecting Sam invited him back into the process.

"How about her cup size?" she asked.

"How should I know?"

"Guess."

"It's not like I measured her."

Sam sighed then turned so Thorbin could see her profile. She arched her back and held her shirt down with her hands so he could comparatively measure. He looked and his judgment didn't feel right.

"OK, that's enough show," she said, letting her shirt loose. "Now tell."

"Bigger," he said.

"Bigger?" Sam said, amazed. "She's smaller and shorter than me and has bigger tits?"

"I think so," Thorbin said, a little put off that the word 'tits' was embarrassing him.

"You think?" Sam said, finding his embarrassment a little endearing. "You know," she said calling him out. "You're not fooling anyone. She's been running around in nothing but your shirt, and you're telling me you haven't gotten a good look at the boobies?"

Thorbin had no response; he just stood there, failing to not visualize Lorilei's breasts.

"How much bigger? A lot or a little?" Sam said, tossing him a reprieve.

"Just a little," he answered, and Sam almost skipped back into the shopping. When she was done she returned to him so he could judge her selection. It all it looked fine to him.

"OK, now for actual clothes. Here, hold these." She handed him an armful of panties and bras. Thorbin glanced from side to side; what would the pirates think if they saw him like this? "Do you know what she likes to wear?" Sam asked, disturbing his insecurity.

"I've only seen her in my shirt. She probably likes girlie clothes."

"Girlie?" Sam said. "Like what, ribbons and teddy bears?"

"No, that's not what I'm saying…well…maybe. I don't know."

"I need a little more than that," Sam pressed.

"Well I don't think she'd like overalls."

Sam smiled. "Are you suggesting I'm not girlie?"

"No, I didn't mean anything like that."

"I like these," She said, pulling on the buckles of her straps. "Besides, look at you. When's the last time you shaved?" Then she leaned forward and sniffed him. "Or bathed?"

"It's been a while."

She stared suspiciously at him. "I'm girlie," Sam told him, just to make sure he understood.

"Cute as a button," he confirmed.

"Yes, we know this. So anyhow, twenty-ish and girlie. Let's have a look at some skirts, pants might be hard without knowing her size." Sam was having fun spending some else's money, even if it wasn't for herself.

"Nothing slutty," Thorbin stated.

"Shoosh," Sam answered. "Come with me," she said as she cocked a finger at him.

"Yes ma'am."

As Thorbin followed Sam around the shop, he wasn't sure if he should feel grateful or ashamed, so he felt both. He made himself feel better by keeping an eye out for danger. The idea that at any moment he may have to leap into action gave him comfort. Unfortunately, there were no pirates. Just a store full of woman gawking at the dirty man who was trying to hide pretty under things by mashing them betwixt other women's clothing, which just made him look more like a pervert. In what felt like an eternity, Sam finished and they made their way towards the registrar. Standing there in line, something caught Thorbin's eye. A sundress, a very simple sunflower print but nice, he thought.

"How about that?" he pointed, asking Sam.

"It's cute. You think she'd like it?"

"I dunno, I like it."

Sam smiled.

"Well, I picked out everything else, let's have a look," she said and left him standing in the line. She shuffled through them until she found one that matched the mystery girl's size, then returned and displayed it for Thorbin.

"I think this should fit her," Sam suggested. Thorbin reached out and felt the material, imagining Lorilei wearing it and looking sweet, maybe innocent; the thought put a smile on his face.

"I hope so," he answered.

Soon it was their turn to pay. The merchant rung them up then took down their delivery information. As the vendor reached to pack the sundress away Thorbin spoke up.

"We'll take that with us. Oh, and those too," he said, eyeing a package labeled 'Candles, lilac scented'.

Soon afterwards they were headed back down the promenade. Sam's attitude had cheered up a lot in the store.

"That was fun, Thanks for that."

"Sure, actually, thank you. I think you may have made for a very happy girl. I'd probably have just made her look like a clown or bought things that were too small."

"So what's next?" Sam asked enthusiastically.

"Right there." Thorbin pointed to an arms dealer.

"First you want panties now you want guns? Typical male. What's wrong with the one you got?"

"Nothing. Just, I could use a few more things," he answered as he led her over. They entered the arms dealer's, and it was now Sam who looked and felt out of place as she followed Thorbin around, holding a sundress.

"I liked shopping for clothes better," she said while they were standing over boxes of ammunition with markings on them that meant nothing to her. Thorbin walked over to the dealer, who greeted him.

"What can I do ya for, son?"

"I'd like a few boxes for this guy," Thorbin said, patting his side arm.

"Fifty rounds in each box."

"I'll take ten, FMJ please," Thorbin said looking through the counter's display glass.

"OK."

"Can I take a look at that, the three fifty-seven?" Thorbin said, tapping on the glass.

"You got a good eye. There are cheaper revolvers that would give you the same bang for less buck," the dealer said as he placed the revolver on the counter. It had a black matte finish with an ornate synthetic python-skin grip.

"This will be fine, I'll take five boxes of FMJ for it too please. Oh, and shotgun shells?"

"Slug, buck or birdshot?"

"Buck and slug please, twenty boxes each."

"OK, and if I may suggest, how about one of these?" the merchant said, placing his hand on a small box.

"What's that?"

"Hygiene kit."

"Oh yes," Sam interjected. "He'll take two of those." The merchant smiled at Thorbin.

"Yes please," Thorbin verified, looking down at the kits which were displayed next to, of all things, several copies of the Bible. Thorbin grabbed one and placed it on top of the hygiene kit that had been pulled aside for purchase.

"In these troubled times," the shopkeeper commented.

"Yes," Thorbin responded.

"Anything else, sir?"

"Maybe. Let me take a look at that three-O-eight."

The shopkeeper turned and pointed to a rifle hanging on the wall behind him amongst some others.

"The walnut?"

"No, synthetic, the black one."

The shopkeeper took the rifle down from its vertical display, opened up the chamber and set it on the counter. "Semiautomatic, three-O-eight, synthetic black matte stock. It's lighter than the wood stock so there's a bit more kick, but there's padding to compensate."

Thorbin picked up the rifle and held it perpendicular on the counter. He released the slide and it slammed forward with authority. He slid it back again and it locked into position. Sam watched, concerned about their potential future.

"Are we going to war?"

"You're not," he said with a reassuring smile.

"I assume your gonna want a sling for that too?" the merchant asked.

"Do you have any fully automatics?" Thorbin answered.

"No, sir, this shop abides by the law."

"Then yes please."

"OK, it comes with two thirty-round magazines. Is that good?"

"That should be fine."

"Anything else?"

"Case of three-O-eight please."

"You got it, anything else?"

"I think that should do. What's the damage?"

"The total is 2,675."

Thorbin counted his remaining funds. "I'm short."

"Whatcha got?" asked the shopkeeper.

"About twenty-six. Well twenty-four really, I was hoping to not spend everything I got."

The shopkeeper thought about it for a minute and Thorbin looked away, not wanting to pressure him. As the keeper mulled it over, Thorbin caught something in his periphery. He kept it to himself so as not to alarm Sam. Just outside the shop, the dark man from the Jaded Harpy was watching them.

"You're a pilot?" the shopkeeper asked, disturbing Thorbin's observation.

"Yes, sir," he answered.

"Were you at the Battle of Earth?"

"Yeah," Thorbin said, turning his head casually to get a better look at the dark man. He was gone. The shopkeeper also looked.

"Ah hell," the merchant said. "I can knock off a few bucks for one our boys. What kinda holster you want for your revolver?"

"Shoulder if that's OK."

"Not a problem, son. Where you want the stuff delivered to?"

"The Victoria please." And Thorbin counted out the money. "Do you think I could take the rifle with me now?"

"Well that's against the rules," the shopkeeper said, glancing towards the window. He had seen the dark man too. "Who was your friend?"

"I don't know."

"OK, I'll put the sling on for you and fill up a mag, but don't go and get me in trouble."

"Yes, sir," Thorbin said understandingly.

The shopkeeper fitted the sling and filled a magazine with thirty rounds then handed Thorbin his new weapon. He gratefully accepted it with a smile, loaded the firearm then placed it around his right shoulder.

"Take care of yourself, son," the shopkeeper said, extending his hand.

"Yes, sir, you to. Thank you very much," Thorbin responded, shaking it.

As they exited the arms dealer's, the dark man was nowhere to be found, which didn't bother Thorbin as he looked around and re-secured his rifle.

"All right, Sam, let's go see if we can find Ben."

"Who's Ben?"

"Victoria's captain."

"You really don't know where he is?"

"No, but we'll find him."

Thorbin led Sam, who was still being followed by Spot, to the place where he and Ben had parted ways.

"We were here when he went that way. I went over there and met you," Thorbin explained.

"That was a few hours ago," Sam observed.

"Well, let's see what's in the direction he went."

Ben's direction led them to a small casino called Jacob's Card Club. It was a decent size for a gambling establishment in the middle of space. Thorbin had never been to this particular oasis before, but he had been to others, and the casinos were where all the action usually was – where a lot of the business transactions took place, aside from the marketplaces. It was also where most of the non-business transactions took place. It was thick with the multitudes in exodus to Mars. No doubt every variety of human predator was taking advantage. There were scores of tables full of gamblers losing their fortunes.

They waded through the crowd until they found Ben. He was playing poker; high-stakes poker apparently, and he was doing well. He was sitting at a table surrounded by spectators so thick that Thorbin and Sam couldn't get near him. There were five other players at the table. By the look of Ben's stack, they were the suckers. The player sitting directly across from him was a familiar face – it was the nicely dressed pirate from the harpy. He had lost his pert blonde hooker, one of the many symptoms of a poor gambler. Money wasn't the only thing he had lost to Ben. Apparently his nice shirt and slacks were valuable because Ben was wearing them. Behind the man were the rest of his boys, looking angry but keeping their composure because behind Ben was half a dozen Syndicate inspiring them to behave.

"That's him," Thorbin said.

"What, the guy playing poker with pirates?" Sam was a touch concerned.

"Yes, playing poker with the pirates. I don't think we're going to get his attention right now. Perhaps we should go to the ship and wait for the deliveries. He told me to meet him there later anyhow."

"OK."

Sam and Victoria

"So, are you going to introduce me to your 'sister'?" Sam said coyly as they stepped through the first door in the walkway that led to Victoria and headed down the corridor.

"I'm sure you'll just love her," Thorbin responded as they reached the second door and waited for the first to close.

"Is she nice?" The second door began to open.

"Yes, very nice."

They walked into Victoria's cargo bay, but Lorilei was nowhere to be found. "I'm surprised she's not here at the door."

"Do you think she's being shy?"

"God I hope so."

"Thorbin?" a sweet Lorilei voice said from behind a piece of debris.

"Yes."

"Thorbin!" Lorilei gleefully squealed as she came from her hiding place. "You were gone forever!" she said as she hit Thorbin with a full on hug that almost knocked the wind out of him. All the excitement stirred a bark from Spot that caught Lorilei's attention. "Puppy!" she said, running over to him. He was very excited to see her too, wagging his tail with such vigor his rear was thrashing from side to side. There was petting and snorting, laughter and licking. If Lorilei had a tail it would have been wagging too. They were a match made in heaven, both equally enthusiastic about meeting each other.

"She's Mosot," Sam attempted to clarify.

"Yes. Hey, Lorilei, come meet Sam."

Lorilei broke away from her puppy love fest and walked over.

"Sam? That's a boy's name," she accused.

"It's short for Samantha," Sam said, already annoyed by Lorilei's presence.

All the while smiling prettily, Lorilei considered this new woman, and what she meant to her. Then tactfully proceeded. "Samantha? That's pretty," Lorilei affirmed, then made a point of looking her over. "You're very pretty, Samantha," she complemented for the sake of making friends, then held her hand out for shaking, standing as upright as she could. Sam was caught off guard by Lorilei's flattery and smiled as she shook her hand.

"Thank you, Lorilei. It's nice to meet you."

"I have a present for you," Thorbin announced.

"For me? Wow! There's pretty Samantha, puppies, *and* presents. Victoria is the best ship ever."

Thorbin handed her the bag he was carrying and she quickly opened it up.

"Oh fantastic!" she said as she pulled the sundress out. "I'm going to put it on right now!"

Thorbin started to suggest that she put it on in privacy, but she was too fast. She had already pulled his shirt off over her head and was having a hard time negotiating the proper way to put the sundress on. The simple dress might have been the most modest piece of clothing she had ever worn to date. Sam walked over and helped her out.

"Well at least she was quick about it," Thorbin said wryly.

Sam was thoroughly amused. "It looks great on her," she said as she picked up his shirt and handed it to him. Seeing Lorilei appropriately clothed was a relief to Thorbin, and she looked pretty.

"She's right, it does look nice on you. Do you like it?" he asked as he stuffed his shirt in the bag then pulled out the second gift. Lorilei sensed that he wanted her to like it.

"I love it."

"I have one more thing for you."

"There's more?"

"Well, yes, there's actually more clothes too, they just haven't arrived yet. But I thought you might like these," he said, handing her the candles. She smelled them.

"They smell nice, what are they?"

"They're candles."

"That's soooo nice," Lorilei said in an appreciative but clearly not understanding voice.

Thorbin explained. "They can be lit to make fire. I thought you might like to use them for your prayer songs."

Lorilei's confusion melted away as she stared at them, touched. Then she looked up at Thorbin with gratitude. She clutched the candles to her chest, beside herself and at a total loss.

Thorbin smiled. "You're welcome," he said, hoping that she wouldn't be inappropriate in her gratitude. She placed her arms around his waist, gave him a sweet hug, kissed him softly on the cheek then let him go.

"Thank you," she said, looking back down at the candles. "I'm going to use them right now. My first prayer will be for you." Then she turned and headed down Victoria's main hallway.

"She's a handful, isn't she?" Sam acknowledged as they watched her flow away.

"Yes, she is," Thorbin agreed.

"You want to hate her, but you just can't."

"Exactly," Thorbin confirmed, then clarified, "Ben can."

They then felt a subtle draft and heard the catwalk doors open.

"Speaking of Ben," Thorbin said as Victoria's captain entered the bay riding a golden mule. He rode it to the rear of the bay before dismounting. He looked much better now that he had gotten some new clothes.

"Did you take his mule too?" Thorbin asked.

"Yep, sucker to the end. Kept him thinking, a few more hands, and he'd get me back. I'll tell you one thing about pirates, they don't know when to quit. Every hustler for ten sectors showed up to fleece people. Candy from a baby. They never saw Ben comin'. I doubled up my cash, got this pretty mule here, and even got some new clothes." He was very pleased with himself. So was Spot, who ran over and leapt up on his knee.

"What the...? I specifically told you *no strays!*"

"He came with Sam."

"Sam? Who's that? Her?" he said, pointing at Sam whilst trying to swat Spot away.

"Yes," Thorbin answered.

"Sam?" he said, a little upset.

"It's short for Samantha," Sam clarified.

"Well, who the hell cares?" he said, trying to approach them with a dog attached to his leg. "What good is she?" he said, battling with Spot for control of his leg. "What good are you?"

"I'm an engineer," she said, feeling very unappreciated.

"An engineer?" Ben said, coming to his polite senses, wondering how he was going to get his ignorant self out of this one.

"Don't mind me, I'm an asshole sometimes, just ask Thorbin," he said as he smacked Spot on the top of his head. He didn't really hit the dog that hard, but Spot acted like he had just been struck a mortal blow and collapsed to the ground, rolling over with a whimper.

"What can I do for you, miss?" Ben said, changing his tone and hoping he could pull off charm.

"I was hoping to get passage to Mars."

"Well right this way, pretty lady," Ben said, extending his arm.

"Are you drunk, Ben?" Thorbin asked.

"Yes. And stoned. Now leave us alone while I show this fine young lady, Samantha, around."

Sam was unsure about being escorted by a completely inebriated Ben anywhere. She cautiously accepted his arm and looked back at Thorbin for reassurance as Ben began to lead her towards the port turbine. Thorbin nodded with a smile and a reassuring wave.

At the turbine hatch, Ben struggled with the hatch release, and even fell once, requiring Sam's help to regain his footing. Eventually they were able to get into the turbine room. Sam stood in awe, seeing the chrome and titanium masterpiece.

"Wow," Sam said, struck by the splendor of it. "This is incredible."

She walked over and put her hand out to touch it, then pulled it back. "I want to touch it, but I don't want to smudge the chrome."

Ben smiled. "You're perfect. Go head and touch if you want."

Thorbin and Lorilei

Shortly after Ben led Sam off, Thorbin left the bay and went looking for Lorilei. He found her in the forward observation deck. She was kneeling on the deck singing a sweet melody next to three lit candles she had placed to form a small triangle. Her voice was astonishingly angelic. Thorbin leaned against the hatch frame and watched her as she gently rocked back and forth with the subtle melody. Her head was bowed and her eyes were closed, and a few stray tears had trickled down her cheeks. Thorbin was taken aback, had she not been relentlessly trying to bed him for the last two weeks he would have described her as looking…chaste – innocent even, like a child praying before they went to bed. He couldn't understand her song, but it gave him peace. For minutes he sat and appreciated the moment until she had finished.

She opened her eyes, turned back her head and saw him standing there. She looked away and used both hands to wipe away the tears; then she brushed her hair behind her ears before turning back to him and smiling.

"Was that a prayer for me?" Thorbin asked, feeling gracious that such a lovely thing may have been intended for him.

"Yes. And for me and Vicky. It was a song that asks God for safety in dangerous places."

"It was very beautiful."

"Thank you," she responded, a little embarrassed. Then her sweet self-consciousness morphed into perplexity and surprise.

"Sam?" Lorilei asked. Thorbin turned around and there was Sam.

"Umm," Sam began. "The captain just passed out under the port turbine."

Chapter Nine
Little Things

Thorbin

Thorbin sat comfortably in the observation deck, staring out at the stars and watching the oasis traffic. Spot had done a terrific job of entertaining Lorilei until they tuckered each other out in the common room. Eventually Sam joined them and Thorbin, for the first time in a long while, was alone and without a task. Lorilei's prayer had inspired him. In his opinion, it was time for he and God to get on the same page.

He settled himself a bit more into the couch, draped his new jacket over him like a blanket and closed his eyes.

"Lord," he began with a solemn whisper. "I realize that there must be some plan in this chaos. It would be nice if you'd let me in on it. What purpose could there be in the Earth's death? What should I be doing? You took me out of the fight. What good could come of that? I don't understand. And Lorilei? Take Mika, and then make me responsible for Lorilei. I don't mean any disrespect, but that's just wrong." Thorbin yawned. "At least now there's Sam, thank you for that. But still, I'm not supposed to be here, am I? At least give me a hint." He waited for a response, a sign, an epiphany, anything. There was nothing. "Fine, I guess I'll just find out. But just for the record, I think you're screwing with me." He yawned again. "Alien invasion and I'm babysitting an emotionally stunted nympho on a tug that wants to be put to pasture. Is this one of those things that's gonna be funny years from now?" He sat silently for a while until he began to tear up. "I want Mika back. If you were gonna take her away from me, why give her to me in the first place? I didn't fail, you did. I've done everything I was supposed to. I held up my end. I don't deserve this."

He stared out into the stars as if demanding an answer. Still there was none, eventually the weary overcame him and as he faded away he asked. "What do you want from me?"

Sam

Hours later, Sam sat on a chair in the observation deck watching Thorbin sleep as she sipped a cup of coffee. She needed to go back to the room she was staying in off the main hall of the oasis, but she didn't want to go alone. She continued to enjoy her coffee while glancing every so often to see if Thorbin was awake. As she waited for him to stir, she watched the sun rise over the oasis horizon, tracking the cowboys as they danced around in the sun light like insects silhouetted against the dawn. She set her cup next to an empty one on the coffee table and began to refill it from a thermos.

"Good morning, Sam," she heard Thorbin sleepily say.

"Morning, I brought you some coffee," she replied and filled the second cup.

Thorbin sat up and began stretching and blinking himself the rest of the way awake. "Thanks."

"Sure. I also brought you some clothes. They were delivered a few hours ago. And the shaving kit you bought at the gun store."

Thorbin rubbed his beard. "Great."

"I was hoping you'd come with me to go get my stuff."

"Of course," Thorbin said, reaching for the clothes.

"I'd like to thank you for helping me."

"Helping you what?"

"Get a ride, I thought I was going to be stuck here forever. I hardly have any money, and I was kinda stuck in that bar. I was really worried, then you came in."

"No problem, it's nice to have you on board." Thorbin took a sip of coffee. "Mmm, and the coffee's nice. If it helps, you didn't look worried."

"I'm pretty good under pressure. But really, when you told me that I might be able to go with you guys, it was like a godsend."

Thorbin blinked.

"Anyways, I refuse to be seen in public with you if you don't shave and put on some new clothes."

Thorbin smiled. "OK."

"There's breakfast in the kitchen when you're done."

Victoria

When Thorbin entered the galley, Sam was seated around the table with Raj and Ben discussing contractors and Victoria's general condition. Lorilei was sitting cross-legged against one of the walls sharing her meal with Spot, who was pestering her greedily. She didn't appear to mind.

Thorbin had everyone's attention as he placed a package on the table and opened it. From it he pulled out a box of shotgun shells and slid them over to Ben.

"I thought these might work better."

Ben picked up the box with a smile and answered. "Let's hope we don't find out."

"Let's," Sam agreed.

"Right," Thorbin said then removed his jacket and placed it on the back of Sam's chair. Sam watched quietly as he got another cup of coffee while donning his shoulder holster. Then he returned to the box on the table and loaded a revolver that seemed to get scarier every time she saw it.

"Anything special going on or are you just playing with your new toy?" Ben asked.

"Sam asked if I would go with her to get her things."

Lorilei swatted Spot away on hearing the news that Thorbin might be off again. He yelped and spun around before collapsing like a vaudeville player on the deck.

"Be quick," Raj suggested.

Lorilei spoke up while she felt she had the chance. "Anything for me in there?"

Thorbin looked at her and smiled. He took a sip of coffee and enjoyed seeing her squirm while she waited for an answer.

"In the cargo bay."

"Come on, puppy, let's go see our stuff," she said to Spot as they headed towards the bay.

"I want to see if I did any good picking stuff out for her," Sam said, then stood.

"We should inventory," Ben said to Raj, and Thorbin found himself alone with his coffee in the mess.

The pot was empty so he started a new one, and sometime later Lorilei and Sam came back in. Lorilei was giddy in her new clothes and frolicked over to him, tossed her arms around his neck, then kissed him thankfully on the cheek. Thorbin noted that in the presence of Sam, Lorilei was acting noticeably more teen-like; no doubt balancing a need for Sam's affirmation while still laying claim to him. The tactic, however, still didn't stop her from being less than modest with her new shirt's buttons and picking the most flirtatious skirt of the lot. Sam too had cast aside her overalls and was wearing a new pair of jeans and a black tank top. Thorbin remembered buying those clothes for Lorilei and looked at Sam with a knowing eye. Sam smiled back coyly with a feminine charm that could have taught Lorilei a thing or two, than she clarified.

"Don't give me that look. Apparently, not all the clothes we got fit her."

"But they fit you," Thorbin remarked, making a point to look her up and down, "just fine."

"Yes," she said with a counter-smile. "And since they did, Lorilei, being the sweetheart that she is, said I could have them."

Thorbin tried to turn around to get some coffee, but Lorilei was still dangling from his neck.

"Can I get some coffee?" he pleaded.

"OK," Lorilei said, sweetly feigning disappointment as she let him go.

"I'll bet she did," Thorbin said, returning to the conversation with Sam. "Let me guess. All the clothes like the ones you're wearing fit you fine?"

"It's the strangest thing," Sam said as she grabbed a cup for coffee and placed it next to his. "Coffee please."

"I didn't know I was going to have to watch out for you too," he stated pouring her a cup.

"You can watch all you want," she said, heading out the hatch, her charisma not skipping a beat. "That won't stop me though."

"Isn't she nice?" Lorilei said, wanting Thorbin's attention. He looked over at her, and she was posing in hopes of getting a complement. She liked Sam just fine, but she was stealing away far too much attention from Thorbin, and that just wasn't going to do. Lorilei hadn't even gotten in Thorbin's pants yet; he was putting up quite the fight. With Sam around, it was going to be more difficult to get his affections. She was feeling unsure about his commitment to her security, and she had to find some way to seal the deal just to be sure.

"Ya," he said, politely smiling at her. He then turned back to his coffee, wondering how much money he had spent on Sam.

Not dismissed so easily, Lorilei turned off the teen and turned on the sultry, sauntering over to him. He turned back around just in time to have her in his personal space, again. He tried to take a step back but was thwarted by the counter. She slipped her arms around his waist and buried her head in his chest.

"Your new jacket looks good on you," she said, nuzzling the soft leather with her cheek. Thorbin tried futilely to negotiate a sip of coffee around Lorilei's head.

"How do I look?" she asked, being direct and leaning her head back to make eye contact so he couldn't dodge the question. She could sense she was getting the attention that she wanted, and she wanted more. She was prepared to use her full arsenal to get it, and Thorbin knew it.

"Very nice," he said uncomfortably in defense. "I think you may have missed a few buttons on top though," he suggested.

"Oh, did I?" she said, feigning innocence.

"Yeah." He realized where this was going, and he was wondering how to get out of it.

"You didn't *see* anything, did you?" she asked while maneuvering so that if he hadn't, he would.

"Nope," he answered, trying not to stare.

"You did. Didn't you?" she teased. "You were thinking of taking advantage of me, weren't you?" she continued with a smile and swayed from side to side, advancing her flirt.

"No. I wouldn't..." Despite the many cups of coffee he had imbibed, Thorbin found himself unprepared.

"Oh, you wouldn't," she pouted. "But I'm so much fun to take advantage of," she said, eyes all a bat. He squirmed a bit, and then decided to just try and make a break for it.

"Hey! Let's go see what the others are up too," he suggested and Houdini-ed his way out from between the counter and Lorilei before fleeing to the hallway. Lorilei smiled at her small victory and followed.

Thorbin made his way to the cargo bay and found the others. Sam was eluding that she may be able to do some of the repairs to the port turbine; she just needed to get some of her equipment. Ben was overjoyed since Raj couldn't come up with anyone. Lorilei approached from behind and slipped her hand in Thorbin's.

"Hey, T," Ben said, then took notice of Thorbin, looking very defeated standing there hand in hand with Lorilei. "Why don't you take Sam to go get the rest of her things?"

"Right," he replied, leaping at the chance to escape Lorilei. He turned to her. "I gotta go," he said, failing to free his hand.

"But?" she said, disappointed.

"I know, but Sam needs me now."

She reluctantly let go and felt envy that Sam could so quickly trump her. After all the effort she had just gone through in the kitchen, and now just like that he was off with Sam, and happy to be with her. If Sam took Thorbin away from her, who would protect her? She was starting to feel sick, and her head began to ache.

Sam hadn't the slightest clue of Lorilei's inner desperation and was grinning at the whole exchange. It was funny to her, she watched amused as Thorbin struggled against Lorilei's incessant clinginess. Eventually he broke free again and headed to the observation deck to get his things.

"Don't worry, Lorilei," Sam said, not helping Thorbin's cause. "We'll be back soon, and you can have him all to yourself."

"OK," Lorilei said, confused and wondering how Sam would give up such a precious commodity. Sam's brevity quickly departed when Thorbin reentered the bay with his rifle slung around his shoulder and his pistol on his hip; a forceful definition of what it meant to 'go get her things'. She felt timid as she followed him towards the main hall.

Chapter Ten
Boiling

Thorbin and Sam

S am tried not to project discomfort as she sat behind Thorbin on their mule, arms around his waist. The small bands of pirates and Syndicate tucked away between shops and kiosks waiting for the other to strike first gave her cautious pause. While at the same time she wrestled with a specific irony. Sitting there behind Thorbin like a grade school sweetheart she wondered why the closeness made her uncomfortable, but the thought that he may have to shoot someone on her behalf seemed less intimate and perfectly acceptable. Not that she was prepared to see someone shot to death – just less conflicted. She felt she didn't know him well enough to be clinging to him. She wondered what her mother would say if she saw her now.

'Sammy! Don't mess it. He look like make good fat grandchildren,' she'd probably advise. No mention of murder by pirates. So there sat Sam as they made their way to the dingy motel where she kept her things.

They parked the mule outside and entered the lobby. A mildly lit place that only served to exchange funds and funnel people and predators to the elevator that would take them to their future crime scenes. They exited on the third floor and entered a hallway, long and dirty and broken up by faded doorways. Some of the doors were marked, and every so often another hallway would branch off into the same unmotivated light.

They tried their best not to attract attention to themselves as they traversed the hall, encountering only a single pair of pirates. They passed without incident, only looking Sam up and down like she was a piece of meat, rating her tastiness. Apparently at the sight of Thorbin and his long barrel she rated 'Not worth it'.

They reached Sam's room and collected what little she had left in her life. Two tool bags, a backpack full of clothes she had purchased before meeting Thorbin, and a piece of luggage filled with the rest of her belongings. They gathered it all up and were preparing to head back when a ruckus could be heard coming down the hall. Sam turned towards the door, which they had left ajar.

Thorbin grabbed her by the arm before she could step towards it and flipped off the lights.

He pulled her back to a corner sheltered by shadow and stuffed her behind him, then he brought his weapon to his shoulder and peered out the door through the rifle sight. Frantic footfalls beat their way across the hall, followed by three flinch-inducing gunshots. There was a deep thud and a man skidded into view just outside the door with a gunshot wound in his stomach.

Their partial view of the fallen man was complemented by tricks of light and shadow. As he lay there succumbing to his wounds, Thorbin recognized him as the pirate Ben had fleeced at the poker table. Shortly after three shadowy figures in finely tailored suits approached. Two of the three set the man up against the opposite wall, their backs to Sam's room. The two then started beating him mercilessly while the third spoke in a measured tone that was indiscernible but clearly intent. The three men paused and waited for a response from the pirate, but he was being stubborn. The speaking man kicked him in the face, yelling in a thick Slavic accent.

"Where is it?"

The man slumped from the forceful blow. The yelling man motioned to one of the other two, who pulled a metallic device from an inside pocket. He pressed it against their victim, who began to convulse violently before falling on his side. The yelling man continued.

"You will die when I tell you too! Now tell me where it is!"

The pirate whimpered a response then coughed up blood.

"What?" the man prodded him again and all three had to take a step back to avoid flailing limbs.

Begging in agony the pirate cried out, "Victoria!"

Thorbin's finger caressed the trigger as he watched the yelling man lower his face to their victim and whisper in his ear. Then he stood erect and glanced at his partner, who placed the prod on the man's head. The Syndicate applied mortal voltage and held it firm as the man again fell to his side. The twitching stopped with a bit of smoldering and the three Syndicate collected themselves. They straightened out their suits, then looked over one another as if their clothes has been disturbed by a breeze. Satisfied, they leisurely walked away.

Thorbin whispered, "We'll wait a few minutes for them to disappear, then we'll head back to the ship."

"There is no way I'm going back to the ship," Samantha objected. "You heard him. He said 'Victoria'."

"Sam, the Syndicate just killed a pirate. We all need to get out of here as soon as we can."

Thorbin's response was interrupted by footfalls, slower and louder than before. Thorbin again brought is rifle to the ready. As he did so, another large dark figure appeared. It was the dark man. Even with his back turned to them, Thorbin felt threatened and targeted the dark man's center mass. He watched through his sight picture as the dark man stood over the dead pirate. Then he knelt down for a moment, fanning away the smoke from the victim's still smoldering head before continuing on.

"I guess if you want, you could stay here, with him," Thorbin whispered to Sam. She shook her head no.

Chapter Eleven
Kittens Claws

When they returned Ben and Raj were talking to a contractor who was describing his plans for Victoria with large sweeping gestures. Another worker was sitting on a mule with his arms folded smiling at Lorilei, who was sitting on another mule being attractive. Thorbin walked straight over to Ben and interrupted the contractor.

"Ben, we need to talk, now."

Ben noted Thorbin's serious tone and excused himself from the conversation. Thorbin led him towards the hallway.

"What?" Ben asked.

"Three Syndicate just murdered a pirate back at the main hall. They didn't see us, but they were interrogating him about something. It was the man you were playing poker with. The one whose mule you took. After he named Victoria they killed him."

Ben's brow furrowed. "Shit," Ben said with less concern than Thorbin expected.

"We have to get out of here," Thorbin added.

"No, they'll find us."

"So what then? You know we're gonna get a visit."

"If I got something they want, they can have it. I haven't wronged them. Besides, we can't leave till Vicky gets patched up."

"There's going to be a damn war at the oasis."

"We stay as long as we can, T. If it gets bad, we go."

"It is going to get very bad," Raj interjected. "But I will have my men looking out for Victoria."

Thorbin turned to Raj, who hadn't been invited into the conversation, but asked anyhow. "There's a man that I've seen wandering around the oasis. I don't think he's a pirate, but I think he's been following us."

"What does this man look like?" Raj asked, intrigued.

"Big guy. Wears a brown cloak and a black respirator that covers his face."

"I have heard about this man. He is a mercenary of some kind. If you have something on the Victoria that belongs to a pirate that the Syndicate wants, it is hard to say what his interests are."

Lorilei

Back in the cargo bay, Sam had picked up the conversation with the contractor that Ben and Raj had left behind. Lorilei was still feeling anxious about Thorbin leaving with Sam, and her feelings were hurt when he hadn't so much as given her a look when he returned. She had been compensating by flirting from a distance with the second contractor, who was smitten. He couldn't stop smiling at her, and she reciprocated.

Fine, let's see what he thinks about this, she thought. Then she swung a leg over the seat, dismounting the mule, and proceeded to saunter over to the man on his machine.

"Hi there, cutie," he said, being friendly and feeling lucky. Lorilei could sense right through his friendly disposition.

This is going to be too easy, she thought.

"Hello," she said with a sweet smile. "That's a pretty bike." And it was, sleek jet black, with crimson calligraphy on the side that read 'Mother's milk' under a mural of a pin-up girl.

"Thank you," he said to the complement. "She's my girl."

"Oh," Lorilei said, mocking disappointment eyes all a bat and lips a pout. "So you already have a girl?"

The man was taken aback. "Well...." was the best he could muster.

Ben took notice from a distance and yelled over, "Kitten! Stop bothering that man! Hey, man, she's trouble! I'd stay away if I was you."

"You're trouble?" the man said with a smile.

"Just a little," Lorilei said, moving in for the kill. "Nothing you can't handle." She then placed a hand on his shoulder and leaned forward, so the cleavage could flow freely. "They look like fun. Are they fun?" she said innocently.

"Sure," he said, not believing his incredible fortune. "Want to go for a ride?" he invited, patting his lap.

Lorilei was thoroughly pleased with herself. This was exactly how it was supposed to go, she hoped Thorbin was paying attention. But now it was time to pull back a bit, she could sense the man was getting a little too excited. Not to mention that there was no way she was going for a ride.

"I can't. I have to stay here."

The man looked back at Raj and the others. "They won't mind. Come on," he said, wrapping an arm around her slender waist and pulling her close to him.

"Really, I can't."

"That's too bad," he said, his tone changing, not so much changing to disappointment but something else. She sensed this change, lust, not just for her but for money. She tried to take a step back, but the gentle arm around her waist became less gentle.

"Thorbin!" she cried out.

The boys turned to see the man heave her over his lap, turn his mule about and speed out to the catwalk.

Thorbin ran to Ben's machine, and Ben leapt on behind him, shotgun in hand. Then they shot out of Victoria's bay and tore after them.

"Dumb bitch! I told you she was trouble," Ben said, aggravated while catwalk bulkheads blurred past them as they gained on Lorilei and her kidnapper.

Thorbin's adrenaline spiked, the sense of speed invigorated him. He couldn't help feeling enjoyment in the chase. His lips curled to a predatory grin. That man might be used to handling his mule, but he was no match for a man that had piloted the fastest birds ever created by humanity. He tried pointlessly to lose Thorbin and Ben in the catacomb of catwalks; however, his maneuvering was erratic and reckless, while Thorbin's was precise and calculating. He was not getting away.

All the while, Ben was holding on for dear life. He had closed his eyes several turns back and had become Thorbin's back. The main hall was ahead, and the pursuit blazed down the last stretch towards it. The man was a few seconds in the lead and Thorbin was no longer gaining due to their speed being matched on the straightaway.

The man arrived at the main hall and banked left and was out of sight by the time they boys arrived. Thorbin decelerated as he entered the main hall, and Ben opened his eyes, amazed he was still alive. There was no sign of them anywhere. Seconds felt like eternities and Thorbin knew he needed to make a decision. He slowly picked up speed in the direction he had last seen his prey go and scanned the crowds.

Ben tapped his back and pointed. "There!"

In the distance a merchant's cloth roof was tumbling to the ground. The kidnapper could be seen, his mule flailing wildly with bits of shop dangling behind it, and the chase was on again. His reckless piloting continued to work against him as it forged an open path in the crowd for Thorbin to follow. Panicked, the man fled down a less crowded alleyway and they lost sight of him, but they knew where to follow.

After the merchant's booth, Lorilei had been holding on for dear life, hoping her captor didn't crash. The alleyway ended abruptly at a hatch that had been converted into a doorway. The kidnapper looked over his shoulder, and his pursuers were nowhere to be found.

Lorilei pushed herself off the mule and attempted to flee, but the man firmly grabbed her by the arm and painfully jerked her to follow his lead. Struggling with Lorilei he headed towards the door. With a swift kick, it gave way, displaying a narrow hallway that curved out of sight ahead. As they entered the threshold, Lorilei suppressed panic and focused. She concentrated on changing the surface of the arm he was manhandling her by to a coarse sandpaper-like texture, then she lurched her arm out of his grasp, shredding his palm.

He yanked his blooded hand away in pain, giving her the opportunity to try and flee, but before she could his other hand reached for her hair. He wrenched her head back with such force it felt like it might snap right off. He kept pulling, and she kept resisting until she lost her footing and he had to drag her by the hair, which wasn't working out for either of them. He reached his bloody hand around her and pulled her up by the throat while heaving her down the hall by her strands.

She struggled for breath and scratched helplessly as his grip on her throat tightened for better leverage. Choking, she willed her fingers into claws and dug deep into the hand that was suffocating her. This was very effective; he wrenched the hand away from her neck and thrashed her about by her hair in anger.

Lorilei managed to turn herself around and face him. He stepped back as far as he possibly could while still holding a swath of hair, yanking her face down to try and muster some iota of control over her. His mauled arm clutched to his chest, he used it to fumble for a pistol he had in a shoulder holster.

Head down, Lorilei couldn't see what was going on, so she fell to her knees and looked up at him. Terrified of his free hand and its intent, she punched him with all she had in his stomach.

He stumbled back, still holding on to her hair as she stood. The punch was solid, he was winded and disoriented but would not let go of her head. She attempted a kick to the groin but was foiled by his baggy pants.

Coming to his senses, the man again reached for his weapon. Lorilei thrust her body forward, pinning him against the wall and firmly pressing her left hand against his. They came to an impasse; he pulled erratically on her hair, trying to pry her away while she teared her way through pain, making sure he couldn't retrieve his weapon. She attempted another strike to the groin with her knee; again his baggy pants deflected the assault, which resulted in her foot becoming entangled in his pants leg. She stomped down on his foot, trying to free herself.

The struggle wasn't going the captor's way. He couldn't get a hold of his piece, or get the girl off of him, and now his baggy pants were starting to give way.

Lorilei saw an opportunity and slid her clawed sandpaper-like hand down his pants, taking hold of the situation. The man tensed up immediately, surrendering and standing motionless.

With the struggle over, Lorilei looked him intently in the eye, with a squeeze, lest anyone misunderstand who was in charge now, she commanded, "Let…go…of…my…hair!" Her command was immediately obeyed.

She stood there, staring him down angrily, her scalp and neck were burning from the pain of being flung about so violently that she didn't take notice of a second and third man approaching from the hall. Her free hand fumbled about in the man's shirt until she was able to relieve him of his side arm.

The man who was now *her* captive stood compliant. His eyes were shut tense and white as he muttered something that sounded like begging. She was adjusting her grip to solidify her advantage when the approaching men announce themselves with a cold steel barrel on her already overburdened head.

"What's this? Good fortune I'd wager," the man said from behind as he smiled to his accomplice then tilted her head forward with the pistol.

"All right then," he began.

"Don't move, Lorilei," Thorbin commanded as he and Ben entered the hall.

"Thorbin?" Lorilei whined stressfully.

"Don't move," he confirmed. He had a clear shot at the pirate behind Lorilei, and he didn't want her to get in the way. The only problem was getting the shot off before the pirate could. The second pirate had moved swiftly to his companion's aid and pulled a pistol, aiming it at Thorbin just as Ben's shotgun announced its presence. The sound of Ben's weapon sliding forward and back as a round was chambered then aimed directly at the second man was very convincing.

They all stood perfectly still as they analyzed the predicament they had found themselves in. Only Lorilei's victim broke the silence with his whimpering. No one appeared to have enough of an advantage to not lose a comrade. If the pirate shot Lorilei, Thorbin would clearly take him out, but then be struck himself by the second pirate. Who would then be shot by Ben. If Thorbin shot first, Lorilei would probably make it out unscathed. But again, he would be shot by the second pirate, who would then be shot by Ben. Neither Ben nor the second pirate could take the initiative without the results being similar. What a fine mess they all found themselves in. The only thing Thorbin had going for him was that the pirate would not squander his prize away so easily. He was surely trying to figure out how to kill Thorbin and Ben while staying alive for his reward. To take advantage of that, the second pirate would have to be shot first, but Thorbin wasn't aiming at that one, and it wasn't like he and Ben could switch real quick. Thorbin was becoming frustrated, this couldn't possibly get any worse. Then it did.

Down the hall, behind the pirates, a large hope-crushing figure appeared – the dark man. Both the boys and the pirates took notice, not long enough of a notice to eek out an initiative, but enough to be concerned. The dark man was unveiling his own weapon. Everyone wished they could better position themselves for this unknown adversary, but all hands were accounted for in the current stand off.

The dark man slowed his pace as he approached and began to raise his weapon. No one could tell who he intended to shoot. They were all easy targets, and he was taking his time in announcing the next move, which was clearly his.

In a moment like this, there are many things to consider. And when life and death cross paths, death usually occurs because of what should have been considered but was not. Someone was going to die because of something that no one (not even the dark man) had considered. That being how incredibly loud a twentieth century shotgun can be when fired in an enclosed hallway comprised mostly of steel.

Ben simply couldn't contain his anxiety any longer. He squeezed the trigger, letting loose an audible hell that none of them were prepared for. Many things occurred in a short time. First, the second pirate went to meet his maker. Ben's shot was so true you'd have thought he was a good shot. The one-ounce slug struck the pirate right above his navel, folding him in half as he was slung backwards by its force. He landed (nearly in two pieces) near the dark man, who was a considerable distance away from the main fray.

The dark man, who was also in the slug's path, narrowly escaped its wrath as it missed him by a hair. Although not directly struck by the projectile, he was still injured minimally by the shear velocity as it passed by him. He fell against the wall, quickly assessing that his right forearm was still there. The slug then continued on through a wall, and no doubt onward, unleashing further destruction and misery.

The next effect of the powerful blast was from the sound. The first pirate, Thorbin, Lorilei, and the dark man, along with Ben, all flinched in terror. Everyone promptly dropped everything, except for Lorilei and Ben. The clatter of everyone's firearms falling to the ground was then followed by a shriek of anguish, let loose by Lorilei's captive. The blast so frightened her that every muscle in her body tensed to their fullest potential, including the hand that held her kidnapper at bay. Poor fellow. In an instant, from that point forward he became the man that everyone referred to as 'Never being the same again.' He collapsed to the ground wishing futilely that he could just pass out. While Ben, having never fired anything out of that shotgun aside from rock salt, wasn't well versed in its proper use. He hadn't been holding it properly when he fired the fateful shot, and there was a significant gap between the butt of the gun, and his shoulder, which disappeared quickly after the shot, knocking him flat on his butt.

So there still were they all – minus one pirate – all in a daze which the dark man recovered from first. He ran towards the rest, but mostly towards Lorilei. Ben was on the ground still trying to discern what had happened. Thorbin's ears were ringing fiercely and he struggled against the loss of his equilibrium while the dark man closed the distance between he and Lorilei with a few giant strides.

Lorilei had fallen on her side as her victim went down and was then looking up at the dark man descending quickly upon her. She attempted to collect herself and at least try to scoot away when the first pirate grabbed her by the arm, the safe arm. She could really care less that he was pawing at her; the dark man's massive foot fell right between her ankles. It was wider than her leg and was the bottom of a menacing figure that towered above her, seeming endlessly tall from her current perspective.

The pirate turned, sensing the dark man's enormous presence. He let go of Lorilei and reached around his back in search of a blade he kept for just this type of occasion. The dark man had other plans; he came down on him with a thunderous right cross that spun the pirate towards the floor on his belly. The pirate pushed himself off the ground and quickly got to his feet before another strike could land. Lorilei scurried under the dark man, trying very hard to not be stepped on as he tracked his target. The pirate was able to gain enough distance to unsheathe the blade, and he was pointing it at the dark man, being sure that if the man came at him again, he would have to answer to his blade.

The giant lunged forward and was stabbed, a firm shoulder strike, but not lethal. At least not lethal to the dark man, whose massive hand had found the pirate's neck. The pirate gasped for air – he wasn't being strangled so much as his neck was being crushed. The dark man held him out at arm's length as he fruitlessly struck at the arm that held him. He tried to reach for the knife he had lodged in the dark man's shoulder, but it was too far away.

The dark man pinned him to the wall by his neck. Then with his free hand he removed the steel from his shoulder, and with a mortal blow sunk it into the pirate's chest. The stabbing was really just for posterity; the blow alone shattered his breastplate.

The dark man then turned to Lorilei, who had managed to get to her feet but had the dark man between her and Thorbin and Ben. His face was covered by the respirator, so she couldn't see his eyes, but she knew. She could feel them scanning her, and she tried her best to look back at them.

"Please," she begged as he advanced slowly towards her.

"No!" Thorbin asserted, finally joining the fray. The dark man, hearing Thorbin's command, spun quickly, and Thorbin raised his weapon.

"Easy now," Thorbin calmly said, frightened out of his mind. The dark man took an ominous step forward and reached a hand over to his injured shoulder, exposing some of the clothing under his brown cloak. Thorbin could see the uniform of a DC pilot and the insignia of a commander.

"Commander?" he said uneasy. "My name is Lieutenant Monroe."

The dark man shifted his hand over his face and grasped the respirator, pulling it down to reveal a deathly pale and grizzled face with a scar over his right eye.

"Monroe?" Tank breathed hard without the respirator, then began to stumble towards him. "Help me," he struggled to say as he began to collapse forward, but he managed to lean against the wall instead.

"This guy know you?" Ben asked as he and Thorbin rushed over to help him.

"We fought in the battle for Earth together. I thought he was dead," Thorbin answered, then he turned back to Tank. "Hold on, buddy," and they set him securely against the wall.

"What about him?" Lorilei asked, standing over her victim.

"Leave him, Lorilei," Thorbin said as he and Ben searched through the pirates' remains. Thorbin pulled a jacket off of one of the pirates and used it as a makeshift bag. They began filling it with all the weapons, ammo, and everything else of use they could find from the fallen.

Ben stopped and took notice of Lorilei, still standing over her kidnapper. She was engrossed at what he represented. Ben walked over to her and also looked down at the man, who was still conscious.

"I told you she was trouble," Ben said.

Lorilei's face flushed further with anger as she lifted her foot above the man's head.

"NO!" she screamed at him. Her leg thrust down with all the fury and pain of a life abused. Then she began to cry and turned towards Ben, who was closest, and sought a comforting hug.

He looked at her like she was crazy. "Not gonna happen," he said.

Thorbin approached, tying off the arms of the jacket to ensure nothing would fall out, then he handed it to Lorilei. They assisted Tank to where the mules were just outside the door, and Ben took a seat on the contractor's ride.

"He won't be needing this."

Thorbin would have smiled, but he was concerned for Tank.

"Him or her?" Thorbin asked Ben.

"The big guy, or the big slut?" Ben pretended poorly to think it over. "Well, help him on, man, we ain't got all day."

Thorbin helped Tank sit behind Ben, who almost changed his mind when several hundred pounds of nearly dead weight leaned forward on him for support. Thorbin mounted their mule then looked over at Lorilei. She stood tearily holding the tied jacket, trying to not fall apart.

"Get on," he said, trying not scream at her for being foolish. As she approached he grabbed the jacket and set it on his lap before she could. She seated herself behind him, wanting to apologize but afraid to speak a word.

Upon arriving back to Victoria, Raj and Sam made up a bed for the new arrival while Ben cursed at Lorilei – a lot. They gathered in the common room, where Tank had been made comfortable. Sam and Thorbin were tending to his shoulder, while Raj and Ben were discussing the repercussions of 'Lorilei's little joyride', as Ben described it. Lorilei all the while was standing quietly in the back of the common room, straining to contain the oncoming migraine. She was relieved to be rescued, but the near successful kidnapping had stirred terrible memories of what had been, and could have been again. Endless abuse that had ceased only during the few short weeks she had been on Victoria. She had never viewed her life as such until that moment. She had taken Victoria for granted. Now she was sure everyone hated her, and her future was uncertain. So she watched quietly as they tended to the large man.

"Sam, you have to keep the pressure on!" Ben shouted.

"Damn it, Ben. I'm an engineer not a doctor," she replied, distressed.

Thorbin had cut off Tank's shirt only to discover a myriad of wounds and marks. Tank's body was a mass of scare tissue. It looked like a map of broken flesh that led to a lifetime of harrowing tales. It was hard to tell which were old and which were new. Around his midsection was another dirty and bloodstained bandage. Thorbin inspected the bandage and determined it needed to be replaced.

"Tank, I have to take off this bandage."

"OK," Tank responded to Thorbin's surprise.

"How are you feeling," he continued, wanting to keep Tank conscious.

"My shoulder hurts," he replied with anguish, and to Thorbin's delight a little sarcastic contempt.

"What happened on your side?" Thorbin asked, carefully cutting the old bandage and trying to determine the next best course of action.

"Talc got me. I'm poisoned."

"Has anyone given you a blood purifier?"

"You're the first one to take a look, Doc." Tank turned his head and looked Sam in the eyes. "Well, being a dying man ain't so bad if your pretty face is the last thing I see."

Sam, being accustomed to working under the kind of pressure that would bring most people to their knees, almost broke down. The only thing she could do was smile and refuse the tears their advance.

"Only the good die young, Tank," Thorbin pointed out as he removed the old bandage, completely uncovering the wound. It was a partially healed cut, long and deep. The wound was an unhealthy green and the skin around it was dead and dark – an eerie contrast to the remainder of Tank's deathly pale hide.

"Is that wound still bleeding?" he asked Sam.

She nodded yes in response as he acquired a blood purifier from the first-aid kit. He didn't see her response.

"Is it?" he yelled.

"Yes!" she yelled back.

Thorbin tore the hermetic seal and removed the purifier from the package. He then applied the purifier to the infected green flesh and activated it. Needles shot from the device, and Tank flinched as they pierced his skin. However, he relaxed as they began circulating the infected blood through the device while releasing antibodies and painkillers out back out. Thorbin began redressing the wound, but Tank passed out before he could finish. He had tried to keep him awake, but Tank was at death's door.

"Is he going to be OK?" Sam asked.

"I don't know. That's all we got. So we'll see."

They all stood quiet for a moment, considering Tank's fate.

"You!" Ben said, pointing at Lorilei. "Observation deck, now!"

Thorbin wanted to be the one to chastise Lorilei, but he figured Ben had that covered, so instead he just escorted her to the observation deck.

Lorilei clung to his arm the whole way down the hall, hoping for reassurance but getting none.

Ben, Raj and Thorbin sat. Lorilei sat on Thorbin's lap and buried her face in his chest. She could sense that Ben wanted to hit her, and she hoped he wouldn't. Ben was so mad he could hardly organize his thoughts.

"You! Stay outta sight from now on!" Ben scolded.

"I'm sorry," she responded timidly from her hiding place.

"Sorry ain't good enough, kitten. The rest of the time we're at the oasis, you are *banned* from the cargo bay. No one outside of this room and Sam is to know you exist. You pull another bullshit move like that, and *I will* leave you here. Understand?"

"I understand," she said, frightened by Ben's genuine tone.

"You don't understand shit. Everyone in the main hall got a show. Can't put some damn clothes on. Every pirate at the Run is going to be looking for you. Hell, I might not have a choice but to get rid of you. You've put us all in danger."

Lorilei began to softly weep in Thorbin's arms. As harsh as Ben sounded, his aura was ten-fold more furious. He was bombarding her head with anger, bringing on an immense migraine. Hitting her would have hurt less.

"Lorilei," Thorbin said with a gentler tone than Ben's, a tone accompanied by his aura, which pained her even worse. "There were two places in this system where you could live without being property. One is here on Victoria, and the other was on Earth."

She looked up at him, making sure to convey that she was listening, and understood fully.

"I'm sorry, please don't be upset with me, Thorbin," she pleaded.

He placed his hand gently on her cheek, wiped away a tear, then moved it around her neck and softly squeezed to illustrate his point.

"Not as sorry as you might have been." The point sank deep.

"I'll do anything," she beseeched. The collective disappointment and anger from the room was seeping into every facet of her heart and head. She rubbed her brow against Thorbin's chest trying to stay the intense pain.

"Anything?" Ben said. "Good. Get the fuck outta my sight!" And with that last burst of anger from Ben, her head pounded with merciless empathy. She cried out from the pain and a blood vessel in her nose broke.

Thorbin took notice.

"Come on, let's go clean up," he said, standing. He had to hold her as he stood so she wouldn't slide off his lap and fall to the ground. She was in such pain that she couldn't stand, only cry. Thorbin sighed, and then carried her towards the kitchen.

After they left Raj spoke up.

"I am sorry about my guy."

"You got no reason to be sorry."

"Still, I thought I could trust him. I have been able to in the past."

"You can't trust anyone with her around."

"True," Raj agreed. "I think I can make this better. If you can keep her out of sight, I can start a rumor that you sold her."

Then Sam entered. "I got him all bandaged up."

Ben looked over at her and smiled.

"I can't stay here, Ben."

Ben's smile faded. "Ahhhh, don't leave me now."

"This ship is marked, Ben. The dead pirate and now Lorilei," she said, making a very good point.

"If I have to choose between you and Lorilei, she's gone," Ben said, hoping that would be meaningful to Sam. Sam knew Lorilei meant nothing to him, nothing good at least, but she wasn't about to be the reason for anyone's banishment. So she argued, while Ben and Raj tried vainly to assure her that she shouldn't leave.

Thorbin and Lorilei

Thorbin carried Lorilei to the galley. When they arrived he searched for a place to set her down so he could tend to her easily. The tabletop would have been fine, but it was cluttered with parts of Victoria, so he settled for the counter next to the sink. He prepared to clean the both of them up and let the warm water run in the sink as he searched for something resembling a washcloth.

Lorilei leaned forward with her elbows on her knees. She massaged her temples with her hands, trying to rub away the pain, her legs dangled anxiously towards the floor. Thorbin removed his shirt, which was damp with his sweat and other people's blood. The two were preparing for the moment ahead. They were definitely not on the same page.

Lorilei was desperate for Thorbin's compassion. Thorbin was desperate to make her understand the folly of her ways. She knew that his dissatisfaction with her actions had put their relationship on unstable grounds, she was losing her protector – something had to be done. He knew that her actions that had led to her kidnapping occurred because he hadn't made clear with her what the nature of their relationship should be. The both of them were preparing, lines were being drawn, and points were being constructed. Physically they were steps away from each other. Emotionally, it was high noon and they were staring each other down, waiting for the other to draw down. The first move was his.

"Are you hurt anywhere else?" he asked.

"No," she said as he washed his hands then approached her with a warm wet cloth.

His exterior was measured, while his wrath from within screamed at her. It fed her headache, keeping it from becoming less than unbearable. Under normal circumstances, she would have flung herself at him, but she just didn't have the energy. Besides, right now she had his attention. That wasn't the problem; she needed control over this situation, not just attention. He wiped away the blood from under her nose and a little from her lips. The bleeding was minor and had stopped. He then took a second cloth, damp with warm water, and began to wipe away her tears and clean her face. She sighed contently as the warm damp cotton and his warm gentle touch did much to help soothe the ache in her head.

"Lorilei, what were you thinking?" he said, making his next move.

She could sense that he was incredibly angry, and she was amazed at how kindly he tended to her. He began wiping the underside of her chin, and she lifted her head to accommodate. Before he finished she grasped the cloth hand and held it to her heart.

He sighed, it was her turn, he didn't really want to have this kind of exchange, but she was patient and graciously looked at him until he conceded. They sat silent for a while. She wanted to be consoled, and he felt that not yelling at her was consolation enough.

She took a deep breath and bravely asked, "Do you hate me?"

"No," he answered to her relief, and the pain in her head continued to give way to that alleviation. She let the feeling settle in, and she continued holding him in her gaze. Her courage was building momentum; it gave her the strength to dare, she felt she may prevail, there was risk and reward to be had if she played this vulnerable moment right.

"I love you," she tactfully proposed.

Thorbin sighed again as he looked away from her. She held his hand firmly in place, not letting him avoid answer. He turned back to her,

"No. You don't. You need me. There's a difference, Lorilei." Then he tried to remove his hand, but she wouldn't let go.

Instead, she slid herself to the edge of the counter and reeled him in by his arm. When she pulled him close enough, she drew him in further by wrapping her legs around his waist, then her arms around his torso. Her cheek found its home in his chest, and she conceded, "Yes. I need you. Is that so bad?"

"Lorilei. Let me go," he answered with authority.

"No," she refused. "I won't until you're not mad at me anymore."

"Lorilei, this is not the way. I know it scares you that I'm upset with you. But why didn't you think of that before you started with him in the cargo bay?" An excellent point on his part. How could she possibly refute such astute logic? Clearly she had to answer for her actions; there was no possible way for her to pass blame.

"He seemed nice, I would rather be with you, but I have to get kidnapped to get your attention," she said, defying astute logic. She proceeded on her track by softly massaging his back and nuzzling his chest with her cheek in such a way as to be pathetic and sweet all at the same time. "I'm just frustrated, I need you so much, and you don't need me at all." The cheek tactic was her favorite when it came to Thorbin; it always seemed to loosen him up. This time was no different. She could sense his anger faltering, being replaced by comfort. It was a direct hit; she was beginning to shape some form of control again.

Thorbin placed his chin on top of her head; it was hard not to take comfort in how she expressed her longing for him, even if it was a charade of sorts. She just wanted security and safety, and he could appreciate that.

"We all have different needs, you're just looking for someone to protect you. I...well, just like you can't meet my needs, I can only do so much for you, Lorilei," he said.

She leaned her head back away from his chin and looked into his eyes with sincerity. "There's *nothing* I can do for you?" she wasn't so sure about that.

"No," he answered.

She still wasn't buying it, but she really wanted an answer to her next question. "So if there's nothing I can do for you, then why would you do anything for me?" The thought that he would risk his life protecting her and ask nothing in return was mind-boggling.

He took a deep anxious breath; the only answer he could come up with was dangerous. "Because I like you," he answered.

That made no sense to her. "So you'll protect me because you like me?"

"Yeah."

"Really?"

"Yes," he said with a smile.

"Promise."

"I promise," he said with a sincerity that her empathy confirmed. Despite whether or not it made sense, he was sincere. No matter, she felt the comfort she needed in his honesty, and she readjusted herself around him so she could bask in its warmth. She had even managed to get wrapped up in his embrace. She sat there perfectly content as they shared a heartfelt moment, and like a confirmation of his promise, he reached a hand around and softly rubbed her forehead.

"Are you feeling better?" he asked.

"Yes," she answered, releasing a sigh from his chest, the last bit of ache melted away with his touch.

"Good," he said, forcing a friendly smile. "Can I have my legs back?"

"Just a little longer," she said, wanting to enjoy the moment. He had never allowed her this measure of intimacy before, and she just couldn't let it be.

"Lorilei, this just isn't appropriate."

"Why not?"

"Well…" he said, not wanting to be direct. "I shouldn't be in between your legs."

She looked up at him with a perfectly pretty Lorilei smile and just the right amount of tease twinkling in her eye.

"Why not? Does it make you think naughty things?" she teased, then she thrust her hips against his to add insult to injury. The playful flirt was neither insulting, nor cause for injury. He had done well to keep his body in check throughout this ordeal, but she had hit the spot.

"It does," she said, pleasantly surprised. So she continued teasing with a subtle rhythm, completely reminding him he was a man. "Are you sure, I can't meet *any* of your needs?" she boldly proposed, more with her hips than with her words, which were capable advocates.

"Yes," he answered, feeling weak in the knees. "Please stop," he asked, knowing it would take more than words. He reached one hand behind him to struggle with her legs, which she had locked around him, while the other arm tried to find a hold to pull her body away from his. No matter how he positioned himself to try and make his escape, he only found himself more encumbered.

Lorilei had become downright giddy; she made sure to accent every meeting of their loins with an excited breath and a well-rehearsed tremble.

"Oh," she teased. "That *does* feel good, doesn't it?"

Thorbin felt like an idiot, wondering how the hell he got himself into this mess, and what miracle would come to get him out.

Then Sam walked in and stopped quickly in her tracks at the sight before her. Thorbin saw her, and she was just the miracle he was looking for.

"Sam! Oh thank God you're here."

"What?" Sam wasn't sure what she had to do with this situation.

"Help me out here!" he begged as Lorilei got in a good gyration, causing him to lurch a bit.

"I'm not helping anything. Ugh! I ate off that counter this morning. What are you guys doing?"

"Thorbin's taking advantage of me!" Lorilei answered, giggling.

"I can see that," Sam said, looking at him with accusation.

"Get off of me, woman!" Thorbin said with all the strength his shame afforded him. And this time she obeyed. He took a step back, relieved that he had been set free. Then he turned to Sam, who was smiling at how silly he looked trying to regain his composure, until she took notice of his pants.

"Hey! Point that somewhere else, stud!" she said pointing.

Lorilei bounced off the kitchen counter and readjusted her skirt with satisfaction. Not only had she gotten a rise out of Thorbin, Sam was witness to it – two birds with one stone.

"I'll be in the observation deck," she said with a smug smile as she headed towards the exit. Before leaving she smiled at Thorbin's nether regions. "If you need anything," and she strutted out of sight.

"Sam. We were just talking and…" Thorbin started, really wanting to clarify.

"Don't want to know," Sam said, cutting him off. "I just came to say goodbye, I didn't mean to interrupt."

"You can't leave, Sam," Thorbin said, desperate at the idea of not having her around to help occupy Lorilei. "I really need you to stay."

"OK," Sam said, now the one wanting clarification. "If we're going to talk about this, you need to sit down."

Thorbin quickly grabbed a chair at the table and sat.

"Please, sit," he asked, trying to will himself into submission.

"OK," she conceded.

"Let's talk about this, Sam."

"Fine, but if it's OK with you, I'm going to take my own seat at the table. I talk differently than Lorilei."

Thorbin was beyond frustrated. Did she really think he was taking advantage of Lorilei? The frustration, however, did help, in a way.

"You saw her, twenty minutes ago she was falling apart. We were just talking and she was starting to feel better. Then she just went for it!" he explained.

"Oh that must have been terrible for you. Cute little Mosot girl, throwing herself at you," Sam replied.

"I'm a married man, Sam, I was just... I was being good, she just... before I knew it... Then you walked in. I was trying to get her off of me the whole time."

"What? She just went off, like a slut bomb?"

"Yes!" he confirmed, as if she was the one he was married to, trying desperately to assure he was faithful. "I was hit by a slut bomb!"

"OK. I believe you. Not like I care either way. What you and the little hooker do is none of my business. I was just coming in to say goodbye."

"You can't leave, it's not safe for you out there."

"It's not safe here either."

"I can take care of you here."

"I can take care of myself, and keep my clothes on doing it," Sam said with a jab.

"You won't last an hour back at the oasis. What do I have to do to convince you to stay?" he rebutted, ignoring the jab.

She stopped and leaned back in her chair, thinking for a moment before she replied, "Assure me I'll be safe on Victoria."

"I assure you, you'll be safe on Victoria," he quickly answered with confidence.

"Don't believe you, Prince Charming."

"Well," he thought, and there was another moment of silence. "At least sleep on it, you don't have to go this second."

Sam thought about it, he was right. Besides, she didn't really have a plan, aside from leaving Victoria. There was no place for her to go. She certainly wasn't going to return to her previous lodgings.

"OK," she said, reluctantly relenting. "But only because I got no place to go. And just to be clear, keep it off the counter."

Chapter Twelve
The Bathtub

Ben and Sam

"All right, ten percent, and I get to take a bath whenever I want," Sam said to Ben.

She was feeling quite refreshed, she had just finished bathing and was toweling off her long black hair as she sat comfortably in a new pair of sweats and a comfy shirt that Thorbin had unknowingly purchased for her recently. She liked them, and after the bath she decided that from now on they would be her comfy clothes. Ben like them too, a blessed reprieve from what had been Ben's only female companionship for what seemed an eternity, Lorilei. Unlike Lorilei, Sam was a woman, intelligent and quick-witted, not to mention handy with a toolbox, and appropriately feminine. A sweet breath of fresh air.

Ben quickly became fond of her. He needed her to stay on board, and his will had no mercy. He had been incessant as they worked on the port turbine, appealing to every aspect that he could conceive. He touted professional camaraderie alongside irrefutable reason. All mixed with a healthy dose of shameless flattery. Then, as if sent by heaven, the bathroom unit was delivered, and they broke away from the port turbine to install it. Upon completion of the install, Ben tactfully sealed the deal without knowing it when he suggested a break to *test* the new bathroom.

It was the warm water that sealed the deal. It was the only secure, alone time Sam had experienced since the Talc invasion. She acknowledged to herself that she might be crazy sacrificing a little more safety for luxury, but the water was so very nice. After all, life without some form of pleasure or comfort is no life at all. Ben had yielded the bath to her as he took a shower in a separate part of the unit, then waited outside for her. After the enjoyable soak, she continued to let Ben bathe her in complements as they sat outside continuing to negotiate.

Outside his tact had not ceased; he stood behind her, genteelly helping her dry her lovely hair.

"Prettier than satin, and softer than silk," he said, then let the hair towel fall as he began to massage her scalp. She was in bliss, she had thought she had reached the pinnacle of relaxation in the tub, she was wrong.

"Mmm," she sighed, closing her eyes to be fully absorbed in the head rub. "Is this appropriate?"

"If it keeps the prettiest woman in the universe on Victoria, it's not just appropriate, it's the captain's duty," he said with a grin.

That was it, ego climax.

"OK, that's enough," she said, raising her hands above her head to stop his magic fingers. "I can't take it anymore, it's a deal."

"Well, that's good," Ben said with a laugh. "That was my ace."

Sam ran her fingers through her hair, shaking out the goose bumps Ben had left on the top of her head.

He circled around in front of her with a gregarious Ben smile, then held his hands up and flexed his fingers. "Free head rub whenever you want."

Sam shuddered playfully. "No thanks, you'd have way too much power over me."

"I would never," Ben said sheepishly. "It would be like soiling a masterpiece, or closing the window on a sunset."

Sam smiled, eyes closed, basking in the glow of Ben's compliments. She took an over-dramatic breath then smiled.

"You're right, Sam is beautiful. We know this."

Thorbin and Tank

Thorbin had been awake for a while and finally decided to open his eyes and check up on Tank. He looked better on account that he was sitting up now as opposed to actually looking better.

"Morning," Thorbin greeted. Tank looked in his direction and nodded. Thorbin sat up, stretched a bit, and then removed his blanket.

"How are you feeling?"

"Them's sum good painkillers," Tank said slowly, still under the influence.

"Only the best for Tank, that's what I told them."

Tank smiled, somewhat. "Well, still breathin', suppose that's good, uh?"

"Lie back down," Thorbin said as he began to inspect the bandage. "Have you seen anyone else in the squad besides us?"

"Romanov, he got picked up by the same transport as me. Lost track of him when the Talc attacked it."

"Too bad. I hope he's OK. There were a few Talc on Victoria when Ben picked me up."

"Ben?"

"He's the boat's captain. You met him yesterday. Helped me get you to bed?"

"Oh, OK," Tank said, not remembering Ben at all. "How many were there?"

"Just a few, not much of a problem."

"Yeah, but they keep comin'."

"Their ship was destroyed before I got here, so it was just the few."

"Not on the transport. We held 'em for an hour or so until the big ones showed."

"How big?"

"Hmm," Tank considered, very little was big compared to Tank. "Six feet maybe. Wore body armor and carried firearms. Nasty ones too, some kind of energy weapon."

"How did you get cut?"

"Turned the wrong corner, four of the little bastards rushed me. Only had time to shoot one before they were pokin' at me."

"Wow."

"Yeah, that was a few minutes before we exchanged with the big ones. Shortly after I was off in another pod with some of them transport boys."

"And Romanov?"

"He was there when we got into the pods, 'cept he had to jump in a different one. That was the last I seen him. After that we got picked up by a Separatists' boat and they dropped us off at the oasis."

"Separatists?"

"Yeah. It was the damnedest thing. Picked us right up courteous and all. Then dropped us off with a handshake."

"Never thought Separatists would be the helpful type."

"Well, it was the end of the world as we knew it."

"Right," Thorbin confirmed, hoping to quickly repress the thought of it.

"What about the girl?"

"We picked her up from a pod. She's adjusting from her former life, kinda. What she needs is a psychiatrist."

"Not her, the other one?"

"Sam?"

"No! The woman, that was here last night."

"Her name is Sam."

"Well, that's not the name I woulda put on that pretty face."

"One track mind?"

"Sex and violence – if one don't get me the other one's bound to."

"I'm betting on violence."

"I dunno, I'm pretty good at violence. So what is she, Chinese?"

Ben and Sam

"Korean!" Sam said, insulted that Ben thought she was Chinese.

"Just taking a guess. Didn't mean nothing by it. With a name like Sam, it's hard to tell where a lady is from."

"Well you could have asked where I was from."

"OK, where are you from?"

"Castro Valley."

"Where's that?"

"Near San Francisco."

"That's in America, right?"

"Yes."

"I visited New York once. Way too many people for me. Probably would've liked San Francisco better. I always wished I'd taken Jessica to Disneyland, she would have liked that."

"Disneyland is nowhere near San Francisco," Sam said, irritated.

"Is there anything I can say to get us back to friendly?"

"Tell me how pretty I am," she said with a sheepish smile.

"As pretty as," Ben paused, trying to come up with a complement. "Ah hell, I already used up all my good ones."

Sam laughed, "Figures, you got what you wanted, molested my head and everything. Men are all the same."

"Just can't keep us out of your hair," Ben retorted.

Sam laughed again. "How many times have you been to Earth?"

"Over my whole life?" Ben thought about it for a moment. "Well I've been in orbit plenty of times, but actually on the Earth…maybe a few days. New York, Tokyo, Jessica and I honeymooned in Kauai. That was nice. Otherwise Earth is way too crowded. Made me feel constrained to be in city with millions of people."

"I can understand that. You've spent most of your life in space. Out here I feel like I'm hopelessly lost in the middle of nowhere."

"It's not nowhere. It's grid O 584."

Sam laughed. "OK. You should have visited the Midwest."

"Um excuse me?" Lorilei said from the bridge entrance below holding a towel.

"Hey, Lorilei," Sam greeted. "Did you sleep well?"

Ben didn't let her answer. "What do you want?"

"Could I go into the cargo bay?"

"Cargo bay is off limits to you."

"I just want to take a bath. I'm stinky."

"You sure are. NO!" Ben said, reaffirming his authority. Lorilei stood there with her towel disappointed. "Use the office sink," Ben suggested.

"No one's on board, Ben. Give her a break and some privacy," Sam sympathetically interjected.

Lorilei threw in a pathetic, "Please?"

Ben said nothing for a moment then conceded. "Twenty minutes. Clock starts now, and don't do anything I'm going to make you regret."

"Thank you," she said gratefully before rushing down the hall with a giddy shriek.

Thorbin

Earlier, Thorbin had also discovered the installation of the bathroom unit and had just finished showering. As he was attending to the beard that was trying to re-conquer his face, he found himself inexplicitly humming a tune. He caught himself and pondered what the tune was and why he was humming it. His silence revealed the answer. He could faintly hear Lorilei singing in the bathtub.

"God, I hope she doesn't know I'm in here," he whispered to himself.

"Lord," he prayed, feeling this moment necessitated prayer. "Please." The distraction caused him to nick himself with the blade. "Agh!" he cried out, inspecting the cut in the mirror. Not bad.

"Thorbin? Is that you?" Lorilei yelled to him from the bathroom. "Are you OK?"

Thorbin thought for sure he heard God laughing. He remained silent, hoping she would think she was hearing things. He waited a moment then quietly continued to shave. Shortly after, the singing recommenced. He sighed, then took pleasure in it. It reminded him of her prayers a few days back. Her voice had a soothing quality in general, but when she sang, it was relaxing. It was a nice moment without stress or consequence, and the beard was soon gone. He leaned back, inspecting himself in the mirror. He rubbed his face and neck with his hands to be sure he hadn't missed any spots. The singing stopped and Thorbin's moment was shattered by a knock on the stall door. He closed his eyes and took a deep breath.

"Good morning," he said cheerfully, hiding his anticipation that it was very likely a naked Lorilei on the other side of the door.

"Oh," Sam replied surprised. "I was looking for Lorilei."

"She's in the tub," Thorbin said, relieved as he opened the door.

"Morning, Romeo," Sam teased as she looked Thorbin up and down. "Looking good," she continued, impressed at seeing Thorbin clean-shaven, filth free, and dressed in clothes neatly tucked in and whole. A smile came across her face. "You fly boys clean up good. Hell, all the men on board do," she concluded coyly as she knocked on the correct door. "Lorilei, time's almost up, if you don't hurry, Ben's gonna drag you out."

Thorbin visualized Ben dragging Lorilei out of the tub. A half-smile appeared on his face, then it disappeared with the acknowledgement that afterwards she would fling herself at him for comfort and reassurance. He then knocked on the door in hopes of quenching a dilemma before it began.

"You'd better not tempt fate," he said, hoping she would listen.

"OK."

He heard her muffled answer through the door. He turned and looked to Sam standing beside him. "You're not looking half bad yourself. And, I must say, I wasn't sure I'd see you again. Did you decide to stay?"

"What can I say? Ben's a tough negotiator."

"Yeah, I suppose he must be."

Then Sam turned to the door again. "Lorilei, you're going to be sorry," was all she could say as Ben and his wrath entered the cargo bay.

Thorbin and Sam parted like the Red Sea as he approached the door and banged on it with authority.

"All right, kitten, you're done, get the fuck out," he yelled then fumbled with a set of keys.

"Ben, she's getting out," Thorbin pleaded as he took notice of the keys. Ben snapped his head and looked at Thorbin sternly. Thorbin caught himself taking a step back.

"I gave her an extra five minutes, I'm gonna learn her ass this time."

Thorbin blinked, and he realized that this wasn't going to go well for him at all. It would only be a matter of time before she was weeping naked in his arms. Fearing the inevitable, he went and fetched a towel. When he returned to the bathroom door Ben had just turned its handle and opened it.

The bath segment of the bathroom unit was very nice, oversized with all of the amenities. The tub sat in the center of the room and there were plenty of shelves and mirrors along the walls.

When Ben entered Lorilei was still in the bath, she had managed to use some shampoo in order to get a healthy level of bubbles going. She had taken her candles and lit them in a triangle around the bathtub. Her wasteful use of shampoo would have been enough to enrage Ben, however, the candles really pissed him off.

"Are you stupid?" he yelled at her as he scrambled towards the tub.

"No!" she defended jolting upright in the tub, preparing for the worst. Her tender soapiness had no effect on him; he quickly snatched up the candles from the tile floor with such a force their flames extinguished.

Lorilei tried to leap out of the bath and grab the last one before he got to it, but the soapy water caused her to slip and hang precariously over the lip of the tub.

"Where did you get these?" he yelled at her, waving one of the candles in her face.

She grabbed onto his hand and tried to free it from his grasp. "Thorbin gave them to me!" she cried out.

Outside the bathroom Thorbin heard the exchange and closed his eyes, it was going to be worse than he thought.

"T!" Ben yelled out to him.

Thorbin slowly leaned into the bathroom threshold, holding the towel in front of him.

"What the hell were you thinking?" Ben yelled at him, struggling to hold the candles as far above his head as he could. He scowled at Thorbin as he turned about, trying to stave off Lorilei, who was tugging on his elbows whilst trying to climb him at the same time.

"She uses them to pray," Thorbin answered calmly in hopes of not exacerbating the situation.

"She's going to burn the ship down," Ben said, engaging in a tug of war with his own arm against Lorilei until he got in a motivated thrust that pushed her back. Her soapy feet lost their footing and she fell to floor hard, landing on her backside with such a force, a shockwave rolled from her bottom to the top of her head. Ben looked down at her, not the least bit concerned that she may be hurt. "Cry all you want, then come to the kitchen for your punishment." Then he stormed out with a last word to Thorbin. "Make sure she's quick about it."

Thorbin watched Ben as he exited. He then turned back to Lorilei.

Here it comes, he thought to himself. And before the thought was finished she was headed straight for him. He held out the towel and she flew right into it and buried her tear-laden soapy face in his chest. This was her unhappy position. Thorbin had figured it out. When she was sad or scared, she would always throw her arms around his waist to maximize the cheek to chest position. It was a sharp contrast from her happy position, which was the arms flung around the neck, so she could pull his face close – the better to try and steal a kiss.

He struggled a little with the towel, trying to figure out how best to attach it to her. He figured it was good for now and simply held it together with his hand, knowing she was going to be here for a while anyhow. She was wet and soapy, and now he was wet and soapy. So while she stood there crying into his chest, he did his best to dry off her back and shoulders, being sure not to touch her posterior. He felt like some odd kind of servant toweling off a princess.

Then he bolstered himself. *What else am I supposed to do?*

She sniffled deeply and finally spoke.

"It's not fair," she said with the only breath she could catch, then her lungs forced the air back in, causing her to heave as they abruptly refilled.

"I know," he said sympathetically as he continued to rub her back.

"My bottom hurts," she sniffled, one arm let go of him, then moved the towel out of the way and rubbed a cheek softly with her hand. "I think it's broken."

"It's probably just bruised," Thorbin said, he didn't know for sure, but he certainly wasn't going to look into it.

She looked up at him in the way only Lorilei could, sweet and attractive despite all the tears and conflict, then she placed her arms around his neck.

"Oh, come on," he said to her. She nodded, pulled the hand back and reinserted the cheek.

Back in the kitchen, Ben stood by the counter furiously drinking coffee. He had fought the urge to throw the candles away, and instead he just hid them. Sam had excused herself, sighting too much testosterone, and gone to get some shuteye. So Ben stood there stewing until Thorbin entered the room and they eyed each other quietly.

Ben swirled the coffee around in his cup, and Thorbin leaned against the hatch, head tilted to the side, arms crossed.

"So this is it," Ben said softly with an aggressive tone. "It has begun. She's gotten into your head."

"No," Thorbin replied. "I just think you're wrong, that's all."

"So you gonna challenge my authority too?" Ben said as he stood up straight.

Thorbin didn't budge; he just looked him in the eye from across the room.

"You're the captain, you want to make Lorilei miserable. Well, you're the captain."

"The situation with you and Lorilei is getting out of hand."

Thorbin took note of Ben using her proper name. "She's drawn me in a little, just like you said she would. But only as is necessary, this is not about me and her. You took something very special away from her."

"A level of control needs to be maintained," Ben pointed out.

"She's changed a lot since we first picked her up."

"Really? She wasn't wearing a thing!"

"She was in the tub."

"Whatever. You need to figure it out; the situation is about to get more complex. Your buddy Tank, we're going to pick up a mechanic who's a young man, and a mercenary who also is male. No telling what she'll do or how she'll act, and what that might lead to. She has a way of...becoming a problem," Ben said, stating the obvious.

"We're going to what?"

"Raj found us some passengers. They'll be waiting for us at the Harpy in a few hours."

"Why not bring them here?"

"I want to check them out, make sure I'm not picking up any more trouble."

"A mechanic, and a mercenary," Thorbin confirmed.

"And a saleswoman, Raj really came through. The lady's willing to pay big. The mechanic and the merc don't have much to pay, but they'll definitely come in handy."

"What kind of merc?" Thorbin asked, cautiously concerned.

"Corporate," Ben answered.

Thorbin took a deep breath and reflected as he loosened up and headed to the counter to get some coffee himself.

"I don't know if that's a good idea, Ben."

"Yeah. I was just thinking, we get any more fury visitors, a corporate merc on board would be nice."

"You're right about that," Thorbin answered, still not comfortable with the idea.

Thorbin had dealt with many mercenaries. The DC would hire them from time to time to help with pirates. So would the Syndicate. Corporate mercenaries were the best of the best. Thorbin's overall impression of them was that they were soulless.

Corporate mercs were genetically selected from birth and weren't raised so much as produced. The selection process was actually prohibited on Earth, so they were manufactured on Mars. The corporate scientists would select candidates based on a variety of genetic predispositions, all centered around growing an organic weapons system. There were woman whose occupation was to breed them. They would then be weaned by the corporate bosom of discipline and regiment. Kept in seclusion from the rest of humanity, raised by scientists and militants. A life wholly dedicated to serving the corporation as a solider of fortune. They were extremely effective in small groups with specific objectives, and they met the DC need for quick and inexpensive deployments against pirate settlements and concerns. The corporate mercenary was a product that met the consumer's demand. A biological weapon, a merc.

"It'll be all right, T," Ben said, breaking Thorbin's introspective silence.

"Let's hope so," he responded as he poured himself a cup of coffee then sat at the kitchen table. "Well, Tank's not going to be a problem. He's seen a lot in his time. Corporate mercs are chemically and mentally castrated. They're not real familiar with the concept of love and intimacy on any level."

"Wow, really? I know they're a bunch of hard-asses, but his parts don't work?"

"Part of the corporate procedure. Instead of contending with the sexual instinct, they remove it. Figuratively."

"Harsh, no wonder." Ben paused to think about this for a moment. "Well, the mechanic, he ain't been neutered and he ain't wise to the world, as it were."

"We'll just have to see."

"Wise to the world," Ben repeated. "I guess that's one of those sayings that's gonna have to be rephrased. Anyhow," Ben said softening himself, "you've done a halfway decent job of keeping her out of trouble. Joyride aside, until she fully adjusts…"

"I know," Thorbin began feeling a headache coming on. "I'm surprised you haven't gotten rid of her here at the oasis."

"Me too," Ben said, displaying a brief moment of sympathy for her. "I gotta punish her."

"What are you going to do, spank her?"

"She has to know what I say goes."

"Well, taking the candles from her is a sentence she will not soon forget."

"They're that important to her?"

"It's a religious thing."

"Religious? She's too stupid to believe in God." Ben had to pause, he wasn't sure if *he* believed in God, and often times felt people who did were just worshiping strange fairytales. It was odd the predicament he found himself in. Thorbin began a rebuttal but then stopped when Lorilei entered the room, still in her towel.

"Damn it, woman! Clothes!" Ben said, then he headed to the hatch that led to the hallway. "I'll be in the cargo bay," he said to Thorbin as he left.

Lorilei smiled at Thorbin.

"What?" he asked. She approached him and put her arms around his waist again, head in his chest.

"It still hurts," she whimpered.

"Well I'm not going to rub it if that's what you're looking for."

"Oh," she said, a little disappointed but not surprised. "More hugs then?"

Chapter Thirteen
Looking For Something Special

Ben sat down on a folding chair a few steps away from the container that was Jessica's makeshift tomb. In a few moments, he and Thorbin would be off to pick up the passengers Raj had booked for him. Until then, he reminisced about Jessica and apologized that he hadn't spent any time with her lately. After a short while of reflection, he reached into his shirt and caressed the Aum Raj had given him. He decided he needed a smoke and pulled his pipe, which he had pre-packed, from a pocket.

Frustration began to set in when his fumbling didn't reveal a lighter and sadness fell across his face. He was about to let it take its toll when he was interrupted by the confident rhythm of footsteps on the cargo bay deck. He didn't bother to look up. Each calculated step prominently declared their owner. A closed hand reached around from behind him then opened, revealing a lighter and a courteous flame.

"What's in the container?" a Slavic accent inquired. Ben accepted the fire and took a hit. He closed his eyes then released his despair in exchange for fear as he turned his head to see the man with the flame. Syndicate, three of them.

"Thank you," he made sure to say, then answered. "My wife and crew."

"Your reputation precedes you, Benjamin. So I'm going to assume you're not lying."

"Killed by the Talc."

"My condolences," the imposing figure said as he offered the lighter to Ben, who accepted it. "Keep the light."

"Thanks again, what can I do for you gentlemen?"

"We have reason to believe…" The man placed his hands in his pockets than continued, "That you have something of ours on board."

"If I do, I was just keeping it safe for you."

"Good man, do you mind if we have a look around?"

"Not at all, if you tell me what you're looking for, I'll get it for you right now."

"You're alive because you don't know what we're looking for. It would be a shame to kill an asset such as yourself. We'll have a look ourselves if you don't mind."

"I'm at your service."

"Thank you. Who is on board? What is on board?"

"Two DC pilots. One severely injured and lying in the common room. My engineer, and a Mosot girl running around somewhere."

"Mosot?"

"Yeah."

"Hmm." He grinned, looking around Victoria. "Times have changed. What about these things?" the man said, pointing to the contents in Victoria's hold.

"Supplies for our trip to Mars and parts for Victoria."

The man motioned to his associates, and they began their search. One of them pulled a scanner from his pocket and surveyed the container; he then nodded, affirming Ben's declaration of its contents. The other was sifting through the boxes of supplies with a scanner of his own.

Thorbin walked in leisurely then froze in his footsteps, startling one of the seekers, who quickly turned and palmed his pistol. Thorbin displayed his unarmed hands. He immediately recognized the three men. They were the Syndicate that he and Sam had witnessed murdering the pirate back in the motel.

"No trouble here," Thorbin said. The man's intense look melted into a half-grin.

"DC." Then he proceeded with his search.

Ben looked over at Thorbin and stared at him, hoping that he got his 'no hero bullshit' message.

"Thorbin, this is Dima and his men. He believes that we may have something of his on board."

"I see," Thorbin said then cleared his throat.

"Your DC pilot?" Dima asked him.

"Yes, Ben picked me up after the Battle of Earth."

"You did well."

"We lost."

"We haven't lost yet. The Mars fleet is intact. Separatists have been chipping away at the remaining Talc, slowing their progress to Mars. The trap is being set. We would have no chance if not for the courage seen at the Battle of Earth."

Thorbin was taken aback by the patriotic tone of his response.

"Perhaps you think I am the bad man. War makes for interesting friends, no? My home is also gone."

The man who had scanned the cold storage container and other items approached Dima and shook his head no. To which Dima replied with a motion towards the bow of the ship. The man then headed towards the hallway.

Thorbin stepped aside and leaned up against a nearby bulkhead, hoping all would go well.

Ben finished his smoke and leaned back in the chair, watching the Syndicate inspecting the contents of the cargo bay. He observed that electronics were under particular scrutiny, especially small circuit boards and components. He was trying to understand what he could have that they wanted. At first he had suspected that this was just an excuse to take Lorilei. But the search was with intent. They were looking for something electronic.

Sam entered the cargo bay sleepily in her PJs, obviously distraught. She went straight to Ben, who gave her a consoling smile and squeezed her hand. Dima looked at her.

"Sorry to disturb you. We'll be done soon."

Sam nodded, not wanting to engage further with the gangster. Moments later she was followed by Lorilei with the Syndicate trailing behind her. Dima took notice, and Thorbin held his breath.

"The Mosot," Dima said, taking pleasure in her beauty. "Come here lovely."

Lorilei did as she was told.

Dima kept his hands in his pockets as he slowly took her in. "Turn around," he instructed, and she did. He looked at her backside and smiled, then causally walked around her until they were facing each other.

Lorilei wasn't sure how to act, his demeanor was without emotion, but his aura was lusting for her. His intent was so strong her skin tingled unpleasantly wherever he eyed her. So she remained silent and as motionless as possible, avoiding eye contact.

"Typically perfect," he concluded at the end of his inspection. He removed a hand from his pocket, and she held her breath as he slowly lifted up her chin.

"Lavender. My favorite."

Lorilei was constraining terror, and the eye contact wasn't helping. She had no power over this man, and he was inspecting her like a prize possession. The intense memories of captivity flooded back into her mind, faltered in her eyes, and ran down her cheek. Dima wiped the tear away with his thumb while still holding her chin up. "I like that too."

Thorbin stood up straight, and Ben focused completely on soothing his anxiety. With every fiber in his being Ben was begging Thorbin not to act. Sam, however, was scoping out a place to hide for the impending gun battle.

Dima gently slid his palm across her cheek and tucked a loose strand of hair behind her ear. Then he inspected the crease in her towel where it was folded at her chest. He tightened the fold.

"If you're not careful, you fall out of these," he said, smiling at her. She didn't smile back because she sensed that a return smile wouldn't demonstrate the necessary submissiveness he demanded.

"To whom do you belong?"

Lorilei was petrified. She knew she couldn't answer or she'd be claimed.

"She's freed," Thorbin answered for her.

Without taking his eyes off Lorilei, Dima responded, "I see." He inspected her further then asked, "Would you like to come with me?"

Lorilei couldn't tell if he was really asking or commanding, no one could.

"You would be safe with me. I have many nice things. Unlike the pirates, I know what a Mosot likes. I know what you need. I have these things if you would like to come with me."

Still she couldn't tell if she was being asked or told, but either way he was waiting for a response.

"Do I have to?" she asked meekly.

"No, but you should," he responded. "My bed is warm and soft. My hand can be gentle. My home is beautiful. I will make sure you have the desires of your heart. And any man, anything, that would harm you I could destroy."

Lorilei could tell by his presence and the presence of others around him that he was indeed a force to be reckoned with. The fact that he could come to Victoria and claim anything as his possession was proof that he could meet her needs. Her abject fear melted away into curiosity, and she contemplated his proposition.

"Well?" he prodded. "These days there are few who possess the power that I have. Even fewer that would care for you the way I would. Where is a *freed* Mosot going to be safe in this system without Earth?"

Lorilei scanned deep for deception; it was starting to sound too good to be true. There was none. Dima was genuine, at least as far as she could tell, which was a skill of hers. What did Victoria have that could compete with his offer? With him she would be comfortable and safe. Her needs could be met. On Victoria she was poor and had already been kidnapped once. Emotionally, Thorbin concealed himself and Ben yelled at her...a lot.

The man was obliviously a bad guy, but if he was good to her, would that matter? Thorbin was a good guy, but that didn't mean she'd be safe with him. The more she thought about it, the more she discovered, she couldn't come up with a reason not to accept Dima's offer. Except one, which really wasn't a reason at all but an unexplained feeling, unnamed yet significant. The first time she had ever felt it was on board Victoria. At first she hated it; it was lonely and unfamiliar, and very frightening. With time she had grown accustom to it, and it was bearable. She wondered why that terrifying feeling was the only thing keeping her from quickly accepting Dima's offer. His offer appealed to her core. But still, she knew that he didn't have this one thing for her. It was only here, on Victoria, and it suddenly seemed more important than comfort and security.

Though she couldn't name this feeling or even completely understand its relevance, she knew it was right.

"No," she answered.

Ben was sure that after Dima's offer he was about to be minus a Lorilei problem. He was amazed. It appealed to everything he thought she was, but she declined.

"This is no place for a pretty thing like you," Dima objected.

"Victoria is first-class accommodations these days, Dima," Ben replied for her.

"Very well then," he said, turning away from her and looking intently at his comrades. One of them answered.

"It's not here."

Dima nodded several times in consideration then turned back to Ben.

"Farewell, Victoria, travel well," Dima concluded and the three of them exited Victoria.

"I can't believe you didn't go with him." Ben said to Lorilei, quite impressed.

"Yeah," Sam interjected. "I kinda wanted to go. Except he's slimy."

"Don't be silly," Thorbin said as he wrapped his arms around Lorilei, who graciously sank into them.

"No kidding here. Why the hell did you turn him down? You know you're never going to get a better offer than that," Ben continued.

"You're not going to get rid of me that easy," Lorilei answered Ben, who smiled at her, and that still-unnamed feeling returned. Still frightening and unfamiliar, but good. It was the real answer to Ben's question, but she didn't understand it enough to explain. She did, however, know that it was guiding her properly because it led to other feelings that she could name – like respect, and it was coming from Ben. Although this one had a name that she knew, she had never really felt it before until this moment. And it was good.

"Lorilei," Ben insisted. "Why did you say no? The truth."

"There's something here that he doesn't have. No one has it for me. It's only here on Victoria, and I need it, I think."

Ben couldn't argue with that. He had felt that way many times. He looked at her in amazement.

"Go put some clothes on."

Chapter Fourteen
All Aboard That's Comin' Aboard

Ben and Thorbin gathered a few things then mounted their mules. As they slowly pulled forward waiting to exit Victoria, Thorbin asked, "There's three of them, we only got two more seats."

"Just one more thing to figure out," Ben answered. "In and out. Let's get to 'em, do the thing and get back."

They rode cautiously down the catwalks towards the main hall. Scores of previously filled docks along the way were empty, with no signs of filling anytime soon. Soon they reached the main hall, which also felt abandoned. All the merchants were gone and the hall was eerily dim. Some of the shops weren't even closed, just left behind. The still emptiness made the fairway seem even larger as their mules dusted a trail through the litter and loneliness, leaving a swirling wake behind them.

Every so often they would pass a small band of Syndicate conversing with each other. Thorbin took a good look at the arms dealer's shop as they passed; it appeared to have been locked before forcibly entered. A little further down five Syndicate were seated across the hall from a dozen or so pirates, no doubt anticipating a fight. If ever there was a calm before a storm.

When they arrived at the Jaded Harpy it was no different. The creaking from the double doors as they entered shattered the silence, immediately gaining the attention of the few people in the bar. Ben and Thorbin stopped at the entrance and sifted through the patrons for their passengers. A half-dozen Japanese Syndicate were at the bar – one of them serving drinks to the others due to a lack of bartending. It was apparent they had been charged with the security at the harpy. One of them approached.

"Konichiwa. You are captain of Victoria?"

"Yes," Ben replied.

"Over there," the man pointed, "quickly."

Ben had already spotted the mercenary and a familiar blonde woman, who were both sitting at the same table. He nodded respectfully to the Syndicate and then made his way to the potential passengers.

The merc stood as Ben approached and adjusted the strap on his assault rifle. He was all business, urban fatigues from head to toe, polished black boots, and lightweight body armor that was hardily distinguishable from his uniform. His face was concealed by a sleek black mask, which contoured his features in a generic, emotionless way. The two holes, filled in with tinted safety glass that allowed the warrior to see his prey, were barely noticeable. Looking at his face was like looking into an ominous dark mirror that reflected back into one's own soul, where a person would be memorized by their own frailty. Intimidation was all part of the product, and this guy delivered.

The armor was a near transparent cloth and had a dull silky texture that was ghost-like. It was very strong and light – the best armor money could buy. It was flexible like cotton, but under extreme pressure it hardened to become as solid as steel. This protected the warrior from explosions, gunshots, and even kicks and punches. Punching a man that wore this stuff was like punching a brick wall. A square foot cost a small fortune, and he was covered from head to toe. His weapon was also state of the art, an M-series smart rifle. The weapon was able to distinguish friend or foe all by itself and fired rounds that could change trajectory in mid-flight. Those were just a few of its impressive features; it too cost a small fortune.

He was in stiff contrast to his tablemate, who leaned confidently to the side in her chair. Her blonde hair flowed from under a tattered straw hat, with jeans and a T-shirt wrapped around a dangerously attractive figure.

Thorbin wanted to tell Ben that he had seen this woman before, but Ben had already proceeded to the table, so he turned his attention back to the entrance and took a position over by the bar in case Ben needed cover.

Ben took a quick look over his shoulder and took notice of Thorbin leaning against the bar, then approached.

"My name's Elizabeth, people call me Liz," the blonde woman said.

"Saleswoman huh?" Ben inquired. He knew full well who she was.

"Yes, sir," she answered.

"Weren't you the one all over that fish in the casino?"

"Fish?" she said, pretending not to understand.

"Sales?" Ben reiterated.

"Look. That's my business, can I get a ride or is my money no good here?"

"I just prefer to know who my passengers are. Prostitution isn't sales."

"Sure it is, not that it matters, I'm not a hooker. Enough with the questions. If I can't come along, then I want to get the hell out of here."

"You're good for now, but we'll be talking about this more."

"Fine. Can we go?"

Ben turned to the merc. "10k," he confirmed. The merc nodded.

"Where's the other guy? The mechanic," Ben asked Liz.

"Just us. No one else has been here."

Ben turned and scanned the rest of the sparse patronage. No one met the description.

"OK, let's go," Ben instructed, but the merc raised his weapon.

"Incoming!" a deep melodic voice declared from behind its mask, followed by the clatter of automatic fire.

Several pirates had charged in the front door, weapons ablaze. A few of the Syndicate were caught completely off guard and were hit. The remaining, along with Thorbin, had leapt over the bar. The merc's weapon let lose a cruel volley as he knelt into a better firing position. Thorbin recognized the unique sound of the M22's fury. The smart bullets made a distinct and unsettling sound when they hit flesh and exploded. The agony of those unfortunate enough to feel the weapon's wrath lay on the Harpy's floor, that is the ones unlucky enough to have survived.

Thorbin looked to his right and made eye contact with a Syndicate. They acknowledged each other and rose up to join the fray. Many shots were exchanged and the pirates were forced to retreat to the main hall. There was a brief ceasefire.

The Syndicate were franticly calling for back up and the pirates were regrouping outside the Harpy. Thorbin heard one of them curse with dismay about engaging a mercenary. Ben was also cursing profusely as he fumbled with his shotgun. It had jammed up on him and was being very uncooperative. Liz was franticly offering advice, trying to help, which didn't help at all. Thorbin took this opportunity to conceal himself behind the bar and reload his semiautomatic rifle. He pulled a few rounds from inside his jacket, pushed them one at a time into the magazine, then set it in place and let the bolt slam forward. In his periphery he could see a commotion so he turned his head to see the Syndicate franticly leaping to the other side of the bar. It caught him completely off guard until he heard one of them bellow. "Gre-n-ade!"

Thorbin was frantic, looking about for it, but it was too late.

Ben looked on terrified as the grenade exploded in Thorbin's proximity across the room. A brilliant flash of light and a defending explosion.

Thorbin was slammed against the bar, completely disorientated, blinded by the flash, his ears screaming. He wondered if he was alive. He decided he was, but he wasn't sure.

Ben wanted to go to him, but a second wave of pirates was rushing in after the blast. The merc nailed several of them but needed to reload himself, which was difficult now that he was the focus of their fire. His body armor was serving him well, keeping the bullets from penetrating, but still, being shot made reloading very complicated. The Syndicate that had evaded the grenade fared no better on the other side of the bar. They were easy targets and now lay among the fallen.

Thorbin's vision blurrily began to return while the ringing in his ears was relentless. He was lying on his back trying to look at his hand. He knew it was in front of his face, but he just couldn't completely make it out. The three hands he had seen slowly melted into one, and he put it down. Behind it a pirate was standing on the bar yelling at him. He couldn't hear him, but he could see that he was yelling. The man fired a few shots to his left then pointed the weapon at Thorbin, screaming something at him. Thorbin slowly raised his hands in acquiescence, but the man was growing tired of the encounter and had decided to shoot him. He took aim, but was then startled when the merc's weapon began to sing again. He flinched and looked in the merc's direction only to catch a flying beer mug with his face. The glass mug shattered with the impact and Ben shouted in victory.

"Ha! Gotcha!"

The pirate dropped his weapon after the impact and was knocked on his ass, straddling the bar. His hands dashed to his face, hoping to relieve the pain of the attack. Then the mercenary shot him center mass, and the exploding round opened him up gruesomely. He slumped forward like an un-stuffed rag doll.

Thorbin was startled when Ben grabbed hold of him.

"You're OK. It was just a flash bang," he reassured despite Thorbin not being able to hear him. For all Thorbin knew Ben was screaming. 'Dear God your legs!' Or, 'so this is the after life.' He tried to read Ben's lips, but all he could make out was something about an orangutan.

Thorbin replied, more than a little confused. "What? There's no orangutans."

Ben stood him up and inspected him for missing parts and extra holes. There were none except for in his new clothes; they weren't new anymore. Ben picked up Thorbin's rifle and hung it over his shoulder. Thorbin was gently swaying as he spied the merc standing by the Harpy's entrance firing into the main hall. There was something strapped to his back, a case of some sort. It was very large, and if Thorbin didn't know better, he could have sworn it was guitar-shaped. Liz rushed over, instructed by Ben to help.

"Hey! I know her," Thorbin said, struggling to point a finger at the woman.

"I'm a popular girl," Liz replied. The three of them headed towards the front door.

"Is it clear?" Ben asked.

"No," the merc answered. "But I see Syndicate coming. The pirates are pinned down in the shop across the hall."

Every few seconds the merc would fire a shot into their hiding place, targeting something that would make the most ruckus when it was hit. The suppressing fire was effective; the pirates didn't so much as display a bit of themselves so as not to have that bit shot off.

Ben and Liz were tiring of holding Thorbin up so they sat him down and began searching the fallen pirates. Liz took a pistol, every piece of jewelry she came across as well as any money. Ben also procured a pistol after engaging the safety on his shotgun and slinging it over his back with Thorbin's rifle. He was mostly looking for keys. He had briefly peered out into the main hall and noticed that one of their mules had taken heavy damage. He scanned the room for a likely candidate and noticed that Liz was searching a Syndicate.

"Don't," he instructed.

She sighed and moved on.

Moments later the merc updated everyone as to the status of the pirates, "The Syndicate have arrived, they are trapped."

"They should just give up now," Liz commented as she cautiously peeked out the entrance.

"The will never give up," the mercenary responded. "They will die."

"Shit!" Liz said. "Dima! Damn it! Can we get out of here before he sees us? Fuck! Here he comes." She slid back into the Harpy trying to find a place to stash her pistol. The back of her pants was going to have to do.

When Dima and his men entered Ben apprised him of the situation. Only two of the Syndicate were still alive. One of Dima's men had some degree of medical training and after tending to them he began giving Thorbin a field check. Halfway through the check up, several explosions were heard followed by shots.

The merc concluded, "It is done." His tone was righteous.

Dima was standing over the shoulder of the man tending to Thorbin, who reported, "He'll be all right. He'll likely be deaf for many hours, maybe a day, but there should be no lasting effects."

"Good," Dima said then turned his attention to Liz. "Come here," he commanded, pointing to the ground at his feet.

"No," she replied.

Dima's eyes narrowed and two of his men advanced towards her.

"OK," she said, putting her hands up, moving towards Dima and stopping at a comfortable distance.

Dima closed the distance, setting his imposing figure in her personal space. He moved his face close to hers, and she didn't turn away or move in the slightest. He stayed there and stared her in the eye, commanding respect. All she could muster was a defiant blank face.

"I thought we understood each other," he stated.

"I guess not," she replied.

"That's fine. I suppose an understanding isn't necessary. But you will do as

I say." There was a brief moment of exchanging breath until Dima spoke up again. "I'm going to hit you in the face for your defiance. Then you're going to stand back up and we'll start again." She didn't flinch.

"Dima," Ben spoke up.

Without moving Dima addressed Ben. "Is this your business, Benjamin?"

"Yes, Dima, it is," Ben replied.

Shocked at Ben's apparent defiance Dima stepped back and turned towards him. "Explain yourself."

Ben gulped slightly. "This woman booked passage on Victoria, safe passage. No disrespect, but I ask that you not hit my passenger."

Dima's lips, already pressed together, tightened even further. He then turned back to Liz, this time walking right into her, forcing her to take a step back. He slung an arm around her back, pressing her firmly against him, and a sadistic smile crossed his face.

"My hand stays temporarily," he said, firmly sliding his hand down her back, increasing the pressure of his unwanted embrace. His hold on her had caused her to stand on the balls of her feet. After grasping the pistol, he removed it from its position in the small of her back. Then his lips drifted to her ear and he whispered, "I will long to see you again." He let go and she fell back onto her heels.

As Dima exited the Jaded Harpy he handed Ben the pistol and bid them farewell saying, "Be mindful of that one." After he left Liz exhaled.

"Thanks," she said to Ben.

"I didn't do it for you, blondie," he said with a tone previously reserved for Lorilei. "Let's go."

After loading up Thorbin on the back of Ben's mule, Liz and the merc procured their own rides and they all headed back to Victoria.

Lorilei

Sam was asleep in the office upstairs and Lorilei was in the common room with Spot watching over Tank. When Ben entered assisting Thorbin, the dog lost his mind with enthusiasm.

"Didn't this damn thing run away?" Ben said, displeased.

"He came back," Lorilei said, a touch more pleased than Ben. Thorbin collapsed on the couch and Lorilei hurried over in concern.

"What happened?" she asked, kneeling by Thorbin's side.

"He got a little shook up. He'll be OK." Ben leaned over and got Thorbin's attention. "Don't worry." He mouthed more than spoke. "Nurse Lorilei's gonna take good care of you."

Thorbin's brow wrinkled as Lorilei scooted herself onto the couch, pushing him back to make room.

Ben grabbed her by the arm. "You're comin' with me."

"But I have to…"

"Nope! Comin' with me."

As they left Spot was nuzzling Thorbin's arm, fishing for attention.

As they entered the cargo bay Ben instructed Lorilei to man the cargo bay control room, and he had the merc and Liz help secure the room for immediate departure. After sealing the hatches they joined Lorilei.

"All right, kitten. I'm going to the bridge and we got no one to remove the catwalk, so we're just going to have to pull away from it. After it's broke off, you pull this lever, got it?"

"Got it," Lorilei confirmed.

Ben went to the bridge and was grateful that Sam hadn't turned off the turbines. The port was running at thirty-three percent.

"Good girl, Vicky. This might sting a little, but you'll be happy once we get outta here, baby." Ben coaxed Victoria further and the catwalk tore away from her cargo hold like paper.

Lorilei watched as the emergency seal of the catwalk slammed shut on the oasis side, and she pulled the lever as instructed. Ben's head popped in from the office entrance.

"OK, good, kitten. Everybody to the bridge."

They traversed through the office to the bridge, no one taking notice that they had disturbed Sam's sleep. When they got to the bridge Ben was about to speak when Liz interrupted.

"Can I have my pistol back?"

"Like I was about to say – no weapons on Victoria."

"What about him," Liz protested, pointing to the merc.

Ben extended his hand, demonstrating that the merc had to hand over his weapon. He removed the magazine, ejected the round in the chamber, inspected the chamber to assure it was empty, and handed it to Ben with the slide open. Ben placed it on his lap.

"What I say goes," he said and began his standard rules of the road speech.

Lorilei was empathically reading the new arrivals. Liz was highly strung at the moment, and it was making for a difficult assessment of her aura. The merc, however, was clear. His presence was as bold as a light in the dark. He had the least confused human essence she had ever sensed. He was confident and possessed the aura of a skilled artisan. He was so focused that he was mentally drawing her in. She reached an arm out and touched him to get his attention. He calmly turned his masked face towards hers, and she felt his eyes look into hers through the dark wall between them. His attention on her allowed her to focus more deeply, she almost felt like she could see his soul. It was the most intense empathetic experience she had ever felt. She wanted more. So she needed to interact with him.

"What's your name?" she asked.

He removed the mask from his face, revealing a handsome complexion of brown skin similar to her own, and when he spoke the words came out almost lyrically.

"Sariel," he answered. As the words passed his lips the connection she desired was made, and the images of hundreds of his victims flowed into her mind like a damn giving way. She could sense how he had killed each and every one, as if it had been her own hands. She fell to the floor as if struck by lightning.

"OK," Liz broke in. "She's crazy." She turned and looked to Sariel, certain that he wouldn't have given up his weapon so easily so that she could have kept hers. "I thought you guys never gave up your weapons, so you're ready to kill at any time, and duty, and all that stuff."

"I don't need my weapon to kill," he responded.

"No," Lorilei confirmed as she shivered, trying to get the visions out of her head. She nervously removed the strands of hair that had fallen in front of her face and tucked them behind her ear.

"Oh," Liz sighed in contempt. "You've got to be kidding me. A Mosot?"

Lorilei paid no attention to her. She braved a look back to Sariel, who had covered his face again, not wanting to disturb her further.

"Hey, kitten, you OK?" Ben asked, surprisingly concerned.

"Oh! Kitten! Is that your cute little pet name for it?" Liz continued, disgusted by Lorilei's presence.

"It sure is, Blondie," Ben snapped back.

"Fine, just keep it away from me."

Sam's upper body burst into the hatch. "Hey I'm trying to sleep, guys."

Sariel's head snapped in her direction, startled by her entrance. Sam took one look at him and almost panicked.

"Oh, God, are we being hijacked?"

"No," Ben assured her. "These are our new passengers."

Lorilei stood, still shook up. "I'm going to check on Thorbin and Tank."

"Yeah, me too," Sam said, feeling Lorilei's sentiment and following her lead.

"Observation deck is below us. The kitchen's down the hall," Ben continued. "You can have anything you want except things marked 'Ben'. The common room is the sleeping area. The office behind us and the turbine rooms are off limits. You can go into the cargo bay if you want, but I'd wait until the atmosphere returns. Welcome aboard Victoria and enjoy your stay."

Chapter Fifteen
Sardines

Lorilei

Lorilie was sitting on the floor next to the couch that Thorbin was lying on. Sam had given him some of the painkillers Tank was using, and he was out of it. When Thorbin was awake, Lorilei had tried to talk to him, but he still couldn't hear anything. Though distraught with concern, she finally concluded that he would be fine. That was what Sam said before she went back to sleep, and he looked way better than Tank, who was still alive.

Sariel's disturbing visions had left Lorilei shaken, she wanted to crawl into Thorbin's arms, but he was completely out of it. Besides, he'd be mad when he came to. He had made it clear that he wanted a platonic relationship. *Whatever that means,* she thought. She knew she could change his mind, but she was going to have to take it easy on him. She had finally gotten to the point where she could touch him and he wouldn't be completely evasive. After Dima had tried to tempt her, Thorbin had come to her and hugged her without invitation. Which was progress, but just to get a voluntary hug out of him, she had to be threatened by gangsters. The contact was very minimal and always cautious. He still wouldn't look her in the eyes, and he would quickly become distant when she tried to kiss him, even on the cheek. She figured by now she'd be giving it to him on a regular basis. She had never even had to try before, much less have a plan. She had been on Victoria for weeks now and not even a single grope, except when the kidnapping contractor ran off with her.

She turned her head and looked over her shoulder at Thorbin. He was rubbing his forehead to quell the discomfort. His new shirt was tattered, and she wondered if he'd let her take it off. Probably not. She looked at his pants. A whole month and she hadn't even seen it. That had to be a record. She knew he responded to her touch. The little incident in the kitchen confirmed that he wasn't lacking. Which was good, she was starting to doubt herself, but still, functioning manhood aside, he was keeping it in his pants. She started to wonder if it even mattered, which confused things even more. Humans liked sex, especially the males. *How could it not matter?* It was too much to wrap her head around, so she stopped trying. *Of course it would make a difference. If I could just get him to want it.* She inhaled quickly with frustration and fell back against the couch. It startled Thorbin, and he noticed she was sitting there. He put a comforting and opportune hand on her shoulder. She nuzzled it graciously with her cheek.

See, he reached out for me, she thought, but there was no sexual intent. She could stir some up, but it wouldn't lead anywhere. She closed her eyes and continued to softly sway her cheek across his hand. *What do I have to do?* she wondered. She felt powerless.

Sam made a sleepy noise and Lorilei took notice. *They like Sam, they adore her, and she hasn't even been on board for a week. Sam's not even trying. She's pretty, but not as pretty as me*, Lorilei thought. *What's she doing that I'm not? Everything's wrong, nothing's the way it's supposed to be. Everything I've been able to get, I've had to take. Except that,* she thought, looking at the sundress Thorbin had bought for her. She knew he had bought her the clothes because she didn't have any. Which again was strange, nobody ever cared if she was naked before, but the dress was special somehow. He thought she would look nice in it. *How is that supposed to make me look sexy?* It was pretty and fit well, a little bit of cleavage, but not much. It was leggy, which most men liked, but it just wasn't that kind of dress. It made her look like a schoolgirl. When she first tried it on, she thought maybe that was what he was into. She was wrong. Nevertheless, he got it for her because he wanted to see her in it.

Lorilei kissed his hand, placed it on the couch, then stood to change into the dress.

Thorbin

Thorbin was contemplating the position he found himself in, again. Humanity was fighting for its very existence, and he was lying on a couch. His biggest concern was the endless advances of a Mosot girl, with a distant second not being killed in the occasional gun battle. It was the girl, though, that really bothered him. He was an ace; he fought at the Battle of Earth and survived. As a constable he was part of the thin blue line that separated civilization from chaos. He had faced death, apprehended it, then handcuffed it, several times. This girl, though, was more than he could handle. She was relentless and determined to have him, despite him trying not to be a part of it. He smiled as he thought to himself, *I'd rather be fighting pirates.* And that was another thing. His best friend was a tug captain by day and most likely a smuggler by night. He helped procure passage for a prostitute a few hours ago and was admired by a dirty Syndicate gangster. It was very likely that the Battle of Mars would occur long before they got there. What then was he destined to be, a drifter? That wasn't the plan. *How the hell did this happen?*

Lorilei came over and tried to talk to him, she looked concerned and he appreciated that. However, nearly being blown up had taken all of his Lorilei-dealing strength away, not to mention the fact that he couldn't hear a word she was saying. Eventually she just sat down and leaned up against the couch he was lying on. It was a nice break, he thought, for sure she was going to snuggle right up next to him. The young irresponsible man inside of him came forth and mocked him. *What are you, a sissy? Go ahead. She wants it. Give her a go. You call yourself a man?* It was ironic because that young irresponsible him almost never got any. Now, the married, responsible, respectful him, had access to what the other could only dream of.

Lorilei gently slammed herself into the couch, she looked frustrated, and so Thorbin placed his hand on her shoulder. She nuzzled it graciously with her cheek. *She's built for sex. All I would have to do is ask, and I'd be taken care of,* he thought. *Eventually I'm going to need some attention. What the hell am I going to do? I really hope I'm nowhere near Lorilei when the itch screams to be scratched. Be strong, man, remember, Mosot don't love humans, they survive. It's all an act, eventually she'll find something better, and it won't be an issue anymore.*

At the same time he acknowledged that she was a person, completely helpless without them – without him. She wasn't evil. She may be a *playful* creature, but that didn't mean she deserved to be some asshole's property. Other Mosot had adapted to human culture just fine. She could even be a pleasure to be around if she would just stop with the advances and be herself. When she did, she could actually be quite adorable.

Like a sweet innocent little girl, he thought. Which wasn't entirely true, but it was Thorbin's wish. That's how he liked to view her. That's how he kept himself from crossing the line.

Like a sweet innocent little girl, he reiterated to himself.

Then Lorilei stood and began to undress.

Sweet innocent little girl! he screamed to his irresponsible self.

Sam

Sam had finally gotten some sleep and was dreaming of better times until she was disturbed by Lorilei gently slamming herself against the couch Thorbin was lying on. Sam knew she was frustrated and felt sympathy for her. *She's definitely out of her element. Which is a good thing, but still, it must be tough,* she thought. *She's not the only one. How did I get myself on Victoria? A month ago I was in a comfy office in Milpitas polishing off a new spyder design. Now I'm one room away from a mass murderer, and it's probably the best thing I got going for me. God I miss my kitties,* she thought as tears welled up. *Debra always said I was going to be one of those crazy old cat ladies. Oh, that used to piss me off so much! Now it sounds like the life. Oh, calm down,* she petitioned to herself. *Ben and Thorbin are nice. Thorbin's a little much with the guns. And Ben's got dead people in the cargo bay! He talks to them! He's the one I trust the most and he's crazy. I'm a design engineer I don't belong here. I should be sitting at a desk with piles of paper worried about whether I'm going to eat lunch. Jesus, I could be killed by aliens, or raped by pirates!* Her closed eyes tensed, and she tightly squeezed a pillow she was holding in her arms. *You're going to be OK,* she told herself. *I want my bed,* she responded to herself. It went on like this for a while until Lorilei stood up. *What the hell is she doing? She's taking her clothes off, and walking over here!*

Sam sat up.

"Hey, Sam, sorry to wake you," Lorilei said as she sat on the couch next to her and continued to disrobe.

"What are you doing?"

"I'm going to put on my dress."

"Oh," Sam said, relieved. Then she proceeded to assist Lorilei. Out of the corner of her eye she thought she noticed Tank sleeping with one eye open and turned her head to take a better look. She was about to chastise him, but both eyes were closed.

They slid the sundress over Lorilei's head and Sam gingerly removed her hair from the back of the garment. By nature Sam wasn't the nurturing type, but Lorilei, as odd as she was, brought it out in her. Sam knew Lorilei was fostering this emotion in her, but she didn't mind. It was nice, and despite giving Thorbin a hard time, which she enjoyed very much, she could understand why he had grown protective of her. She felt a little protective of Lorilei herself. After fiddling with Lorilei's clothes, she readjusted her own pajamas and made herself comfortable as she sat up by draping a blanket and pillow over her lap. Lorilei leaned over and laid her head on the pillow, and Sam gently stroked her soft brown hair.

"So you just decided to change clothes?" Sam asked.

"Yes," Lorilei answered.

"Why?"

"Because he likes this dress."

"Well it looks nice on you."

"It's not very sexy."

"I don't know about that, but he certainly didn't get it for you because he wanted you sexy."

"Why not?"

"You know why."

"Yes…I know why, but I don't understand. How come he doesn't want me?"

"Because...it's not what he needs right now, wanting you wouldn't be good for him."

"How does that make any sense? I wouldn't hurt him."

"Not on purpose I'm sure, but you could."

"But if he doesn't want me, he's never going to need me."

"That's not true. Besides, he doesn't have to need you in order to want to protect you," Sam said, wanting to get to the point. Lorilei grabbed Sam's hand and placed it under her cheek. Sam smiled, admiring her charisma.

"Why would someone protect you if they don't need you?" Lorilei asked, struggling to understand.

"He likes you. He'll protect you just because he doesn't want to see you get hurt. And we're all in this mess together. We're all going to need each other to do our part. Protecting you is part of his part."

"Well, what's my part?"

"I don't know, Lorilei. I'm not even sure what my part is."

"You fix things," she said with an air of admiration, and a tinge of jealousy.

"I guess."

"And they like you."

"Thorbin likes you. You just need to relax a little. Most everything is out of our control. Out of your control. You can't put on a dress and lap dance your way into someone's heart."

"I could before."

Sam laughed. "Not with men like Thorbin and Ben. Thorbin's all duty and honor and 'let's shoot stuff'. Ben's all about getting it done, then smoke a bowl. They don't need a Lorilei accessory."

"What about you?"

"I don't know. I'm just trying not to get killed."

"Me too."

Sam smiled and stroked her hair. "You could have gone with Dima to do that."

"I didn't want to."

"Right, but if all you wanted to do was survive, you would have been better off with him."

"I don't know."

"I do, you don't need the things you think you do, Lorilei."

"So what do I need?"

"Freedom? No, independence."

Tank

Tank was hungry and needed to go to the bathroom.

Man I'm starvin', he thought, *and I gotta take a crap. Can I even stand? Oh! Hot damn! The little cutie's takin' her clothes off! She's walking over to angel face. Oh ya,* he thought, the excitement mounting. *That'll do. Shit! I've been spotted! Pretend to sleep!*

So Tank lay there listening to Lorilei and Sam's conversation. It started of promising and then got boring. *Blah, blah, blah, independence*, he thought. *Man, I really gotta go.* He faked an 'I'm waking up' noise in order to declare himself. Sam ushered Lorilei away and went over to his side.

"Hey, you doing OK?"

"I gotta go to the john," he answered, a little distressed.

"OK, do you need help?" she asked.

"Maybe gettin' there." He slowly sat up and began to remove his blanket then stopped. "Hey...ah...where's my clothes?"

"Your shirt was ruined, and your pants needed to be washed," Sam replied.

"Still got my drawers."

"I can only do so much."

"So ah," Tank grinned. "Were you takin' advantage of me?"

"You wish," Sam smiled back. "I couldn't take the smell anymore."

"It's OK. Was I good?" Tank teased. Sam picked up a pillow from the couch and threw it at him.

"You can go in bed, pervert."

He caught the pillow as it hit his chest and was preparing to throw it back, but the arm movement disturbed his wound. The pillow dropped and he winced in pain. Sam, turned back to him and saw him, teeth clenched and shivering as he held his side.

"Sorry!" she said as she rushed to his side. "Is it bad? Did something bad happen?" she asked.

"Ugh...No. Should be fine, I gotta go now."

She grabbed his arm and put it over her shoulder.

"Lorilei, get on the other side."

The ladies slowly helped Tank to his feet and Lorilei was reminded just how big he was as the bottom of his chest brushed against the top of her head. He slumped forward in order to utilize their assistance, which put great stress on his stomach wound. It was laborious escorting him to the cargo bay, but still in time they made it. The bathroom stall was the only room they could get him into. They sat him down on the toilet.

"OK you should take a bath too. I'll be right outside if you need anything," Sam said at the door.

"Thanks," Tank replied, feeling emasculated and exhausted from his trip down the hall. He couldn't lift his arms, but using the bathroom didn't require any lifting. He just had to sit there. Pulling his boxers back up was a chore that required bending forward. It was excruciating, but he wasn't about to call the girls back in to help him get his underwear on.

After Sam closed the door, leaving it cracked just a smidge, so she could hear Tank if he called to her, she and Lorilei stood there for a moment quietly. Lorilei was disturbed by the helpless feeling she had sensed from Tank. She recalled when she had first seen him not long ago in the hall at the oasis. He was monstrous and hardly seemed capable of being incapacitated, and yet he couldn't go to the bathroom without her help. Sam was contemplating the same thing. It made them both feel very vulnerable in a mortal sort of way.

Sam tapped Lorilei on the arm and pointed at Sariel. He had made a space in the cargo bay and was kneeling with his ankles crossed behind him. He had removed his body armor and the button-up top of his fatigues. They were neatly folded by his side, topped off by his mask. His boots lay on the opposite side from his other belongings. His green undershirt was tucked neatly into his pants, whose cuffs had been rolled up. With hands folded in his lap and head bowed, he was quietly reciting the same indiscernible sentence over and over again.

"Hey, sweetie, can you hear me?" Tank said, gasping for breath.

Sam cracked the door a little further. "Yes, are you good?"

"Yeah, I'm good."

She opened the door and he was sitting right where she had left him. There was a towel on the floor at his feet, evidence that he had reached over to the nearby sink to wash his hands. The girls went over to him and assumed their positions.

"Thanks, ladies, back to bed if you don't mind," he asked.

"No," Sam said softly. "You need to take a bath."

"Oh, I don't think I'm up for that, hun," Tank refuted.

"You're stinky," Lorilei confirmed from under his right armpit.

"I know," he said, not wanting to be firm with her, especially after she had helped him so tenderly in his time of need. "It's just I can't reach all that well right now."

"Lorilei," Sam said with authority, "we're taking him to the tub." And that was that.

The girls slowly approached the tub lengthwise, and Tank stepped in with Sam and Lorilei guiding him in from outside. He stepped in with a nervous shake, hoping desperately that he knees wouldn't buckle. With the girls help, he slowly began to sit down with his back straight so as to not exaggerate the wound.

As his weight reached a critical point his feet gave way and he fell. Fortunately, he was only a short distance from sitting anyhow. The sudden drop temporarily put all his weight on the girls, and they collapsed under his arms as he fell. Lorilei's elbow hit the tub perfectly to make it numb.

"Ow," she cried out as she clutched it, still under the weight of Tank's massive arm. He looked over to her so quickly that it disturbed the wound, but he buried the pain, distraught that he had injured Lorilei.

"I'm sorry, sweetie."

"It's OK," she said back to him with a smile, inwardly she felt terrible, making him feel like he had hurt her. "It's nothing, I was just startled."

"Oh, good, sorry I startled you." Then they all sat silent as they contemplated the next best course of action.

"Well, you gonna have to turn the water on, I can't reach, sweetie," Tank directed. Sam reached over and took care of it, making sure the water was at a comfortable temperature.

"I'll help as much as I can, but are you going to be able to take care of your…" She paused, trying to think of a polite way of expressing her thought.

"My man parts?" he said, saving her the effort.

"Yes, those."

"You still have your boxers on," Lorilei noted.

"I think I'll just keep them on for now, cutie," Tank said with a reassuring smile. "When the water's full, I think I can take it from there."

The girls sat silently, being sure to be respectful, preparing him as best they could for his bath. As the water level rose, it became dank with days of soil and sweat, gunpowder residue and blood, some of it not his. It was reaffirming to Sam, she knew her decision was right; he couldn't heal properly with all this dirty mess caked on his body.

With the bathtub full, they decided to let it empty out and take most of the first layer of filth with it, and then they began to refill it. Sam was becoming more comfortable with the situation, and it didn't seem to bother Lorilei in the least. As the water level began to rise, this time there was less cloudiness in its depth until tank stirred and his boxers polluted the water. They were going to have to re-drain the tub again. This was going to take all day, which also wouldn't be good for his wounds. Sam rubbed her forehead, forcing the words out.

"You need to take them off," she braved.

"Well," Tank started to answer, knowing what she was getting at. "I don't mind, but are you sure? I think we should just leave it, there's no way I can reach over and get them off."

They sat silent for a minute until Tank spoke up again. "Hey, it's OK, look, I'm way better off than I was, let's just call her clean and head back."

"No," Sam said. "This has to be done. If you get any more infected you'll…" she didn't want to mention that he might die, so she quickly continued, being persistent. "I'll do it, I just need a minute."

"I know," Lorilei said, feeling smart. "If we run new water I can put bubbles in it."

Sam smiled with relief. "Of course, why the hell didn't I think of that?" And, before they knew it Tank was up to his armpits in bubbles. Moments later and pleased that they were able to work things out, Sam scooped a handful of bubbles by Tank's feet and playfully placed them on his head. Tank smiled, and Lorilei giggled.

"OK," he said, feeling heartened. "You guys dun your part," and his hands sank below the surface and his face grimaced. They waited, looking at him, and the surface of bubbles expectantly, as if the lady of the lake was about to reveal a dirty cotton Excalibur. He slowly leaned forward, then wrenched back in pain, clutching his midsection.

"Agh!" he gasped. "I think I'm bleeding," he said as he caught his breath.

Sam quickly brushed away the bubbles and inspected the water, she noticed no blood, and that he had made no progress with his shorts. She readjusted the bubbles so he was covered again.

"No bleeding," she reassured. She was starting to perceive that he may not be as comfortable with them watching him as he declared he was.

"OK, now what?" he said, a little disappointed that he wasn't bleeding.

"Oh come on!" Lorilei said. "I'll do it," and before Sam could object, Lorilei was elbow deep in the bubbles fumbling around. Sam felt an instinctive need to chastise Lorilei, but she said nothing, also finding herself a little relieved at Lorilei's initiative.

"Oops," Lorilei said innocently a few seconds later.

Tank flinched then smiled. "Sorry about that," Lorilei said, to be polite, not because she really was sorry.

"Oh, that's OK, little lady," Tank said, suddenly feeling much better.

Sam was disgusted. "Just do it!" she commanded.

Lorilei gave Tank an apologetic and disappointed pout, then retrieved a dirty pair of soapy drawers from the bubbles and grimaced at them.

"Put them in the sink and stand outside," Sam commanded, and Lorilei did as she was told, no longer able to hold back her mischievous smile. Tank sat there, watching Lorilei leave, somewhat satisfied with himself until Sam grabbed the soap and a washcloth and plunked them in the water with a scowl. "Wash!"

Then she went and lowered the toilet seat lid and sat down while he did so, only looking over at him every so often to make sure nothing bad was happening.

Slowly Tank was able to wash most everything. Every so often Sam would drain a bit of the water for him and replace it. That kept the water warm and the bubbles high. And so it went for a while until he was reaching down for his knees and the pain shot through his wound defiantly. He quickly stiffened back up and kicked the tub with a thud. Sam leapt over to his side to check on him.

"Are you OK?" she asked, concerned.

"No, I've got a big hole in me that's not spossed to be there."

"Aside from that."

"I got everything I could get, including the man parts," he confirmed. "What you want to do from here is up to you," he said, hoping she would let him get out. No such luck, she grabbed the soap and rag.

"Can you lean forward a little?"

"Yes," he said reluctantly and leaned forward. She began to wash his back. Each stroke with the rag was like a paintbrush on a bare canvas as she brushed away the layer of dirt.

"You don't have any smart ass remarks?" she said, trying to start off a conversation and hoping it might pass the time.

"I got plenty," he said. "But I wouldn't dream of biting the hand that washes me." Sam didn't really know what to say after that. "Hold on," Tank gasped. "I gotta lean back," and she yielded, helping him to slowly lean into position.

"Are you OK?" she asked again.

"No," he said with a quiver in his voice. "I can't even take off my own drawers." His words had too much pain for Sam to ignore. She sat on the side of the tub and looked into his defeated eyes.

"You'll be OK."

"I don't want to live like this."

"What?" she probed.

"I'm tired of living," he said solemnly.

"That's a terrible thing to say," Sam said, a little disturbed.

"Oh, not because of this, and I'm not saying I'm going to do myself in or nothing like that. It's just, life's a bitch and then you die. Only I'm still alive. Lots of good men died. And I'm alive and not doing well. What the fuck, huh?"

Sam empathized, he was depressed and she wished more than anything that she could do something for him.

"Oh," she said, having a revelation. "I know what will make this better."

"Lorilei already did it, and I don't feel better," he said.

"No perve, this," she said, and she squirted a portion of shampoo on his head and began to rub.

"Ohhhh," Tank said as his eyes rolled. "Oh, that's good."

"Isn't it great?" Sam said, beaming.

"That's amazing," he affirmed as she massaged the goose bumps forming on his head.

"Doesn't it just make you want to live?"

Chapter Sixteen
Full House

Thorbin

The ringing in Thorbin's ears was beginning to subside and the most subtle of movements no longer caused him pain. He slowly inspected himself again, ensuring that he was all there, then he took note of his tattered clothes and gunpowder fragrance. The intense smell of grenade residue was making him nauseous. He slowly propped himself up, then held his head as the blood rushed from it. He was struck by a sudden dizziness, then his ears popped and the dizziness faded to a dull hum – the hum of Victoria's turbines. He sat still so as not to incur any unnecessary wrath from his body and appreciated the sounds he heard. He looked over and noticed a bag of his things. On the top was his unloaded revolver sitting atop the Bible he had purchased at Jacob's Run. He reached for it and opened it. He searched for a while for something consoling until Tank slowly entered the room. A makeshift cane in one hand and Lorilei in the other. She turned and smiled at Thorbin, happy that he was sitting up then continued to assist Tank to the bed.

"Thanks, sweetie," Tank said gratefully.

"You need more bandages, I'll get Sam."

"No. Don't bother her, just hand them here. We can take care of it ourselves. If ya don't mind, cutie." She liked how Tank called her 'cutie'.

"OK," she agreed. She looked over at Thorbin who was still looking through his Bible.

"I've seen him reading it before," she observed out loud.

"They call that the good book, sweetie. Lota good it's doing him now though, huh?" Tank's cynicism didn't skip a beat.

"I can hear," Thorbin responded, looking over at them.

"Well good fer you, rookie."

"Feeling better?"

"A little, thanks to yer girlie here."

Lorilei smiled. *Thorbin's girlie*, she liked the sound of that.

"Are you feeling better?" Lorilei asked Thorbin.

"Much better," he replied.

"Good," she said, seating herself next to him. "You smell like, blown up. We just finished with Tank, now let's get *you* bathed," she said, grabbing his hand and tugging him towards the door.

"I can do that myself," he said as she lifted him off the couch.

Lorilei turned and looked him in the eye authoritatively. "Are you going to be able to reach everything?"

"Yes, ma'am," he said, then put down his Bible and rummaged around for a change of clothes. As he headed out the door he turned to Tank.

"You...you didn't really let her bathe you? Did you?"

"Yep," Tank said with a full on shit-eating grin. "The little cutie and Sam did a hell of job too. Very thorough."

Lorilei smiled a naughty smile and leaned up against Tank.

"But I guess you'll be OK bathing without me," she said, pouting. "That's OK, I'll stay here with Tank."

Tank was thoroughly amused. *This little one is all right*, he thought.

Disturbed and sore, Thorbin headed towards the cargo bay. Halfway there, it hit him. "No way did Sam participate in that nonsense, he's just screwing with me."

When he reached the bathroom unit, Sam was just outside the door.

"Oh hi," she said. "How are you feeling?"

"Just fine, thank you. I'm about to take a bath."

"Oh, OK," Sam said, then abruptly turned to the door. "Hold on, I left Tank's underwear in the sink."

Thorbin blinked.

A moment later Sam came out holding a pair of boxers that clearly could only be filled by Tank. "OK, all yours," she said casually as she walked away.

Liz

Liz sat alone on the observation deck. Unlike the others, she and Ben hadn't rested after their near tragic escape. Ben had been at the helm since they had departed Jacob's Run, and aside from the cargo bay and common room, Liz had the entirety of Victoria to herself. She had started, with a coveted soak in the tub, then dried off in the observation deck while watching the stars go by to the comfort of a cup of coffee. She painstakingly brushed her long, still moist, blonde locks, but they struggled against her will to tame them. She conceded to let it dry a bit more and returned to her coffee in thoughtful solitude. She couldn't believe that she had actually pulled it off.

Of course I did it, she thought to herself. Nonetheless, she was impressed with herself.

With a cautious eye she glanced over her shoulder to ensure no one was watching then undid the top two buttons of her pants. She reached slowly into a pocket she had sown just inside, fumbled for a moment, then retrieved a small velvet pouch. She held it up by its pull string and smiled at it.

"Hello, meal ticket," she said sweetly to her prize. "I'll bet Dima is still looking for you. But don't you worry, that nasty bastard will never see you again. Not until it's too late." She flicked it with her finger, and it spun by its pull string, then she continued being amazed with herself. After a while, she was done gloating, so she returned it to its hiding place. She buttoned up her jeans and enjoyed her coffee.

Before long she had finished. She wanted another cup but couldn't find the motivation to get out of her seat. It had been days since the opportunity to simply sit and rest had presented itself. She attempted to convince herself that she could come back and sit down again after she refilled her cup but was unsuccessful. As if in answer to a prayer, Ben opened the hatch from the bridge above her and descended the ladder with a thermos in his hand. When he reached the bottom he took notice of her empty cup and offered.

"Coffee?"

"First you get me outta hell, now you have coffee. That's it, you're officially the man of my dreams."

Ben smiled as he filled her cup. "Yup, I get that a lot." Then he sat down on a nearby chair.

"Are we clear?"

"Yeah, we were part of a convoy, but Vicky still can't keep up."

"Vicky?" Liz smiled. "You have a nickname for your ship?"

"Well ya, don't you have a nickname for…" he paused "…whatever it is that you do?"

"No, and I'm not a prostitute."

"Look, missy, I don't care. You're a paying customer and your business is your business."

"Well good, but I'm not a prostitute, so don't get any ideas."

"Five seconds ago I was the man of your dreams."

"Fifty pounds and you could be again."

Ben Laughed.

"Just kidding," she said with a smile. "So how's Vicky?" she asked with the slightest tease in her tone.

"Banged up real bad. But still capable. She'll get us to Mars if that's what you're asking."

"It was, but aside from that, she could use a new coat of paint."

Ben perked up. "Was just thinkin' 'bout that, candy apple red with chrome trim and deep black rigging. The kind of black that has that under tint of blue. After I get the lower deck replaced of course. New Nav and com, something nice."

"Sounds nice," Liz said, dropping her mocking tone.

"It's Vicky," Ben said with loving sincerity. Liz held up her coffee cup and proposed a toast.

"To Vicky."

Ben accepted the toast and they drank for a moment in comfortable silence until Ben spoke up again. "I realize that I may be contradicting myself, but now you've got me interested. If you're not a working girl, what were you doing with them pirate boys in the casino?"

"Do I look like a whore?" Liz asked, wondering if she did.

"Well, not now," Ben said, pressing the issue passively.

"I liked him," Liz said off the top of her head.

Ben could clearly tell she was lying and decided that if she didn't want to talk about it, he wasn't going to get the truth.

"OK," he said, dropping the issue. "Are you hungry? How 'bout a bite?"

"That sounds good."

Ben and Liz entered the kitchen to find that Sam was already there munching on a piece of toast.

"Thought you were sleepin'," Ben inquired.

"Lorilei woke me, then Tank needed help."

"Uh, want some sausage?"

"Yes, please," Sam replied.

"How's Tank doing?" Ben asked as he rummaged through the fridge to prepare breakfast. Liz sat down at the table across from Sam and gave her a polite smile of acknowledgement.

"Better, still not good though."

"He'll be all right," Ben concluded, so he could focus on cooking. He hadn't prepared a meal this large in a long while and was looking forward to it.

As he did so, Sam and Liz shared an uncomfortable silence at the dining table. Sam had never spent time with a prostitute and didn't know what to talk about. Even though this wasn't Liz's profession, Sam thought it was, and it was making her a little uncomfortable. Liz all the while was completely disinterested in Sam. She didn't dislike her, she could just care less if they interacted or not. As a result she was bored sitting at the table and began tapping her fingers on its surface to pass the time.

Sam felt the need to say something and offered an olive branch.

"I like your hair," she offered, the complement being genuine.

"Thank you," Liz replied, again politely acknowledging Sam's presence before turning her chair to face Ben.

"Whatcha cookin'?" she asked.

"Aside from sausage, still workin' it out." And so Sam and Liz sat quietly while Ben cooked sausage until Sariel entered, guitar in hand.

"I smell sausage," he observed.

"Hungry?" Ben asked.

"No, Captain," Sariel answered. "I have come to play music while you eat. If you like?"

"Oh, that would be nice," Liz said, jumping at the opportunity for a little entertainment, and also curious what type of music a person of his profession would make.

Sam's earlier thoughts about Sariel returned, and she decided to try and make herself as small as possible. Sariel's ominous presence seated itself, and he began strumming a gentle melody.

Thorbin

When Thorbin returned from his bath, Lorilei had finished assisting Tank with his bandages. He was on his back wrapped up in blankets, showering Lorilei with gratuity in the form of sweet nothings. She lay next to him on her stomach sweetly swinging her legs to and fro and enjoying the attention. Thorbin looked at the both of them, still not sure what to make of it all.

"Nothing happened," Tank reassured.

Lorilei looked at Tank, playfully disappointed. Thorbin sighed with relief, which caused Lorilei to give him a disgusted look.

"Like you care, I should sleep with Tank."

"Yeah, you should sleep with Tank," Tank agreed. Then he brushed her cheek with the backside of a single massive digit. Lorilei closed her eyes and soaked up the attention.

"I'll bet that would be fun," she said matter-of-factly.

"Go ahead," Thorbin said in his best 'I don't care' tone of voice. Lorilei's eyes snapped open and peered at Thorbin again, that made her angry. "Well!" she began before Thorbin cut her off.

"Where's everyone else?" he asked as he sat back down and reached for the Bible again.

"They're all in the kitchen, including Sariel. That's why I'm in here," she explained, "with Tank," she added, paying attention to see if Thorbin responded. Which he did a little, nothing visible, just a little emotional tweak she picked up on, then it was gone.

"Sariel," Thorbin said to himself. "That kinda sounds like a Biblical name."

"Really?" Lorilei said, taking notice. Thorbin opened his Bible to the index and searched for the name. Lorilei got up and sat next to him, curious.

"Is it in there?" she asked.

"No," he answered.

Lorilei asked, "What's so good about it?"

"What?" Thorbin said, confused.

"The book, what's so good about it? Why do they call it the 'Good Book'?"

Thorbin paused, he had heard what she said, but he was taken aback that she asked. "Well some people call it that because there's lots of good advice in it."

Lorilei was puzzled but interested, so she asked, "Like what? I tried to read it and it didn't make much sense to me. Adam and Eve and God, I understand that, but then people started begetting people. What is 'begetting'?"

Thorbin smiled. "It's an old Earth word. It's not all that important to the good parts."

"So then what kinda good stuff is in it?"

Thorbin thought for a moment how best to approach an answer for her.

"Well the most important part is about a man named Jesus."

"Jesus?" Lorilei asked. "That's a nice name," she said, getting ready to hear a story.

"Oh brother," Tank chimed in, putting a pillow over his head.

"Tank doesn't like the good book?" Lorilei asked, suddenly it occurred to her why Tank behaved differently to Thorbin.

"Some people don't believe in it, or they think it's obnoxious."

"Obnoxious? Like me," Lorilei said with a probing smile. "So tell me about Jesus."

Meanwhile back in the kitchen, Ben was nearly done cooking the meal while Liz and Sam sat there quietly listening to Sariel play beautiful Spanish guitar. With every note he played, Sam was certain he was going to kill her. He strummed the guitar with a passion that disturbed her.

Liz, on the other hand, was coming up with a story and a plan. She looked across the room and thought about everyone on board as she incubated a scheme. *Sariel,* she thought. *Dangerous but predictable. If you don't threaten him or his concerns, you'll live.* While on board, Ben and the safety of Victoria were his concerns. *Sam,* she thought. *Mostly harmless, of no use to me at this time. The less I talk to her the better. The Mosot girl,* she thought. *A problem waiting to happen, but not necessarily my problem. Her value could come in handy in a pinch if necessary. Thorbin,* she thought. *Could be a problem. He used to be a cop and he's DC. Too much information and he might be on to me. Best to avoid him if at all possible. If I give him a story, I should stick with it. Damn! I should have just gone with the hooker thing. Everyone really believed it. Too late now. Ben,* she thought. *He definitely calls the shots. Be his friend and that will reap dividends. That other guy they got bandaged up. He's DC too. Better stay away from him too.* For a brief moment she made eye contact with Sam, who smiled then looked away. *I'm going to be on this ship for a long while. I should just resurrect the prostitution angle; maybe it's not too late.*

Her thoughts were disturbed when Ben spoke up.

"Sariel, are you sure you don't want no sausage? There's plenty."

"No thanks, Captain. I'm a vegetarian."

Ben stopped cooking, turned around, and looked directly at Sariel in disbelief. "You're shitting me."

Sariel stopped playing and answered, "No, sir."

"What? You're against killin' animals?"

"I don't need to kill to eat, I just do it for fun," he answered.

Sam closed her eyes and tried not to shudder. Liz, however, took the road less traveled.

"You're crazy. Killing for fun is Evil."

"Evil is relative," he casually responded.

"You see? That's what crazy people say," she said, pointing at him.

Her hand hadn't returned to her side when Lorilei burst through the kitchen hatch in tears. Thorbin was right behind her.

"Lorilei! Wait! Let me explain!"

She spun around and stomped one foot on the ground, with tears streaming down her face she accused, "That's a terrible story, humans are evil! How could you do that to him?"

"I didn't do it," Thorbin defended.

"He healed people! And loved everyone! And you killed him!" she said, stomping again with her whole body.

"Who was killed?" Sariel asked.

"Jesus!" Lorilei answered with anguish. "Humans are horrible!"

"Ah, you see?" he said, looking at Liz. "A death that many consider good."

Liz rolled her eyes while Lorilei looked at Sariel, mortified. She could hardly breathe she was so upset. She held up a finger and slowly pointed at everyone in the room. Then breathed, "E-v-i-l," and stormed out nearly knocking Thorbin over. He quickly got his footing and stuck his head out the hatch, trying to get her attention.

"He came back!"

"Hold on," Ben said before Thorbin ran after her.

"Yes?"

"Here," Ben said, handing Thorbin a plate. "OK, now go deal with your mess."

Thorbin and Lorilei ate sausage, in the observation deck while he concluded, then explained, the remainder of the story of Christ. Sam eventually joined them after checking up on Tank, and the three of them spent a few hours together enjoying each other's company. They talked about Tank, who they agreed would be OK so long as he was able to rest. Sam and Lorilei were in agreement that Sariel was going to kill them all, despite Thorbin ensuring them that mercs always act that way. Before long Ben popped his head down from the upper deck, where he had been looking after their course.

"Hey, you guys wanna play cards?" Ben asked with a gleam in his eyes.

"I don't have any money," Sam clarified.

"I'll spot you, we'll play tournament style. Twenty buy in."

"Me too?" Lorilei asked, not knowing how to play cards but thoroughly interested.

"Sure," Thorbin said. "Sounds like fun."

Before long, the four of them had cleared a space in the middle of the observation deck, and Ben was divvying out chips and raspberry wine. Sam and Thorbin went to check in on Tank and invite him to the table, which was easier then getting him there when he agreed. Liz was there when they returned, and even Sariel left his solitude to join the game.

Lorilei listened intently as Ben explained the rules. She noted, as they played a half-hour of practice hands, how everyone was letting their guard down. Ben, for the first time, was treating her as an equal. She would ask questions, and he would politely answer them, engaging in friendly, almost paternal conversations with her. Liz appeared to be relaxed for the first time that they had shared spaced, and Sam seemed to be relieved by a break in the monotony. Tank almost seemed more comfortable sitting around the table than he had been lying alone in the common room. Sariel appeared to be less menacing as a part of the group. And Thorbin, he was sitting next to her without any reservation about her presence. At this table she felt included, and it felt great.

She was amazed how a simple game could reveal the complexities of everyone on board. Sariel played confidently though he rarely bet. His style of play was consistent with his trade. He was overly conservative and only stayed in if he felt certain that he couldn't lose. His tight playing style slowly drained his chips until he didn't have enough to reap the benefits of a good hand. Not playing a hand until he was certain that he wouldn't lose caused him to be the first person to bust.

Sam lacked confidence as she played. Not unlike the confidence that had eluded her ever since she had been torn from her life and recovered by Victoria. The game was new to her, and she often found herself in an unfamiliar position. While she quickly picked up the technique, which allowed her to win up a few pots, the finesse of drawing people into her winning hands was lost on her; an effect of having little experience. In time she would likely gain confidence and be formidable. After she lost her chips she sat near Ben like an apprentice.

Thorbin was a completely different person at the card table. He was relaxed. He enjoyed Ben's wine and the game in subtle moderation. A complete juxtaposition; he didn't take the game seriously at all. He wasn't concerned with her safety, or with Sam's, Tank was just across the table, recently bathed, and looked his best since he had been found. Thorbin had no worries at this table; his only concern was to play. He was just having fun and Lorilei couldn't have been happier. Even after he had lost all his chips his spirit wasn't broken. He didn't even get up from his seat at the table next to her. And Lorilei discovered that by playing dumb she could coax him over to assist her with her hands. She leaned into him while he held the hands that held her cards and whispered friendly advice into her ears that rode on raspberry wine breath. All without reservation, she was smitten with the experience.

Even Liz, whom Lorilei had barely interacted with since coming on board due to her abrasive attitude, was being openly friendly. Lorilei didn't like Liz at all until now. When she spoke to Lorilei, which she rarely did, she was rash and made it clear that she wanted nothing to do with her. Lorilei could sense that she was attempting to hide some facet of her nature from everyone else. She didn't really care what Liz was trying to hide; she just wanted her to be nice. Like she was being now. Liz, like Thorbin, seemed to care less about winning and was just enjoying the game. When her last bet was made, and subsequently lost, she politely excused herself from the table and went to bed.

Tank, despite being sick, had a healthy chip stack by the time this happened. Ben, who was obviously the most superior player at the table, was very impressed by him, and her. No one seemed to catch on to the fact that one of the people playing at the table had a mild empathic ability. Lorilei wasn't really the cheating type, but she figured it wasn't a problem since Ben didn't mention the use of empathy when he explained the rules of the game. In fact, he had stated, over and over again throughout the whole night, that poker was a game of information, and you 'had' to use your 'abilities' to gain any advantage you could in order to play well. So that was exactly what Lorilei did. She let the boys knock Sariel out early, since she didn't want to use her abilities on him for fear of passing out. Sam played herself out of the game, as did Thorbin and Liz. Now Tank was difficult, and Ben was very good. Tank was completely unpredictable. He would often say one thing while feeling something else, then acting in a way that was contradictory to both his words and feelings. Her empathic abilities were of no use against him. Even Ben appeared to be struggling to understand his playing style as the three of them traded pots.

Ben dealt five cards to the three of them, and after he had finished, Lorilei took a look at what she had: two queens, a seven, a five, and a three. It was Tank's turn to bet.

"I'll raise twenty," he said as he placed the bet into the pot. Ben matched the bet then looked to Lorilei, who was thinking.

"The bet's twenty," he confirmed.

Thorbin leaned over her with his hand on her shoulder; she showed him what she had then looked at him. She had already decided that she was going to stay in but wanted to feel his reassurance. He nodded, and she placed the bet.

"Two please," Tank said as he tossed two cards face down on the table.

Ben dealt him two cards then said, "Dealer takes three."

"I'll have three please," Lorilei asked, and then received the three cards. She looked at her new cards and smiled, which Ben took note of, she had received two tens and a jack.

It was Tank's turn again. "Check," he said, passing the bet to Ben.

"How much you got left?" Ben confidently asked.

Tank laughed then started to count. When he was finished he answered, "A hundred and two."

"How 'bout you, kitten?" Ben asked.

"Ninety-eight," Lorilei answered.

"OK then," Ben said, counting out chips. "I raise 102."

"Ah… shit," Tank said to the bet.

"I'll see that," Lorilei said, pushing in her chips.

Ben smiled then they both looked at Tank, who thought for a moment then responded, "Fuck it, all in. Whatcha got Capt'n?"

"Two pairs, jacks and nines," Ben answered.

"Beats me," Tank responded then plopped his cards on the table.

Ben looked at Lorilei, who was grinning from ear to ear, Thorbin was behind her, concealing is own smile with a hand.

"What?" Ben said, knowing he had lost the bet.

"Yaaaa! Two pairs, queens and tens!" Lorilei gleefully exclaimed then reached across the table to the cheers and jeers of the onlookers.

Tank leaned back in his seat.

"Watch out for her, capt'n." Ben handed her the cards. With the win she was just behind Ben in the chips.

She awkwardly dealt both of them five cards. After she dealt the cards she turned them over and took a look: a ten, a five, a two, and two aces. She tried not to show the emotion in her face, and tried to sense Ben's. They looked at each other, as each was deciding their course of action. She sensed confidence and felt that he was going to bet. He didn't.

"Check," he said, passing the bet to her.

"Pass," she quickly answered.

"Check, sweetie," Ben corrected.

"Oh, sorry, check," she said, correcting herself.

"I'll take two," he said, and she dealt the cards.

"I'll take three," she said and dealt herself three cards, keeping the aces. She turned over her cards, and to her delight there was another ace, along with a king and a three. Ben paused and everybody was in anticipation. He looked at her, and for a second, she thought maybe *he* had empathic abilities and was trying to use them on her.

"Check," he said.

Lorilei sensed he was confident, but he was always confident. Instead of trying to read him, she read the bet. He bet nothing, so maybe he has nothing.

"All in," she said, pushing in all of her chips to the excitement of the room. Ben took note of her aggressive bet and took into account her previous win.

"Another two pair, huh?" he said with a smile.

"Only one way to find out," she answered with a sweet smile that Ben rather enjoyed.

"OK…I call," Ben said, he was thoroughly enjoying himself, and immensely impressed with Lorilei for providing him with a good game. "What do you got?" he called. Lorilei placed her cards on the table.

"Three aces."

"With a King kicker," Ben added. Nodding at her well-played hand.

"What do you have?" Lorilei asked. Ben smiled then placed his cards on the table for a win.

"I got a full house."

Chapter Seventeen
Things Unknown

After a few days Ben was able to produce a routine that kept everyone out of trouble. He didn't create a schedule per se; he simply encouraged people to find their niche. He knew it was important that everyone have something to do, otherwise the monotony of slowly traveling through the desolation of space would eventually overcome them.

He would generally wake, take a shower, then have a smoke in the cargo bay while spending time with Jessica. Sariel was almost always there, and often times would be meditating or training. Ben hadn't needed to influence Sariel in any way. He was a wholly dedicated mercenary; he had more discipline than rest of them combined. He spent the majority of his time in solitude in the cargo bay. His only means of socialization was his guitar, and he would spend hours strumming classical masterpieces of his own design. The music was both captivatingly melodic and haunting. Ben enjoyed it, especially when Sariel took notice of him with Jessica. He would often times stop his routines and play a lament for Ben. After his mandatory session of mourning, Ben would collect himself and head to the galley. There, one by one, people would slowly meander in.

Ben would try his best to be positive as everyone gathered to eat breakfast. As captain he set the tone not only for each day, but for the whole of their journey. His prime task at hand was the safety of all on board Victoria. His wit and charm were invaluable at maintaining a healthy morale; the first step in assuring that all went well.

After breakfast he would usually spend the rest of the day with Sam, keeping Victoria from falling apart around them. Every day he grew more fond of Sam. She didn't belong in space, which to Ben made her very endearing. Aside from that small detail (which wasn't a liability in Ben's book) she was heaven sent. Her engineering expertise made the daily maintenance and daily mechanical catastrophes a burden that was bearable. While she often expressed panic in the face of life and death circumstances, she never faltered. She was capable of performing well under great stress and discomfort. And in quiet moments together, Ben allowed himself to appreciate her. She was perfect at providing just enough feminine intimacy without threatening the cherished memories of his dearly departed. In return, he was her mentor, educating her on her new life in space. While everyone on board played a role in each other's survival, great or small, Sam kept him sane.

Thorbin spent most his time in the bridge. He was allotted the task of keeping Victoria on course and confirming repairs made by Ben and Sam. When not in imitate need of confirmation, he would oversee scans and listen for news from Mars or from other ships that passed them by, and of course he was still responsible for Lorilei.

Lorilei had been given the most time-consuming task of all, keeping Victoria shipshape. The timely part meant cleaning; Victoria hadn't been properly cleaned for years. The initial cleaning took three days. After that, Lorilei (who was amazingly well organized) just had to do a few hours of maintenance a day. She took this in stride and enjoyed getting to know every nook and cranny Victoria had, with the exception of the turbine rooms. The cleaning, however, was not her first responsibility. Ben had also entrusted her with the task of tending to Tank, which was fine, as they seemed to get along well. Other than that, she was the mistress of the random task. Anything that needed to be done that someone else didn't have time to do, or didn't want to do, was Lorilei's job, and you can be sure, random tasks had never been accomplished so attractively.

Ben

Ben was making his way down the hall towards the cargo bay to find a part that he and Sam were in need of when he nearly stepped on Lorilei. She was bent over on hands and knees with her head in a compartment that Ben had forgotten Victoria had. As usual, she couldn't do a thing without being less than absolutely fetching. She was wearing skirt, of course, as was standard apparel for whatever mechanical task she was doing that Ben didn't remember asking her to do. A frilly thing that cleverly hid nothing from the imagination, especially at this angle. Ben watched silently for a while as her pert posterior jiggled to and fro as she struggled with whatever she was fighting with in the compartment. Ben smiled, pink panties, at least she was wearing some. Then his smile broadened as he thought about how much fun it would be to kick her right in her ass. However, he relented with a mild tinge of guilt. She had been behaving recently, and that just wouldn't be nice. So instead he yelled.

"Damn it, Ace, what the hell are you doing?"

Lorilei's assets dropped to the floor, and she quickly slid backwards out of the compartment and looked up at him from the floor, withholding anxiety. She knew she was about to get a good yelling at before she could even get a word in for her defense. Luckily for her, she was mess; hair pulled back in tangles, face smudged by grease, including a spot of oil and dust that had settled on the tip of her nose. Ben couldn't help but smile at her.

"I was realigning the number thirty-nine gravity inducer, it's been making a funny noise. I think I've almost got it," she said. She wanted to say more but didn't want to push it; instead she just blew a tangled mass of her pretty brown hair out of her face.

"Who the hell said you could do that?"

"No one, but Sam said it needed to be done. She said it was easy and no big deal, but she didn't have the time."

"So you thought you'd give it a go."

"Yeah, but it's not as easy as she made it sound."

"Very well then," he said sternly. "Carry on." Then he reconsidered. That wasn't nearly enough chastising for this encounter. "Did you ask if you could borrow that wrench? You better make sure you put it back where you found it when you're done."

Lorilei tilted her pretty face to the side and her eyes narrowed in mild defiance.

"You got something to say to me?" she said, standing up.

Ben's mind raced as he thought of all the things he had to say to her. Where should he start? He tried to accept this invitation to rip her a new one, but all his thoughts mushed together in his brain in such a way that none of it could get out. Lorilei stood there with her hands on her hips, tapping a foot as she waited for his response.

"You're! You! Sluttish! Getting' in the way!" is all he could mange to force through the mush.

Her face became flushed with anger and her brow furrowed. It was then that Ben knew he had pushed a little too much. The work that she was doing was extraordinary, and his efforts to keep her on her toes may have just backfired. But she had asked!

Lorilei pressed her lips together and inhaled a deep breath through her nose before letting the breath out as graciously as it had entered.

"I forgive you," she said, striving to be big about the circumstance.

"Forgive me?" Ben asked. He hadn't been prepared for that. Usually when he pushed too much she cried, this time she seemed angry, but in the end she was forgiving him despite him not apologizing. This approach was far more unsettling.

"Yes," she clarified. "I forgive you."

"What?" he said, for lack of a better response.

"Ever since I came aboard Victoria, you've been very mean to me. At first it was because I did things that I shouldn't have because I didn't know any better. I can accept that. Then it was because I did things that I shouldn't have even though I knew better. That was wrong. I'm sorry. Now you're just being mean," she said, laying out the history of their relationship very astutely. "But I forgive you," she concluded with a nod.

Ben was again awestruck but kept his game face on. Should he yell, or concede?

"At least I didn't kick you in your ass like I wanted to."

Lorilei gasped. "You see, that's mean!" she said, pointing as she stomped a foot.

"You're right," he said, working an angle. "I'm mean, it's just the way I am."

"I know," she said, confirming his angle. "And for that, I forgive you."

Ben was astonished; this wasn't going his way at all. The plan had been to give her a hard time then be on his way. His mind told him the best course of action would be to bail, but Ben rarely paid his mind any attention when it came matters of stubbornness. Still though, he felt the need to retreat. All he had to do was get in one good last word.

"Button up your shirt!" was the last word he decided on.

In true Lorilei fashion she had left the top few buttons of her shirt undone. Lorilei was steadfast; she reached her hands to her shirt buttons, looked him squarely in the eye, and defiantly undid a button. She cocked her head, waiting for a response. Ben gave up, stubborn or not, he hadn't been prepared for her to stand up for herself. He softened.

"Why do you do that?"

"I'm pretty, it's just the way I am," she said, using the same tone of voice he had used with her.

Defeated Ben began to walk away and muttered, "Good job with the gravity inducer."

Thorbin

Thorbin climbed down the ladder from the bridge into the forward observation deck. Normally that was where Liz was. Generally when he came down for his breaks they would engage in small talk, then she would politely excuse herself. He knew she was avoiding him, but he really didn't care why. This time, however, any such pleasantries were avoided because she was absent.

Ben really only demanded two things of Thorbin during the routine day — fly the ship and keep Lorilei out of trouble. Flying the ship took very little effort, and Lorilei had been behaving herself recently. That left him more time to fly the ship. He was intent in his effort to scrutinize every reading and listen intently to every broadcast. The effort, however, came at the price of boredom and a strain on his eyes, for which he would take breaks, like this one. It wasn't because he was tired, but because boredom presents a special challenge to focus which requires monotony to be broken every so often.

Since he was alone he decided it was time for exercise. He removed his shirt and began a regiment of pushups and sit-ups along with other calisthenics. Space travel didn't take much energy, so this was his only means of staying in shape. He kept up a steady pace for twenty minutes and broke a sweat. *Good enough for now,* he thought and drank out of a bottle of water he kept in the observation deck for just this reason.

Lorilei entered from the hall holding a bucket and sponge.

"Hey, Lorilei," he greeted, and she flashed him a pretty smile. It had been some time since they had left the oasis, and she had been trying very hard to keep their time together 'appropriate'. The extent of which she didn't believe was being realized. Thorbin looked at her shirt, of which there were a few buttons undone. What he didn't know was that she had fastened the one that she defiantly opened for Ben and then another on top of that because after all, he was captain, and she had promised to be good. And now, Thorbin was looking at her like she was testing him. Truth be told, working on the gravity inducer was a hot affair. She had almost taken her shirt off entirely to try and deal with the heat but decided that would most definitely be misconstrued, so she settled for undoing a few buttons. And still, Ben gave her a hard time, and now Thorbin. It was a testament to her struggle, which made her well behaved but not very happy.

So there she stood, looking at Thorbin. He was shirtless and smiling at her, sweaty and glistening in the starlight. Her pretty brow furrowed again – it had been doing that a lot lately.

"Hey," she said with every fiber in her being longing to wrap her arms around his neck. "I just came to wash the window."

"Oh," he said, moving away from the window towards the couch and sitting down. Lorilei constrained herself, she was here to do work, not play. She turned her attention to the window.

The window was clean; she made sure of this. However, the observation deck was one of the most frequented spots on Victoria. Often times the others would place their hands on the dome glass and stare out into the stars, leaving their oily fingerprints behind. Sure enough, as she inspected the glass, fingerprints everywhere. She scrubbed away at them as if they were her nemesis. It only took a few moments before she stood back, satisfied that the offending marks had been destroyed.

After the observation deck window she had tasked herself with checking the bridge window, so she turned towards the ladder leading up. As she did Thorbin came back into view, still shirtless. He had put his legs up on the couch and was leaning upright against a pile of pillows checking his PJU for mail, there was none. Her brow furrowed again. He was just lying there, being handsome, the contours of his chest and abdomen, complemented by shadow, accentuating the forbidden fruit that was screaming at her to be bitten.

Oh, enough with being well behaved, she thought and set the bucket down.

The splishing of the sponge dropping in the water got Thorbin's attention, and he turned to see Lorilei approaching. He prepared himself with a sigh. Before the sigh was finished she had lifted up his right arm and fastened herself into a prime cuddling position, her head softly nuzzling his chest. She then brought the arm down around her and positioned his right hand back in front of his face so he could continue with his PJU.

"Lorilei," he said with patient authority.

"Why not?" she pouted from his chest. "You're lying here anyway."

"You know why."

"I've been good," she said, advocating for herself sweetly.

Thorbin knew she was right, and really she didn't appear to be up to much. Besides, her soft brown hair brushed quite pleasantly on his bare chest.

"OK," he conceded. "But just until my break is over, and only if you behave."

It was like music to her heart. She reached a hand up to her shirt and fastened yet another button as a demonstration of her sincerity. Then she melted into his arms and the chest nuzzling recommenced. Thorbin wondered if she was all right. He thought she was up to her old tricks again, but she was just lying there. He shifted the PJU into his left hand and brushed some of her hair behind her ear.

"Are you OK?" he asked.

"I am now," she replied, closing her eyes and taking pleasure in the beating of his heart.

"Do you want to talk about it?" he asked, not knowing what needed talking about.

"Shhhh," she whispered. His voice was soothing, but she wanted to hear his heart. So with contentment she repositioned her head to the center of his chest. She then slid the hand she had fastened her shirt with around to the small of his back. She felt comfortable enough to sleep, but dared not lest the moment pass too quickly.

Thorbin watched her for a moment, weary at first, but this appeared to be it. It was apparent that she just needed a moment.

Why not? he thought to himself. And soon she had fallen asleep. Her warm steady breath rolled softy across his skin, and he felt her chest contract and expand softly on his stomach. It was very nice, and asleep she was angelic. *A sweet innocent little girl,* he thought. As she lay there he continued to sift through pictures on his PJU.

An hour had passed, and his self-regulated break had long since ended, but he hadn't moved from the couch. Within that hour Ben had come in and almost disturbed Lorilei's sleepy time but was promptly shushed by Thorbin. Ben felt accountable, he was sure that his earlier interaction with Lorilei was responsible for this somehow, and he let it be without a word.

Lorilei stirred, and as she awoke she snorted a bit and sleepily wiped her mouth, she had been drooling slightly. When she opened her eyes, Thorbin's PJU was flashing pictures of people and places she had never seen. Thorbin reached a hand around and placed his undershirt on his chest near her face, wiping away a little of what she had left behind.

"Sorry," she said as she stirred and nuzzled a bit more.

"It's OK."

She grabbed the undershirt and wiped away the rest of her dribble.

"What are you looking at?"

"Just some old pictures, from back home," he answered.

She smiled as his breath raised and lowered her head. She wanted to know if he would show her pictures of Mika, but she was afraid to ask. The subject might disturb the happy place she was in. She wanted to look up at him, but even that might be too much. She returned her hand back around to the small of his back, which evidently was acceptable, and watched the pictures as they changed.

After a few had come on gone a lovely brown-haired woman appeared, she was wearing a pretty red dress, and Thorbin had his right arm around her waist as they smiled for the picture.

"Is that her?" Lorilei braved, then held her breath.

"No," Thorbin answered softly, his demeanor unchanged.

She let the breath go. Thorbin felt her anticipation. "Would you like to see a picture of Mika?" he asked, thinking that might be helpful in some fashion. He navigated through the files as Lorilei watched expectantly. "That was Michelle, she was one of Mika's bridesmaids." Then he purposely pulled up a wedding picture.

Lorilei reached her hand out and placed it on his so he couldn't change the picture. Mika was beautiful, and the sight of her in her wedding dress made Thorbin's heart beat a little faster.

Lorilei sized her up, Mika didn't have Lorilei's perfect hourglass shape, in fact quite the opposite, but her smile beamed out towards Lorilei, who couldn't help but smile back. She a little shorter than Thorbin, and she was slender in an athletic sort of way. The dress was simple white and complemented her face and figure with grace. She was a typical bride, perfect, the center of attention, and obviously the center of Thorbin's world. Lorilei moved her hand.

"Pretty," she commented. "Are there any more?"

"Yes," Thorbin answered, happy to showcase his life so she would better understand him. He showed pictures of them on vacation, and pictures at home. Pictures of formal events, and pictures of silly moments. She reached her hand out again to stop him when a particularly relevant and intimate picture came up.

It was of the both of them, Thorbin lying on a couch shirtless, and Mika with her head on his chest. Her lovely face looked most content. Her hair, which was almost identical to Lorilei's, lay lazily around his torso, and Thorbin also looked very content. She looked at his face in the picture, then turned her head to look at his face above her. Not the same. Her heart hurt.

She didn't have to say a word; Thorbin knew what was on her mind.

"It's not same," he confirmed, and Lorilei took a very deep breath. Now she understood. She let her empathy loose to better understand. She could tell when he was thinking about Mika, and when he was thinking about her. His emotional aura leapt wildly back and forth. When he thought about Mika, he seemed warm and complete. When he thought about her, he seemed warm…and incomplete. This was certainly love she felt from him, but he didn't feel it for her.

"Thorbin," she said, uncertain, and she quickly stopped looking at him, placing her cheek back on his chest. She was fighting an impulse to cry.

Thorbin considered, maybe this was too much for Lorilei, maybe now would be a good time to get up. He knew she got the point and was sure she was about to do something desperate. Before he could act she looked back up at him.

Too late, Here it comes, he thought and prepared himself.

Lorilei retrieved her arms from around him and placed them on the couch, pushing herself off. He watched, amazed as she stood up and sat down on a chair facing the couch. Her face was pained, but she wasn't crying. He sat up and faced her. She was changing right before his eyes; she was really hurt, in a permanent way, and he felt like a monster.

Still holding back tears she bravely collected herself, straightening out hair and clothes as she sat up perfectly straight, poised and graceful in her distress. Before Thorbin sat a different woman. They looked each other in the eye.

"Are you OK?" he asked.

"Yes," she said, knowing full well that if she said no, he would gladly wrap his arms around her and try to make it better.

"I'm sorry, Lorilei," he said with gentle understanding. "Is there anything I can do?" Again, he tempted her, and her head turned sharply to the side. She sniffed, pulling in more courage before turning back to him.

"What's it like?" she asked, eyes shimmering.

"What's what like?" he clarified as he clasped his hands.

"What's it like…" she began to ask again, a single tear finding its way down her cheek, "…to be loved?" Her poise and grace collapsed, and she fell forward, the last of her strength used to force the question out.

Thorbin's heart broke. He stood and approached her with his arms open. Lorilei sensed his approach and shot both arms out, holding up her hands to stay his advance.

"No!" she begged, and he stopped in his tracks, arms slowly falling to his side.

"You need a hug," he said, desperately wanting to make it better.

She stood and took a few steps away from him. She spun suddenly around, yelling at him with a deluge of tears.

"Stop it! Answer the question!"

He didn't really know what to say to her. Anything he said was bound to make her feel worse. He didn't love her the way he loved Mika, but he didn't hate her.

"Mostly, it's wonderful," he began. "The best feelings you'll ever have. Sometimes it's terrible, the worst hurt you'll ever feel."

Lorilei stood there in pain, the most pain she had ever felt, and remembered how Thorbin felt wonderful looking at pictures of Mika. The most wonderful she had ever sensed from him. He approached her again, but she jumped back.

"Don't touch me!" she screamed at him. "If you don't love me," she continued softly then proceeded to sob, struggling for breath, "then don't touch me."

Thorbin was in shock. They stood still, soaking in intensity. He wanted her to understand, and now she did, but he didn't want her to feel unloved. What was he to do now? He really wanted to hug her and tell her it would be all right. If he did, would she misunderstand? If he didn't, would she be OK? She was Mosot; too much of this kind of hurt could be really bad for her. He closed his eyes and approached her. *Here goes,* he thought.

He took one step towards her, and she flung herself into him and collapsed. With her head in his chest, her sobs slowly faded away. He rubbed her back to help soothe them out and kissed the top of her head.

"Take it easy, I do love you," he said, and she felt it, wonderful and hurt all at the same time. "Not like I love Mika," he clarified, "but I really, truly, love you, Lorilei." She sensed his honesty and understood.

Love was love; sometimes it was wonderful, sometimes it was pain. Sometimes it was physical, and sometimes it was friendly compassion, like now.

"I love you too," she whimpered.

He smiled at her. He felt it.

"You're going to be fine, baby steps, OK?"

Ben

Ben was on the bridge sitting at the helm. He had heard the whole exchange. He couldn't help but wonder if Lorilei was being sincere, or maybe she was the best actress he had ever heard. He tentatively settled on sincerity; their encounter in the hall was the deciding vote. His mind drifted, contemplating the question that was Lorilei.

Had she never really been loved, he considered. *It's possible.*

Sam entered the bridge from the office, and Ben turned to look at her. She smiled at him and mouthed the word. "Wow," Ben nodded an acknowledgement. Evidently, parts of Thorbin and Lorilei's conversation had been loud enough for the whole ship to hear.

"How's the compression now?" Sam asked, and Ben turned his attention to the console. He began doing calculations, and Sam put her hand on his shoulder. Ben looked up at her.

"Don't touch me unless you love me," he said with a huge grin.

"OK," Sam said, returning the smile and removing her hand.

After a moment of continued monitoring, Ben answered Sam's original question.

"The new manifold is working fine." Then his smile returned. "But I'm so loveable."

"My loss," Sam said, nodding her head with a playful smile.

The console beeped, demanding Ben's attention.

"What's that?" Sam asked.

"Someone wants to talk." Ben tapped away at the screen. "Looks like a transport."

"…is Ellis, captain of the Marisol. Can you hear me?" a voice said from the com. "I repeat. Victoria, this is Captain Ellis of the Marisol, can you hear me?" Then they heard a second voice that sounded distant from the speaker.

"Their com might be down, they look pretty beat up too, Captain."

"OK, set a course to intercept," the captain answered. Ben finished opening the com.

"Captain Ellis, this is Victoria, we hear you."

"Great," said Ellis. "We're in a real bad spot, Victoria, any chance you can assist?"

"What's the problem?"

"Our environmental filters are crapping out on us and our turbines quit a few days ago."

"OK, Marisol, we'll see what we can do."

"Great, thanks a lot."

"No problem, Victoria's actually a tug if you need a tow."

"We may, unless you got some saline KP."

"We might," Ben considered.

"We'd be happy to trade ya. I got a crate of cigarettes."

Cigarettes, Ben considered, pleased.

"OK, deal," Ben said as he set a course. "Looks like we should intercept you in an hour or so.

Thorbin entered the bridge from the observation deck below to reassume the helm.

As Ben stood Sam asked, "Cigarettes?"

"Yeah, can you believe that?"

"I don't know Ben, saline KP is going to be pretty hard to come by. It doesn't sound like a good deal to me."

"It isn't, he's getting screwed. Back at the run, a carton of smokes was priced higher than an ounce of gold. He's giving up a whole crate. I'm guessing that's around a hundred cartons. Shit, I got gallons of hydraulic grade saline."

"Hmm," Sam replied in disagreement.

Lorilei entered the bridge through the office with Spot frolicking on her heels. She had just finished checking up on Tank, who was doing better, and was making her rounds. She had a new perspective on love after her and Thorbin's conversation. During her visit with Tank, she had told him that she loved him, and he had told her that he loved her too, and then there were hugs. After that, she was feeling the love, and part of the round making was to see who loved her. Sam was the first to greet her and be sucked into the love trap.

"Hi, Lorilei," she said.

To which Lorilei tossed her arms around Sam and declared, "I love you Sam."

Sam rolled her eyes. "I love you too, Lorilei."

Lorilei smiled. *Score!* she thought. *That's three out of four.* Thorbin, Tank, and now Sam. When she had asked Liz, Liz had promptly told her to fuck off. Lorilei counted that one as neutral.

She turned to Ben.

"Ben," she began, this one could go either way.

"No," he briefly said before she could get out the whole sentence. She didn't finish.

Hmm, she thought. *That's two neutrals.* Then she tossed her arms around Thorbin's neck.

"Love?" she asked.

"Now you're just being silly," he answered.

She tilted her head and eyed him with a 'That's not an answer look'. Like

Sam, he rolled his eyes and answered penitently, "Love."

"Love!" she cried out happily as she pushed herself off of Thorbin and spun around.

Spot enjoyed spinning, so he joined her. Lorilei considered, "You love me, don't ya, puppy?" Spot barked and Lorilei eeked happily, "Five!" With a hand on her hip and a finger thoughtfully on her lips she thought. *Anyone else?* Sariel had clearly been left out of the love train. "I'll go ask Tank some more." Then she frolicked away, with Spot following, back into the office.

An hour or so later, they were bearing down on the Marisol, which looked to be in a similar condition to Victoria. She was a small transport vessel, almost shaped like a perfect rectangle, about Victoria's size expect much longer. Thorbin sat at the helm and diagnosed her through the sensors.

"The Marisol's taken a lot of damage." Ben nodded. "Their hydraulics appear to be fine."

"He may not be having trouble with the actual hydraulics – he mentioned something about his environment filters."

"Get the spyder ready, Sam," Ben ordered. "Just in case."

"Victoria," a voice from the Marisol said through the com. "We've got a hatch just under our bow."

After much effort Thorbin maneuvered Victoria under the Marisol so that the office was just below the other boat's bow. The ships mated and the hatches were prepared to be opened. Ben, Thorbin, Sam, and Sariel were in the office. Sariel addressed Ben.

"Captain, my weapon please."

Ben considered what Sariel suggested, but he was certain it was unnecessary. Thorbin, however, was not. Ben worked the hatch and confirmed the seal, then began the arduous process of opening it; Thorbin went to the common room to procure his pistol.

As the hatch opened a faint odor of rotten eggs entered from the other ship. Ben looked up and the Marisol's hatch was also open, a clean-shaven bald man was peering down from above.

"Victoria's captain I presume?" he asked.

"Yes, Ben," Ben answered. The smell was becoming stronger and Ben held his hand over his nose. "What's that smell?"

"Smell?" the man began. "Oh! Sorry about that, one of our recyclers got banged up when the Talc attacked. It's been leaking sulfur dioxide. Don't worry. It's not at a toxic level. Hell, I must have gotten used to the smell." Then his head disappeared and a brown box soon replaced it. "Comin' your way," the man said, then pushed the box down the hatch, where it fell, bounced off the lip of Victoria's hatch and fell through on to the office floor. Shortly after the man unrolled a rope ladder and began to climb down. Ben held it tight until the man was firmly standing on Victoria's deck.

"Thank you, Ben," he said politely and extended his hand. "Captain Ellis at your service."

"Welcome to Victoria, Captain," Ben said, shaking the hand.

"I'd invite you on board the Marisol." Captain Ellis took a deep breath and smiled. "But it smells better on Victoria."

Ben smiled back, Sariel's suspicions had him wondering, but Ellis seemed OK. *Still*, he thought, *better keep Lorilei tucked away*.

Thorbin returned, his pistol concealed but available if necessary.

Captain Ellis looked down at the box he had dropped. "There's your smokes. A whole box of cartons still factory sealed."

"Separatist?" Ben asked.

"You know it," Ellis replied. Then his face turned to a questioning expression.

"Oh," Ben said. "Where are my manners, sorry, haven't had much contact since we left Jacob's Run. I got the saline KP."

"Oh," Ellis smiled. "It's not that, I'm sure you're good for it, I just…" and the face returned. "Well, I'd hate to impose, but I imagine my crew would love to breathe a few hours of fresh air."

"Certainly," Ben responded. After a few seconds he wanted a few hours of fresh air.

"Great," Ellis said. "Dinner's on us." Then he turned to a radio he had fastened to his left shoulder and held down a button as he spoke.

"Hey, Demarco, gather everyone up, along with dinner for…?" he looked towards Ben.

"Five," Ben answered, not including Lorilei into the count. She would have to hide for a few hours. Her comfort was negotiable; Captain Ellis's crew had no doubt been suffering bad air for weeks.

"Dinner for eleven," Ellis said as he added the sum of both ships. "Victoria has invited us aboard for some fresh air."

"Excellent, Captain," the man said from the other side, obviously excited about the fresh air.

In ten minutes the five crewmen were headed down the rope ladder; handshakes, thank yous, and introductions were being doled out. Everyone seemed pleased to be meeting new people. Ben had only one problem, he had no way to communicate to Lorilei that she needed to stay out of sight.

Like a bad habit, she entered the office from the control room. *Damn*, Ben thought. *I hope this goes well*. Captain Ellis took immediate notice.

"A Mosot," he said, pleased to look at her.

"Yes," Ben answered. It was too late to hide her presence now.

"What do you want, Lorilei?" Ben asked, displeased. Lorilei didn't answer, she just looked at the new arrivals with a pretty smile. Then she sensed something and her mouth dropped.

"Ben!" she yelled. "They're lying, they're gonna do something bad!"

In an instant, seven hands reached for seven concealed pistols, only one of them belonged to Victoria. Captain Ellis sighed.

"Put it down, cowboy," he said to Thorbin, who was outgunned six to one and had to concede. Two of them had their pistols firmly affixed to Sariel's head, completely aware of what he was. The other four had the rest of the room covered.

"I was hoping to actually have dinner first," Captain Ellis sighed. "Oh well. OK, here's the deal. Nobody moves." And at that Lorilei ran back into the control room and down the stairs to the cargo bay, closing and sealing the hatch behind her. Captain Ellis looked frustrated. Ben smiled.

"She don't listen very well," he said, inwardly happy that she had gotten away. She had uncovered whatever plot they had and was now definitely off to tell Tank, who for all intents and purposes, Ellis and his men didn't know about.

"Demarco, take Eddy and Turner and go get her. And be careful." He turned to Ben. "She don't listen very well." Then he continued with what he was originally going to say.

"We know you guys have the system board. That blonde bitch stole it from my buddy before that asshole Dima showed up. If you give it up now, without any trouble, I'll only kill blondie." He paused for a moment. "And take the Mosot."

Sariel assessed the situation. *One more,* he thought. *There were six, then they split up. Mistake the first.* In Sariel's way of thinking, anyone could correct a single mistake, a single mistake meant life or death. Two mistakes meant death. So he waited for the second mistake. He already knew that Thorbin was primed, and Ben, who could not act quickly, would still likely not hesitate. Ellis had prepared for two of his men to cover Sariel, which was no misstep on his part; if he hadn't, that would have been the critical second mistake. Ellis himself kept Thorbin and Ben at bay from a distance while frequently keeping an eye on Sariel. Ellis was out of reach to everyone, but the two guarding him were within arm's distance. Effective killing range for Sariel without a weapon. The mistake was going to be Ellis's.

Ellis waited nervously; so far everything was working out, despite not going quite as planned. He had planned his treachery to occur after dinner. No matter, he was flexible.

Ten minutes passed and Ellis was beginning to get concerned about the others. Victoria wasn't that big, how hard was it to find one little Mosot girl?

Then from downstairs there was a bang. Sariel watched, Ellis didn't flinch.

Then came barking. Ellis didn't flinch. Then there were gunshots. Ellis still didn't flinch. Then over the radio Demarco reported. "We found her, she ran into the kitchen; it won't be too much longer. Oh and there's another guy in a room down here."

Ellis turned his head to speak into the radio, keeping an eye on Ben and Thorbin, but not Sariel.

Sariel smiled. *Mistake the second.* In that second Ellis heard a whoosh from Sariel's direction. He turned his head to see what it was. Sariel had turned around and now held each of the guards' pistol hands in one of his own and was pulling them forward, off balance. Ellis raised his pistol to take aim at Sariel, but Ben and Thorbin tackled him.

Sariel held the men firmly in his grasp by their shooting hands, making sure each weapon was pointed in a safe direction. He flung his right leg up and kicked the left assailant in the head with the ball of his foot, then he thrust it right and kicked the right assailant with his heel. He let their hands go as they let their pistols fall, which Sariel caught by the barrels. Flicking both wrists, the pistols danced and spun into his grasp. With a fluid motion his fingers met the triggers, and he killed both men with their own weapons. *Beautiful,* he thought. *Three hundred ninety-eight.*

Ben and Thorbin were wrestling with Ellis, who was being beaten senseless. The simultaneous gunshots cause all three of them to flinch. Thorbin turned to see if Sariel was alive, but he was gone.

Sariel entered the kitchen pistols first and saw one of Ellis's men hopping in circles trying to shoot Spot, who had bitten him in the ass and locked his jaw. The pit bulls violent thrashing made him difficult shoot. Sariel shot the man in the ear and turned to see Lorilei. She was struggling with another of Ellis's men – the only one left in the room. In an instant Sariel had closed half the distance. The man took notice of Sariel's approach and spun Lorilei around, holding her with his free hand and aiming his weapon at Sariel.

Mistake the first, Sariel mentally counted, *considering me his greatest threat. He should have shot the girl first.* The man's arm wavered as he struggled with Lorilei. *Mistake the second.* Thinking he was skilled enough to wrestle Lorilei and take an accurate shot at Sariel. The man fired three times as Sariel closed the distance. Each missed shot brought Sariel closer to his victim. It wasn't that Sariel was faster than the bullets, but he was faster than the man.

Sariel seized the man's pistol hand and wrenched it in a safe direction as Lorilei took the opportunity to grow fangs and drive them deep into his neck, effectively setting herself free. After which she fell to the floor in order to get out of the way. Now Sariel *was* his greatest threat.

The merc forced his palm up, leading his arm forward and his body off balance. Then he reached his other hand around to the man's elbow, pulling down on his hand as he slammed the elbow up, snapping the arm at the joint. The pistol fell from the man's hand as he cried out in agony.

Unskilled and twenty percent incapacitated, Sariel calculated. He grabbed the left side of the man's face by jamming a thumb in his eye and smashed his head into the wall behind.

Twenty-five percent, he recalculated.

Sariel then removed his thumb and held the man's head firmly against the wall by his brow. He attacked the eye again, sinking his middle and index fingers into it all the way to the knuckles. Then, from behind the man's face, Sariel reached around to the other eye socket, one hand pushed against his brow while the other pulled on his nasal cavity. Bone and cartilage gave way and the man collapsed to the ground with the bridge of his nose still in Sariel's hand.

The mercenary flicked the bloody mess at him, picked up his pistol and shot him with it.

"Four hundred," Sariel breathed methodically.

From the floor Lorilei cried out with concern.

"Tank!" she said.

Sariel spun around and was out the door.

When Sariel entered the common room Tank was asleep. Although instead of lying on his back, as he normally did, he was on his side. In his hands was a pistol. To his left, leaning against the wall, was the last man. He was shivering uncontrollably, his arms and legs were broken, which was nothing compared to his spirit. Sariel stood over him.

"I surrender," the man begged.

Sariel lifted his weapon and aimed at the man's face.

"You can't." His begging intensified. "I surrender!"

"Four hundred and one," Sariel said as he ended the man's life. He turned towards Tank. "Ninety-nine more to go." He gently removed the pistol from Tank's hands and headed back up to report to Ben.

Lorilei had fled immediately to Thorbin. She was terrified that he might be hurt.

When she arrived Captain Ellis had been hogtied with duct tape. Thorbin turned to her, and she assumed her reassurance position in his arms, head in his chest. She was certain Ben was going to be furious with her. She had been behaving, and now all her effort was about to be for nothing. Slowly, everyone in the office gathered as a plan was formulated and questions were asked. No one said one word to Lorilei, and she kept her mouth shut. Eventually it happened.

"Lorilei!" Ben said to her grumpily.

Immediately she responded from Thorbin's chest. "I'm sorry, Ben!"

Ben was confused. "Sorry for what?" he said, pissed, but not seemingly at her.

"I put the whole ship in danger again?" she said, not understanding why he wasn't upset with her.

"You're always putting us in danger," he said, confirming her fear that she was about to be severely reprimanded. "But this time, it's not your fault, Ace. Can you tell me what this guy was talking about when he said he knew we had the system board?"

"Well," she began; Ben really wasn't upset with her. "I can't read minds, only emotions," she said, wishing she could be more helpful. "But if you ask him a question, sometimes I can tell if people are lying."

Ben walked over to Ellis and tore the duct tape off of his mouth.

"What system board were you talking about?"

"System board?" Ellis replied, surprisingly coy under his circumstances. "I don't know what you mean."

"He's lying!" Lorilei confirmed.

Sariel entered the office and approached Ellis. With both hands he held his new pistol and was taking careful aim at the man's head.

"Hold on," Ben ordered. Sariel removed his finger from the trigger and looked at Ben, waiting for the OK to execute Ellis. "I got some questions for him." Sariel unloaded the pistol and set it on a desk, then he retrieved a knife from his belt and came upon Ellis, stabbing him in the shoulder.

"What are you doing?" Ben asked as Ellis screamed then whimpered in agony.

"Interrogating him, Captain," Sariel explained as if they had an understanding.

"How 'bout you go check his ship and make sure it's safe."

"Yes, Captain," Sariel said standing erect. "May I have my weapon?" he asked. Ben fumbled in his pocket until he came across his keys. He tossed them to Sariel.

"In the cargo bay on the port side of the bathroom, green locker," Ben instructed. Sariel headed immediately towards the locker.

When Sariel returned he was in full battle regalia. He climbed the rope ladder and was gone. Ben and Thorbin continued to question Ellis to no avail. Sariel returned and insisted that he could get Ellis to talk. Ben wasn't too keen on torture, but this was the second time his ship had been boarded in search of the same item, which was intolerable.

Sariel instructed that the bathroom would be the most suitable location; it would be easiest to clean up. The bathroom, however, was a holy place, so he settled for the cargo bay.

Sariel

In the cargo bay Ellis lay on his stomach, hogtied and alone with Sariel. By this time Ellis was rather concerned for his well-being. Sariel had positioned him on an empty space on the floor and sat quietly in front of him crossed-legged. Ellis's duct tape gag had been removed so he could give information at any time. He was terrified of Sariel and remained quiet. Sariel had procured his PJU and was recording the day's events. As he did so he thought out loud, which was not his way, but he wanted Ellis to hear.

"Four shots fired," he began and then wrote, "Two strikes, one kick. Five kills," he calculated. Then he thought to himself for a while. After consideration he continued, "To thine own self be true. Three assists – Tank, Lorilei, canine."

Sariel addressed Ellis. "Truth is all that exists. Honor is all that is required. Deception is frail, dishonor is self-defeating."

"A murderer speaks of honor," Ellis said, taking the bait.

"I am nothing without honor," Sariel answered.

"Honorable men don't torture," Ellis said, refuting Sariel's position.

"Honor," Sariel explained. "The Latin word is 'decus'. It means integrity. Integrity means truth. The search for truth requires honesty. Extrapolation of the facts, removal of deception. Sometimes honesty is painful."

"What?" Ellis responded, sorry he had opened his mouth. Sariel looked up from his PJU and stared at him.

"Pain is honest. It cannot be denied; there is no deception in it. Pain is honorable."

"Oh shit," Ellis responded.

"I am without deception and without dishonor, therefore, I am truth. You question my honor, however, if you did not deceive, we wouldn't be here. You see, deception is frail, easily broken by honesty, which is pain."

Ellis hung his head in despair. "I'm going to die."

"Ah yes, death," Sariel said with a smile as if he were talking about a dear friend. "The ultimate truth. Now matter how you add all the portions of any life, in the end, its sum equals death. Death, like pain, cannot be denied, it, like truth, is without deception. Death equals truth. Pain equals honesty. Life equals deception. A deception that continues frail until broken by truth." Sariel walked over to Ellis and crouched down; he sat on his heels and waited for Ellis to look up at him. When he did, Sariel concluded, "I seek truth."

"If I tell you what you want to know, will you spare my life?"

"No, you can never be spared from truth," Sariel answered. "However, less deception requires less honesty."

"The system board is part of a weapons system, it was stolen from the DC.

Then stolen from the Syndicate, who want it back. I've been hunting it down for six months. I found the processor; the system board is on Victoria. The only other portion is the firmware. I don't know who has it. I got a tip that it may be at Kenton's Crypt."

From over the intercom Lorilei gleefully confirmed, "He's telling the truth."

Sariel joined Ben, Thorbin, Lorilei, and Sam in the office. Thorbin spoke first.

"If it's a DC weapons system, we need to get it to them as soon as possible. They may need it for the war effort."

"Yes," Ben agreed. "And the last piece is at Kenton's Crypt."

"Kenton's Crypt?" Thorbin asked.

Ben breathed then gave his explanation. "It's one of the asteroids the miners pulled from the belt. It wasn't mineral rich, so they hollowed it out and used it as a facility. It's like an oasis for the mining companies. I've done plenty of work there. Lots of Syndicate, although who knows now. It's on the way."

"Do we have to get involved?" Sam asked. "We got two pieces, let the DC get the rest."

"I am the DC," Thorbin said, feeling purpose. As far as he was concerned this was too much coincidence not to be of divine intervention. He was resolute.

"It may be a mistake," Sariel added. This made Sam nervous about sharing an opinion with him, but she didn't have much to say. She just looked at Thorbin, hoping the desperation in her eyes would convince him. It didn't.

"I understand if you don't want to go. I'll take the Marisol and go alone, it's not a problem," he said offering a solution.

Lorilei leapt at him. "It's a huge problem!" she said.

Thorbin didn't even look at her; he just instinctively put his arms around her as she approached. "You're not going anywhere alone," she said.

"Ellis said he had the processor. Sariel, see if he'll tell you where it is," Ben asked.

"He also said we already have a piece," Sam interjected. "He said the Syndicate wanted it back. Dima searched the ship thoroughly, and it wasn't here, so really we only have one piece."

"Unless it came on board after Dima searched the ship," Ben said, adding it up. "Perhaps with a certain mysterious blonde passenger."

"Where is Liz?" Lorilei asked.

Nobody knew.

Ben stepped into the bridge, and a moment later he rushed back into the office. "The Marisol!"

"Not to worry," Sariel said. "I disabled the engines. Shall I go and get her?"

"In one piece please," Ben instructed.

Sariel rearmed himself before ascending the rope ladder once again.

Liz

When Liz awoke she lay hogtied on her stomach in the cargo bay alone with Sariel. She was rather concerned for her well-being. Sariel had positioned her on an empty space on the floor and sat cross-legged in front of her.

"Honor," Sariel explained. "The Latin word is 'decus'."

Twenty minutes later Liz was no longer hogtied, instead she was handcuffed with Ellis, securely held to the cargo bay wall. Both of them had a single cuff on, which was secured around one of the rails meant for securing cargo with rope. They had been placed in such a way where they could stand or sit so long as they did it at the same time. Liz was flustered but had collected herself. Sariel's interrogation of her had only hurt her pride. After she had told him where she was hiding the system board, he retrieved it – while everyone watched. Thorbin had then produced the handcuffs and now they were all in the cargo bay inspecting the two pieces. Except for Tank, who was still in bed.

Thorbin and Sam considered the two parts of the device.

"Think you can figure it out, Sam?" Thorbin asked her.

"It looks pretty straightforward. The processor goes into the board. Apply proper power. Install firmware, which is odd, firmware is usually…well…firm. As in part of the hardware, which I'm holding."

"It's part of a weapons system, no doubt the firmware isn't installed yet for security reasons. I'd also be willing to bet that there's a fourth piece," Thorbin replied.

"What's that?" Sam asked. She was fairly certain she was the expert in these matters.

"Training, once you put it together, it won't do anything unless you know how to use it."

"Well I'll check it out anyway, it'll be a slow process, or maybe I'll just leave it alone. I don't know what it is. I could break it."

Chapter Eighteen
Breathing Room

Lorilei

Once again, Lorilei was in the hall working on the number thirty-nine gravity inducer. She had found a manual and now knew exactly what needed to be done in order to get that infernal humming to shut up. She lay on her back stuffed into the maintenance compartment up to her belly button, sweating profusely as she wrapped her arms around a conduit that blocked her view of the necessary repairs. She strained against her sore arms as she blindly fumbled through the work.

"Ben and Sam make it look so easy," she complained as her arms demanded to be put down. She negotiated her limbs from around the blind spot and laid them by her side. They tingled as the blood reentered them. As the strain in her arms subsided the ache in her back and neck became more noticeable. She squirmed a bit, trying to find a more comfortable position. It didn't help.

"I'm going to fix you," she said to the inducer, flapping her shirt rapidly to try and coax the cool air in from the hallway. The fresh air wafted in, refreshing her moist skin and bolstering her resolve, but it did little for her aching muscles. She took a deep determined breath and commanded her arms to get back to work despite their disdain.

"Oww," she complained, acknowledging them, then she smiled, "Vicky, don't be difficult like Thorbin." She giggled to herself.

"Knock it off," she heard Ben say from the hallway. Then she felt something nudge her foot.

"I already did most of my chores; I really want to get this thing fixed," she explained towards the hallway. She then felt a tug on her shirt.

"Can you do anything without losing your shirt?"

"It's hot in here," she whined.

"If you can't stand the heat, get out from under the kitchen."

She felt a large object being placed on her lap – with care.

"What's that?" she yelled, curious.

There was no answer.

"Ben?"

She reached her arms out and held what felt like a box, then she shimmed her top half out of the compartment and scooted herself across the floor until she could lean up against the wall.

With the box in her lap, she looked down both sides of the hallway; Ben was nowhere to be seen. Apparently something else needed yelling at. A sweet and curious smile crossed Lorilei's lips as she tugged open the box's flaps.

"Oh," she breathed, seeing its contents.

The box was full of candles. Her lavender candles were there, as well as a dozen white ones with crimson writing. She plucked out one of the white ones and read the single sentence aloud.

"Merry Christmas, Jessica, Love Ben."

"Oh," Lorilei breathed again. She inspected the rest of them and shuffled them about until she discovered a note at the bottom of the box. She quickly pulled it out and read it.

"Sorry, Ace. It's just the way I am, Love Ben."

"Oh," she breathed once more, this time with tears in her eyes.

She immediately felt the need to rush off and give Ben a great big hug, but she reconsidered.

If he wanted a hug, he would have stuck around, she decided. *I'll get him later.* She looked back at the maintenance hatch. *I think I'm done with you for now. I'm filthy, I should go take a bath, and then I can pray with my candles, that would be nice. I might miss Thorbin's break.* This didn't appeal to her. *I don't really have time for that anyway, I gotta check up on Tank too.* She smiled at the thought of Tank.

As Tank's health returned he was more active and becoming pleasantly lecherous. She had considered just giving in to his advances, but it just didn't seem right in that it didn't fit with winning Thorbin's affections. So she pretended poorly that he was being inappropriate, forging a blurry line that he shouldn't cross, blurry enough for a great many pleasant misunderstandings. It was an effective technique that pleased them both and allowed for her to claim that she was a pure chaste victim of his naughty carnal desires, which had been fine until recently, but it seemed less appropriate each time she tended to him.

If Tank's going to be pawing at me, I should take a bath, she sighed.

Thorbin and Ben

On the bridge, Thorbin was seated at the helm and Ben was standing over his shoulder as they confirmed Victoria's heading. Thorbin had been reinvigorated with purpose. This caused Ben great concern.

"What's your plan?" Ben asked, he didn't really want to know, but a captain's prerogative didn't include ignorance.

"I get the firmware then head to the closest DC vessel," Thorbin answered. Ben considered this and was a little relieved.

"Well most of the DC are at Mars by now. So I guess you'll be with us for the long haul."

"What's your plan?" Thorbin asked. It had occurred to him before that they would eventually have to say goodbye. Until the discovery of the device, it seemed distant. Now Thorbin had purpose and a plan, that most definitely meant saying goodbye to Victoria, whom he had come to appreciate.

"Get Vicky to a proper dock. Fix her up, clean her up, new coat of paint. Then, I don't know. There may be a surplus of tugs, in which case Vicky and I need a new occupation."

"Or there could a serious lack," Thorbin refuted.

"In which case, I'm in the money," Ben agreed.

"What about Sam?" Thorbin wondered out loud.

"Well, I don't know," Ben answered. "There's gonna be a need for design engineers. It's a good occupation, most of them were on Earth." He took another moment for consideration. "Although I would really like her to stay on board. I'm gonna have to get a whole new crew. It would be nice if she was a part of it. How about you? What are you going to do with Lorilei?"

"Damn," Thorbin hadn't a clue, and he had been trying hard not to think about it. "Fighters only have one seat," he observed in an attempt to write off the conversation. "She's going to have to take care of herself eventually."

"I'm sure she'd happily sit on your lap," Ben jabbed.

"Pretty sure that's against regulations. I have no idea."

"Well, DC's got a plan for everything," Ben said.

"Yeah, doctrine of contingency," Thorbin clarified. "It's one of the DC's missions. I don't think Lorilei's part of it."

"Well I'm sure they have a plan for family members," Ben said. While he was starting to like Lorilei, he didn't want her around indefinitely. "You might be able to declare her as a dependent," Ben suggested. "Then you two could get a nice place on base. Play house." Thorbin looked at Ben.

"Or," Thorbin said, "she could stay with you on Victoria."

"Or," Ben said back, "you could quit the core altogether and the two of you could live happily ever after in some dank but comfortable shack on Mars, and Victoria will never have to worry about slutty little alien women ever again."

Thorbin laughed. "When we get to Mars, are you going to wait for us to land before you kick her out? I thought you guys were getting along better."

"She's all right," he began. "But she'll always be a little too much for me." They sat silently for a moment considering Lorilei's fate.

"They probably have a facility for transitioning captive Mosot. That would probably be the best place for her," Thorbin said, coming to a reasonable conclusion.

"It was probably on Earth," Ben said with a tone that clearly stated 'she's your responsibility; if you go, she goes with you.'

"I'll figure something out," Thorbin said, wanting to end the conversation. Ben understood.

"How long until we get to Kenton's Crypt?" Ben asked.

Thorbin analyzed the helm console. "Approximately twenty-two hours."

"You should do a double shift. Go to sleep in twelve hours. That way you're rested right before we arrive. I'll go talk to my guy. Then we'll take it from there."

"What about our guests locked up in the cargo bay?"

"I don't know if we should drop them off or take them with us. I'd like to be rid of them sooner. Although I don't think we have that luxury. If we let Ellis go, he'll squeal first chance he gets. Maybe Sariel was right."

"No, someone at the core will be interested in them. You know Ben," Thorbin said considering, "the Defense Core has a policy of rewarding people that give them intel."

"Hey, you're right!" Ben started to think about a big fat government paycheck.

"Hey, Ben, can you hear me?" Sam asked through the intercom.

Ben tapped the com button on the helm console and answered, "Yeah, what do you need?"

"I found a stress fracture in the kitchen floor."

"Shit!"

"Are we OK?" Thorbin asked as Ben headed down the ladder into the observation deck.

"If I get to it now!" And then his head disappeared down the hatch.

Tank

Tank lay alone in the common room staring at the ceiling. It had been a while since anyone had come in to check up on him, namely Lorilei. Sam would check in now and again, but she had become increasingly preoccupied with keeping Victoria afloat, and in one way or another everyone else had responsibilities that kept them from visiting. While he was feeling less like an invalid, he still couldn't run about, and he depended on other people, namely Lorilei. This was fine with him, he was becoming quite fond of her. She was tender with him in a way that he could accept without feeling emasculated, and she was easy on the eyes, which was nice. All this, wrapped up in a chemistry that he rather enjoyed. A reluctant beauty and the beast sort of thing, where the beauty only pretended to be reluctant to a point. Less a point and more like an inkblot open to interpretation and misinterpretation, where the word 'no' was sometimes declared with an encouraging giggle, and other times with sincerity, but never with clarity. She was a fantastic tease, although he was starting to get a little disappointed that it appeared as if he would never get the whole enchilada – just a taste that kept him wanting more. It was starting to make him feel like a back-up plan in case she couldn't seal the deal with Thorbin.

No enchilada for you unless Thorbin doesn't want it, he thought.

Which really pissed him off because Thorbin was leaving it cold in the microwave, and Tank wanted to eat it!

I must be hungry, he thought.

Then Lorilei walked in, looking very tasty in her yellow sundress.

"Good morning, Tank," she said, flashing her sweetest smile at him.

"Morning, little cutie," he replied, happy to see her.

"How are you feeling?" she asked as she approached him.

"OK, better now that you're here." He shifted his legs off the bed and sat up slowly.

Lorilei stood between his knees and began a regimen of looking him over, feeling his forehead and tipping his head from side to side inspecting, for what she didn't know, it just seemed like the thing to do. Tank wrapped an arm around her waist, drawing her against him.

"Everything check out, Nurse Cutie?" he asked, looking up at her with a smile. She smiled back.

"You're not going to molest me, are you?"

"Of course not," he said as she felt a massive Tank paw slip under the back of her dress and grab hold of a cheek. She squirmed a bit, not in the usual playful attempt to not really get away, but in a reluctant 'maybe this isn't right' kind of way.

"What's the matter, cutie?" Tank asked.

"You really shouldn't," she said, a little disappointed.

"Really?"

"Yeah," she answered.

"I'm sorry," he said, letting her ass go and leaning back from her. "I thought…" he began, a little confused.

"Not this time."

"I thought it was OK to fool around?" he asked, they had never actually discussed it.

"I am…I was. It's not your fault. It's just…" she tried to explain.

"Thorbin," he said for her.

"Yes."

"Sweetie." He put his arms back around her. "That ship ain't gonna sail. You know that, right?"

"I guess."

Tank took a deep reflective breath.

"Cutie, he ain't interested. I know you was just lettin' Tank fool round with ya because he wouldn't, and that's OK with me. And if yer changing your mind about that, that's OK too, no hard feelings, but you just gonna make yourself crazy chasing Thorbin."

Lorilei looked penitent and distressed.

"I never met anyone like him."

"I don't know what all the fuss is about."

"He's wonderful," she sniffled.

"Oh no, don't do that."

"Stupid wife."

"Yeah, monogamy is a motherfucker."

Lorilei chuckled.

"That's better," he said. "Look, little cutie, Tank loves you," he said, giving her a squeeze.

"Even if I don't let you play with my ass?"

"Absolutely. Although if you need that sort of thing, I'm here for you."

Lorilei grinned from ear to ear. "That's what I like about you, Tank, you're a giver," she said, throwing her arms around his neck and planting one on his cheek. Then he watched disappointed as she headed to the hatch.

"I'm going to the kitchen, need anything else?" she asked.

"I'm a little hungry," he answered.

"OK, any requests?"

"Enchilada," he said coyly.

"What's that?" Lorilei asked.

Tank smiled. "I'll just have whatever Thorbin's having."

In the Galley

Meanwhile, in the kitchen Thorbin was distributing platefuls of lunch to Sam and Ben. Then he prepared a plate for himself and sat. Sam had been in the kitchen for about an hour. In that time, she had managed to cover half the table with various electronics and a mound of papers bleeding with calculations. Most of them scratched out. Thorbin set a plate on the table for her, and she set her work aside to eat.

"Any luck figuring out what it is?" Thorbin asked.

"Yes, lots," she replied, pleased with herself. Then she returned to the plate. Thorbin and Ben looked at each other.

"Well?" Ben asked.

"Oh, of course," she said. "The system board isn't a system board. It's an expansion card. Typical, I figured that out right away, except it's different. Most expansion cards use an ECS 15 slot, but this one uses a much bigger pin out. I thought I'd never seen it before, then I realized that the optic bus wasn't the ECS standard. It's DC."

"What?" Ben asked.

Sam sighed as if she were explaining to a child that 'A' stood for apple and they weren't getting it.

"DC," she said slowly so he could understand. "Defense Core, it's a military design, which makes perfect sense. Since it's a weapon, or whatever. Anyhow, I matched the card; it's similar to one that we were using in a project back home. Then it hit me," she said, demonstrating with a hand smacking her forehead. "This is a control card for a robot. I messed with it some more, and I realized that it was designed for 128 volts input. I felt like such an idiot, it was so obvious I can't believe I didn't see it right away."

"Uh huh," Ben responded this time. The word 'what' was obviously the incorrect word choice for following along with this conversation.

"I know!" Sam said. "I must be losing my touch. So anyway, I compared it to the spyder we have on Victoria, and it was a perfect match. Except our spyder isn't military so it won't work. But that's OK. Anyone with half a brain can mock up a DC optic bus."

"Yeah, I did that yesterday," Thorbin intervened.

Sam stopped. "You did?"

Thorbin half-laughed then continued. "Sam, you're smarter than we are. We don't know what you're talking about."

"I understand perfectly," Ben said. "But why don't you dumb it down for T."

"The card," Sam began, trying to break something complex into something simple. "It's made for a military spyder."

"What does it do?" Thorbin said, now following along.

"It connects the processor to the spyder."

"What does the processor do?"

"It runs the program that tells the spyder what to do."

"What does the program do?"

"I don't know, we don't have that yet."

"OK," Thorbin said. "So it's part of some new type of spyder?"

"Yes, a really small one, like the size of your hand."

"Well, we don't know what it does, what would the DC want a really small spyder for?" he asked.

"I don't know, the DC already have the best spyders money can buy, and probably the best money can't buy. They're really quite amazing, they can fix anything – the new ones can even do surgery on organic tissue."

"Tank wants an enchilada," Lorilei said as she entered the kitchen. Everyone snapped out of their futile attempts to guess at the nature of the DC spyder.

"Really?" Sam said. "That's good. Do we have any, Ben?"

"No," Ben answered.

"That's too bad," Lorilei said, wishing she could offer him an enchilada, whatever that was. "Well, he'll take some of this," she said, walking to the counter and taking a few bites for herself. As she prepared a plate for him she thought about Ben.

"Ben," she said, formulating a heart-felt thank you.

"No," he cut her off.

Not content, she continued overflowing two plates. When done, she turned, holding a plate in each hand, and looked at Ben.

"What?" he said to her stare.

"I sang one for Jessica."

"I bet she liked that," he said.

Lorilei nodded then headed out the hatch with food in hand.

Lorilei

Lorilei delivered the food to Tank, who accepted it graciously and quickly ate most of it. Then she took the other plate to Liz and Ellis. She hadn't been assigned this task, but she felt sympathy for them. She didn't like to see anyone chained. To her, it was a fate worse than death.

She always made sure Sariel was present and close by when she approached them. Their arrangement was awkward. Ellis was an absolute scoundrel. This provided Lorilei with more sympathy for Liz, who she still detected deceit in. Liz was still hiding something. Whatever it was wasn't nefarious. She had tried to express this to Thorbin, but he assured her that Liz was shrewd and not to be trusted. Whatever she was holding inside caused her much more pain than being handcuffed to the cargo bay wall. Which pained her plenty. Ellis however, wasn't the least bit upset at sharing not enough space with Liz. She was more than capable of keeping him at bay, but he kept her on her toes.

Lorilei approached cautiously. She set the plate on the floor just outside of Liz's reach. Then she slowly slid it on the ground until it appeared to be within her reach.

"Thanks," Liz said as she reached out with her free arm and drew it in.

"Better make sure it's not poisoned," Ellis said, glaring at Lorilei.

"You say that every time," Liz complained. "It was obnoxious enough the first time."

"This time it might be," he insisted.

"Well let's hope so," she said pointedly at him. "Then I can be rid of you."

"Do you guys need anything else?" Lorilei asked.

"Yeah," Ellis said, stirring up the sarcasm. "Think you could get us the keys to these cuffs?" Lorilei ignored him and looked at Liz.

"Anything?"

"Is there any way I could get my own space?" Liz asked. Ellis wrapped his free arm around her.

"Ah, then who will keep me warm at night?"

Liz jabbed him in the ribs and he grunted. "I told you, no touching."

Ellis removed his arm and used it to rub his ribcage. Liz started eating some food as she looked at Lorilei, who was still watching her.

"Everyone else on board could care less if we eat or not," Liz said to her. "Why do you?"

"Because I don't like to see people chained," Lorilei answered.

Liz nodded, looking at Lorilei significantly for the first time, seeing her outside the light of her prejudice.

"Ahhhh, isn't that sweet," Ellis started in again. "Hey Lorilei."

"What?" she answered, knowing he was about to say something terrible.

"When I get out of here, I'm going to take you with me and sell you to the highest bidder."

Lorilei's eyes widened at the terrible thought.

"Fuck you," Liz said, elbowing him even harder in the ribs.

This time Ellis responded by hitting her square on the jaw. Lorilei took a step back and abruptly hit Sariel, who was approaching the coming feud. Without looking at him she stepped to the side.

As Sariel approached Ellis, he attempted to stand; the attempt was thwarted by his arm cuffed to Liz's.

"What?" he yelled at Sariel. "You fuckin' dog. You can't do shit to me. Captain's orders."

With a flash Sariel struck Ellis in the throat and he collapsed. Lorilei slipped away and continued on with her duties.

Chapter Nineteen
Kenton's Crypt

Thorbin

Twenty-two hours later, Victoria was still in one piece. A welded, taped, and willed together piece, but still whole. Thorbin had enjoyed his rest after a double shift. It had only been disturbed once, by Lorilei, who had attempted to make up for lost affection opportunities. Thorbin was able to convince her that he needed his rest for the danger that lie ahead; she relented, but only after stealing a kiss.

He sat once again at the helm. The flying had become increasingly interesting as the asteroid farm had come into view. Traffic between the enormous rocks was far sparser than Thorbin had imagined. These mines had once been the only source of raw materials outside of Earth. The mining corporations had collected the asteroids from the belt and brought them closer to Earth in order to close the distance between mining and refining. Then the Mars settlements began to flourish and the asteroid barons moved the farm precisely between Earth and Mars. Mars proved to be far more mineral rich than anyone had guessed. Plus there was an added benefit to mining on Mars. Since the majority of the colony was underground, after miners had excavated all the riches, they were left with prime real estate – twice the profit for the same cost. After that, the asteroid farms were abandoned and were only useful as an oasis.

As Victoria entered the field, Thorbin was cautious traversing the giants. They had been long since abandoned by industry. Like large gray tombstones marking the death of an era, they floated sorrowfully. The decrepit frames of buildings and scaffolding lay strewn about the asteroids like leaves and sticks unattended in a graveyard. The sun's light was mocked as its rays were forced to reflect off unnatural surfaces as larger boulders eclipsed smaller ones. The deeper into the field Victoria traveled, the less light there was. On occasion other ships passed onward to better places, disturbing the eerie glow like birds flying against the moon. As Victoria forged into the heart of the field, Kenton's Crypt was visible like a mausoleum visited only by those who tended to it.

Kenton's Crypt was an average-sized rock in the field; it had no distinct qualities except for its history. It, like every other asteroid, was chosen from the belt because it was assessed to be mineral rich. The asteroid baron Kenton had plucked it from its natural resting place in hopes of revitalizing his failing company. He had chosen poorly. R389 (as the asteroid was called in his day) was not mineral rich, a fact that he ignorantly disputed. He had developed a technology that tunneled more effectively than others through the hardest stone. Back then no one wasted time with such thorough mining. Not when there were easer ways to go about it. He thought his technology would give him an edge. Deeper and deeper he dug, still thinking he was right. He was wrong, he dug until had no capital left to invest, and no integrity left to sell. Like many who came to the asteroid farms in search of fortune, he died unpleasantly and poor. He had believed in the riches that could be found in asteroids and scoffed at those who felt Mars was a better opportunity. After all, it was twice the distance from Earth. After his death irony struck hard. His technology was paramount in the excavation of Mars, which eventually proved his beliefs wrong about the value of asteroids.

Also, after his death, there was an asteroid that had been excavated more than any other in the fields. Positioned by coincidence near the middle, it was the perfect place for asteroid farm commerce. Kenton's Crypt, they called it. On Earth, authors wrote books and directors directed films about his life, or how he haunted the asteroid. They too were made wealthy from his endeavors. In the end, his greatest contribution to humanity was a cautionary tale.

As Victoria came upon it Thorbin was able to spy one of the entrances and paged Ben, who quickly made his way to the bridge.

"That's gate seven," Ben informed him. "We should be able to enter without trouble. The gates are automated."

"People seem to be expecting us wherever we go."

"The ship stalls are pretty secure; it's outside Victoria that we could come across trouble," Ben advised.

As they spoke, Victoria pulled close enough to the gate that it began to open. It was a large metal door that was recessed into the mouth of one of the asteroid's cavernous entrances. It slowly slid down, allowing Victoria to enter. As she passed it, on the other side was another door that waited to open until the first was closed. Then behind the second was a third, and then a fourth. And at each, Victoria had to wait for the previous to close, until the last door stood before them. In mountainous red letters was written 'Caution – Gravity'. Thorbin prepared the thrusters and prayed that Victoria wouldn't plummet to the ground and smash into a million pieces. Just in case, he decreased altitude as low as he possibly could. The wait for last door to open took considerably longer since Victoria was positioned near the bottom of it.

When it did finally open, the world behind was revealed – an enormous carved-out cavern. Metallic structures lay littered on the ground and in the walls, even embedded the ceiling. It was hard to tell which were in use and which were abandoned; they all looked the same, a patchwork of construction built using the ores that were mined here or in other asteroids. It was oddly sterile in that nothing here was constructed by anything organic. Not a sliver of wood in sight, and perhaps not even out of sight. While at the same time everything was filthy, soaked in rust and dust.

Thorbin was concerned that there was no traffic control broadcasts. Although none seemed necessary, Victoria was the only visible boat in flight. He peered at their surroundings through the bridge window. The ground below was littered with rusting metallic refuse with spots of whole-looking industrial machinery that hadn't yet become refuse. He spied a small group of people cutting sections off a rather large piece with torches, the first sign of life.

He inspected the walls. They were beset with manmade nooks, most occupied by buildings flickering with light from within. Others were organized into slips where various boats were docked. It was apparent that most of the living occurred here in the side of the caverns, far from the bottom. In the far distance he took notice of an ancient Earth vehicle. He recognized it as a dump truck and was instantly interested in it. He had never seen a wheeled vehicle outside of a museum. It was larger then Victoria and had a dusty orange hue with patches of rust. It was backing up towards the lip of one of the nooks, where the edge dropped abruptly towards the cavern floor far below. He watched as it unloaded its fill right over the edge. The garbage plummeted to the ground for seconds before it crashed into a pile on the floor below.

"Keep this heading," Ben instructed as he entered from the office hatch. "I got a hold of my guy. He's on level twenty-eight on the starboard. He said we should dock near the center."

"Which level is twenty-eight and where's the center?" Thorbin asked.

"Twenty-eight from the bottom." Ben began to count levels. After he counted out twenty-eight he pointed down. "There," he said. "About two levels below us. There's a 'one half' marker on the wall in the center."

"Who is this guy?"

"Business associate," Ben answered.

"Is he trustworthy?"

"Not usually, no."

"So we're going to see him because?"

"Because if you need information about what's going on at Kenton's Crypt, he's the one to ask."

"I'm going with you, and we're taking Sariel."

"He won't talk if Sariel is around."

"You're not going without me, and I'm not going without Sariel."

"OK, we'll keep him a secret. He can stay behind us and follow."

"Good enough."

Sam

Sam was in the kitchen. Ben had taken a break to go and speak with Thorbin, so she took the time to go and grab a bite to eat – toast and jam. She contemplated her food, both products of Earth. Eventually there would be no more. She didn't have any great affinity for toast with jam, but she was sad to think of existence without them. She must have looked very sad indeed.

"Don't be sad, angel face," Tank said from the hallway hatch. "I'm right here."

Sam turned and smiled at him. "Well this is a nice surprise. Didn't expect to see you up and about."

"I was thirsty, thought I'd get a drink. Maybe take a bath. Where are the rest of my clothes?" he said, pulling a blanket tighter around his shoulders.

"They should be in there. I'll find them while you're in the tub. Your shirt was…" She smiled while motioning with her food. "Toast," she concluded with a subtle giggle. "Ben got a trench coat from Jacob's Run while he was there. It should fit you."

"Pants?" he asked.

"Lorilei washed them. We were able to patch them up."

"Thanks," he said then turned to the cupboard to get a glass. As he was filling his glass there was a gentle rumble that seemed to be slowly growing more violent. Soon the cupboard doors started rattling and the dishes in the sink began to clatter. Tank turned to look at Sam, who had a white knuckled vice grip on the table, which was also beginning to rattle.

"All hands!" Thorbin's voice said from over the intercom. "Brace yourself, we're about to land."

The rattling sharply turned to violent jolting. Sam was tossed from the chair to the floor, where she met Tank. He threw an arm around her and began to crawl towards the center of the kitchen floor. It was the safest place he could think of, far away from the cupboards, which were flinging their contents onto the deck. Once in the center of the floor, Tank rolled slightly to one side and squished Sam underneath him, securing them both in his blanket.

The quaking continued and all manner of kitchen debris was flailing about. Tank was doing his best to shield himself and Sam from harm. He was doing fairly well; mostly they were being pelted by little items until the kitchen table decided to attack. In true Tank fashion it quickly learned its lesson and fled out into the hallway, followed by a chair.

The quaking continued to intensify until there was one last final great jolt. It was Victoria's last drop to the ground, and she fell quickly. For a second Sam and Tank were airborne and fortunately Tank had the wits to brace himself with his hands as he landed so as not to crush Sam. The shaking abruptly stopped and only the sound of their rapid breathing could be heard.

Sam looked up at him.

"You OK?" he asked.

"Yes," she answered.

Victoria

After the rocky landing, everyone gathered in the cargo bay. Ben and Thorbin were pleased to see Tank join them. If only for a moment before he went to the tub.

"Sam, Lorilei," Ben began. "Me, Thorbin, and Sariel are going to go and take care of business. I need you to check to see how bad that landing banged up Vicky. Fix as much as you can. We may need to get outta here in a hurry, so get it done."

"OK. Where are you going?" Lorilei asked. "In case we need to know."

"To go meet up with a friend, after that, I don't know. So you got some time to get things straightened out here. Just don't mess around, OK?"

"OK," she answered.

"What do we do if something happens? Shouldn't one of you stay here? Just in case?" Sam asked.

"Here's the key to the weapons locker. Tank should be able to handle it," Ben said, handing the keys to Sam.

"But…" Sam began.

"Sam," Ben interrupted firmly, "I need you to check Vicky, *now.*"

"OK," she said, still unsure.

"We'll try to take it easy," Ben consoled. Then he took notice of Ellis. He was fast asleep, awkwardly dangling from Liz. "Does he normally do that?" Ben asked.

Liz looked over to him. She had made it a point to ignore Ellis completely, so she hadn't noticed. "That's odd," Liz said then began to feel a little sleepy herself.

Ben was then startled when from the corner of his eye he noticed Sariel bolt towards his gear. He looked back towards Liz, who was now also dangling awkwardly. He found himself staring at her for no good reason. Then his vision began to blur and he felt himself stumbling to the ground.

Chapter Twenty
A Fate Worse Than Death

Lorilei

Lorilie's head hurt something awful when she came to. She wanted to open her eyes but decided that would be a painful course of action. Instead, she sat silently and enjoyed the comforting caress of a hand on her cheek. She wasn't sure what had happened. Evidently she had passed out somehow. She could feel a pillow under her head and a stomach against her cheek. No doubt Sam was nursing her with compassion once again. She sighed as the gentle touch helped to relieve her headache.

"Oh, you're awake," a sweet and unfamiliar voice observed.

"What?" Lorilei answered, surprised that it wasn't Sam's voice.

"You're awake, you've been asleep for a very long time," the sweet voice answered. "My name's Lili," it continued. "What's yours?"

"Lili?" Lorilei answered groggily.

"No, silly," the sweet voice giggled. "That's my name. What's yours?"

"Who are you?" Lorilei asked, tensing her closed eyelids, still debating whether or not to open them up.

"No one," Lili answered. "Just a Mosot like you."

Lorilei's debate was over. She forced her eyelids open and was greeted by a pretty brown-haired Mosot with crystal blue eyes. She wore the uniform all too familiar to Lorilei. Light blue, seductive and opaque, outlining a typically perfect feminine form, and around Lili's neck was a thin silver chain. Lorilei began to panic.

"Oh," Lili breathed pleased to see Lorilei's eyes. "Lavender, how pretty."

Lorilei sat up quickly, her heart pounding. Her hands flew to her stomach to see what she was wearing. To her relief, she still donned her yellow sundress. The revelation allowed her to catch her breath.

"Well, are you going to tell me your name?" Lili asked again.

"Where am I?" Lorilei demanded, snapping her head in Lili's direction.

"In the resting chamber," Lili answered.

"No!" Lorilei breathed. She looked around, confirming what Lili had said. She was in a medium-sized room decorated in pastels and littered with numerous pillows of varying size. It had a single door, which was closed.

"No," Lorilei repeated as her heart fell.

"Don't be afraid," Lili said, fighting to suppress the panic that Lorilei was empathically inundating her with. "The mistress is a kind woman."

Lorilei's eyes widened with terror. She stood, and then ran towards the door. She franticly grabbed at the knob that wouldn't turn.

"You just got here," Lili said, starting to be overcome by Lorilei's panic. She could sense that Lorilei was about to scream. "Please don't, that will make Mistress angry."

Lorilei screamed. "Let me out!" she shrieked as she banged on the door.

"You're going to make her angry!" Lili insisted distraughtly, but it was too late, the knob began to turn.

Lorilei prepared for it to open; as soon as it did she slammed her body against it, violently thrusting it open. On the other side stood a tall thin woman with a displeased look on her face.

"I told her not to!" Lili cried out in fear. The woman paid Lili no attention, focusing on Lorilei.

"Stand back," the woman calmly commanded.

Lorilei ignored her and tried to run past, but the women caught her by the arm and dragged her back into the room. Lorilei tried to change the texture of her arm to defend herself, but she was immediately thwarted by a stabbing pain from within her head. The woman thrust Lorilei to the floor then closed the door behind her.

"I'm sorry!" Lili cried out.

"Shut up!" the woman barked before turning her attention back to Lorilei. Lili slunk to the opposite side of the chamber and found a large pillow to cower under while she cried.

Lorilei stood back on her feet, trying to figure out how to escape.

"Let me go!" she yelled at the woman.

"After what I just paid for you," she laughed. "I think not."

"I'm freed, you have to let me go!" Lorilei demanded.

"Freed?" The woman frowned. "You've got spirit. That's going to be annoying. Let's have a look at you now that you're awake."

"No," Lorilei yelled. "You let me go right now!"

The woman's eyes grew large with anger and her hand delved into a pants pocket. From the pocket she retrieved a small device with a myriad of buttons on it and pressed one. From around Lorilei's neck stirred an intense burning pain that quickly spread to her head, causing her vision to blur and her muscles to tense. One of her legs gave way and she fell on its knee. She placed a hand on the ground to catch herself before she fell completely. Convinced that she had made her point, the woman stood over Lorilei and explained.

"You are not going to escape. You are going to do as I say. The only reason I haven't put you to work yet is because that basterd Ellis didn't know whether or not you've had your shots. So you will behave yourself until I can rectify that. Now take off that silly dress, or I will rip it off you as you cringe in pain from your collar." The woman let go the button and Lorilei caught her breath. "Do we understand each other?" the woman asked pointedly.

"Yes," Lorilei whimpered.

Victoria

"I got nothing to do with this!" Liz begged. Thorbin held her with one hand by her throat while the other pressed his pistol firmly against her forehead.

"Then I got no use for you," he growled as he pulled back the hammer. Liz watched frightened as the carriage revolved and she saw the round that was about to go through her head slide in line with the barrel.

"Motherfucker!" Ben yelled from behind them as he entered the bay from the main hallway with Sam trailing behind.

"Ben we can fix it!" she insisted.

"I fixed the damn thing last week."

"Captain!" Sariel answered in full battle gear. "My weapon please, I will retrieve the device." And with that, everyone began angrily voicing their opinions about priorities and plans all at the same time.

"Now hold on," Ben spoke with authority, getting everyone's attention. "We don't even have a full picture of what's going on," he said, trying to organize the chaos, but before he could continue, the door of the bathroom unit flew open and smacked against the wall, diverting everyone's attention in that direction.

Tank slowly emerged from the bathroom unit wearing his patched up pants and dripping from head to toe. Everyone watched as he exited then stood erect and stretched his massive arms infinitely upward. As he brought them back down he flexed his fingers as if summoning power to them, and the muscles in his forearms twitched alive. His head swayed from side to side as he cleared his mind and began looking for something to wear so he wouldn't be bare-chested for what was coming next. He spied the trench coat, approached it, tore off the arms then squeezed into it.

Everyone kept a respectful distance as their eyes followed him around the back of the bathroom unit to the weapons locker. Ben fumbled in his pocket for his keys, but Tank didn't ask. He simply placed a hand on top of the lid and the other around the lock and pulled. His pale face flushed red as the green container creaked metallically in pain and the latch gave way. He flipped the lid up, reached in the box and pulled out Ben's shotgun. Thorbin noted Tank wasn't smiling; shotguns were the sort of thing that usually made Tank smile. Instead he looked calculating.

"What's the plan?" Thorbin asked cautiously. Tank answered with a quiet determination that even caused Sariel to take pause.

"I'm going to find Lorilei, kill every pirate I see," he paused. "Then maybe get the device." He walked to a mule and slung a leg over it. The bike sank as he sat on it.

"Tank," Sam said, approaching him with concern. "You're in no condition..." she started to say, but she was interrupted by a gentle look from Tank that was like a calm before the storm.

"I may not want to live," he said softly, "but now I have a reason not to die." And with that Tank headed out into the hallowed recesses of Kenton's Crypt.

"Sariel," Thorbin said, addressing the mercenary. "Follow him."

Sariel looked at Ben, who nodded, and then he mounted his own mule and went after Tank.

Thorbin went to the weapons locker and began procuring his own gear. Ben stood over his shoulder.

"So where we goin'?" he asked.

"You're not going anywhere," Thorbin responded. "You and Sam need to stay here and get Victoria patched up. I don't think Tank is going to find Lorilei or the device, but he *is* going to kill a lot of pirates. I'm going to try and get Lorilei and the device back before he brings the whole rock down around us."

"By yourself?" Ben said astutely.

"I don't really have a choice, do I?" Thorbin responded.

"You do," Liz said from her confines. They both looked over at her. "Take me with you."

"That's a great idea," Thorbin said sarcastically.

"I'm the best there is when it comes to finding things that people don't want found."

Thorbin considered for a moment then reached into his pocket for the cuff key.

Lorilei

"Why not try it on?" Lili asked, looking up at Lorilei from the pillow that had been placed on Lorilei's lap for Lili to rest her head on. Lorilei took a generous bite out of apple they were sharing and swallowed.

"I prefer to be naked," which she was, "than ever wear anything like that again," she answered, scowling at the pink under things the mistress had left behind after confiscating her sundress.

"I think it would look cute on you," Lili said, hoping to convince Lorilei not to be defiant. Lorilei smiled at Lili and offered her a bite of apple, which she accepted.

Lorilei's defiance and panic, along with the mistress's rage, had frightened Lili something awful. So Lorilei had suggested Lili rest her head so that she could stroke her lovely brown hair and tell her everything was going to be all right. She didn't tell her so much as she envisioned it. Mosot found it much more effective to communicate empathically with feelings and mental pictures, vocalizing only in a supplemental way.

As Lili calmed down Lorilei considered her and pitied her a little. She was a sweet girl, eager to do her owner's bidding, and she wanted nothing more than to be safe and feel reassured. In truth, Lorilei saw herself in Lili and was disgusted. She thought about this in the privacy of her own mind. But being Mosot Lorilei wasn't privy to private thought while Lili was around.

Lili responded by painting a picture of how happy she was here because she was safe and the mistress treated her well.

"It only hurts when we misbehave. So we don't and it's good here."

Lili told Lorilei about some of her favorite regular customers and about Kryst, another Mosot that lived there as well.

Lorilei rebutted Lili's perception of 'good here' with her own, showing Lili Victoria and trying vainly to advocate that Victoria was a far better place than with the mistress. Lili didn't agree. Victoria seemed like a dirty scary place. Ben seemed very mean, and while Lorilei embellished a little when envisioning Thorbin, Lili didn't understand why they weren't sleeping together. Lili was, however, very interested in meeting Spot, and while the idea of not having to wear her collar seemed foreign, it had a certain appeal. Still, it didn't sound safer than with her mistress. In the end, all they could agree on was that they were happy to meet each other.

A short while later Kryst entered the room, another typically ravishing Mosot with black hair and pretty gray eyes.

"Who's this?" Kryst said, excited at seeing Lorilei.

"This is Lorilei," Lili introduced, eager to do so.

Kryst ran over to Lorilei and threw her arms around her. "It's so nice to meet you! It's going to be so much fun having a new friend."

"It's nice to meet you too," Lorilei said with a smile. Despite being in such a terrible place Lili and Kyrst's affections were very comforting.

"How did it go?" Lili asked Kryst, looking up at her from the pillow.

"Fine. It was Mr. Feeday," Kryst answered from around Lorilei's neck.

"Really? But he usually comes at the end of the week."

"Usually, no matter, it's always nice to spend time with him."

"Mr. Feeday is another regular I didn't tell you about," Lili told Lorilei. "He's nice man." Then Lili painted a mental picture for her. In it Mr. Feeday looked to be a kindly old man. "We always have fun," she said. The picture changed showing Lili bent over the man's lap happily receiving a spanking.

Lorilei frowned.

"He doesn't spank hard," Lili assured. "You'll see."

"I don't want to be spanked," Lorilei clarified.

"Oh really?" Lili said with a mischievous smile then changed the participants in the picture to Lorilei and Thorbin.

"Stop it," Lorilei said, embarrassed.

"Who's Thorbin?" Kryst asked, and Lorilei began to tell Kryst about Victoria.

Tank and Sariel

Sariel had eventually caught up with Tank and informed that he had been ordered to follow. Tank didn't really care as long as Sariel didn't get in the way or try to steal any of his kills.

The two of them sat silently in the shadow of a crevice set in a rock wall that overlooked a very large crater. In the crater was a pirate encampment, an old production facility that they had commandeered. Near the center was a control tower several stories high. Around the tower were warehouses and other smaller buildings. And throughout the whole complex were little pirate-shaped targets that Sariel and Tank were considering.

"If I get down to that there building," Tank said, pointing to one of the buildings on the perimeter. "You could start picking them off from up here. The first few will never see me coming. After that the rest will be screwed."

"Hmm," Sariel considered. "That's a fine plan," he said with tact in order to lessen the impact of his oncoming criticism.

"But?" Tank said, not really wanting Sariel's input.

"It allows a means of escape," Sariel answered. "You're assuming that they won't flee, but I think they will. We would be giving them an easy way out from the other side of their camp."

"You're right," Tank said, appreciating Sariel's logic. "There's only a few dozen down there. It will only be a matter of time before they start shitting their pants and try to puss out."

"I think I can get to the other side of the encampment without being noticed," Sariel said after some consideration. "If you wait here, we can attack from both sides. That will decrease their options for retreat."

"We won't be able to communicate. We'll need a more thorough plan."

"Yes," Sariel agreed.

"I'd be willing to bet that whoever is in charge is in that there tower."

"Agreed," Sariel answered.

"If you get over by them buildings," Tank said, pointing to the far side of the encampment. "And I start here. Then we can work our way towards the center. A few might still get away, but if we move quick like, we should get to the tower before the big fish gets away."

"Good," Sariel confirmed as he readied himself to move out.

"How will I know when you're ready?" Tank asked as Sariel started to head to his position.

"I'll send you a signal."

"What kind of signal?"

"A big one," Sariel assured then headed out.

Thorbin and Liz

Thorbin and Liz parked their mules outside a building in what looked like the main square for this floor. Ben had suggested this location as a good place to start. Liz dismounted gracefully by swinging a leg around the mount then sliding off, landing firmly on the ground. Thorbin began to dismount.

"You stay here," he said.

"You stay here," she mocked sarcastically. "You forget, I'm going in."

Thorbin looked at her dismayed.

"Easy, cowboy, you better let me handle this one," she said then stretched a bit by rotating her shoulders.

"Why would I stay here?" he asked.

"You couldn't look more like a cop if you tried," she said, smiling at him.

"Your point?" he asked.

"You already scared off half of our leads just by being here. If you go in there, the other half will be gone before the door closes behind you." She winked at him. "So you just stay here and look 'rugged', and I'll go find out where Lorilei and my device are hiding."

Thorbin leaned back on his mule and crossed his arms. "You're not going in there alone," he insisted.

"I'm not Lorilei," Liz said as she began to adjust her cleavage. "I don't need your protection."

"I'm not worried about your protection," he said. "Let me be clear. I don't trust you."

Liz stopped in mid adjustment. "Funny," she began, speaking to herself. "My father used to say the same thing." Then she turned to Thorbin, presenting her properly aligned cleavage. "Do they make you feel like talking?" she asked.

"What?"

"Oh never mind," she said, leaning over the mule so she could see her reflection in the glossy paint job. "I prefer to have more than two tricks up my sleeve, but I only got the two," she explained. "Isn't that right, girls." She smiled at the reflection. Then standing erect she addressed Thorbin again. "If you'll kindly allow me to borrow your pistol."

"I thought you didn't need my protection?"

"I don't," she clarified. "I just need your piece."

"That *would be* my protection," he clarified. "Looks like you're just going to have to be a one-trick pony."

"Fine," she said pointedly. "You just keep that mule ready in case they lack the ability to be charmed."

Thorbin watched as she turned around and swaggered towards the entrance.

Ben and Sam

"Ah damn it all to Hell," Ben said furiously while standing in the cargo bay reading a diagnostic on his PJU. "We got stress fissures all over the place."

"At least Vicky didn't break in half when she landed," Sam said, trying to get him to look at the bright side of a dim situation. She was adjusting the pressure on a tool she was about to use to reinforce the fissures Ben was complaining about.

"The damn AC invertors are out of alignment again too," he said with a frown. That was a direct hit to Sam's patience.

"I just fixed those."

"I know," he said.

"It took me five hours," she said disgustedly as she powered on the tool.

"At least we won't need them to get off this rock," he said, now it was his turn to show her the bright side.

"How many fissures do we have?" Sam asked, starting to seal one up.

"Twenty-six in the cargo bay, five in the kitchen, eighty-two outside," he said as he rummaged through a toolbox.

"Will the spyder be able to repair the ones on the outside soon enough?" Sam asked.

"No, I'm going to have to do it myself. Tommy's working on the starboard thruster again."

"Tommy?" Sam said. "You named your spyder? You never told me that before."

Ben sighed. "I didn't name the damn thing. Lorilei did."

"Oh," Sam said sympathetically.

"I hope she's OK."

"Yeah," Sam agreed. "She'd be able to help me with those AC inverters."

"Yeah," Ben said solemnly, looking into a full toolbox as if it was empty.

"Thorbin is going to find her, Ben," Sam said, hoping she was right.

Without another word Ben went into the bathroom, later returning with a candle in his hand. He took it over to a card table next to the container Jessica was in and lit it.

"The last time I seen her, I yelled."

Thorbin and Liz

Thorbin waited outside the building for what seemed an eternity. He had contemplated that Liz may have given him the slip, or that maybe she was in trouble and couldn't signal him. He hated just sitting out there waiting. He wanted to barge right in and tell everyone to keep their hands where he could see them. His imagination was running away with him about all the terrible things that might be happening to Lorilei, and he was just sitting there – dependent on Liz of all people. She was right of course. He wouldn't be able to get a bit of information out of anyone in any kind of effective way. Sure, he'd get one person to talk after a lot of effort, but they would probably be the wrong person. Meanwhile, the right person with the right information would be long gone.

Thorbin's thoughts were shattered as a man exited the building via a window, as opposed to the traditional way. The man landed on the ground face first in a way that he would probably later regret. Shortly after, Liz and the girls came flailing out of the proper egress in a tremendous hurry. On her heels was the source of their discontent – three apparently excitable lads that clearly thought Liz was leaving much too soon.

Thorbin turned on the mule and drifted in Liz's direction. By the time they met, one of the men had nearly caught her. Thorbin reached a hand out, ready to pull her on board at the same time the man caught hold of the back of Liz's shirt.

"He can't come," Thorbin told her as he drew his pistol. Liz spun around, knocking the man's hand away with hers as she turned. Then with power and grace she kicked the inside of the man's knee. The knee gave way and the man fell. The other two men, who were quickly closing in, were encouraged not to interfere by Thorbin's revolver.

"Time to go," Thorbin instructed.

"Hold on," Liz managed to respond despite being winded. She placed her hands on the back of the man's head and thrust down as she shot her knee up. Liz was mounted behind Thorbin before the man finished collapsing. She threw her arms around Thorbin's waist and hung on as he kicked the mule into gear and sped off.

Lorilei

"You fix things?" Lili said, excitedly curious.

"Yes. I can fix all kinds of stuff," Lorilei said happily. She had of course exaggerated how proficient she was, but, nonetheless, she had learned quite a bit about electronics and mechanics.

"I would love to learn how to fix things," Lili said, daydreaming. She empathically projected that daydream to the others. She painted a sweet picture of herself in overalls like the ones Lorilei had described Sam wearing, only on Lili it didn't look like work apparel. She imagined herself repairing a console by brutalizing the screen with a mallet. Lorilei laughed.

"That's how Ben fixes things sometimes, except you forgot to curse."

"Ben," Kryst said, painting a picture of him in her mind and inserting herself into the scene hugging him graciously.

"Ben's gonna love you guys," Lorilei said, losing all sense of reality.

"I'll bet I could get Thorbin to sleep with me," Kryst interjected. Then she changed Ben's character in the dream-let to Lorilei's representation of Thorbin. Lorilei had exaggerated most in her description of Thorbin. She had rebuilt his image in their minds the way she saw him – a dashing prince charming type, larger and taller than he really was. While he was a handsome man, the picture she painted for Lili and Kryst was more like something you'd see on the cover of a romance novel, Lorilei, of course, always painted herself buxomly flowing from his arms. Kryst's declaration of her prowess in thinking she could bed him made Lorilei laugh.

"Good luck."

Kryst smiled, now she was the comely maiden painted into Thorbin's arms being kissed passionately. Lorilei's mirth melted away.

"Oh I'm sorry," Kryst said, sensing she had vexed Lorilei. "I didn't mean anything by it."

"That's OK," Lorilei conceded. She let it go, not wanting to disrupt the momentum she had built.

"Let's see," she continued, trying to come up with a scene that would further her cause. Then she smiled as a wonderful idea came to her. She had been attempting to sell Victoria as a wonderful place where they could be free and independent. She had forgotten how unnerving the discovery of independence had been for her. And in reality, it was still unsettling. For a moment she lost focus and wondered if independence ever stopped feeling lonely.

"What?" Lili asked, not understanding Lorilei's thoughts.

Lili's question refocused Lorilei and affirmed her idea. Explaining independence would have to wait until they got back on Victoria. For now she would play to the audience.

She cleared the canvas of their minds and began to draw the bathtub. She filled it to the top with bubbles and inviting warm water. Steamed up the tiles and mirrors with condensation, and there, in the tub, she placed Tank. She omitted a few scares and made sure his hair was neat and his face clean-shaven. Lili and Kryst were being mesmerized by the picture. Lorilei kept painting Tank the way she saw him, a playful and gentle giant with a large warm smile, a big kind heart, and a healthy appetite for lovin', a huge beast of a man more than capable of looking after the wanton pair. Then, when she felt their interest and curiosity was peaked, she plopped the two of them right into his arms. She had hit the mark dead on. Lili and Kryst giggled as they took control of the daydream Lorilei had constructed for them. Soon the imaginary three were frolicking in the tub and Lili and Kryst were sold. Tank seemed to be all the fun they could stand and all the protector they could ever need.

Lorilei conceded that playing into their tendencies in this way wouldn't help them better understand independence, but she had to start somewhere. The concept was still murky at best for her, although being around them cleared it up a lot.

Being around Lili and Kryst had also cleared up something else for her. A feeling she had felt in Thorbin that she wanted desperately from him, a sense of purpose. Thorbin had clarity, especially after they had found the device. When she had been set free from captivity, she had lost all sense of purpose in her life. She didn't know where she fit in. Being with Lili and Kryst was affirming to her, in the sense that she was sure where she didn't belong. And now she knew, that meant there was somewhere that she did belong. Lorilei smiled.

The door to the rest chamber creaked open and the mistress entered with a fat slob of a man close behind her. The woman took notice that Lorilei hadn't donned her uniform.

"Why haven't you dressed yourself yet?" she asked, angry at Lorilei's defiance.

"I'm not going to wear that," Lorilei said, glaring at the woman. "You might as well give me back my dress."

The woman reached into her pocket and Lorilei held her breath anxiously but didn't show any sign of backing down.

"I don't mind," the unkempt man said, gawking at her breasts. "I'll take her."

Lorilei felt dirty and grabbed a few extra pillows to cover herself.

"Unfortunately, she's not available today," the woman said.

Lorilei could sense the evil woman was truly disappointed that she couldn't let this man defile her. "But Lili and Kryst would be eager to please you, isn't that right, ladies?" she continued. In reality she was commanding, and Lili and Kryst jumped to the height specified. They rose from their seats on the pillows and embraced the creepy man, feigning perfect delight. "This is Mr. Kine, girls. If you're real nice to him, he may come and visit you often. How does that sound?" the woman said, smiling to the ugly man, who was enthralled with the affection Lili and Kryst were thickly laying on him.

"That sounds great!" Lili said, inwardly gagging at the idea.

"He's so handsome," Kryst followed up, kissing him on the cheek. The man began to breathe heavily and Kryst got a glimpse of what he wanted. She pulled her hands from around him and took a step back.

"We don't have to do that," Kryst said.

Lili hadn't caught on and was afraid that Kryst was about to be punished for acting poorly in front of a perspective regular client. The hideous man indeed was frowning.

"Oh of course we do," Lili said, hoping that she was recovering for Kryst so the mistress wouldn't punish her.

The woman eyed Kryst, at first she thought about chastising her. She figured Lorilei had been a bad influence, but of the two of them Kryst was the better behaved.

"What are you talking about?" the woman asked Kryst.

"He wants to hit during sex. We don't do that."

"This one says she does," the man rebutted, putting his arms around Lili so she couldn't get away.

"No," the mistress said. "No, I can't have that."

"I'll pay extra," the man said, afraid that he wasn't going to get his way.

"Lili is a good earner. On a good day she makes me fifteen thousand. I simply can't allow it. She'd be no good to me for a week. My regulars don't want a bruised-up girl."

"A week," the man said, disappointed, then considered for a moment. "That's a hundred and five thousand. I'll pay that much."

The mistress's eyes grew large with greed, but she quickly caught herself.

"I don't know," she said in a wheeling and dealing sort of way.

The man look frustrated. "Come on that's more than fair."

"I don't think I can allow it," she said, holding firm.

The man inhaled. "OK. One fifty. But that's it."

"Done," the mistress said, satisfied with her haggling skills. That was a good chunk of what she paid for Lorilei, who would be available in a few days at most. "Lili would be happy to please you. Isn't that right, Lili?" the mistress said, commanding the girl to play along.

Lili was terrified and speechless. She didn't dare defy, but she was too frightened to speak.

The man looked down at her with a yellow grin.

"It's OK," he said. "You don't have to pretend to like it. It's better if you don't."

"No!" Lili cried out as the monster led her out the door with the mistress right behind them.

Kryst flew into Lorilei's arms and began to weep for Lili. In moments it began, and they could sense Lili's panic through the walls. They could feel every terrible hopeless moment. Lorilei would have described what she felt happening to Lili as inhuman, if she hadn't known better. The sharp pain on skin as clothes were torn and ripped, the desperation of being forced into position. They could feel the sting of being slapped in the face, then the breasts, then between her legs. They felt Lili's hope disappear as he prepared himself, and with a terrified scream her empathy went silent.

"What happened?" Kryst asked, sobbing. She feared the empathic silence meant Lili was dying. Kryst focused, trying her best to reconnect with Lili.

"No," Lorilei said. "It's better this way, she just went somewhere else. She'll be back." Her lavender eyes began to well deeply.

"She didn't go anywhere!" Kryst said, beginning to argue.

Lorilei put a finger on Kryst's mouth. "Shh," she said. "Don't make her come back."

Chapter Twenty-One
Kinda Like Good Guys

Ellis sat comfortably in a circular glass room atop a control tower that overlooked an old mining facility, which was a large complex nestled in the center of a crater. He sat at a table opposite the pirate lord he had come to see.

The man wore an eye patch, which was odd; as far as Ellis knew both of his eyes functioned fine. No matter, the man's fashion choices were of no concern to him. All Ellis was interested in was the large sum of money he had in a shoulder bag sitting on his lap. Their business was done and Ellis was waiting to be excused. Normally Ellis wasn't concerned with being polite, but the pirate lord had a small army and wasn't a person with whom to be short. So Ellis politely and patiently honored the man sitting across the table. The pirate was amused at the tale Ellis had regaled him with and wouldn't let it go.

"I can't believe that they actually brought you here with both pieces of the weapon," the pirate said.

"I know, it's amazing," Ellis said with a smile. "I thought for sure when they killed my crew that I was screwed."

"Here's what I don't get," the man said, leaning back in his chair and unwrapping a pack of cigarettes. "How did you know that you'd wake up before anyone else?"

"Ah well, normally I wouldn't say anything about the gas, I use it as a last resort. But since I'm already rich from selling their little slut, and what you've paid me for the weapon, I'll indulge."

"You're gracious," the pirate replied.

"You see, being the type of person I am can cause sleeping to be difficult at times. I've been using a pill form of the stuff for years now to help me sleep at night. I've built up a tolerance."

The pirate laughed heartily. Then lit his cigarette. "They killed your crew, and you had them all asleep, and you didn't kill them?"

"I wanted to," Ellis answered. "But business before pleasure. All in all I stood to make a mint. That can buy a lot of vengeance," Ellis said as he petted the pack on his lap. "To be honest, what I really wanted to do was to have a go at the Mosot before I sold her."

"You didn't?" the pirate said, admiring Ellis's apparent focus.

"A mint," Ellis reiterated. "Hell, if I want too, I could go back there and buy her back."

"Is that the plan then?" the man asked with a smoky exhale.

"Nah," Ellis said with a causal wave of his hand. "I'll get one later, she was kind of a pain in ass anyway."

The pirate stood and walked to a cabinet. He opened it and grabbed a bottle of whiskey and two glasses. He set the glasses on the table and opened the bottle.

"Really I can't," Ellis said, risking offense.

"Eighteen years," the pirate said. "This isn't being made anymore. You would refuse my hospitality?"

"Oh no," Ellis said, backpedaling. "It's just…I still have a lot of business to conduct."

"What business?" the pirate said indigently. "You have another multimillion transaction you have to get to? Do you know what this device means to me? I am now the most powerful man in the solar system. My whiskey isn't good enough for you?"

"I meant no offense. Please," Ellis said, trying to figure out how he was going to get himself out of this one. "Forgive my arrogance. I'm tired and not thinking straight. You are the only man I need to talk to."

The pirate didn't respond.

"I need a ship, and a crew. I don't know why it didn't occur to me to ask you." Ellis did know why. He hated dealing with pirates and didn't like to deal with anyone who knew how much money he had to offer. The only reason he was here was because this man was the highest bidder. But now, finding himself in need of pacifying the situation, he offered the pirate something he wanted. Money, the pirate had just given him a big chunk of change and would love to get some back.

"You're right, you are stupid, I have access to the best ships for sale in the Crypt." Then he poured the glasses and was about to berate Ellis further when his eye patch started speaking.

"Sir, we have intruders!" a panicked voice reported through the patch. "I think we're being invaded."

"What?" the pirate asked. "Who the hell would invade us?"

"I…" the voice began but went silent at the same time a tower-shaking explosion erupted in the north section of the complex.

Ellis and the pirate stood and ran to a north-facing window. One of the exterior buildings in the compound was engulfed in flames. A dozen of the pirate lord's men were franticly firing at a target the two men couldn't see. They watched as one by one the pirates fell to the unseen assailant.

"Sir!" the patch cried out again. "They're attacking from the south as well."

Ellis and the pirate lord moved to a southern window. They could see another dozen or so pirates scrambling in a frenzy around the buildings. They looked lost.

"South guard, what the hell are you doing?" the pirate lord asked.

One of the distant figures, who was standing on a rooftop, turned and looked towards the tower, then waved a hand at them. "They're around here somewhere. We can't find them."

Ellis squinted his eyes to look at the man and noticed a rather large figure climbing up on the roof behind him. The figure was massive, and once on the roof, it closed the distance quickly to its victim. Ellis watched as the figure heaved the pirate off his feet and flung him off the roof to the ground below.

"This is north gate!" the patch cried out. "We need reinfor...." The broadcast went silent.

Ellis and the pirate turned their attention back through the north window. A great number of pirates were converging cautiously on one of the larger buildings below.

"Hold your position, north gate," the pirate lord commanded. Then he closed his un-patched eye and set two fingers on his temple. The pirates below stopped their advance and took cover. After a few seconds the pirate lord continued his commands. "There's only one, and he's in the building. North gate, charge in there and kill him now."

"Aye!" the patch responded and they watched as all the pirates who had stopped and taken cover dashed madly towards the closest entrance to the building. There was a minute of silent inactivity then the building flicked from within with small arms fire as windows burst and walls were pierced. Suddenly the gunfire ceased. Not long after, one of the pirates exited from a door facing the tower and waved up to them.

"You see, Ellis, not to worry, they got him. North gate report," he commanded, but there was silence. They watched as the pirate below smacked the top of his head, indicating that his gear wasn't working. Then his chest exploded and he fell to the ground. From out of the very same door he had exited appeared a dark ghostlike figure that seemed to float as it moved towards the center of the complex.

"Shit!" Ellis said. "It's the mercenary. He's a corporate merc."

"All men," the pirate lord commanded with this news. "Fall back to the tower and take defensive positions."

"Hey there," a strange large sounding voice said from the patch. "Did I hear ya right? Did you say Ellis was up in that there tower?"

"Who is this?" the pirate lord demanded.

The voice on the other end laughed. "Hey, Ellis," it said. "Do you have any friends that aren't easy to kill?"

The two men moved back to the south window. There in plain sight the large figure slowly ambled down a main path towards the tower dragging a dead pirate along with him by the foot. "Tell you what," the voice said, "if you tell me where Lorilei is, I won't make you eat your own asshole."

Ellis became nervous. "How do we get out of here?" he asked the pirate lord, who had moved back to observe the north window.

"Don't let him shake you. They're not getting in here."

"My ass they're not getting in here," Ellis said, starting to panic. "How the hell are we gonna escape them."

"There's only the two of them. I have over fifty men down there." The pirate watched as the dark ghost paused in an open area. "What's he doing?" the pirate lord said, almost amused. Ellis stood next to him and looked down at Sariel.

"He's up to something," Ellis answered.

"What?" the pirate asked. Then the glass shattered and the pirate's headless body fell to the ground.

Lorilei

Lorilei and Kryst sat together, silently watching over Lili. She had returned to the chamber a while ago bruised and bleeding. She didn't say a word. She wasn't crying. She just limped to the nearest large pillow and lay on it. Lorilei slowly approached and put a comforting hand on her shoulder. Lili shifted and pulled her shoulder away from Lorilei's touch.

"Sorry," Lorilei said, trying to probe into Lili's mind, but it was still blank, she hadn't returned yet. Lorilei was all too familiar with this scenario. She knew Lili had to be brought back. Her body would heal; her mind, however, may not if she stayed gone. She'd seen others of her kind die from less emotional trauma. At best, Lili would be scared for life. Distraught with concern Lorilei crossed her arms and stood over her.

Kryst was silently reading the mental picture Lorilei was unintentionally drawing.

"We've been together our whole lives," she said mournfully.

"She's still with us," Lorilei said unconvinced. "Maybe you could bring her back," she said, turning towards Kryst with an outstretched arm. Kryst stood and accepted her hand.

"What should I do?"

"Give her a reason to come back, something that's greater than the hurt."

Kryst sat next to Lili. "Lili," she probed softly. "I love you."

Lili responded by digging her head further into the pillow and towards her chest. Kryst looked up at Lorilei, who motioned to keep at it.

"Come back to me, Lili," Kryst pleaded with a whisper and a tear. "I don't know what I'd do without you."

Lorilei felt Lili's presence return like a timid breeze. She took a deep breath, relieved that maybe Lili wasn't going to be lost.

"Lili," Lorilei interjected at the risk of causing her to withdraw. "You're going to be all right."

Lili began to sob softly, and Kryst put a comforting arm around her. Lorilei felt the subtle breeze turn warm with hope as Lili softly spoke.

"I hope Thorbin comes to rescue us soon."

"Me too," Kryst said, glad that her dear friend seemed to be recovering. Then Kryst turned her head back and faced Lorilei. "Do you think he'll rescue us soon?"

"I don't know," Lorilei said. Her brow wrinkled as she began to build up enough strength for the three of them. "I think maybe we may just have to rescue ourselves."

Thorbin and Liz

Thorbin and Liz tore down a stone highway at a blistering pace with a pair of pursuers hot on their tails.

"I thought you said you could lose them!" Liz accused, holding on to Thorbin firmly as she looked back at the two men chasing them.

"I'm trying," he answered calmly as he quickly banked right into a smaller roadway. The pursuers matched them perfectly.

"Still there!" she reported. "I think they might be gaining!"

Damn! They're good, Thorbin thought to himself. Then he heard shots ring out and felt a round fly past his head. The near miss almost caused him to jerk his mule to the side, but he was able to keep focused.

Liz's hands raked across his stomach then inspected his belt from buckle to hips.

"Where the hell is your gun? They're shooting at us!" she said, franticly searching.

"Under the left shoulder!" he yelled back as he tore down another passage to the left.

Liz lifted herself from her seat and reached an arm around his neck and under his left shoulder. With a fluid motion she seated herself and took aim behind. Another round of shots flew past them as Liz tried to orientate herself to fire back. She couldn't aim properly with her torso awkwardly twisted. Sparks erupted off the mule as their pursuers shots were truer.

"I can't get a good shot off!" she yelled in frustration. "Hang on!" she told him.

"Hang on?" he said as he felt Liz's weight shift behind him. Her left hand slid across his belt to his right hip. Then she forced her fingers between his belt and pants and into this right pocket, where she grabbed a handful of material and pinched a little skin.

"Ow!" he cried out. "What are you doing?"

"Hang on!" she commanded. With her arm anchored, she swung her left leg under her and sat on the back of the mule sidesaddle, leaning into to Thorbin's back. A moment later Thorbin heard his Magnum's thunder followed by the sound of a nasty mule crash.

"Got one!" Liz cried out in victory.

Their mule charged onward and the passage ahead opened up onto a deserted highway. The riders cut a swath of dust down the old road as they lurched into high gear. Thorbin and the pursuing rider banked wildly around rusty debris as the man and Liz exchanged fire. Up ahead a wall of abandoned garbage was quickly approaching, threatening to slow them down. It didn't look impenetrable, but it didn't look inviting either. Large pieces of cut-up ships and parted-out industrial machinery were stacked atop each other in some senseless order. As Thorbin screamed towards it he noticed a few openings that appeared to be large enough for their mule to enter. Where they led, however, was a complete mystery.

"Why are you slowing down?" Liz yelled at him as she fired off another shot that missed their pursuer but did cause him to bank sharply behind some abandoned containers.

"End of the road," Thorbin answered. He looked at all the entrances that led into the garbage heap and picked two that seemed the best. "Left or right?" he said, decelerating more.

Liz still had her eye in the general area she had last seen their pursuer; behind and to the left.

"Right," she answered, and with her answer Thorbin leaned right and entered the debris.

On the other side of the entrance were messy rows of crushed and whole machinery stacked on top of each other. Thorbin picked a path that led between the rows and rode down it as fast as he could. The row turned subtly to the left and reached a point where it branched out. Thorbin picked the left branch to be inconsistent if their pursuer had seen them enter. Before long the new path branched, then branched yet again. After a while Thorbin was sure their pursuer had no idea where they were because he had no idea where they were. He slowed down to a coast and the mule's turbine quieted to a gentle hum, allowing them to take in the full ambiance of the dump they were now lost in.

A dirty wind whistled softly through the refuse as they intently listened for the other rider's turbine. The rows of junk creaked angrily at them for disturbing their peace, but the pursuer's turbine seemed to be silent. Thorbin cautiously approached a four-way intersection in the trash. He stopped and considered for a moment.

"If he followed us in here," he whispered to Liz, "we might be able to get out without being noticed."

Liz caught on to the thought and whispered her reply. "By the time he heard us leaving it'd be too late. He'd have to find his way out, and we'd be long gone."

"So which way leads back?" Thorbin whispered, looking down the three new paths.

"Maybe that way?" Liz said, pointing to the left.

Thorbin turned the mule and traveled slowly, assuring that the noise from the turbine never exceeded the noise of the wind. The row slowly slid by as they listened intently for any sign of their pursuer. At every intersection they stopped and cautiously looked down all possible paths for danger and the best way out.

Suddenly from the right they heard a rusty crash as one of the distant rows gave way. Then from the same vicinity they heard their pursuer curse loudly.

"Where the hell did you go?"

Thorbin smiled. The man was his equal in piloting a mule but apparently had very little patience. They continued forward silently.

After a short while they heard another smaller crash just ahead of them.

"How did he get up there?" Liz whispered.

Thorbin shrugged. The next chance he got he would turn left. Then there was another small crash far to their right.

"Those two couldn't have been the same guy," Liz observed.

Thorbin frowned. "Maybe he got back up?" Then from above a small piece of debris sailed by and crashed into one of the rows hidden on their left.

"It's still just him. He's trying to flush us out. He's definitely to our right."

Thorbin nodded in agreement and slowly eased the mule forward. Painstakingly slow they came to one intersection after another and made their best guesses as to which path to take. All the while their pursuer kept throwing debris in hopes of flushing them out. Now and then Liz would throw a piece herself, just to mess with his head.

Thorbin cautiously approached another four-way junction. He had got into the habit of leaning forward over the handlebars to peak around the corners before proceeding. Liz, tense with the suspense of it all, would also lean forward to see, but Thorbin would always sit back before she could see anything.

This intersection was no different. Thorbin slowly slid the mule forward and leaned over with Liz pressed against his back like a child who wanted to see too. He looked down the right passage and quickly leaned back, frantically reversing the mule.

"What?" Liz whispered.

"Pistol," Thorbin whispered and held his hand over his shoulder. Liz handed him the firearm. "Hang on," he told her as he cocked the hammer and aimed it towards the path to the right. Liz nervously tightened her hold around his waist and felt him take a deep preparatory breath. Thorbin gently kicked the mule into gear.

As they went across the intersection Liz grabbed onto Thorbin's belt with both hands as she saw what he had. Their pursuer was slowly traveling down the row with his back to them. Thorbin stopped the mule and reached his left hand over to hold the pistol firmly as he aimed. He closed one eye, exhaled, held his breath, and just then the man began to turn in their direction. Thorbin smiled at him and the man's eyes widened in shock and fear – he knew he was done for. Thorbin squeezed the trigger.

Click! was sound the hammer made as it struck a previously spent round. Thorbin's eyes widened in disbelief and the man smiled.

Thorbin kicked the mule into gear and paid no attention to the sound of the turbine. Liz gripped tightly as the garbage rows went from well-defined refuse to blurry gray streaks around them. The chase was on again and they hadn't made it out yet. Thorbin managed to stay one turn ahead of the man, exposing them only for a second or two as they headed around the next turn while the man bent the previous one. Each time he would take a shot at them.

Thorbin found himself blazing down a particularly long row. He heard shots from behind and banked from side to side to be a more difficult target. He saw a right intersection ahead and turned hard into it as the man fired another desperate shot at them. Shortly after there was another intersection and Thorbin turned left down it. Soon he had lost the man again and decided to quiet the turbine once more. They heard the other mule overshoot them on a parallel row before slowing down and going silent.

"Damn it!" the man yelled out.

Thorbin slowly made a three-point turn to silently head in the direction they had come. Liz restrained herself from nervous laughter. A piece of metal garbage sailed over them, confirmation that their pursuer had lost them.

Thorbin guided the mule back to the long row and slowly headed back down it. Something told him that this might be a main path.

Then, from the left they heard another small crash. The crash turned into a creak and then a rumble. The left wall of the long row trembled as the row on the other side crashed into it.

"Thorbin?" Liz whispered, concerned about the wall slowly leaning over in their direction.

"Damn!" he answered and kicked the mule into gear. The turbine screamed as they hurtled down the path with the collapsing row chasing them. Thorbin was desperately tying to make it to the intersection ahead. He was sure that if he reached it in time, the break in the wall at the intersection would allow them to escape being crushed to death. He tried his best to maintain speed while dodging the various lumps of debris that littered the ground. The collapsing wall was catching up to them. They were about halfway to the intersection when the lean of the falling wall started to overtake them. The garbage on the ground cleared a little, and Thorbin was able to keep out from under the wave of falling debris, but he was unable to catch up to the lean ahead.

As the wall ahead started to give way their path became steadily narrower, and Thorbin had to drift dangerously close to the right-hand wall. They had almost reached the intersection when the left wall began to overtake them again. Thorbin drifted further to the right until the mule's handlebar began to scrape against the right-hand wall. He felt Liz maneuver behind him, shifting herself low and left. Scraping against the right wall was slowing them down and causing the mule to want to careen into it.

The handlebar was beginning to dig a trough in the garbage. Thorbin let go of the right handlebar to save his hand from being ripped apart on the wall. He then used both hands to furiously pull back on the left bar to keep the mule straight. His arms started to feel weak, and he felt like he couldn't hold the mule steady enough to make it to the intersection. It seemed really close, but not close enough.

The left wall began to lean further over them, and Thorbin and Liz had to lean back so their heads wouldn't scrape against it. They were drifting even more to the right, so Thorbin pulled his right leg up and braced it against the right side of the handlebars near the center and pulled back on the left as hard as he could. Sparks and debris shot out from the right wall and were deflected back down on them from the collapsing left wall above. The intersection was just a mule's length ahead, but there was no way they were going to make it. The drag from the right handlebar was slowing them down too much – they could almost run faster. Thorbin thought for sure that this was it, but just as the wall was about to over come them the right handlebar snapped off and was left behind. Thorbin's death grip on the left handlebar caused the mule to flip violently into the left wall, throwing him and Liz forward into the intersection. Bruised and cut they looked back from the ground to see their mule crushed by the wall of junk.

"I got ya now!" they heard from nearby.

"What now?" Liz asked.

"Pistol," Thorbin asked, holding out his hand.

Liz gave a half-smile and pointed back towards the collapsed passage.

Thorbin smacked his forehead, annoyed more than upset. "Fine," he snapped. "Lie right there. Play dead," he commanded and began to climb up the fallen wall.

Soon after, their pursuer came across Liz's seemingly lifeless body in the middle of the intersection. He stopped, dismounted from his mule and aimed his pistol at her. He didn't trust the scene and was going to make damn sure she was dead.

However, before he could squeeze the trigger Thorbin fell on him from above. They were soon rolling around on the ground wrestling for control of the pistol. Both men grasped at it, attempting to point it at the other. Thorbin, weak from straining during the mule ride, was quickly becoming overpowered. The man crouched over him and the pistol slowly turned in Thorbin's direction until Liz's fleet foot kicked the man in the face, turning the tide. His hands faltered and Thorbin quickly gained control of the piece, letting loose several shots. Their pursuer fell slain on top of Thorbin, who fell back to the ground breathlessly in relief.

Liz grabbed the dead man and rolled him off Thorbin.

"Do you think we'll make it to a place where people won't try to kill us?" she asked as she offered her hand. Thorbin accepted it and stood.

"It is getting old, isn't it?" he said, inspecting himself. "Please tell me you got some kind of useful information from all of this."

"Exclusive red-light district," she answered. "Three floors down."

Ellis

Ellis had decided that he wasn't going to wait in the tower to die. He was franticly making his way down the interior stairs to the base of the tower. The clatter of small arms fire periodically rose then went silent with each passing step. In his right hand he held his pistol, in his left he firmly held the strap of his bag of money.

When he finally reached the bottom, the stairwell unfolded into a hallway that led in two directions. As he considered which way he should go, he slung the bag snuggly around neck and shoulder.

With palms sweaty, his pistol led the way as he cautiously followed. The hallway curved then straightened out, revealing a door with a broken exit sign above it. He approached slowly and was only steps away when the clatter of gunfire recommenced from just beyond. He turned and headed down the other side of the hallway.

Soon he reached the bottom of the stairwell and passed by quickly. Like the other, this hallway curved a bit then revealed a door labeled 'exit'. The crimson backlit letters flickered ominously, casting shadows against the subtle red glow. Again he proceeded towards the door cautiously. A few steps away he paused and listened. It was silent. He approached the door, placed his hand on the push bar and was about to open it when he had second thoughts. He placed his ear against the door just to make sure there was nothing there and listened for a moment longer. He heard something.

He wasn't sure if he was satisfied that his intuition to listen further was right. The sound was odd – someone was grunting as if exhausted. He determined that this sound was better than what lay behind door number one. He readied his pistol and placed his free hand on the door's push latch, preparing to open it and shoot whoever was on the other side. The latch clicked as the lock loosened and the door was free to open. He prepared himself to thrust it open.

Three, he mentally counted.

Two, he inhaled anxiously.

"One!"

He screamed like a terrified little girl as something thunderous crashed into the door, locking it back into place. Ellis leapt back, frightened, and swung the pistol towards the door. Whatever had hit the metal door had bent it right down the middle from top to bottom.

Again something crashed against the door, causing it to fold inward down the length of the bend and start to give way. Then something truly disturbing happened. As the something on the other side began to force its way through the door, cracks formed, then bled.

Ellis mustered the manliest scream he could and yelled, "AHHHHHH!" as he fired into the cracks until his weapon was spent. He nervously released the magazine, and it fell to the ground with a metallic clatter. Before he could get new rounds in, his battle cry was answered by a roar that clearly sounded like hell's minions wanted his ass, and the door was thrust upon again. This time the cracks were forced open and through the biggest a battered and broken pirate head had been shoved.

Ellis turned and ran. He quickly passed the stairwell as fast as he could and rounded the curve back to the first door. He had managed to get his weapon reloaded by the time he reached it and fired without discretion as he approached. His shots were quickly answered as four perfect hits destroyed the doors hinges and lock, sending them careening in his direction. He decided not to wait to see what would pop through this door. As the door started to fall inwards he was heading to the stairwell. The tower was his only hope.

When he reached the bottom of the stairs, he discovered Tank had already beaten him there. The grim beast of man had Ben's old shotgun in one hand and a headless pirate battering ram in the other. The two men made eye contact and Tank smiled.

Lorilei

Lorilei lay on a pillow by the door pretending to sleep. Across the room Lili lay stoically in Kryst's nervous arms. Kryst sat, anxiously comprehending what Lorilei was trying to tell her. It seemed like a good idea at first, but seeing it mentally the way Lorilei was drawing it for her was very frightening.

"I can't do that," Kryst told Lorilei meekly. "I'm not that strong."

Lorilei didn't stir a muscle from her faux sleep but responded more emphatically.

"You say that," Kryst responded, "but really, you don't know me that well. I'm not brave like you." Kryst's nerve broke and she started to shake, causing Lili to stir with a sigh of discomfort.

Lorilei grabbed Kryst's attention, making the mental picture more vivid and disturbing.

Kryst began to cry. "Please stop it."

Lorilei didn't stop.

"I don't know what I'm going to do," Kryst answered, frustrated. "Next time, I'll go, so Lili won't have to."

Lorilei modified the image to accommodate Kryst's answer. Kryst shuddered under its implication. She looked down at Lili.

"I'm sorry. I love you, but I'm not capable."

The door opened and the vile mistress entered.

"Kryst," she began. "One of Lili's regulars is here, you'll be taking care of him."

With every bit of strength Lorilei had, she pried into Kryst's mind and screamed at her. *"Now!"*

"No!" Kryst screamed aloud. She was screaming at Lorilei, but the mistress thought she was being defiant – which was actually the plan.

The evil woman turned to Kryst. "Great, now she's gotten into your head," she said, taken aback by Kryst's apparent defiance. She reached her hand into her pocket and pulled out the collar remote.

Lorilei leapt at her from behind and entangled the woman. Lili quickly rolled off of Kryst's lap to the ground and Kryst jumped forward, batting the device from the mistress's hands.

"Julio!" the mistress bellowed while fighting to get out of Lorilei's entanglement, "Get in here now!"

Lorilei looked about for something sturdy to hit the mistress with, but the furnishings comprised entirely of pillows. She shot a picture out to the others; in it she commanded Lili to get the device and Kryst to hit the mistress in the head. Lili responded and scurried towards its resting place on the ground. Kryst, however, was nowhere to be found.

A large man entered the room, not sure what he was needed for until he saw what was going on. The mistress had managed to free herself from Lorilei's grapple but was still struggling to contain her.

"The collar control!" the mistress barked at him as she started to get the upper hand over Lorilei.

"Kryst, you have to stop him!" Lorilei yelled out to her, wherever she was.

"I can't, he's too big," a shivering pile of pillows responded.

"He's gonna get Lili!" Lorilei insisted.

"No!" Kryst said and leapt from the pillows, startling the man.

He didn't really expect her to try and stop him, but try she did. She was no match for him, every time she approached he would bat her away or pick her up and toss her to the side, but she kept at it. He couldn't get to Lili because Kryst kept coming.

"Lili, turn them off!" Lorilei said.

The mistress had overcome Lorilei but couldn't let go of her.

"Lili," the mistress commanded. "You give that to me right now."

Lili looked up from the device and stared the mistress squarely in the eye, then she defiantly pressed a button.

Lorilei shrieked in agony as the collar pained her.

"Not that one!"

"Sorry," Lili responded then turned back to the device, trying to figure it out. She pressed another button and was startled when the man cried out in agony. "You're wearing one?" she said to him.

He lifted his hand up and swung down at Kryst, whose teeth had sunk into his ankle. He hit her square on the top of her head, knocking her out cold. Then he turned to Lili, more than a little upset.

"I'm going to fuck you up," he said as he got his hands on her.

She looked up at him, and he paused as he watched her pretty blue eyes turn blood red, her soft brown skin turn scaly and sickly green and her fetching smile widen to display a rack of fangs.

Thorbin and Liz

Thorbin parked the mule in front of an unassuming building that he and Liz assessed to be the one. They dismounted and headed towards the entrance.

"What's the plan? You gonna pretend to be a client? Something like that?"

"No," Thorbin responded. "I'm going to burst in and tell everyone to keep their hands where I can see them." Thorbin had had enough excitement and wanted nothing more than to find Lorilei and get back to Victoria.

"OK," Liz shrugged.

When they got to the door Thorbin found himself annoyed by it and kicked it open furiously. He then rushed in, weapon ready, and yelled with conviction, "Hands where I can see them! If anybody moves, so help me *God*, I will kill you." He was very impressive – fierce and menacing. And if anyone had been on the other side of that door, they would have been stunned into submission.

Liz casually walked in behind him and smiled at the empty room. Then she turned the smile to him.

"Not a word," he said and proceeded towards the back of the building.

As they began to investigate, a blood-curdling scream filled with absolute terror could be heard. It led them back to a large room – a waiting room of sorts. There were couches and tables, and one section was partitioned off into a reception area where there was a desk with a door behind it. From behind that door came the screams.

Thorbin could tell they weren't Lorilei's screams, and again he seemed to be annoyed that something other than finding Lorilei was going on here. As he prepared himself to investigate the door it swung open and a large man scurried franticly out. His clothes and skin had been savaged horribly, and he collapsed on the desk, breathing heavily.

Seeing Thorbin and his weapon he begged, "Help me!"

Then behind him, from the door, appeared a frighteningly terrible little green monster which oddly enough appeared to be wearing light blue under things. It leapt on the man's back and proceeded to rip and bite into him.

"Ugh!" Thorbin said, startled at the sight. The little green monster's head snapped up and its menacing red eyes stared at him. Thorbin began to raise his weapon but stopped when the ugly thing smiled at him. The eyes turned crystal blue and the skin de-scaled and became much easier on the eyes. Before he knew it, he was staring at a very pretty Mosot girl.

"Thorbin!" she said, excited to see him. Then her eyes squinted. "You're a lot shorter than I imagined."

"Thorbin?" another sweet and unfamiliar voice said from within the room. Then from the door appeared another pretty Mosot with black hair and captivating gray eyes. She ran out the door and flung herself at him.

"Ow," was all he could muster.

She looked up at him, graciously batting her pretty gray eyes. "You're skinnier than I imagined."

Thorbin was bruised and sore from nearly being crushed by a wall of garbage and now some strange Mosot girl was squeezing him.

"Oww," he said again.

"It doesn't matter," the gray-eyed Mosot continued. "You came to rescue us, that's all that matters."

Thorbin's brow furrowed. Then from the door appeared Lorilei, naked as a jaybird.

"Lorilei!" he said, happy to see her.

She didn't even look in his direction; she was preoccupied with finding something. He watched as she rummaged through the desk drawers, than checked under couch cushions, becoming increasingly distraught until the formerly green Mosot called out to her.

"Lorilei, here it is."

Lorilei walked over to the girl. She picked up her yellow sundress and put it on. She then inspected herself and to her great dismay found a small tear in the fabric.

"That bitch!" she snapped as she headed back into the room from whence she came.

Ben and Sam

Ben and Sam sat in the cargo bay. The last fissure had been repaired and Victoria was as good as she was going to get for now.

"You know," Ben said. "I thought Kenton's Crypt was gonna be more exciting."

"I know," Sam said, then she held her breath and handed Ben his pipe and lighter.

"Not for nothing," he continued. "But we been here half a day and haven't been shot at once."

Sam coughed as she exhaled. "That's got to be a record," she confirmed, straining as she inhaled fresh air. "You probably just jinxed us."

"Nah," Ben said as he took a hit from the pipe.

"Where'd the dog go?" Sam contemplated.

"I dunno. He was round here a while ago."

"Hey, look who's back," Sam said as Liz pulled into the cargo bay on an unfamiliar mule. Seated behind her was a Mosot that wasn't Lorilei. Shortly after Thorbin pulled into the cargo bay on another unfamiliar mule. Behind him was another Mosot that wasn't Lorilei, and there, making herself comfortable on Thorbin's lap, was Lorilei.

Ben looked displeased. "Who are they?" he asked…displeased.

Lorilei leapt off her seat and frolicked over to Ben, giving him a gracious Lorilei hug. Soon after Kryst was upon him and Ben found himself armpit-deep in disgustingly sweet Mosot lurv. "Ah! You guys couldn't have just been followed by pirates, could you?" he complained.

Then, by extreme coincidence in rode Tank. He didn't even bother to get off his mule, he just stood up and the machine went on its way, gently crashing to a stop. He spun around, setting one knee on the ground and assuming a firing position. On his back was a large bag; Ben didn't recall him leaving with that.

"Time to go! Sariel ain't gonna hold 'em forever."

Ben broke free and headed for the control room while Thorbin ran to bridge.

Tank held his position and when Victoria began to lift off he whistled. Soon after Sariel came running towards the cargo bay doors trailed by angry natives and gunfire. Tank afforded Sariel the freedom to jump on board with a bevy of well-placed shotgun shells, and Ben closed the door behind him. Victoria soon left the deck behind and Ben cursed every bullet that pelted her hull until they were out of range.

"We've got company!" Thorbin said over the com.

Ben ran through the office and onto the bridge. "What now?" he said, looking at the console.

Thorbin snapped his fingers in front of Ben's eyes to get his attention then pointed out the window towards a ship coming straight at them.

"Fuck!" Ben said. "I did jinx us."

The ship had an unpolished black finish. It was Separatist fighter class, fully armed and very menacing, and behind it were eight more.

"Victoria, this is Wing Commander Singh of Dog Squad. We have orders to escort you to H Carrier Muir. Do you copy?"

"Wing Commander," Thorbin began, not knowing how he was going to get them out of this one. "This is Lieutenant Monroe of the Defense Core, we are on special assignment and cannot comply."

"Lieutenant," the Dog Squad commander answered. Thorbin thought that he heard a tinge of humor in the man's voice. "You have new orders. Prepare to receive a video file."

Thorbin looked down at the console and saw that the fighter was transmitting something to them.

Thorbin and Ben waited for it to download and nervously watched as the Separatist fighter squadron surrounded them. They looked out the bridge window to the squad leader on their starboard side. The cockpit glass revealed a young man that looked a lot like Ben's friend Raj from Jacob's Run, only younger, fitter and clean-shaven.

"This is bad," Ben spoke up.

"At least we don't have to worry about pirates anymore," Thorbin said sarcastically. The console dinged, demanding attention and declaring that it had finished downloading the file.

Thorbin opened it and they watched the camera focus and display a DC officer sitting at a desk.

"This message is meant for Lieutenant Thorbin Monroe. If Monroe is deceased then it should be passed on to a…" The officer paused as he looked at a piece of paper on his desk. "Benjamin Reagan, captain of the tug-class ship Victoria, or whomever is currently her captain. This message is a direct order to Lieutenant Monroe.

"First of all, on a personal note, Lieutenant, I hope that this message finds you alive and in good health. The Core has gotten intel that you may be in possession of a very important device. I am currently stationed on the Separatist Horticulture Carrier Muir. It is my mission to recover this device by any means necessary. If you *are* in possession of the device, you are to make your way to the Muir without delay. Under no circumstance are you to lose the device. You will keep it safe by any means necessary. The captain of the Muir has been kind enough to dispatch a wing of fighters to escort you back. I realize that if you are alive and receiving this message, you may find it strange that an admiral is issuing orders from a Separatist carrier. Times have changed, the Separatists have agreed to a joint defense force to protect survivors against the impending Talc secondary invasion.

"If you receive this message and you are not Lieutenant Monroe, then we ask that you carry these orders out on his behalf. I realize that you may not recognize my authority, but the Separatist wing is also under my orders to recover the device at any cost. If you do not comply, you may be destroyed. If you do comply, you will be dully rewarded.

"Let me be frank, to whomever this message concerns. The device may mean the difference between the survival or extinction of humanity. I do not envy the possible hardships it may have brought you, but, if this be any assurance, if humanity survives, history will forever honor you."

The message ended. Ben and Thorbin were silent with consideration. It seemed genuine and plausible, but it could also be a charade. It didn't really matter though; Victoria was no match for a squadron of Separatist fighters. Nothing was except a squadron of Defense Core fighters, of which none were present.

"Lieutenant Monroe, this is Wing Commander Singh. Have you received the video?"

Thorbin responded. "We have."

"Follow our led. We will escort you to the Muir. She's just outside the farm."

Thorbin shrugged. "So, Dog Squad has been sent to look after us?" Thorbin asked.

"Yes, sir," the commander replied. "Dog Squad's got your back. Aaa Whooof!" the commander sounded off.

Eight other pilots immediately responded, "Aaa Whoof!"

Chapter Twenty-Two
Slow Ride

Thorbin

Thorbin sat at the helm cautiously infused with purpose. The arrival of the Separatist squad and the message from the DC brass had reaffirmed his belief that he was still a part of the fight. His wayward journey on Victoria had purpose, a purpose that had eluded him. But now, it all seemed to be falling into place. His personal defeat at the Battle of Earth seemed less like a failure and more like destiny, which started to wash away feelings of inadequacy and replace them with resolve.

Furthermore, he was piloting Victoria amongst a fighter squad. They weren't DC pilots, but it didn't matter, they had his way about them. Nine finely crafted birds executing a precise escort pattern around Victoria. One raptor above and one below, one in front another behind, and one to port and to starboard. The remaining three formed a spearhead and circled in wide arcs around them, creating a defense perimeter. All the while efficient pilot chatter emitted from their com channel. Every so often the squad leader would address him, and he would respond in kind. Thorbin figured it was a matter of time before he was strapped into a cockpit unleashing hell on the enemy, where he belonged.

Ben entered from the office hatch behind him.

"Vicky ain't well. How long till we arrive?" he asked.

Thorbin tapped the console and opened the channel. "Dog Squad," he said, feeling like a real pilot. "What is our ETA?"

"Victoria," the squad leader replied. "At current speed, two hours seventeen minutes."

"Should be all right," Ben surmised, "So long as we don't run across any trouble."

"Clear," Thorbin responded.

Tank

Tank stood outside one of the shower stalls preparing to wash the battle away whilst coming down from a considerable adrenaline high. He could hear Sariel a few stalls over recounting the fight to himself. Tank inhaled a deep and satisfied breath and his chest settled loose. He proudly looked himself over in the mirror. He didn't see the gray in his hair or acknowledge the pain in his joints. Instead he watched his chest rise and fall with each mighty breath he took. He turned to the side and flexed an arm. Then smiled as little Tank came alive – he felt like a god.

He opened the stall door and stepped in. It was his first shower in a long time, as he hadn't previously had the strength to stand long enough to take one. Now, however, he felt sturdy. He reached for the shower door and started to pull it closed.

"Damn," he said to himself. He was too big; he couldn't get the door to close all the way. He turned, twisted and squeezed but to no avail.

"Fuck it," he conceded. "The floor's just going to have to get wet."

He turned on the water and felt defeated as the showerhead sprayed comfortable warm water on his chest.

"Ah come on!"

He tried pivoting the nozzle up and was able to get the spray just under his chin. He tried to lean over and find a way to compensate, but it was just a painful exercise in futility.

"This is bullshit," he said, turning the shower off. All he wanted was to stand there in the shower godlike as the water rained down on him. He stepped out of the stall, conceding that a bath would be just fine, although he felt like he was conceding to mortality. He wrapped a towel around his waist and sulked towards the bathroom door. As he turned the corner Lorilei and the black-haired Mosot were standing there. Lorilei was holding a skirt against her waist, judging size.

"This should do," Lorilei commented at the skirt with a nod of her head.

"You guys gonna use the tub?" Tank said, defeated.

They looked up at him. Lorilei could see his huge frame dropping in disappointment.

"I was just going to have her wash up and put on some decent clothes," she answered. "But we can wait."

"No, that's OK," Tank said, disappointed.

"No really, it's fine," Lorilei insisted.

The gray-eyed Mosot giggled and smiled at Tank.

"No," Lorilei said to her.

Tank was confused.

The Mosot sauntered over to him and flung her arms around his waist.

"Or," the black-haired lass began to suggest.

"No," Lorilei said more firmly.

"But you promised," she protested.

"Promised what?" Tank asked, feeling less disappointed with her arms around him.

"That we could take bathes with you," she answered, eagerly looking up at him.

Tank's god complex swiftly returned. One hand held the towel while the other scooped his soon-to-be tub mate up and over his shoulder.

"Absolutely," he said as he opened the bathroom door.

"Tank!" Lorilei whined.

He ignored her and stepped into the bathroom unit.

"I suppose I should know your name?" he asked his willing captive.

"Kryst," she said, pleased with herself.

Sam and Liz

Sam was in the kitchen packing up the device, a little sad that her mystery object was going to be taken from her. Liz walked in and headed to the fridge. She opened the door and addressed Sam without looking at her.

"Keeping my device safe?" Liz wasn't being particularly condescending, but Sam felt insulted that she wouldn't even look at her.

"*My* device is just fine. Thanks for asking."

Liz pulled a carton of orange juice from the fridge, closed the door and leaned back on it looking at Sam. She was amused by Sam's tone. She spun the cap off the carton and took a sip.

"I've chased that thing from the Battle of Earth to Jacob's Run, through Kenton's Crypt, all the while being stalked by killers. Do you really think you can keep it from me?"

"Right now, it's over here," Sam said, finally having enough of the blonde bitch, "and you're over there. Do you really think you can take it from me?"

Liz smiled. She found Sam's wrath quaint.

"What?" Sam said, giving Liz some serious stank eye.

"Nothing."

"What are you smiling at?" Sam said, growing furious. She knew Liz was some kind of badass, and Sam really wasn't the fighting type, but she felt right at this moment that she could lay her out with one punch.

"I'm sorry," Liz offered. "I can't help it. I wasn't trying to start a fight. It really doesn't matter who hands it over, I'll get mine either way."

"Yours?" Sam asked.

Liz thought for a moment, she really had no reason to be elusive, it was almost over. It would be nice to have a friend. She walked over to the table and sat down. Sam grabbed the pieces of the device and set them on her lap under the table. Liz smiled at the effort and Sam scowled at her. She wanted to tell Sam how cute she was when she was angry, but she thought better of it. She took another sip of the orange juice.

"I'm a professional thief," she confessed to Sam.

Sam heard her and wondered what the angle was. She was a little lost, it almost sounded like Liz was trying to start a conversation with her. She was wary, but after some consideration, the idea of having a conversation with another woman sounded great. Conversations with Lorilei weren't exactly give and take. She let her guard down slightly.

"Really?"

"Yup, there's more to it than that, but that's the gist of it."

"So you're going to steal the device from us?"

"I was," Liz said. "But now I don't have to. You guys are taking me and it to my employer."

"Your employer?" Sam asked.

"Uh huh, the Defense Core."

Sam was confused again. "But it belongs to them, what kind of thief returns things to their rightful owners?"

"The kind that's paid to," Liz answered quickly, then took another sip of her juice.

"So you're like a cat burglar?" Sam asked, vicariously excited.

Liz laughed. "I don't wear skintight latex and sneak around dropping in from the ceiling," she confirmed. "At least not professionally."

Sam laughed. "You make a living doing this?" she asked.

"It's not so much that I make a living doing it, as it is that I live to do it."

"It sounds really exciting."

"Don't sound like you don't know what excitement is," Liz said to her. "It can be. Though it's mostly hours of boredom followed by short moments of sheer terror. And on occasion I get caught, which isn't so much fun."

"What do you do when you get caught?"

"Figure out how to get uncaught. It's not usually that difficult. Just like the rest of the job, it's all about opportunity," Liz answered, putting the orange juice on the table. "Orange juice?" she offered.

Sam took the bottle and took a sip as if they were sharing a bottle of scotch.

Liz smiled. "So you're an engineer, what's that like?"

"Mostly hours of boredom followed by moments of sheer tedium."

"It can't be that bad."

"No, I was just comparing, I like it really. I figure out how to make things work."

"Hmm," Liz said thoughtfully. "Putting it like that, really, that's all that I do. Figure out how to make things work."

Lorilei entered the kitchen beside herself.

"Have you guys seen Lili?"

"Is that the black-haired one?" Sam asked. Not that it mattered, she hadn't seen either of them.

"No," Lorilei answered. "She's taking a bath with Tank."

"Huh?" Sam said shocked. "She's been on board for an hour!"

"Jealous?" Liz teased.

Sam gave her a friendly dose of stank eye and then considered. "Yeah, a little, I mean, not about Tank, but I've been solo since before Earth was zapped."

"Have you seen her?" Lorilei broke in.

"No," Sam said, and Lorilei left the kitchen.

"Well that's got nothing to do with you," Liz consoled. "Pickin's is slim round here."

"No kidding," Sam confirmed. "All the good ones have issues or are murderers."

Liz almost choked on her orange juice.

Tank

Tank lay in the tub, god complex satisfied. Softly, he fondled both of Kryst's breasts with a single hand as she lay back against him. They both lay content in the moment, quiet and comfortable in the warm water. Tank kissed her on the top of her head, to which she responded with a sigh.

"That hit the spot," he said to her.

"Yes," she agreed. "Want some more?" she asked, turning her head and kissing his chin.

"Later," he assured. "I'm good just like this here." And he gently squeezed a breast.

"Umm," she purred. "Me too."

Kryst rolled over on her side and slid a hand down his chest, carefully navigated across his wounded stomach and returned Tank's fondling in kind.

"Are you going to take care of me?" she asked.

Tank let out a half-laugh. "We can take care of each other," he answered, placing a finger under her chin and raising it so he could kiss her.

"OK," she said satisfied with another kiss. "Will you take care of Lili too?"

Tanks brow furrowed.

"Look, little cutie," he said. "I'm a simple man. If somethin' angers me, I treat it poorly. If somethin' makes me happy, I cherish it. You don't need to work your magic on me."

"OK," Kryst said, not sure what he was getting at.

"Now," he continued. "If all you're lookin' fer is Tank to bash all your troubles away, you ain't gotta play naked rodeo with him to get it done."

Kryst was confused, she wasn't sure what 'naked rodeo' was, but it sounded like fun. She felt the need to clarify.

"I take care of you," she said, gently squeezing him. "And you take care of me," she offered.

Tank smiled, she didn't get it, what the hell did he care anyways. "Sure," he agreed.

"And Lili too," Kryst added.

Tank nodded, then wrapped his arms around her and pulled her in close.

There was a knock at the bathroom door, and they both looked over.

"Yeah?" Tank answered.

"Tank, I need you," Lorilei said from the other side.

"He's busy!" Kryst answered.

Tank stood up and Kryst fell into the water.

"Hold on, I'll be right out."

Lorilei waited impatiently outside for a moment until Tank opened the door.

"Good, you're dressed," she said and grabbed him by the hand.

"What's going on?" he asked, allowing himself to be led.

"Oh! Don't think I don't know!" she said angrily at him.

"I didn't do nothin'," he defended.

"Don't lie to me," she scolded, leading him up the stairs and into the office. "I felt the whole thing. Kryst can't keep her mind to herself. Ugh!" she shivered.

"Oh that," Tank said coyly.

"Oh that!" Lorilei said, dragging him into the office.

"Well, Tank," Lorilei said, head cocked, arms crossed and foot tapping after they stopped by a desk. "Time for you to hold up your end of the bargain."

"OK," he said, afraid to cross Lorilei. "What exactly am I doing?"

Lorilei pointed sharply under the desk. "She won't come out," she said angrily at him. Then she inhaled a deep breath and exhaled softening. "She's afraid. You just promised to take care of both of them," Lorilei said, looking past his eyes and into his shame. "Lili needs taking care of, and not the way you took care of Kryst," she clarified. Tank looked where Lorilei was pointing.

"Under the desk?"

"Under the desk," she repeated. "Right after we took off and the pirates started shooting at us she got scared and hid. I just found her right now, and she won't come out."

"Maybe we should leave her be," Tank suggested.

Lorilei shook her head no and pulled her arm back before snapping it forward with conviction.

Tank turned around and got on his hands and knees to look under the desk. There he saw Lili huddled as far back as she could get. Her arms were wrapped around her knees and she was shivering. He reached a hand out and touched her shoulder. She frantically lurched away, pressing herself against the wall, then turned a tear-stained face towards him and started to say something, but the words choked her and she heaved for breath.

Tank pulled his hand back and gave her a sympathetic look.

"Hey, dumpling," he offered. "It's OK, nothin' gonna hurt ya now."

She sunk back even more and started to hyperventilate.

Tank backed away and gave her some room. "It's over," he offered.

She struggled and caught her breath, but the shivering started again.

"Lorilei's a lair!" she yelled at him. "Victoria's scary. I want to go home."

"Dumpling," Tank said compassionately, "you don't want to go back there."

"Not there," she whimpered. "Home," she clarified with a teary nod.

"Which home, sweetie," Tank asked.

"My home world," she answered.

A shiver ran goose bumps down Tank's spine. Her home world had been decimated, worse than Earth. He wasn't about to say that, so he sighed.

"Me too," he said.

Lili looked at him awkwardly. "You want to go to my home world?" she asked.

Tank smiled. "Yup, we can go there together if ya want."

Lili used the whole of her arm to wipe the tears out of her face. "OK," she said meekly.

"Good," he said. "Now how 'bout you come out from under there?"

"No," she pleaded. "It's better here."

"You say that now," he said. "But if Ben catches you up here…."

Lili's eye's started to fill with terror.

"Just kidding," Tank said, hoping to cut off the flood. "You know what?" He said changing the subject. "It is kinda nice under here." Then he started to shimmy his way under the desk. Lili had to move to the side to accommodate him.

"You don't fit," she said, smiling at how silly he looked trying to get under the desk with her.

"Sure I can," he said as he rolled over on his side. His shoulder lifted the desk off the ground while most of him stuck out from under it. "See," he said.

Lili was grinning from ear to ear, Tank looked silly all squished under the desk next to her. His face was turning bright red and he couldn't really move his upper arms.

"You're too big," she sniffled.

"I think you're right," he agreed, admitting defeat. "I may need your help getting me out of here."

She placed a hand on his cheek. "You're turning all pink."

Thorbin

Thorbin still sat at the console; his eyelids were getting heavy when in the distance he saw her – the Muir. He looked down at his controls and confirmed that they were still a good half-hour away. He was amazed and his eye's widened.

She's huge, he thought. Then the sinking feeling that this was possibly all a trap came back. He brushed it away. There was nothing they could do. He watched for a few minutes as the Muir grew larger in the distance. He turned on the ship's internal com.

"I have visual on the Muir. She's enormous," he announced to the whole of Victoria.

In less than a minute everyone on board came to the front of Victoria. Ben entered the bridge first and stood next to him. Then Lorilei, who leaned against the captain's chair. Everyone else was in the forward observation deck.

"So this is it," Ben said.

"Cross your fingers," Thorbin responded.

"I don't think they were lying," Lorilei said, she wasn't really sure though. For all she knew the Separatist pilots were just following orders and not asking questions.

Ten minutes later the Muir had gone from distant vessel to lumbering space giant. They could see Separatist fighters swarming around her like bees around a hive.

"Victoria, this is Dog Squad," the com said. Thorbin opened the channel.

"Go ahead, Dog Squad."

"This is the end of the road for us. We will escort you a few more kilometers then control will guide you in."

"Thanks," Thorbin responded.

"Ahh Woof," the squad leader sounded off then cut the com channel.

A few minutes later Dog Squad was gone and Muir loomed even larger. Thorbin had seen horticulture vessels before, but this time it looked different. She was a large rectangular carrier, a dull silver color with black trim where smaller pieces had been brought together to make the whole. There were a great many windows, some lit others dark, all scattered across her hull. This he had never seen before. He guessed that the windows were probably always there, just hidden. Possibly because every other time he had seen a horticulture vessel trouble was afoot. Now there was none.

She must have her guard down, he thought. *That bodes well for us.*

In the center of the large carrier was a mess of glassy tiles. It seemed to run across a good portion of the ship. He looked closely and saw that the glass mesh was moving on an axis to the ship, as if posturing for sunlight.

"What's that?" Ben asked, addressing the mesh.

"I'm not sure," Thorbin answered. "Maybe solar panels."

"Hmm," Ben answered. "Maybe, that technology's pretty old though. I'm sure they got plenty of turbines to power that thing."

As they continued to move closer they noticed that the mesh was transparent. Their eyes strained to make out what was beyond the glass, but the sun's reflection was overpowering.

"Victoria. This is tower Muir, do you copy?"

"Tower Muir, this is Victoria. We copy."

"Good, Victoria, release helm to us and we'll bring you in."

Thorbin hadn't done that with Victoria before. He struggled to find the right commands but eventually got it done.

"Tower, you have control."

"Affirmative, Victoria, sit tight."

All the while this exchange happened the Muir grew larger and they struggled to see what was behind the large glass mesh. It stretched upward for many stories and ran at least half the length of the ship. Thorbin couldn't help himself, he had to know.

"Tower, this is Victoria."

A few seconds later the tower answered. "Victoria, go ahead."

"Please excuse my curiosity, but what is all that glass on the side of the Muir."

"You can't see?" the tower responded. "You're only a couple hundred meters away."

"No," Thorbin responded. "The sunlight is blocking our view."

"Hold, Victoria, let me see if I can get permission to change your heading so you can see." A few minutes later the tower came back. "Victoria, I'm going to bring you about."

After the broadcast Victoria started to bank to the starboard. For a minute they couldn't see anything at all. The massive vessel was underneath them. Then the control tower stopped turning the ship and proceeded to level her out.

As the Muir came back into view, the blinding sunlight dissipated displaying the contents of the great glass mesh. All hands on board lost their breath, as before them in the cold of space, countless miles away from decimated Earth, in the belly of the Separatist carrier they laid eyes upon a beautiful redwood forest.

Sam burst onto the bridge from the observation deck below; she was ecstatic and tears were streaming down her face.

"Redwood trees!" she screamed as she threw her arms around Ben. "Ben! Redwood trees! Just like home!" Then she collapsed in a mess of tears and happiness.

Lorilei had never seen Sam so happy. She didn't know what redwood trees were, but looking at how beautiful they were she understood why Sam was so happy to see them. Thorbin on the other hand couldn't believe his eyes.

"Jesus," he said into the console to the control tower. "Is that really a redwood forest?"

"Yes, sir," the tower responded. "Why do you think they call this a horticulture vessel?"

Ben watched silently as Victoria cast a shadow through the glass onto the canopy of the trees as they cruised to the aft of the Muir. Sam was pressed against the glass, naming things for Lorilei.

"Which ones are the trees?" Lorilei asked.

"The tall ones," Sam answered.

"They're really big," Lorilei commented. "Are they friendly?"

Sam smiled. "Yes."

"What are those?" Lorilei asked, pointing.

"Those are deer," Sam said, surprised to see them.

"What's that white stuff?"

Sam's shoulders fell and another tear escaped. With a warm heart she answered, "Fog."

Then Lorilei spotted a brown speck emerging from the fog and pacing Victoria.

"What's that?" she said, pointing to it. "I think it's following us."

"That's a hawk," Sam said.

"An animal that flies?" Lorilei asked amazed.

"Yes."

"Wow," Lorilei said. "I wish I could fly."

Sam put an arm around her and they watched the forest go by as the hawk escorted them to the end of the glass before disappearing into the fog. As they left the forest behind and neared the end of the Muir, Sam turned and leaned up against the glass contented. She made eye contact with Thorbin, who smiled warmly at her.

"It's nice, isn't it?"

"Wonderful," she responded.

Soon Victoria was turning about to face a hangar door that was opening for them.

"Well, here goes," Ben commented and Victoria entered.

The control tower still had control and guided them slowly into a busy hangar. It was full of every kind of ship they could imagine. Separatist fighters stood proudly in line next to each other across from transports and cargo vessels. Thorbin even pointed out another tug to Ben. It was a newer model, but Ben insisted it was garbage compared to Vicky. Nobody argued.

"Look," Thorbin said as he pointed at a column of soldiers running in rank.

"Marines," Ben said with a smile. Ben knew all too well why Thorbin had pointed them out. It meant they hadn't been set up. Ben's smile grew large.

"I can do ya one better," Ben said, pointing in another direction.

"What?" Thorbin said and he followed the line Ben made with his finger. There on the deck, a squad of DC fighters were being taxied into position. As the others looked on to see what could be seen, Thorbin couldn't stop staring at his destiny.

Chapter Twenty-Three
The Muir

"Victoria, this is tower Muir."

"Go ahead, tower."

"Prepare to dock."

"Clear," Thorbin confirmed then opened the ship's internal com. "All hands prepare for docking; it might get a little bumpy."

Ben

While everyone else on board found a sturdy seat and waited anxiously for the landing, Ben was in the control room where he had gone to open the cargo bay doors just in case. The last time Victoria had landed she nearly shattered, so there in the control room he waited in tense anticipation.

Control was bringing Victoria down slowly, but that was no guarantee of gently – Victoria had been through a lot. The fact that she remained space worthy was either a testament to her design or a sign of the utter strength of Ben's faith in her.

As she came down Ben could see the flashing lights of the emergency vehicles standing by. Rescue personnel in bright orange jumpsuits and medical blues were preparing to leap into action if needed. Victoria rumbled a bit as she neared the deck, and Ben reached a hand to the console and gently stroked it. With compassion he encouraged her.

"Just a little more, Vicky."

Then there was a slight jarring that was easily absorbed by his legs and Victoria came to a halt – she had landed. Just outside the cargo bay doors Ben could see the rescue personnel watching intently, their shoulders relaxed and their arms fell casually to their sides still holding the equipment they were prepared to utilize. One of them made eye contact with Ben and waved. Ben waved back with a relieved exhale. However, just as he turned and faced the hatch that headed into the office Victoria started to groan eerily.

He felt her start to lean and the groan turned into a painful metallic shriek.

Ben had to readjust his footing as the deck started to lean precariously towards the cargo bay. Victoria continued to creak and the deck continued to lean. He grabbed onto the hatch to steady himself as he took a look over his shoulder. The rescue personnel had taken a few steps back, and the tension had returned. Ben winced as he heard Victoria continue to creak in agony as she began to slowly tear. The ceiling just beyond the office hatch he was holding onto opened up. His eye's widened and his jaw dropped as the front half of Victoria slowly separated from the back half right where he was standing. Through the widening crack in the floor he could see Sam staring back up at him from the galley below in mutual disbelief. Then they both flinched as Victoria's bow and aft cleanly separated with a shriek and two separate monstrous thuds on the Separatist deck. Ben and Sam stared at each other, neither daring to speak, afraid that the sound of their voices might cause further disaster.

Despite the calamity and chaos, in moments the rescue personnel managed to get everyone out of Victoria mostly whole. Thorbin, Ben and Sam stood outside, inspecting the two halves of Vicky while paramedics argued with Tank about his general condition. They futilely insisted that he needed urgent medical care while he assured them that he always looked that way. All the while Lili made sure she was safely tucked away in his girth while Kryst insisted to a handsome paramedic that she was in need of immediate medical attention.

Lorilei appeared from behind Thorbin and sunk into him as she saw the worst.

"Is Vicky going to be OK?" she asked, concerned.

Ben didn't answer, so everyone remained silent until Sam wrapped an arm around him. "She'll be fine."

"Lieutenant Monroe?" a voice addressed them from behind.

They turned to see two sharp-looking officers. One a young female DC lieutenant in dress whites, the other a Separatist man who would have normally looked very imposing if it weren't for the welcoming smile on his face.

"Lieutenant Monroe?" the young officer asked again, looking at Thorbin. "I presume?" she added when he didn't answer.

"Yes," Thorbin finally said, to which she responded by raising her hand to her brow in salute, holding it firm.

"Welcome to the Muir, sir."

Thorbin hadn't received or given a salute in a long time and he wasn't prepared.

"Of course," he answered then snapped a hand up and let it fly down with finesse and a smile. "It's good to see you."

"It's really good to see you, sir," the young lieutenant answered. "I'm Lieutenant Wice, this is Commander Patel. I've been ordered to take custody of the device and get all of you settled into your quarters. The admiral regrets that he was not able to welcome you personally, but he will be at the debriefing tomorrow morning. Right this way, sir," she said, turning to the side and extending a hand towards a personal transport parked just off the runway.

"Thank you," Thorbin answered, then looked over to Sam.

Reluctantly she pulled a pack off of her back, opened it up and began to pull out the pieces of the device.

The Separatist man spoke up. "The device?"

"Yes," Sam confirmed as Defense Core marines accepted the equipment with friendly smiles.

"DCI," Lieutenant Wice ordered, and the marines left as instructed.

"Doctors are a pain in the ass!" Tank said as he approached.

The young lieutenant offered him a salute, which he lazily returned unimpressed. "What now?" he said, looking at Thorbin.

"We'll show you to your quarters, sir," Wice answered, unfazed by the causal salute.

"I can't leave Vicky," Ben said.

"We'll get her patched up," the Separatist commander answered.

"Not without me you won't," Ben answered.

"Of course," the man replied in an understanding tone. "We'll come get you when we start. But for now, she's not going anywhere. We've set aside some of our nicest quarters. You've all been thorough a lot; the Muir is a most gracious hostess. Please, allow us the honor."

Ben looked at him suspiciously. "You ain't gonna lay a finger on her unless I'm here."

"I give you my word," the commander answered sincerely and offered his hand.

Ben shook it, finally convinced. "All right then."

The commander nodded then extended his hand in the same direction as the lieutenant, who had seated herself in the driver's seat.

The transport was a low-profile vehicle which held its passengers in with nothing more than seat belts and a roll cage. The Separatist commander seated himself shotgun and Lieutenant Wice drove the transport off the flight deck and through a series of hallways that led to a thoroughfare which seemed to run the length of the horticulture vessel.

Victoria's people sat comfortably, trying to enjoy the ride. With the exception of Lili and Kryst, who were attempting to hide in Tank's folds, they all felt a sense of relief that security was now someone else's problem. Thorbin didn't have to drive for once – someone else was doing that. Sam and Ben no longer had to run around patching up Victoria so she wouldn't fall apart. None of them had to worry about being captured by pirates because they were already captured, and it didn't seem too bad. So instead they watched the Separatist world go by.

The large ship had an odd way about it that would have been disturbing had they visited it prior to the attack on Earth. It was a militant place wrapped in a blanket of humanity. They spied large gun emplacements that clearly declared, 'Come anywhere near this vessel and we will end you.' Then in juxtaposition just outside the emplacements were comfortable-looking couches and coffee tables where people were sitting and sharing warm smiles and friendly conversations because the gun emplacements offered nice views of space. Often times they would observe the gunners leaning causally back in their turret seats sipping coffee and acknowledging stargazers with a nod and a smile. Normally you wouldn't see civilians have this level of access to military ordinance, but the guns were safe, and unless you were really hairy the soldiers could be fairly confident that you weren't an enemy spy.

At one point foot traffic forced them to a slow crawl next to the entrances of makeshift barracks constructed by the Separatist for a battalion of DC marines. The proud insignias of companies hung by the entrances, symbols of bloodstained blades and fierce animals underlined with mottos like 'Death before dishonor' and 'Do or die' were set next to crayon masterpieces of stick figures captioned with 'Me and mommy in the trees,' and 'I love you, Daddy.'

The entire atmosphere declared, 'We will not go out with a whimper, but with a roar. However, in the meantime, we'll enjoy some tea and biscuits while we wait.'

During that moment of slow travel, Lorilei undid her seat belt and slid close to Thorbin, who put an arm around her.

"It looks OK here?" she asked.

"I think we'll be fine," he agreed.

Then Thorbin's pocket began to vibrate and chirp at him.

"What's that?" Lorilei asked.

"My PJU," Thorbin answered, a little surprised as he retrieved it.

Lorilei leaned over and watched as he tapped on the screen, waking it up. It prominently displayed '17 messages'. "My Com Link service is active again," he said in further surprise.

"Yes," Wice interjected. "Most communications service providers have been able to reestablish connections, and the Separatists networks have been included into Earth's infrastructure."

Thorbin tapped away, navigating through his PJU until he came to his mail, which displayed the new messages. For a moment he was excited at the possibility that he might have been contacted by a loved one, maybe Mika. The excitement faded when the only message of any importance was from the Defense Core – a mass mail that instructed everyone to report to the closest DC facility. Then another reporting that the DC and Separatists had made a peace agreement and reporting to Separatist vessels was acceptable. The rest were spam and automated messages informing him that his bills were late.

Thorbin let out a disappointed half laugh as he closed the mail program.

"Looks like the mortgage is past due."

Lorilei felt his sadness and rubbed his shoulder with her cheek until her eyes lit up with excitement and she squealed and pointed. "Little humans!" she said, sighting a column of children holding hands and being led like ducklings by an adult. She had shrieked loud enough to get their attention and they stood wide-eyed and excited at the sight of Tank, who waved casually. A little redheaded one at the end, being the only one with a free hand, waved back. Lorilei's smile beamed at them as she continued to shriek at how cute they were until they were out of sight.

"I've never seen humans that size before," she commented to Thorbin.

"We were all that size once."

"I know," she answered. "You must have been cute when you were a small human."

Thorbin desperately felt like he needed to find a way out of this conversation. "Lieutenant," he said, leaning forward. "Where are we going?"

"Your quarters, sir," she quickly responded, not trying to be rude, but she was driving and didn't want to be distracted.

The commander turned in his seat. "We've assigned you with some of the finest quarters the Muir has to offer."

"That sounds nice," Lorilei said. "What are they like?"

"You'll be very pleased," he said, excited to describe Separatist accomplishments. "You'll be staying at the Hall of the Honored Dead."

"What?" Lorilei said, confused. That didn't sound like a nice place. She noticed Sam looking over and taking an interest in what was being said.

"At the Hall of the Honored Dead," the commander repeated.

"Is that a graveyard?" Lorilei said, failing to not sound disappointed.

The commander looked at her and tried not to be offended. The hall was sacred to him, like most Separatists he went there often. Also like most Separatist he had never had the honor of staying there.

"It's not a graveyard," he said sternly.

"Don't mind her," Thorbin said. "She doesn't understand," he clarified, although he didn't quite understand himself.

"Of course," the commander conceded. "The Hall of the Honored Dead is holy place," he told her. "Every horticulture vessel has one. It's the part of the ship that overlooks the terrarium. The hall connects us to our past, reminds us who we are, and guides us into the future. *It is* the place where we leave our bodies when we travel to the next life. It is also where we celebrate every great moment in our lives. Not just death, but also birth, and marriage." Then he turned to Sam and looked at the pack she was carrying before continuing. "And hope. Every Separatist life is reflected at the hall – past, present and future." Then he turned back to Lorilei. "You'll be staying in one of the nicest quarters."

Lorilei leaned back into Thorbin feeling ashamed.

"Thank you," she said with a penitent smile.

"It's an honor for us to have you stay there," the commander said, accepting her smile and offering one back.

Soon after, their ride ended at a set of large glass double doors set in a marble wall. The lieutenant and commander stood and soon everyone followed. As they approached, the doors gracefully opened inward, inviting them into the rotunda of the Hall of the Honored Dead.

It was beautiful. A large circler plaza with marble floors and walls decorated with gold inlay set in dramatic patterns. Marble benches lined the walls filled with hundreds of people entranced by ornate video screens sunken into the stone. Their hosts didn't rush them as they walked by, often times stopping to see what was on a particular screen. Each played a different biographical video where the person on screen described themselves or were described by others as they told the story of their lives. Some of the biographies dated to the founding of the Separatist movement on Earth, whereas others were more recent. Most were in between.

As Vicky's people walked by they heard brief moments of a hundred tales of farmers and fighter pilots, holy men and laborers, all telling what they regarded as the most important parts of their lives, the most important lessons they had learned, the greatest achievements they had accomplished, the most profound advice they had to give, and lots of charming personal moments. As soon as one biography ended another began. Before they knew it, they had spent hours learning about strangers. Although by the time each video ended they didn't seem like strangers.

The commander and lieutenant eventually gathered everyone up and led them to an elevator which took them up to the fifteenth floor, where they were escorted down a similar marble hallway to their quarters.

Waiting at the door was a middle-aged man in slacks and a fine silk shirt.

"Good afternoon, commander," the man greeted the Separatist officer.

"Afternoon, Leonard," the commander answered with a respectful nod.

Lieutenant Wice turned to Thorbin and Tank.

"This is Leonard. He'll see to it that you have whatever you need. Your orders are to report to debriefing at O-eight hundred tomorrow. I'll be here at seven to escort you there. Have a good night."

Everyone thanked the lieutenant and the commander, then Leonard gave them a tour of their quarters.

Their quarters would have been a luxury home on Earth. The living and dining room areas combined into a single large space with vaulted ceilings. Every furnishing in the room seemed to be a finely crafted masterpiece designed to be pleasing to the eye and touch. A large oak table stood proudly containing a bounty of snacks – cheese and crackers, wine and berries, fresh vegetables and delicious dipping sauces. It was set upon immediately.

Soon after the snack feast everyone began to divvy up rooms. It started when Liz entered one and declared it to be entirely hers. This created a small problem since there weren't enough rooms for everyone to have their own. Lorilei graciously offered to share one with Thorbin, just as Tank graciously offered to share one with Kryst and Lili. Which left the remaining two for Ben and Sam, who would have shared but didn't argue about having their own space. Sariel spoke with Ben and they agreed that their contract to Mars was insolvent due to Victoria's condition. Sariel departed without so much as saying goodbye as everyone else settled into the their spaces.

The rooms were as extravagant as the living space. Each contained an immense bed and private bathroom, in addition to a small work area that included a desk and workstation. And most impressively a large balcony that faced out towards the redwood forest.

Thorbin

Thorbin entered the room that Lorilei had picked for them. He eyed the bed; he hadn't slept in a bed in months. He didn't like the idea of sharing it with Lorilei, so he looked at the couch. It looked comfortable, but it wasn't the bed. He wondered if he could talk Lorilei into sleeping on the couch, but he felt guilty. He wondered if he could talk Lorilei into staying with Sam, and then he felt guilty some more.

His thoughts were disturbed when from the balcony he heard Lorilei squeal with excitement. He looked over to see that a dove had landed on the railing, and she had tried to pet it. The squeal was her response to it flying away from the crazy woman. Thorbin watched her and smiled. He thought for a moment. Maybe he should just resign himself to his fate. Mika would want him to be happy. He looked back at the bed. Then realized it wasn't a matter of Lorilei. He just wanted the bed to himself. Lorilei frolicked back into the bedroom gleefully beside herself.

"Thorbin!" she said. "Did you see the hawk?" Thorbin laughed.

"That was a dove," he answered.

"Oh," she said then wrapped her arms around his waist and buried her head in his chest. She sighed. "It's really nice here."

"It is," he agreed.

"What do you want to do now?" she asked from his chest.

"I think," he said thoughtfully, "I'm going to take a shower, then lie on the bed. Maybe drink some wine."

"That sounds like fun," Lorilei replied. "I'll get the wine," she said and started to let go. Thorbin held her firm and she looked up at him.

"What?" she asked.

"If you don't mind," he asked, "I think I'd like to be alone for a while."

Lorilei looked hurt. "OK," she said and he let her go.

"Come get me when it's dinner time."

"Sure," she answered then stopped at the door. "I'll still get you some wine if you want."

"Thank you," he answered with a smile. "That would be nice."

Lorilei almost closed the door but stopped and asked, "Do you want me to ask Sam if I can stay with her?"

Alone in another room Sam suddenly felt uncomfortable for no reason at all.

"No," Thorbin answered. "I just need a little time alone."

Sam's random feeling of discomfort subsided.

"Hey," he said, stopping Lorilei at the door once more. "Maybe Sam will take you for a walk in the woods."

In the Living room

Ben and Tank sat on couches surrounding a coffee table in the living area with Lili and Kryst. The men had quickly consumed a fair amount of wine and for the first time were getting to know each other. Ben let out a bellow of a laugh.

"You should have seen him," Tank said with a laugh-inspired tear in his eye. "He didn't know what to do with himself. I was one side and Sariel comin' down the other."

"Good riddance," Ben said, lifting his glass.

Tank accepted with a clink and they both finished their glasses.

"More?" Ben asked, grabbing the bottle.

"Fill her up," Tank answered.

Ben attempted to fill his glass and discovered the bottle was empty.

"Shit," he said to himself. Then looked over to the table. It was all the way over there. "I gotta get another bottle," he said, disheartened.

"Nope. I got ya covered," Tank said, pulling a bottle out from under the coffee table.

Ben was drunkenly touched and speechless. Tank just smiled.

"Yer welcome," he said then struggled to open the bottle around Kryst, who was sitting on his lap. Ben grabbed it.

"I'll take care of that."

"Thank ya kindly," Tank responded as he readjusted Kryst, much to their mutual delight.

Ben leaned back comfortably and unscrewed the bottle. Lili slowly approached him and sat down. He looked at her.

"What?" he asked.

She shrugged.

"You ain't gonna try and get up on me, is you?"

Lili shook her head no.

"OK good," Ben said and leaned forward to fill two glasses.

"Is it good?" Lili asked.

"Oh," Ben said, taking a sip. "Mmmmm." He paused. It was good. "You don't want any of this," he told her.

"Oh, man, that's fucked up," Tank said, then he turned to Kryst. "Go get two glasses from the table and a few more bottles."

"OK," Kryst said happily as she leapt off his lap.

"I don't think that's a good idea," Ben said, not wanting to break the jovial mood.

"Why the hell not?" Tank asked as Kryst returned.

Ben sat back and took an uncomfortable sip as Tank poured two more glasses.

Tank looked over at Ben and saw his discomfort. "I'll bet they'll be cute all shit faced."

Kryst's face scrunched in disgust.

"I don't want anything like that on my face!" she objected.

Ben couldn't help laughing.

"They're your responsibility," he clarified.

"My pleasure," Tank said, handing Kryst a glass.

Lorilei exited the bedroom she had chosen and grabbed a bottle of wine and a glass. Tank took notice.

"You guys don't want to join us out here, little cutie?"

"No. Thorbin wants to be alone," she said then took the bottle to the room.

"No way," Ben said in disbelief.

"It's about figgin' time," Tank commented. "I don't know how he held out this long."

Ben took a big sip. "Fine," he said to Thorbin. "Here's to ya." He toasted and took another sip. Tank scooped Kryst up and placed her back on his lap than poured two more glasses.

Lorilei

Lorilei gently nudged the door open with her hip, hands full of gifts for the bearing.

"Thorbin?" she explored as she cautiously poked her head in the door. There was no response. She smiled to herself as she found him lying on the bed. Apparently she had taken too long – he was fast asleep. His arms and legs splayed wildly under the covers, attempting to consume every inch of comfort.

She set the glass and bottle on a nightstand and took a seat next to him. He looked peaceful in a way she had never seen, and it looked good on him. She had felt rejected when he said he wanted to be alone, but she felt better seeing him relaxed. She could sense that he was stress free and decided that she probably shouldn't climb in under the covers with him like she wanted. Instead, she scooted a little bit closer and gently ran her fingers through his hair. He mumbled something incoherently and rolled over in her general direction. She continued to stroke his hair and softly whispered to him.

"I talked to Sam and we're going to go for that walk. You enjoy your nap." She was certain he couldn't hear her, but nonetheless she felt she had to tell him. Through the haze of sleep he responded.

"OK, honey," he slurred and tossed an arm around her.

Honey? Lorilei thought confused. *He's never called me that before.*

"Thorbin?" she whispered. "I thought you wanted to be alone?"

Thorbin breathed deeply whilst rubbing her leg, and Lorilei wondered if something wonderful was about to happen.

"I love you, Mika," he groaned sleepily.

"Of course," Lorilei sighed. "I love you too."

Chapter Twenty-Four
A Walk In The Park

Sam

Sam had packed up some water and snacks for her and Lorilei to take with them on their walk in the woods. She hadn't expected Lorilei to take this long to get ready, but she wasn't surprised, so she sat around the coffee table with Ben and Tank and the two new Mosot. Really she was sitting alone. Tank was busy being inappropriate with Kryst, while Ben was telling Lili about how much Lorilei and her kind are a pain in the ass. Sam gave Lili credit for being a good sport. She was sitting there quietly holding a full glass of wine politely paying attention to Ben's tirade. Sam felt the poor girl needed rescuing.

"Are you gonna drink that?" she asked Lili.

Lili quickly turned to Sam and smiled. "Oh, no," she said, looking at the glass. "It's bitter."

"What?" Ben said. "This is some good wine!"

Lili turned back to him. "You can have it if you want," she said, offering him the glass.

Ben considered. "You don't have any diseases?"

"Nope," she answered, completely un-offended.

Ben finished his glass, again, and then accepted hers.

Lorilei exited the bedroom looking somewhat distracted.

"Hey, Lorilei," Sam said. "Are you ready?"

Lorilei nodded and Sam gathered her pack. "We'll be back in a few hours," she said to the room. "Leave some for us, OK?"

Tank laughed. "Have fun and watch out for polar bears."

"Oh, and take the damn dog with you!" Ben said, using his outside voice.

"OK," Sam said. "Come on, stupid," she commanded to Spot, who had been prepared from the word 'walk'.

"Polar bears?" Lorilei asked Sam as they opened the door and started down the hall. "Are they friendly?"

"I don't think you could call them friendly," Sam replied. "They've been known to eat people."

"Really?" Lorilei said, taking slower steps down the hallway.

Sam looked back over her shoulder and smiled.

"There's not going to be any polar bears."

Lorilei was consoled by the smile, but she was still unsure.

"How do you know?" she said, running to catch up, inspiring Spot to dash madly down the hall ahead of them with unabashed abandon.

"Polar bears live in the snow."

"What's snow?" Lorilei asked.

"Not important. There probably won't be any snow, so no polar bears."

"OK," said Lorilei.

As they approached the elevator a very formal-looking guard was standing next to it. "Just as long as there's no polar bears," Lorilei clarified. The guard smiled.

"Where are you ladies off too?" he asked.

It hadn't occurred to Sam that they might need directions, she had gotten used to living in a space that could be lapped at an amble in less than a few minutes.

"We want to see the trees," Lorilei said to the guard.

He looked at Sam.

"Yes," she confirmed. "Trees please."

The guard smiled again and pressed the elevator call button. Then he made a fist, brought it up to his face and spoke to it. "This is honor guard E fifteen." He waited.

They could see he was listening to someone they couldn't hear. "I have two VIPs From Victoria and the dog. They need an escort to the terrarium." A few seconds later the door opened and the guard held it open for them.

"Your escort will be waiting in the rotunda, ladies," he informed them.

"We really don't need an escort," Sam said, feeling over-watched. Lorilei disagreed. There may not be polar bears, but it was better to be safe than sorry.

"Sorry, ma'am," the guard said. "It's for your own safety."

"Are we in danger?" she asked.

"Probably not," he answered.

"But?" she led him on.

"Well," the guard said, a little embarrassed. "You're kind of…" He paused, not wanting to sound like a star-struck idiot. "Famous."

Sam was caught completely caught off guard. "Famous?"

"Yes, ma'am," he confirmed, feeling confident that he had avoided geekdom. He let go of the door and before it closed he added, "That and the polar bears."

The ride down the elevator was long for Sam, trying to convince Lorilei that they were not going to come across any polar bears in a redwood forest. It was hard arguing with Lorilei's 'But the guy said!' argument. She eventually settled her down by telling her that polar bears are deathly afraid of dogs like Spot. Which worked out well. Now she didn't have to watch Spot. Afterwards, Sam decided that it was fun to answer Lorilei's incessant questions with outright lies.

Ben and Lili

"Lorilei says she fixes things. I want to do that," Lili said to Ben. "Maybe I can help fix Victoria," she sincerely inserted.

Despite Ben's predisposition to hate her with his whole being, he was warming up to her. It must have been the wine, or the destruction of Victoria, or his relationship with Lorilei, but she seemed all right. Besides, anyone who offered to help fix Vicky couldn't be all that bad.

"Let's not talk about Vicky right now, OK?" he said, he didn't want the depression that came along with that topic.

"OK," Lili said, happy to be talked with, as opposed to being talked at. "Are they going to be OK?" she asked again, then looked at Kryst and Tank.

Kryst had passed out twenty minutes ago, and while Tank was still conscious he wasn't moving. He just kept looking up at the ceiling while commenting on how it was spinning.

"Yeah, they'll be fine," Ben told her. Then there was a knock at the door. Ben stood, tried to balance himself, then sat.

"You should probably get that, kitten," he said.

Lili smiled. She liked kittens. She went to the door and opened it to find Leonard standing outside.

"Hello," he said, pleased to see Lili, who greeted him with a pleasant smile.

"Hi," she answered, sweetly shy.

"May I come in?"

Lili looked over to Ben, who waved him in. As he entered Ben stood. Tried to balance himself, then sat.

"Great place you guys gave us," Ben said, suppressing a slur.

"I'm glad you like it," Leonard said as he noticed Kryst and Tank. "I see you all enjoyed the wine."

Ben gave Leonard a thumbs-up. "Very nice."

"Should I have some more sent up?"

"Oh, we don't want to drink all your wine."

"We have plenty, perhaps I'll send more up with dinner. Speaking of which, since I mentioned it, tonight our chefs are delighted to serve you a fine meal. I believe I heard them say that we just received several dozen fresh lobsters from our sister ship, the Marianas. I hope seafood is to your liking?"

"You're kidding!"

"No, sir," Leonard answered.

"You're going to serve us lobster?" Ben clarified, starting to sober up a bit.

"Yes, sir," Leonard answered.

"You have lobster? For eating?" Ben said, still amazed.

"Well, we don't husband them here, but the Marianas does."

"The Marianas?" Ben asked.

"Yes, sir," Leonard said with a smile. "She's like the Muir only her terrarium is an aquarium. A series of aquariums really."

Ben started to understand. "So all the Separatist horticulture vessels have different parts of Earth on them?"

"No," Leonard answered. "Most of the vessels' terrariums are dedicated to crops and cattle. Very few of them are like the Muir and the Marianas. We do, however, have one horticulture vessel specifically designed for each of Earth's macro eco systems."

Ben smiled. "So the Marianas has whales on it?" he asked.

"No, sir. Unfortunately, some species require far more than we are capable of. We do, however, ever have a sample of DNA from every species. Including the ones that we were unable to husband. As a matter of fact, every horticulture vessel in the fleet carries sufficient samples of all of Earth's life."

Ben shook his head in amazement.

Leonard waited a moment with his proud smile in case Ben had any further questions. When none were asked, the smile faded and he continued, "That really wasn't the reason for my visit, sir."

"Oh," Ben said. "What can I do for you?"

"You've done enough, I assure you. I have a matter to discuss with you." Then he looked around at the others in the room. "Of a personal nature."

Ben stood, Tired to balance himself, then sat…yet again.

"Go ahead," he said. "We're all friends here."

Lili smiled, she had never had so many friends.

"Well," Leonard said hesitant. "Please forgive me. I don't want to be insensitive about such matters."

Ben learned forward intently.

"Command asked, sir," Leonard said with a lump in his throat. "If you might perhaps…" He took a deep breath, hoping to deliver his message softly. "…like to lay Mrs. Reagan to rest in the Hall of the Honored Dead, sir."

Ben's head fell into his hands at the mention of his wife.

Leonard took another deep breath. "I'm sorry," he consoled. "Please forgive my arrogance."

"No," Ben said. "That would be nice."

"Thank you, sir. We know where she currently is and can see to it that she's treated respectfully."

Ben began to tear up, and Lili scooted close to him, comforting him with an arm.

"Thank you," he said to both of them.

"It is our greatest honor," Leonard said sincerely. "If there is anything you desire of this matter, please let me know. We have ministers and priests of every faith on board should you need one."

"Jessica was Hindu," Ben said.

"I can have someone from the temple contact you if you'd like?"

Ben nodded.

"Again I apologize. If there is nothing else, I'll go, sir," he said.

Ben didn't answer.

Lili nodded to him and he nodded back before heading out the door.

Sam and Lorilei

Spot dragged Lorilei by the leash Michael had provided for her while she stared open-mouthed at the redwood canopy above. Michael was the nice armed escort who had been waiting for them in the rotunda. He had introduced himself as Sergeant Levit, but Lorilei quickly broke him in and insisted that he was too cute to be referred to by stuffy formal titles, and furthermore, it was impolite to allow him to walk behind them. He found it difficult to refuse her and now walked leisurely between the two ladies. His hands rested casually on the assault rifle that hung around his neck, save for the times when he would reach an arm out to the leash and help Lorilei when Spot got extra uppity.

Staring up at the canopy Lorilei asked, "Are you sure there aren't any bunnies up there?"

"I'm sure," Michael answered.

Sam could barely contain herself. At first Sam felt uncomfortable with the idea of having a heavily armed escort. The discomfort subsided when he commented on how lovely she looked today, and quickly caught on to how much fun it was to lie to Lorilei.

"But if they can fly, how do you know there aren't any up there?" Lorilei asked, a little concerned; she had heard about bunnies before but didn't know how dangerous they could be.

"Oh don't you worry, little lady," Michael said in his best John Wayne voice. "If there's any ravenous rabbits up there, I'll protect you."

Lorilei looked over at him with a nervous smile. He was no Tank, but that sure was an awfully big gun. If anything could take out a bunny, that just might do it.

"OK," she relented.

Sam looked up at the canopy and felt a pleasant vertigo while she focused to see if she could find the brilliant green tops of the infinitely tall-looking trees against the pretty blue sky. She thought she'd never see a blue sky again. She sniffled a happy sniffle and Michael looked over to her.

"Are you OK?" he asked.

"Why is the sky blue?" she asked, smiling to herself.

"Well, on Earth it would have something to do with the way the light reflected off the atmosphere. Here on the Muir it has to do with the filtering on the glass."

Sam hadn't really wanted an answer; she was being reminiscent. "Right," she said.

Unhurriedly they continued on. They learned that Michael had been born on board the Muir and knew every path and secret. He pointed out the various flora and fauna and regaled them with his favorite stories. Eventually he led them off the path to one of his favorite places in the terrarium.

The great trees were large there, so the underbrush was thin and easily traversed. The lush ferns that grew at their base were sparse, and the soft redwood bark covered the ground like a welcoming carpet. They followed Michael to a lake that forced a clearing in the trees. Knee-high grass sprung up around the water where the shadow of the great trees couldn't get to it. Patches of flowers spotted the small field, adding hints of yellow and orange. Michael waited for them and soon Spot was leading the way. They couldn't actually see him, but his leash led them nonetheless.

"Good. No teenagers," Michael commented as they reached a granite sandbank.

"What?" Sam asked and Michael smirked.

"This place is well known. We only have one river, a creek really. This lake is the central point. All the water in the terrarium flows here. You see the island?" He pointed.

Sam looked and spotted what looked more like a large rock than an Island. "You mean that rock?" she asked.

"Yes," he said, still full of smirk. "We call it 'the Island'."

"Cute," Sam commented.

"It's actually an entrance to the pumping stations disguised as a rock."

"Oh," said Sam. "So what's that have to do with teenagers?"

"This place is called 'the Point'. They come here to make out."

"And you have a problem with that?"

"No. Actually I kissed my first girl on that rock. It's a lot more romantic than it looks. At night the water is warmer around the rock and there's a subtle glow from under the surface – from the pumps. Not that any of that matters, it's nice during the day too. I'd just prefer not to have rumors running around about how I brought you and Lorilei out to 'the Point'."

"I see," Sam said with a laugh. "You're right though, it's pretty. You want some snacks?" she said and seated herself in the sand.

"Sure," he accepted.

"Lorilei!" Sam said, noticing that she and Spot were trailing off along the beach. "Don't go too far." Then she worked at her shoelaces.

Soon she and Michael were barefoot, scrunching sand in their toes and sharing cheese and crackers.

"So the guy upstairs said we were famous. What's that about?" she asked.

Michael gave her a perplexed look. "How can a famous person not know they're famous?" he answered. Sam took a bite of cracker.

"No fair answering a question with a question."

"You're one of the Victoria's crew. The engineer. You probably know more about the device than anyone."

"You know about the device?"

"Sure, everyone does."

"I thought it was supposed to be some kind of top-secret thingy."

"Well, everyone pretends not to know about it unless it comes up in conversation. No one knows what it does. At first we just knew that the DC built it, then it was stolen and they wanted it back real bad. Afterwards the DC emissary came to us looking for it. We didn't have it, but soon after the alliance was made and our commanders made finding it a high priority. The whole fleet was looking for it. Then about a week ago it was all over the news. The device is on Victoria. News reports came in about the ship and all the near misses you'd had. Well, it was a good story, and a great mystery. The whole galaxy looking for Victoria. So I don't know what it is, but it's important."

"Are there any guesses as to what it does?" Sam asked.

"Some people think it's a cloaking device. Others think it's a new kind of smart missile. What do you think?"

"Well, it's a spyder design," Sam said, sure of herself.

"Really?" Michael said, a little disappointed.

"Yes, that's definitely what it is."

"Hmm," Michael said, considering. "Not what I expected, especially after all the fuss. Hope it helps when the Talc come back."

"Come back?" Sam asked.

"That's what command is saying."

"Man, just when I thought I was going to live."

Michael looked her in the eye. "They don't stand a chance."

Wow, Sam thought. *He has pretty eyes.*

"Sure they do, we're all going to die," she said with a smile. He smiled back.

Good smile too, she thought.

"We'll be ready this time."

"Are you a murderer?" she asked.

"What?" Michael asked, a little shocked. "No!" he answered.

"Do you have issues?"

"Issues? Like what?" he said, wondering what this line of questioning had to do with the device or the return of the Talc.

"Recently dead wife you're pining over? Murderous side? Bedwetting?"

"Oh," Michael said, finally catching on. Sam gave him cute face, and he couldn't help but be charmed. "Umm, no bedwetting. Have yet to kill. Not currently pining over dead wife," he said, de-gloving his left hand and wiggling a ring-less finger.

'FAT GRANDCHILDREN!' her mother's voice screamed at her.

"Why do you ask?" Michael said, not really knowing what to say and trying not to let his ego get the better of him.

Sam almost advanced, then cowed and looked away back to the lake. A breeze picked up and the grass rustled pleasantly behind them. Michael felt awkward and figured Sam did too.

"You know what makes me feel better in circumstances like this?" he boldly said.

"What's that?" Sam responded, biting.

"Murdering someone. The only problem is, later on that night I usually wet the bed."

"I knew it!" Sam said, pointing at him, and they laughed.

Shortly after Lorilei returned with her bottom half thoroughly soaked. She had discovered that lakes only look like big bath tubs, but really they were much colder. And more slippery.

They sat on beach for a few more hours until Michael picked a pair of California poppies for their hair and suggested they get back to their rooms in time for dinner. They left him in the rotunda with grateful hugs in plain view of a few hundred people and watchful chatter. As the elevator lifted them to the fifteenth floor the Separatist rumor mill kicked into high gear.

They arrived back to their suite with plenty of time to spare. Thorbin and Liz were seated at the table talking. Tank was passed out like a lump on the couch with faint hints of Kryst poking out of his mass of clothes and flesh. Ben and Lili were gone. Lorilei stood behind Thorbin and put her arms around his neck. He looked over his shoulder to talk to her and received a kiss on his cheek.

"How was your nap?" she asked.

"Good," he answered. "You're not upset that I wanted alone time?"

She pointed to the flower in her hair. "Flowers make things better. But you're sleeping on the couch tonight."

Liz laughed.

"Where's Ben?" Sam asked.

"He's a little upset right now," Thorbin answered. "Leonard came and asked about Jessica. He's been in his room."

Sam shot Thorbin some serious stank eye. "You left him alone?"

"No," Thorbin said defensively. "Lili's in there with him."

The stank eye grew stankier.

"We checked in on him, but it just made it worse. Lili seemed to have it under control."

Sam stormed to the door that led into Ben's room, and then stopped and collected herself, letting the anger wash away so she could put on her compassionate face. Then she slowly opened door.

Ben was drunkenly curled up on the couch in a semi-ball weeping in Lili's arms. She was rocking him gently when she looked up at Sam pleadingly.

"See, Ben," Lili said. "Sam's right here. I'm not going to leave you and neither is Sam," she said, still looking at Sam.

"Right," Sam said instinctively as she sat on the opposite side of Ben. He rolled over to her a broken man.

"Jessica, Vicky, all you guys are gonna go your way." Then a sob hit him. "I got nothing."

Sam pulled his head to her chest and kissed the curly top of his head.

"That's not true," she consoled. "I'm sure we'll get Vicky shipshape in no time."

Ben caught his breath. "She broke in two," he sobbed. "My baby broke in two."

Lili leaned over too him and held a hand. "I won't leave you," she said with all the sincerity in her heart. She hadn't known Ben long, but she understood loneliness. Despite all involved, ultimately, it was Ben and Victoria that had changed her life for the better less than twenty-four hours before. Not only did she need Victoria and Ben, it appeared that they needed her.

Shortly after, Lorilei came in and administered a gracious portion of her own compassion upon him, and then informed everyone that dinner was being served.

Victoria's people sat around the large, finely crafted oak table and shared a special meal. They were served food and drink, and shared comfort and hope. They toasted Victoria's health and thanked her for watching over them. They wished Thorbin and Tank the best, knowing that soon, perhaps in just days, they would return to duty. Sam and Lili assured Ben that they would help him with Victoria. Liz was vague but suggested that she would have to move on soon.

It was a fine meal despite the encroaching feeling that it was a last one they would ever share.

Chapter Twenty-Five
Change

Thorbin had woken up on the couch half-expecting Lorilei to be there, having snuck under the covers sometime during the night. She had not; a part of him was disappointed. Instead, she lay on the bed consuming only a small corner of it. He went to get coffee, greeted a hungover Tank, and returned to the room with a package that had been left for him which contained a fresh set of dress whites. Still she slept. He showered and shaved and the whole time Lorilei didn't seem to wake.

Standing in front of the mirror Thorbin buttoned his pants and placed his arms in his shirt one sleeve at a time. The fresh whites were pressed and felt rigid and proud on his body. He buttoned the bottom few buttons on his shirt then tucked it in. He adjusted it so it aligned properly with the white stripe on his pants then buttoned some more, leaving the high collar undone. He checked the time. He still had an hour before his escort arrived.

He sat in the chair at the desk and watched Lorilei sleep as he drank his coffee. At some point since he had woken she had collected all the pillows on the bed and surrounded herself in them. He could just make out the back of her. After a while the pillows spoke.

"I feel you looking at me."

"I'm sorry, I didn't mean to wake you."

"You didn't."

"How long have you been awake?"

"All night."

"Are you OK?" he asked, knowing that she wasn't.

"No."

"Do you want to talk about it?"

"No," she said, wanting to talk about it.

"I'll be off to report to duty in an hour or so. I don't know when I'll be back. It's not likely, but I could be reassigned immediately."

"Reassigned?" Lorilei asked.

"I may be ordered to go somewhere else."

Lorilei sat up and looked at him. He looked handsome in his dress whites, but she hated them.

"You can't be reassigned," she said anxious.

"It's not likely to happen today," he assured, trying to console her, "but probably pretty soon."

"Can I go with you?"

"It's hard to say. Under normal circumstances, no, just spouses and children, even then not during combat missions, which is pretty much every mission at this point in time. Are you even sure you would want to come with me, it would be very dangerous?"

Lorilei tossed the blanket aside and went to his lap. To his relief she wasn't sleeping in the nude but was wearing a complete set of underwear, which allowed him a greater measure of conversational tact.

"I'd follow you anywhere," she said to his chest. "No matter what."

"You're safest here, Lorilei."

She looked up at him, distressed. "I don't care about that."

"What? You don't mean that."

Her distressed face turned to rage. "Don't tell me what I mean."

"OK," he said in defense.

"You really do buy all that nonsense, don't you? That Mosot don't love. You still think it's an act."

Thorbin said nothing.

She held his head with both hands and looked him in the eye. "I love you. You give me a hard time for being a tease, but the whole time part of you lets it happen, lets me be me. I'm not the tease here. Yes, I would go with you. Despite how dangerous it might be. Despite that I can't compete with her. Despite that it may never be." Then she stood up and angrily flailed her arms.

"Ugh! Humans!"

Thorbin was still stunned. "I didn't know that you really loved me."

"I only said it like five million times."

"I thought you meant something else."

She threw her arms up. There was a knock at the door.

"Come in!" Lorilei snapped.

The door opened and Tank stood there in his dress whites.

"What do you want?" Lorilei yelled at him.

"Nothing, ma'am," Tank said and closed the door.

Lorilei crossed her arms and looked at Thorbin. He figured he shouldn't say anything else.

You idiot, he thought replaying what she had said to him in his head. *Five million times.* He had to admit, she had a point. Did she really did love him, did it matter?

"Well?" Lorilei snapped at him. "You got nothing to say to me?"

Thorbin felt inner panic. "I'm confused," he answered.

Lorilei was prepared to give him hell but then stopped herself and nodded.

"OK," she said, forming a calm face. "That's fair." She looked up at the clock. "You've got twenty minutes to figure it out." Then she turned and stormed out the door, slamming it behind her.

Thorbin leaned back in the seat feeling as if he had just finished a marathon boxing match. He relaxed and tried to collect his thoughts when Lorilei came bursting back into the room, snapping his attention back.

"I forgot clothes!" she snapped at him as if it were his fault.

He smiled at her.

"It's not funny! I'm mad! Don't smile at me."

Thorbin stood.

"Come here," he asked, holding out his arms. She looked at him accusingly.

"I already told you. Don't touch me unless you love me. And I don't mean that platonic crap either."

"Twenty minutes, Lorilei," he answered. "Yes, I'm an idiot. You've hit me with a lot. I have to think about it, but you're right, and I'm going to have to go soon, do you want to leave things like this?"

"No," she answered a little pissed that he still had the ability to reason.

"Please," he said, arms still outstretched.

"OK," she relented. "Just because you asked nice, this doesn't mean I'm not mad at you anymore."

About twenty minutes later, there was another knock at the door.

"The lieutenant is here," they heard Tank say from outside. Lorilei was teary.

"I'll be back," Thorbin said to her.

"OK," she said, leaning back from him.

They turned towards the door and Thorbin stopped. "Clothes?" he suggested.

"Oh, right," she answered.

"You might as well go back to bed anyhow. Try and get some sleep, Lorilei."

In the living area Lieutenant Wice waited and gave a smart salute. Then she nodded to Tank and Thorbin in turn.

"Commander," she addressed Tank.

"Lieutenant," she addressed Thorbin.

"Where's Agent Hollis?" she asked.

"Who?" Thorbin queried.

"Agent Hollis," the young lieutenant repeated. "The admiral wanted her to report as well."

Thorbin and Tank just looked at each other.

"We don't know who you mean," they responded together.

"She means me," Liz said from behind them.

They turned and their mouths nearly dented the floor seeing Liz decked out in her dress whites.

"Agent?" Thorbin asked.

"Yes. DCI," she clarified.

"Defense Core Intelligence?" he asked.

Liz smiled. "That's what I said. You really should be saluting me, I outrank you both."

Thorbin and Tank considered then began to salute.

"Come on, flyboys," Liz said, rolling her eyes. "Put them in uniforms and they lose their sense of humor," she commented to Wice, who grinned.

The young lieutenant led them to a meeting room near the bow of the Muir. There they met the Muir's captain and the DC admiral.

"As you were," the admiral said, entering the room and extending his hand.

"Lieutenant Monroe, Commander Tank, Agent Hollis," the young lieutenant introduced. "Admiral Durant, Captain Faust."

"Please be seated," Admiral Durant said. "We have a lot to talk about, but this meeting is going to be short and sweet. First, let me say each and every single one of you has performed in an exemplary fashion. After the Battle of Earth we lost you, but you didn't stop serving, and for that you are owed a debt of gratitude that can never be repaid. I've suggested that the three of you be considered for the Medal of Honor for distinguished service above and beyond." He turned to Tank with a smile. "I believe we may even owe you a few purple hearts, Commander." Tank laughed. "A lot has changed, stand up, Lieutenant," he said to Thorbin.

Thorbin stood and the admiral retrieved two pips from his pocket. "I hereby promote you to the rank of captain," he said, placing the pips on Thorbin's uniform.

"Thank you, sir," Thorbin said.

"Don't thank me yet, son," Durant answered. "After this meeting I'm going to need you to stick around for your new orders."

Thorbin reseated himself and the admiral handed Tank an envelope.

"Sir?" Tank asked.

The admiral pulled another pip out of his pocket. "This is your promotion," he said as Tank stood and received it. "And those are your discharge papers. You've served for thirty years. You can re-up if you want or you can retire with the rank and privilege of a captain."

"I'm not fit to fly, sir," Tank said.

"Maybe," Durant answered. "That would be for the doctors to decide. I sure as hell ain't gonna be the one to make you leave if you're not ready."

"Do I have to decide now?" Tank asked.

"God no," Durant answered sympathetically. "You got six months. And, if you do decide to stay active, I'll see to it that you get assigned wherever you like."

"Thank you, sir."

"My pleasure, Captain. For the time being you may return to your quarters."

"Sir?" Thorbin asked. "Will I be returning to my current quarters after assignment?"

"No, Captain, unfortunately not, we have another meeting then you'll be reporting straight to your next assignment. We'll send someone to get your personal effects, but your time is critical."

"Yes, sir," Thorbin answered.

Durant turned to Liz.

"Agent Hollis," he said and handed her a sealed envelope.

Liz accepted it with a nod.

"These are your new orders, straight from DCI. I'm not privy to them, but a vessel has been assigned to take you to Mars."

"Thank you, Admiral," Liz said.

"If there are no further questions, this meeting is adjourned." No one spoke. "Very well. Captain," the admiral said, turning to Thorbin, "you're with me."

Everyone stood and Thorbin received hugs from Liz and Tank. After which he and the admiral traversed a series of hallways and came to another room. A sign above the door read 'Test pilots only'.

As they entered the briefing room a proud squad of the DC's best stood to attention. The sound of their feet on the deck and their hands raised in salute spoke right to Thorbin's soul. There wasn't a single familiar face in the bunch, but he knew who they were, and he suddenly felt complete, as if he had been without his spirit, which had been patiently waiting for him here.

"Omega," the admiral said. "This is your new squad commander, Captain Monroe."

"Clear," the pilots responded in unison.

"He has more experience flying these birds than all of you put together. Unfortunately, he won't have much time to get to know you before launch." A young pilot raised his hand. "Yes, Bond, what is it?"

"Does that mean we're launching soon, sir?"

The admiral took a deep breath. "Hold your horses, pilot, you'll find out soon enough."

"Clear, sir," the pilot responded. Then the door opened again and the Muir's captain entered with a man in a lab coat trailing behind.

"Please have a seat, Captain," the admiral said to Thorbin, who seated himself.

"OK, pilots," the admiral began. "I know there's been a lot of speculation around here, but what I'm about to say does not leave this room under penalty of treason." No one said a word. "Am I understood?" the admiral clarified.

"Clear," the pilots responded in unison.

"Good," Durant said, collecting himself with a pull of his shirt. "We're calling this one 'Operation Hail Mary'. We've got just enough time to pull it off. Tomorrow, Omega will make the history books. We've retrieved the device from the Victoria and we are going to use it. The Muir is going to Mars to help with the impending secondary invasion. The invasion will be arriving soon. We know this because of intel we've garnered off of Talc vessels. And that's not the only thing we've discovered – we've also learned a few new tricks. Specifically, how to open those portals the Talc use. With that I'm going to turn this brief over to the good doctor."

"Right then," the man in the lab coat said. "Thank you, Admiral. The device, as it is so eloquently described, is this." The man pulled a small spyder from his pocket and set it on the table.

Everyone leaned forward to have a look, but no one knew what they were looking at. It just looked like a small robotic spyder, like the thousands they had seen in their lives, only really small. They looked at the lab-coated man, who held a smirk. He appeared to be the type of man that reveled in knowing what no one else knew.

"That's great," one of the pilots spoke up.

"Yes, it is," the lab-coated one responded. "I'm glad you ascertained its greatness for us. Do you care to tell us what it does?"

The pilot looked at him blankly.

"No? Then I suppose I shall. This, my good man, is the panicle of artificial intelligence. This little guy here is self-aware." The man was so pleased with himself that nobody knew what to do with him.

"To the point, Doctor," Admiral Durant cautioned.

"Yes! Yes, of course. This spyder has an artificial consciousness. It is completely capable of higher reasoning."

"The point," Durant snapped.

"It has the ability to reason and problem solve. It has been programmed to seek out and destroy Talc assets. It is capable of using all available resources, and it is capable of procreation. Given enough time, a single one can create an entire robotic army. Everything you'd expect from a military unit; resource management, weapons, intel, whatever it takes to damage Talc infrastructure. And, even if that army is defeated, as long as one survives, it will adapt and rebuild. It has also been programmed to provide aid to non-Talc species. And…" the doctor began but was cut off by Durant.

"So, pilots, what the good doctor is saying is that this little guy is going to be a big problem for the Talc. That's where Omega Squad comes in. When the next Talc invasion comes, we will be able to open one of their portals to what we think is the Talc home world. If not the home world, close enough. Omega Squad will be carrying a retrofitted missile. Now here's the kicker, we only got one shot. The power source that opens the portals is in Talc space. We can only open one from this side when they flip the switch on their side, which means Omega will have to be in place to strike the exact moment the Talc open their portal. It also means we've had very little time to prepare the device for a proper strike. So we've only got one shot. We think we'll be able to fight off the second invasion, but we're pretty sure we're going to lose Mars. We will not, I repeat, will not, be able to withstand a third invasion. If the device scores, there's a very good chance we won't have to try."

Admiral Durant paused to let that point sink in, then continued, "The retrofitted missile carries three payloads. Once fired, the payloads will deploy in three different directions and guide themselves. After they've reached a set distance, they'll release. Each payload contains one of these little guys along with enough resources to help them be an effective force multiplier. That's ranger speak for one unit having the ability to increase its numbers exponentially. We only need one to find the enemy and it will let the rest know where to go. They will assess the enemy while they increase in numbers. When strong enough, they will engage in clandestine attacks on strategic Talc assets. All the while they will continue to grow in numbers until they determine that the enemy is weak enough to be permanently compromised by a full-on assault. Just to be clear, Omega, a lot of things that could have gone horribly wrong went right for us to have this opportunity. The good doctor here, who invented the device, surviving the initial invasion so that he could be available here at Muir, the astonishing ability of Victoria to not fall apart until we found her, the fact that somehow a dozen of DCI's finest engineers and a hundred or so Separatist technicians were able to get three of these little bastards up and running in less than forty-eight hours despite no one ever actually assembling one before, and probably a great many other happenings we're not even aware of all led us here. The proverbial stars have aligned and are waiting for us to do what we do best, let's not disappoint."

"Clear," the squad answered.

"Good," Durant replied with a smile. "Your squad commander is flying the bird with the payload. Everyone suite up. Launch is in four hours. You'll get more details in flight."

Jessica

Ben sat in the front row teary eyed, listening to the holy man. Sam sat to his right with her arm around him, and Lorilei to his left holding his hand. On either side of them sat Lili and Kryst and towering to the right sat Tank. The holy man had assured them that it would be a small ceremony. So behind them sat the only people on the Muir who had been allowed to attend – all three thousand of them. The rest of the ship was forced to watch the ceremony on video from their quarters or in community centers. The man at the podium was the third to speak.

"Sister Jessica Evette Reagan," the man said. "It is with love and honor that we lay you to rest in the Hall of the Honored Dead." Behind the man a large screen showed pictures of Jessica and Ben, mostly on Victoria but a few on Earth or other ships.

"In the past months we've all felt like we've lost more than we could bear." The man looked down at Ben sincerely. "We on the Muir and millions on other ships and on Mars came to know and personally connect with your loss. The events that unfolded on Victoria summarized what has happened to us all, humanity's most recent parable. And like we, you face a life that always requires the courage to continue, in the shadow of great change. It can feel very lonely." The man smiled at Ben. "But as you can see," he said, lifting his arms to those seated behind Ben and those watching on video. "The prayers and good will of us all have been with you." And at those words a solemn applause ensued.

"And we have come to see," the man said, encouraging the applause to die down. "We have come to see how one life touches another in a series of events that are eternal. Victoria, like humanity, is the sum of all those who are, have been, and will be a part of her. Jessica will always be a part of you, Ben, inspiring love and courage. Love and courage, the two halves of hope, that which she gave you and which you have selflessly given. And when there is hope, the soul can be at peace and is fertile. Becoming a hospitable place in which to reap and sow deeper love and greater courage so that we are prepared for the rest of our journey. Thank you, Jessica Evette Reagan. Thank you, brother Ben. We offer all the love and courage we have, and hope that it grants you peace."

Chapter Twenty-Six
The Big Uneasy

Thorbin

Lieutenant Wice and Thorbin geared up together in the ready room. The young officer was beaming with excitement. She was trying on the special gear made for the experimental aircraft for the first time.

Thorbin sat on a bench looking at his PJU. He was mulling over pictures of Lorilei. Since they had met she had never been away from him for this long before. She had been a persistently needy presence that he couldn't get away from, and now it had been hours. He missed her. But the time without her had given him time to reflect. She had changed a lot in the time since she first leapt on him wearing little more than a smile. He had changed too. He navigated through the pictures and pulled up a picture of Mika in her wedding dress. Lorilei offered him all the love she had, and it was genuine, but she wasn't Mika. Their hair was similar, and sometimes Lorilei created familiar moments, but she could never give him what he had on Earth. He thought about it. That wasn't really fair to Lorilei. No one would ever have what had been lost on Earth. Hours ago he felt like he should relent. He thought about it some more, that was not how love should be. Build a life with Lorilei because he relented – he admitted that it wouldn't be a terrible life. Lorilei would take good care of him, and she really was completely loveable. He wasn't sure if he loved her or not, but if he could let go of Mika, he probably would. He thought that if ever his heart made room for Lorilei, he could definitely fall deeply in love with her. All he had to do was let Mika go, the actual love of his life, the woman who defined him – he was Thorbin and Mika Monroe.

It can never be, he thought. *Lorilei is right. I'm completely leading her on. I do have to make the decision. The longer I wait, the more it's going to hurt her. Whatever indecisiveness is in me isn't helping her.*

"Fuck," he said to himself. He wished he could tell her then, since he was in a moment of clarity. It would have to wait till after the mission. On the cheery side, if he died, he wouldn't have to worry about it.

Wice snapped her fingers in front of his face.

"Focus, sir," she ordered. He looked up at her. She was fully suited up and awaiting inspection, a great big shit-eating grin on her face. He'd have to take care of that.

"You ready to kick some ass?" he said.

"Yes sir," she snapped back.

"Right," he answered. "Just don't get yourself killed."

Her smile faded. "What's that supposed to mean?"

"Do you know who Robert Chin is?"

"No," she answered, feeling like she should.

"He flew your position at the Battle of Earth."

"Damn," she answered. "That's a little dismal, don't you think?"

"You only get a seat in this squad when someone retires or gets killed. You're sitting in Chin's seat."

"Yes, sir," she answered respectfully. "Don't worry, I don't plan on giving up my seat anytime soon."

"Neither did Chin," Thorbin said.

"I hope that's not the pep talk you're gonna give the squad."

"Shit," Thorbin said, the implications of being the lead on Operation Hail Mary fell suddenly upon him.

Ben and Sam

Ben sat on the balcony of his room looking out to the redwoods and smoking his pipe. The whole world had gone and turned itself upside down on him, and he really wasn't sure what to think about it. He had never suspected that he and Vicky were the history-book types – maybe in a statistical way, but never as a topic. He took a hit. The door creaked open.

"Want some company?" Sam asked.

"Only if it's you," he answered.

Sam approached him from behind and began to rub his shoulders.

"Oh yeah," Ben said, letting her magic fingers work. "That's the stuff." Then he reached his hand up and offered her some smoke.

"No thanks," Sam said. "If I hit that, I'll be no good to ya. Where did you get that from anyway? I thought you ran out."

"Separatist."

"Man, they have everything."

"Didn't even have to pay, on account I'm famous and all."

"Yeah," Sam said. "Weird, huh?"

"Makes you wonder."

"It does. I'm never gonna meet a decent man now. I guess you'll just have to do," she said. He reached back and placed his on hers.

"It's a burden I'm willing to bear."

"Do you think they'll name a drink after us?"

Ben laughed. She walked around him and leaned up against the balcony railing. Ben took her in, jeans and a black tank top. Her long black hair pulled back in a ponytail; except a few strands that got away. Ready to work, ready to play. She smiled at him.

"What are you looking at?"

"You're beautiful," he said.

"We know this," she replied with a flip of her hand. "What does that have to do with anything?"

"I'm just enjoying the sight of you while you're still here."

She cocked her head at him. "You keep saying things like that. Like I've outlined my plans on leaving you."

Ben smiled. "You just got nowhere else to go."

"I'm your friend, Ben, have a little more faith in me."

"You misunderstand, sweetie. I know you love me. I know you'll stick around to help me take care of Vicky. But you're a beautiful woman, eventually someone gonna fall in love with you at first sight – somebody good. You gonna tell that man 'No, I gotta stick around with an old crotchety captain and his busted-up tug'?" Sam didn't know what to say to that. "See?" Ben said, accepting her silence as clarification of his point.

"Well, who says you're not gonna leave me?" she answered with a smile.

"I do. You're too damn cute to leave."

"We know this."

Tank and Lorilei

Tank was consoling Lorilei on one of the couches in the common area.

"He didn't have no choice, little cutie. The admiral gave him his orders, he must have told you that could happen."

"He did, but he said he would come back."

"If he can, I'm sure he will."

"No matter what."

"Like I said," Tank assured.

"But what if he doesn't?" she insisted.

"Well then," Tank considered. "You still got old Tank."

"He could get killed."

"We all could," Tank said in a fit of expertise comforting. "I mean," he backpedaled. "It's just as likely that everything's going to be fine." Lorilei looked up at him.

"Thorbin's much better at this."

"Look, unless he's been ordered to launch immediately, he'll be back."

"Really?"

"Yes."

There was a knock at the door, which Lili answered.

"It's good to see you again," said Leonard from the other side.

"You too," Lili said with a charmed smiled.

"You already bummed Ben out once this week, one's the limit, come back next week," Tank said from the couch.

"Oh dear," said Leonard. Tank's shoulders sank.

"Ah hell, man, I was just kidding. What the hell is going on now?"

Ben burst through the bedroom door with Sam on his heels.

"What now?"

Leonard took a step back. "Victoria!" he said in self-defense.

"Ah damn it! Damn it! Damn it!" Ben said.

Victoria

Ben just kept mumbling incoherently all the way down to the flight deck; he wouldn't let Leonard explain, he didn't want to hear it. When they got to the area Ben was pretty sure they had left Victoria, Leonard finally got a word in.

"I tried to tell you, sir," he said. "We had to move her." Then he turned into a hallway that paralleled the flight deck and seemed to be guided by an endless line of people. "After the services for Mrs. Reagan, people showed up in droves on the flight deck to come and see Victoria. Tons of them, they were causing operations trouble. We had to move her. Then the people became upset. We had to do something. These days Separatists aren't the only ones on board the Muir. We have DC and tons of refugees. We were afraid that there might be a riot, so we placed her off the flight deck and let people stand in line." He nodded to the line the transport had been speeding past for the last few minutes.

Soon they reached the front of the line, where a squad of Separatist soldiers stood making sure everyone respected each other's turn. They allowed them to pass into a hangar just off the flight deck from a door on the opposite side. Inside hundreds of people stood in line around Victoria waiting their turn to greet her. When the transport stopped, all eyes were on Ben, who was looking at Victoria in amazement.

She lay in the middle of the bay in a pool of flowers, cards, and a variety of other wish-you-well artifacts. As Ben approached the Separatist soldiers that stood around her snapped to attention like an honor guard, and he spied taped messages on Victoria's broken hull. Hundreds of them, ranging from the handmade get-well card written to Victoria from Miss Kim's third grade class to a full-blown advertisement, '10 cents from the sale of every cup goes to the Rebuild Victoria fund.'

As Ben walked around her he eventually came to a middle-aged woman whose turn had apparently been next. She was leaning forward and holding on to the crack that split Victoria in two and was weeping. Ben's immediate reaction was outrage, but her tears inspired compassion. He was familiar with those kinds of tears.

"Ma'am?" he said.

Her free hand covered her face and from it she spoke. "I'm sorry," she said. "My time must be up; I got carried away."

"No, it's fine," Ben said. "It's just, you have your hand on my crack."

The woman laughed and looked over to him. "Your crack?" she said with a smile. She then noticed who was speaking to her and her eyes widened. "Oh dear," she said. "Oh, dear, I didn't mean…" she began to explain.

"No, it's fine," Ben said. "It's just…what are you doing here?"

The woman nodded. "My daughter worked on a transport," she bravely said. "I haven't talked to her since before." She looked at Ben's face and could tell that he had compassion for her but didn't quite understand. "I know," she clarified. "It's just, my friend Bonnie came here and said she felt a little better afterwards, standing in line with the people, sharing."

Ben smiled and gave the woman a hug. "If Vicky can make it, I suppose we all can."

"Mr. Reagan!" a voice called out from behind Ben.

He turned and saw a man failing his struggle to get past the honor guard. He held a microphone and behind him stood a cameraman.

"Mr. Reagan over here!" another man shouted out to him. "Channel 5, can you tell me, is it true that Mrs. Reagan was in a cold storage container for the duration of the trip?"

A portion of the crowd standing line to pay respects began a collective 'boo' at the question.

"Mr. Reagan!" another reporter asked. "Did you really kill a Talc with rock salt?"

Leonard stepped up to the crowd of journalists.

"Mr. Reagan is not taking questions at this time."

"Is salt poisonous to Talc?" the journalist persisted.

A woman broke through. "Is it true that Lieutenant Thorbin Monroe is currently set to launch on a preemptive strike against the next Talc invasion?"

Lorilei came to the front. "What?" she asked the woman, who scurried around the myriad of microphones, magnetically drawn to Lorilei.

"The Muir is heading to Mars," the reporter said. "We know it's because of the secondary invasion. But a DC squad is being primed for launch. Is it because

Lieutenant Thorbin Monroe is going to lead a preemptive strike on the Talc?"

Lorilei turned away looking for an escape route.

"What do you know about the device?" the woman screamed after her.

The Huddled Masses

Muir locals and recently rescued refugees had flooded onto the perimeter of the flight deck. They waited patiently to see the fabled Omega Squad pilots mount their steeds and deliver hell to the Talc. Even the local merchants came out to distribute water and sodas. A thousand conversations turned into whispers as Omega stepped onto the deck. The news reports said something big was about to happen. The Muir had changed her heading towards Mars. Everyone deduced that the secondary Talc invasion would occur there, and word was that every human vessel was making its way there to join the fight. When the impressive-looking DC fighters were taxied out to the flight deck rumor quickly spread, that it was on. The people would be dammed if they didn't see their heroes off.

The whispers turned to chatter as it was confirmed. The pilots that were making their way down the flight deck were Omega Squad. People hoisted handmade signs and children were reseated on shoulders.

From somewhere in the crowd a man yelled, "Give 'em hell, Omega," and the crowd erupted into cheers. The line of Separatist guards that kept the crowd at bay was forced to take a step back as people tried to get a closer look.

"Please stay clear of the flight deck," the control tower demanded from the loudspeaker system.

Omega Squad waved and nodded to the crowd and had gotten about halfway to their war birds when a ruckus drew the crowd's attention. The cheers turned back to chatter as they saw a guard struggling to hold back what appeared to be a small woman. One of the pilots broke from the squad and was saying something to an armed escort who then spoke into his communicator. The struggling guard seemed relieved when he stepped aside, having been given permission to allow the woman past. She bolted down the deck towards the pilot crying out to him, and the crowd hushed to hear what she was saying.

"Thorbin!" she cried out and thousands of eyes followed her.

She was a lovely young woman with flowing brown hair and a pretty yellow sundress that trailed behind her as she ran. The crowd went silent as she closed the distance to the dashing pilot, carrying with her all the love and hope they wished to bestow on their heroes. A collective smile formed on the hearts of every man, woman, and child as she reached his embrace. Thousands of people watched breathless for a kiss that would infuse all their goodwill and see their brave warriors off to battle.

A. A. von Dessauer

Thorbin and Lorilei

Lorilei's lavender eyes glistened up at Thorbin. Her love washed into him with timeless abandon.

"Hey, Lorilei," he said, happy to have this moment. He knew full well that this might be his only chance to set her free.

"You were going to leave without saying goodbye."

"I didn't want to," he said, squeezing her a little tighter. "Everything happened so fast."

"The people say you're going off to fight the Talc?"

"Yes."

"Not without me," she demanded.

He smiled back at her. "Fighters only have one seat."

"I'll sit on your lap."

"I think that's against regulations."

"So what?"

"Lorilei," he said, preparing for what he had to say.

"When are you coming back to me?" she cut him off.

"We can't be together, Lorilei," he said, and she became teary.

"I'd follow you anywhere. The only thing I'm afraid of his not being with you." She reached her hands up and palmed his cheeks. She was being difficult. He just had to do it.

"Goodbye, Lorilei," he said, and then tried to pull away.

"No," she commanded. She sensed his sincerity and wasn't going to have any of that. "You can't say goodbye without at least one kiss." A kiss would show him that he loved her – she knew it.

"I don't think that's appropriate," he said.

"All the time we've spent together, I've kissed you a hundred times. You never once kissed me. If you're saying goodbye, you're saying you don't love me the way I love you. The least you can do is give me one good kiss. Besides, everyone's watching."

Thorbin looked up. The masses were indeed watching and waiting for a kiss. He knew he wasn't getting away without one last kiss. He wasn't completely disappointed.

"OK," he said. "Go ahead."

"I'm not," she said. "You kiss me. And make it good one."

The huddled masses held each other close as the dashing fighter pilot, the hero of the Battle of Earth, leaned forward to kiss the lovely girl with flowing brown hair in the pretty yellow sundress. She melted into his arms and a leg lifted off the ground as her back arched. As their lips met thousands of hearts skipped a beat, and the love and hope held within erupted into cheers and happy tears. They beamed lovingly at the pretty woman as their heroes mounted their steeds to meet the enemy on the field of battle. Their hearts fluttered along with her dress and hair from the back draft of the mighty war birds as they left the Muir behind to meet their destiny.

Lorilei

Lorilei watched Thorbin mount his steed, and before launch some guards respectfully came and escorted her back towards the line, where she waited until Omega was off.

She was all a fluster with emotion. Thorbin had said goodbye and meant it. But the question of his love for her had been answered – it was in his kiss. She turned and strolled down the flight deck with a satisfied smile. Nothing else mattered. What he had said to her, what he had meant, what he intended. The kiss told all, and he loved her. If they never met again, at least for this one moment, there had been love. She felt like she was floating, elevated to a point that nothing could drag her down from.

Then it happened, an icy cold soda exploded as it burst apart on her face. Lorilei was stunned as the sticky liquid dripped off of her.

"You fucking bitch," she heard a woman scream at her.

She turned to see a lovely woman with brown hair a lot like her own and a second trimester belly braking through the guard line.

"That's my husband!" the woman screamed at her sidestepping a guard with amazing grace.

"What?" Lorilei said as Mika's vicious right cross connected with her eye.

Chapter Twenty-Seven
What Now?

Lorilie was sulking on the couch. Nobody was paying attention to her. They were too busy making sure Thorbin's dead wife was OK. Lorilei hadn't so much as thought ill of that evil bitch from hell, while she on the other hand had received quite the ass whopping. Several punches to the melon, many a good smack, a throttling with her own dress, and even two bites, and everyone was making sure Mika was OK! And to make things worse, the news cameras had gotten the cherry on top of the biggest story of their lives, including all the unflattering juicy pictures of Lorilei's thorough shaming.

"Young lady, you have to sit down," Ben said, still a little in shock at meeting Thorbin's dearly deceased.

She accepted his help and sat on the couch opposite Lorilei. Lili and Kryst had fled to their room when the Mika came in and she screamed something about, "How many of you bitches are there?"

"Can I get you anything?" Sam asked her.

"Peanut butter and tuna fish and pickles, the big ones," Mika answered.

Sam blinked. "I'll see what I can do."

"Can I have a pickle?" Lorilei asked. She didn't know what a pickle was, but if the evil bitch from hell was going to get one, she wanted one too.

"I can't believe you attacked a pregnant woman!" Sam snapped at her.

"She threw a soda at me!" Lorilei defended.

"So you attacked!"

"I didn't do anything to her!"

"You kissed *my* husband!" Mika yelled.

"He kissed me."

"Don't give me that crap."

"No crap!" Lorilei insisted.

"We have peanut butter," Sam interrupted, placing a jar of some good chunky on the coffee table with a spoon. "No tuna fish, but we do have some leftover lobster." She placed a bowlful on the table.

Mika looked up at Sam and smiled.

"No pickles?" she asked, Sam shook her head no. "Oh," she said, disappointed. "I've been craving pickles ever since Earth was attacked." She greedily unscrewed the peanut butter jar and spooned the largest portion she could fit into her mouth.

"Mmm," she said, an expression of pure delight on her face. "Pemut buber." Then she reached a hand out and squeezed Sam's forearm in thanks before scowling at Lorilei. "What are you looking at?"

Lorilei resisted every urge in her body to be mean. "He thought you were dead."

"Is that so?" Mika said, pointing the spoon at Lorilei in a way that concerned her. "So since you're a slut, you decided to have at him."

"I'm not a slut. You ruined my dress."

Mika flung some peanut butter at her. "You kissed my husband."

As if in answer to a prayer, Tank entered. Surely Tank would give Lorilei a great big hug and make sure she was OK. Tank looked her and smiled. Lorilei gave him her best puppy-dog eyes.

"Tank, oh my God!" Mika said, dropping the peanut butter and shooting her arms up at him from the couch.

"Mika!" he said and rushed over to hug her. Tears quickly filled his eyes. "Mika!" he said again as if to say more but unable to get it out. Lorilei sulked further.

"You're pregnant," Tank said as soon as he could catch the breath Mika was squeezing out of him.

"Three and a half months," she said.

"Do you know if…?" he began to ask.

"Boy!" Mika shrieked and there was another hug fest. Tank finally caught sight of Lorilei dropping into the couch.

"What's wrong with you? What happened to your dress?" he asked.

"She's a slut," Mika answered. "She attacked me."

Tank laughed, noticing that Mika didn't have a scratch on her.

"Can you believe she did that?" Sam yelled from the kitchen in the middle of trying to round up some pickles.

Lorilei reformed her sad puppy-dog face, this time involuntarily. Tank stepped over the table and put his arms around her.

"Tank," Mika whined. "You're supposed to be on my side."

Tank nodded and smiled at Mika.

"Lorilei's a good girl, Mika. Everybody thought you was dead. See this face?" Tank said, holding Lorilei by the chin and aiming her puppy sadness at Mika.

"Doesn't fool me for a second."

"What do ya think it did to Thorbin?"

Mika huffed; she wasn't ready to not hate Lorilei yet.

Omega

"Thank you, Admiral," Thorbin said to the console before switching the com over to the rest of the squad.

"Omega, listen up. I just finished getting the last of the intel from Admiral Durant. DCI says they're charging the portal. It will be ready in a little over a day. After that it can open at anytime from one to three hours after it's charged. I'm uploading our new heading. DCI says it should align us with the Talc home world. Once open, I launch the weapon. After that, we're done. We head back and help clean up the mess that will be waiting for us at Mars. Any Questions?"

"I think my NI is acting up, sir."

"The NI doesn't fly for you. You still have to guide with the stick. The NI really doesn't kick in until you start to sweat."

"Sweat, sir?"

"Not literally, pilot. If we engage you'll see what I mean."

"Clear, sir."

"Anyone else?" No one spoke. "We're about to take a shot at the Talc home world and you guys got nothing to say?"

"I gotta pee," said the smart ass.

Mika's Story

Leonard had procured the largest pickle ever produced by man, per Tank's request, and Mika was happily nibbling on it as if it were Lorilei's heart and last nerve all rolled into a tasty green package. Meanwhile, Lorilei had made herself defiantly comfortable in Tank's lap. The defiance lasted as long as it took Mika to point out that Tank was just as big a slut as she was – only charming. Lorilei hadn't said much since, only resenting the fact that she was practically giving Tank a lap dance and he was still chattering on with Mika.

"So you came to the Muir with the refugees?" he asked her.

"Yeah," she said, slurping the pickle.

"I thought you were on Earth?"

"I was," she answered, taking a generous bite and crunching it loudly. "God, this is good. So anyway, the air raid sirens came on. And then the DC broadcasted, saying the Talc were invading and everyone should stay in their homes."

"So you stayed in your home?"

"You know me better than that." She put down the pickle by sticking it into the peanut butter, then reached for the bowl of lobster. "Do you remember old man Moore?"

"Sure, as batshit as they come."

"Remember how he used to talk about the end of the world?"

"Yeah."

"Well, he was prepared. I was making my way to a DC shelter when he grabbed me. Talking crazy." She impersonated the old crazy man. "Them damn aliens ain't gonna get me."

Tank laughed.

"He had an old shuttle and took me and a few other girls from the neighborhood with him."

"He always was kinda a pervert."

"That's a terrible thing to say," Mika chastised. "Look who's talking?"

"You used to say it all the time. You always closed the blinds on that side of the house every time you *felt* him looking at you."

"Well," Mika said, feeling bad. "Turns out he was just a lonely old man."

"Was?"

"Damn aliens got him," Mika clarified. "Afterwards we were picked up by pirates. Then their ship was destroyed. Me and May barely got out in time."

"May?"

"One of the pirates girlfriends, she got jealous when her man got handsy with one of the Johnson girls from down the street. We ended up becoming friends. She bailed when the Syndicate transport found us adrift on the old mining frigate. Man there was a creepy guy on board the Syndicate vessel." Mika shivered. "Dima, I'll never forget that name. Eventually they dropped us off at this wretched place called Jacob's Run."

"Been there," Tank said, following along. "How come you never tried to get in contact with us?"

"I did try. DC reported all you guys as killed in action. Is Charles still alive too?"

Tank shook his head no.

Mika's face morphed from storyteller to mourning pregnant woman.

"You know we're famous now?" Tank said, changing the subject.

"Yes, when I found out Thorbin was alive I mailed him every day at least once. I jumped on a ship that was headed to the Muir, and we had just landed when I saw him walking down the flight deck. That's when I saw this bitch," Mika said, staring down Lorilei, who wasn't looking at her. "I nearly had a heart attack, then when I got my senses back I tried to get down there, but the crowd was too thick. I could only get to her," she concluded in contempt.

"Lorilei!" Ben yelled at her as he exited his room with Sam behind him. She snapped up.

"I didn't do anything," she pleaded.

"Go put some clothes on."

"OK."

"Something to work in, Lili too if she's up to it, and be quick."

Lorilei leapt at the opportunity to get away from Mika and went to find Lili.

Sam headed to the fridge to fill her pack with work snacks when there was a knock at the door.

"What now?" Ben huffed and headed over to the door. Sam smiled as Ben answered the door with a, "What?"

"I…huh…" the poor unsuspecting person on the other side began "I was wondering if Sam was here?"

"Sam?" Sam said. "That's me. I'm Sam," she said poking her head around the corner to see who could be looking for her. It was Michael, the solider that had escorted Lorilei and her through the terrarium, only he was looking less solider-ish in a silk shirt and cream slacks that hung off of him nicely. Sam was pleased, Ben not so much.

"Hi, Michael," Sam greeted with a smile.

"What do you want with Sam?" Ben interrogated.

"Well…um…" Michael began nervously, holding a freshly picked poppy in his hand. He wasn't sure who to address.

"Michael, huh?" Ben continued.

"Who's Michael?" Mika chimed in from the couch.

"What's with the flower?" Sam asked.

"It's for you," Michael said, finding the courage to complete a sentence.

"Sam doesn't like flowers," Ben informed him.

"Oh, Mika likes flowers," Mika suggested, if Sam didn't want it.

"Why is the flower for me?" Sam asked.

"Invite him in," Mika said, twisting about her belly so she could see he who bears flowers. "I can't see him," she complained.

"I don't know," Ben said, eyeing him suspiciously.

"Come in," Sam invited, smiling at Ben.

"Well, I don't know if I should," Michael said, respecting Ben's obvious disapproval.

"I guess," Ben said, finally allowing him room to enter.

"Oh, he's cute," Mika said as Michael stepped into the room, showing Ben as much respect as he could.

"Michael is the solider that escorted us through the trees," Sam explained.

"So what?" Ben clarified, "you take her for one walk in the woods, now you think you're dating?"

"A date?" Sam said, smiling at Michael.

Tank walked by on his way to grab a beer. "You a solider?" he asked Michael as he passed.

"Yes, sir," Michael answered, a little intimidated.

"That'll do," Tank said approvingly.

"Are we going somewhere?" Sam asked.

"I made reservations on the off chance that you'd like to eat."

"I already ate."

"Oh."

"See," Ben said. "She ain't interested."

"Give 'em a break," Tank said from the fridge.

"You should take her to the trees," Lorilei interjected.

"Don't look at her," Mika commanded. "She's a slut!"

Michael couldn't help but look and then wave back when Lorilei waved hello.

"We could do that," he said, looking at Sam for approval, then Ben.

"I should go put on something nice. Wait here," Sam said then headed to her room.

"I heard about them trees," Ben accused.

"Hey, solider boy," Tank yelled at Michael from the fridge. "You want a beer?"

"No, thank you," Michael politely answered.

"What's wrong with beer?" Ben continued.

"Damn, Ben, get out the man's ass," Tank said as he was walking back from the fridge.

Ben turned and walked away, only to be replaced by Tank, who stopped and placed a heavy hand on Michael's shoulder. "Are we having an understanding right now solider?" he asked.

"Yes, sir," Michael answered.

"Have fun, break her heart and I will destroy you." Then Tank took a sip of beer as he headed back to the couches.

"Understood," Michael answered to Tank's back, starting to think he should head for the door and run. But before he could, Sam came out of her room, ready in her cutest pair of worn-out jeans and a pink tank top that she had never worn while wrenching on Victoria 'just in case'. She grabbed Michael by the arm and led him out to the hallway before he could escape.

Sam and Michael in the Trees

Sam was almost skipping as they walked down the path, for the first time in months she felt like a real girl. Michael on the other hand had his hands in his pockets lest they not break anything, resulting in his destruction. He was also pretending that he wasn't taking every opportunity to observe how nicely Sam filled out her cutest pair of worn-out jeans.

"Does he mean he would kick my ass, or actually destroy me, as in decimate…then eat me?" Michael asked.

"Um…" Sam pondered. "Decimate probably. Tank's the decimatin' type."

"Yeah, that's what I thought."

"Why, are you afraid of Tank?"

"Um… yes."

Sam laughed. "Where are you taking me?"

"Well, there are some ruins on the bow side of forest. They're…romantic," he ventured.

Sam looked over at him and smiled. "Are you trying to romance me?"

"That was my original thought," he began.

"But now Sam is dangerous," she said with a slight giggle, weaving her arm through his, despite his hands being thoroughly entrenched in his pocket. "You thought you were all dashing in your uniform, which you were, and that you could just show up with a flower all dressed up and handsome and sweep Sam off her feet then take her to some ruins and have your way with her?"

"I was going to take you to dinner first," he pointed out. "But you already ate."

"Right," Sam accepted. "But now you're asking yourself, is it worth it? I could be… decimated!" she said, bumping into him as they walked. "Am I really interested in this Sam, who is so very cute, but clearly a very tasty forbidden fruit who looks a lot better in this tank top then she thought she would," Sam said trailing off.

"Well," Michael began. "We knew Sam was cute."

"Yes, we knew this," Sam confirmed.

"But I was unaware of her tastiness."

"It's a closely guarded secret."

"So the question is, how does one approach this goddess Sam in such a way as to avoid breaking her heart, and thus avoiding decimation?"

"Many have tried," Sam said, faking thoughtfulness with a finger on her chin. "I think…" Sam said tactfully, "the only way to break Sam's heart at this point in time is to fail to romance her."

Michael laughed. "No pressure. You're a lot more forward than I expected."

"I know," Sam said, a little surprised at herself. "More than I expected too. I guess I've been through a lot, and all kidding aside, sometimes you just have to go for it I guess."

"So you're just going for it?" Michael asked.

"No. But I think you should," she said with a smile.

"Take Sam to the ruins and have my way with her?"

"No. As fun as that may be, Sam likes to take things a little slower than that."

"I figured as much, but…you know."

Sam laughed. "Sure I know, can't blame you for wanting to have your way with Sam. But that's not happening tonight. I would…um," Sam said, suddenly feeling a little shy.

"What?" he asked gently.

"Could we hold hands?"

"As you wish," Michael said with sincerity and pulled his hand out of his pocket. And so they walked amidst the redwoods and ferns hand in hand to the romantic ruins at the bow end of the forest.

Tank

The next morning, Tank lay in bed the happiest he could ever remember being. It was as if all his adolescent dreams had come true. He was sharing a room with three of the loveliest, most eager to please women he had ever met. It seemed unreal. Last night he actually participated in a bra and panty pillow fight. Which was good, it was one of the few things Tank had wanted to experience before he died. See Paris, fight aliens, and participate in a semi-naked pillow fight with sexy woman – check. It was odd that Paris was going to be the unfulfilled experience.

So there he lay, Lili nestled nude in his shoulder with a hand in his boxers. Kryst sprawled at the bottom of the bed like a mental patient that had tuckered herself out. And Lorilei all wrapped up in blankets on the couch like a burrito. He was just waiting for something to come along and mess it all up.

"I think they're growing too dependent on you," Lorilei said.

"Look who's talking?" Tank snipped back. He was growing tired of Lorilei mother-henning Lili and Kryst. It had gotten worse since Mika showed up. "Mika shows up, and you come running straight to Tank."

"I didn't come running. Mika kicked me out of our room."

"Their room."

"Whatever. I'm glad that Lili and Kryst feel comfortable around you. It just seems that they're building an existence around you."

"If the cuties want a little Tank in their lives, I ain't gonna be the one to deny them."

"A little is one thing. Worship is another."

"Hey, the worship is mutual."

"You know what I'm saying, Tank."

"Yeah, I do. Now stop saying it. Besides, you hypocrite, you started this. I'm just holding up my end of the bargain."

"If you don't watch out, they're going to fall in love with you."

Lili shifted, making a content sleepy noise.

"Well, I hope so," Tank said, reaching a hand over to caress Lili's cheek.

"No, Tank," Lorilei said, upset with him. "That's not good."

"Why the hell not? I been shitted on my whole life. I never did nothin' to no one."

Lorilei gave him a 'you're full of shit' look.

"OK," he conceded. "I never did nothin' to no one that didn't deserve it. You think I got all these scares 'cause life's been easy? They ain't nothing compared to my insides. If these two little angels want to give all their lovin' to Tank, he'll take it. He ain't gonna complain, and he ain't gonna do 'em wrong. If you so worried about your fellow Mosot, there's a whole solar system of them out there that need rescuin'. You don't have to worry about these two. If they fall in love with me, it's only right, 'cause I dun fell in love with them."

Lorilei was sure he was wrong but didn't know where to take it from there.

"Look, little cutie, Tank loves you too," he said and smiled at her.

She smiled back. Than Tank, feeling that he was resonating with Lorilei, decided to do a favor Mika had asked him for. As Tank recalled, Mika asked him to make it clear with Lorilei that anything she thought she had with Thorbin was over. Then she asked Tank to kill the little slut.

"Since we havin' a heart to heart and all," he began. "You know that Mika being alive and all really kinda ends any chance you had with Thorbin."

Lorilei began to tear up. "Yes," she answered.

Tank leaned forward and extracted Lili from his drawers then rolled her to the side. "Come on," he said. "Let's go for a walk in them there woods."

Mika

Mika had settled herself in the room that Tank had explained was Thorbin's. The settling had consisted of her going through everything in the room and throwing anything that she perceived as Lorelei's off the balcony then demanded that Leonard send someone up to change the sheets, that way Lorilei couldn't 'infect' their child with sluttiness while she slept. Then she slipped on a pair of Thorbin's boxers and one of his shirts before going to sleep.

As the redwood forest awoke, so did she. With a cup of tea she sat at the workstation and logged into her personal accounts.

"Oh look at that," she said to herself. "The mortgage is past due." Then she stood and rummaged through Thorbin's things until she found a DC cover. She put on some make-up and arranged her lovely brown hair in a fashion that looked cute with the hat on, then sat back down at the workstation, placing the make-up to the side and preparing to send Thorbin another message.

She clicked 'record' and began.

"Hey, honey," she said with a big smile. "Looks like I just missed you yesterday. I can see from my account that you haven't received any of my messages, so I won't hold that against you. I'm here with Tank and Ben sitting in our room. I kicked Lorilei out, I hope you don't mind." She paused the recording and began to cry.

She was more than hurt, but she decided before sending the message that she wasn't going to address the whole Lorilei thing with him until he returned to her. Tank, Ben, and sweet Sam had all explained that he had been faithful and Mika choose to believe that. Seeing Lorilei on the flight deck kissing her husband hurt more than she could describe, but seeing him alive mitigated the pain a lot. As a military wife she was familiar with how important it was to be supportive, and since she believed in his faithfulness, her support for him did not waver. In that spirit she didn't continue the message until she had stopped crying and reapplied her make-up.

"Sorry," she said, restarting the message. "I had to go to the bathroom," she explained so that the abrupt video shift in the middle of her message was plausible. "Carrying your boy around does that to me. Anyway, I hope you get this message soon. I love you so much, and when you get back, I'll be here waiting for you. I can't wait to be in your arms again, warm under the covers where I belong. I was thinking we should name our son 'Thorbin' after his daddy," she said in a high-pitched voice that almost brought the tears back. Collecting herself gracefully she continued. "People would call him 'TJ'."

She went on for an hour or so, affirming her love and longing for him until she finished.

Then Mika clicked send.

Somewhere on Mars

Deep in the catacombs of Mars sat a man at a desk in an unassuming room that didn't officially exist. He wore slacks and a buttoned-up shirt with a tie that had been loosened from his collar and hung down his chest from his shoulders. His sleeves were rolled up, so he could better manage the plethora of documents that besieged his workspace. To his left sat another man, also in slacks and a dress shirt, who was puffing away at a cigar.

"Jesus, White," the cigar smoker said to the other. "Our defensive capabilities have been decreased by eighty percent, and you still got a desk full of shit. Shouldn't less assets mean less paperwork?"

"Turns out losing battles creates more than winning, plus we got all kinds of Separatist intel now that we're buddies and all."

"Well, for your sake let's hope we don't lose the next battle."

The paperwork besieged man looked over to his compatriot. "How's that working out?"

"We got the device. Somehow someway. We got a squad about to be in position; if everything works out, we may just take the Talc with us to hell."

"The device is that powerful?"

"White, you should have seen the contingency scenarios," the cigar smoker said as he leaned back in the chair, placing his arm over the back. "We just better pray this thing doesn't mistake us for the enemy."

"That bad, huh?"

"Oh yeah, that bad, this thing is going to hunt the Talc down to the ends of the universe."

"No kidding?"

"For starters, it self-replicates, it can manufacture any weapon we got so long as it has the resources. If they disable an enemy vessel, they could turn it into scrap for resources, study and use its technology, or just commandeer the damn thing and use it in the war effort. Can you imagine the look on those fury bastards maws when suddenly in the middle of a battle they didn't expect to have one of their own ships starts firing on them?" The man laughed smoke then continued. "And the most amazing thing, if it meets other species at war with the Talc, it will assist them, thereby making allies out of races we haven't even met yet."

"Assist how?"

"It's been programmed to build bases, repair friendly vessels, and share technology. It's like 'The Good Samaritans' message' with a human twist."

"Blow things up?"

"Right."

Their conversation was disturbed by a knock on the door.

"Yeah?" the cigar smoking man said.

The door opened and a uniformed DC officer entered.

"Sir," he said with a salute. "There's a priority contact I think you should look at, and an agent here to see you."

"Send them in," he answered.

The man at the desk rummaged through his paperwork until he found his PJU as Liz walked in.

"Well if it isn't Agent Pink." The cigar smoking man addressed her with a laugh."

"Cute, Caesar," Liz said, eyeing him disapprovingly.

"It's not Caesar around here agent, it's Black."

Liz let out a half laugh and eyed the man at the desk, who smiled back at her.

"White," he said to her. "You have a problem with that, Pink?"

"Just give me my next assignment and shut the hell up."

Agent Black laughed.

"Right, if everything goes as planned with the secondary invasion, we're going to have a big problem with the Syndicate. You're being reassigned to watch those assholes."

"I told those idiots not to forward these to me," Agent white spoke up, frustrated. "I don't have time for this garbage."

"What?" Black inquired.

"Thorbin Monroe's wife is trying to contact him again."

"She's persistent, I'll give her that."

"Block message, mark it as not received," Agent White said casually as he responded to the communication.

"You've been blocking messages to Thorbin from his wife?" Liz said, disturbed.

"Well…yeah." Agent Black answered as if her question had an obvious answer.

"He thinks she's dead."

"We know."

"He's completely heartbroken," Liz said, accusing agent Black.

"Like I give shit about his broken heart," Black said, defending himself from the seat. "In less then twenty-four hours, the Talc are coming to take another shot at exterminating the human race. Keeping those two away from each other has been a bitch to say the least. The device is the only good shot we got, the last thing we need is for some pilot to decide it's time for family first."

"If that's what helps you sleep at night," Liz responded, not intimidated by his tone.

"Don't you have a job to do, Pink?" Black said, dismissing her.

Omega

Omega lay in wait to strike. They had reached their objective and stared blankly into the empty space. Without warning a streak of blue lightning emanated from nothing and spread outward like sporadic fingers trying to find a hold. The electric blue lightning flexed into a frame like an evil window that allowed you to look into hell. On the other side was Talc space.

They saw a dreary-looking gray world that seemed to ooze the wretched crafts that carried the enemy. Millions of them, jumping in and out of scores of similar portals unleashing misery on as many worlds and species as possible.

"Initiate launch, Omega. Be prepared to engage if necessary." Thorbin advised as he quickly began hitting switches.

He wasn't fast enough, dozens of Talc screamed through the portal and Omega began a deadly dance. Thorbin was forced to evade as three came at him spewing fire.

"Omega, I'm being engaged," Thorbin said as he banked hard. "I'm being forced away from my line of fire." Then his war bird was struck.

"Goddamn it, I'm taking fire!" he said, looking over his shoulder at his pursuers. The lead Talc ship exploded and its followers had to pull off to avoid the debris.

"I'm on your six, Captain," Wice answered. "You're clear to fire."

Thorbin rolled his bird to the starboard, preparing the device for launch. He snapped up the cap of the firing control and pressed the button with a smile. The console blinked red at him – it was the misfire indicator. The device was not launched.

"Damn," he said to himself.

Then his dash came alive with warning indicators informing him that the enemy was on him again.

"Omega, I need cover now!" he yelled into the com.

Lorilei and Tank

Tank and Lorilei made quite a spectacle walking through the terrarium trails. Tank wore charcoal gray slacks and a white dress shirt that the Separatist tailors had crafted for him. With the sleeves rolled up and the top few buttons undone he looked like the Herculean arbiter of death after a business meeting. While Lorilei, on the other hand, resisted her urge to regress into complete and total tart-dom and settled for head-turning shorts and a tank top.

"You know, little cutie," Tank said. "It may not feel like it, but you got yourself a moment of clarity. That's a good thing."

Lorilei was a little distracted. "Are you sure there aren't any bunnies?"

"For the last time!" Tank said, raising his massive paws in demonstration. "If we come across any bunnies, I'll squish the livin' shit out of them."

"OK," Lorilei said, feeling better. "You were saying?"

"You give me a hard time about the girls being dependent on me, but you dependent on Thorbin. The difference is, it was never gonna happen with you two. But now, it's done. You free."

Lorilei looked up at him. She wasn't sure if free was the word she would use to describe her situation.

"Tank I don't know what you're getting at. Thorbin is all I have. Now what am I going to do?"

"Exactly."

"What?"

"What do you want to do?"

"Be with Thorbin," she answered.

"If Thorbin didn't exist, ever, and you were still here right now, what would you want to do?"

Lorilei thought about it then answered, "Be with you." She smiled at him. Then she recognized the path they were on. "Oh, hey! Let's go this way. I know this nice place Michael showed me and Sam. No bunnies." She led him by the hand off the trail and into the woods.

As they approached the Point, Tank and Lorilei snuck up on a dozen teenage couples making out. The fact that a man as large as Tank was able to sneak up on them was a testament to how engaged they were. They had almost made it to the beach when one of the young girls noticed him and yelled out.

"Someone's dad!"

A dozen terrified teenage boys all focused on Tank and nearly died of fright.

Tank couldn't help himself; he yelled with delight, "You get yer fuckin' hands off my daughter."

All the boys instantly leapt to their feet and fled for their lives. Soon the girls were gone too. Without so much as looking Tank or Lorilei in the eye, they skittered off to find their wussy boyfriends. Tank laughed the whole time.

Soon Tank and Lorilei had their toes in the sand, and Lorilei had explained her pervious visit.

"I'm sorry," Lorilei said after a short silence. "If I made you feel bad about Kryst and Lili."

"You just tryin' to look after them."

"I want them to be safe."

"Me too," he said.

"Do you really think that there's a lot of Mosot out there?"

"Used to see it all the time," Tank said. "I bet they're even worse off now that the constable force has been disrupted."

"Who's going to take care of them?" Lorilei asked. She suddenly had a profound moment.

"No one," Tank answered.

"Well," Lorilei began to say but was interrupted by a shrieking air raid siren followed by the voice of the Muir's captain.

"All hands to battle stations! I repeat, all hands report to battle stations now!"

The forest began to go dark as the protective shell began to enclose the terrarium from the outside. Lorilei and Tank re-shoed themselves hastily and bolted back through the forest towards the Hall of the Honored Dead. They hit the path and were soon just two amongst hundreds heading off as ordered.

As Tank and Lorilei entered the room, everyone was gathered around the coffee table intently watching the large-screen video. A news reporter was blathering on.

"This is Randle Mashar reporting to you live from the site of the secondary Talc invasion."

Then the screen changed and displayed an open Talc portal, from which the enemy poured forth. The Talc ships emerged from the gate and began to immediately explode. Then the screen zoomed in on one of the exploded vessels and a small triangular object nearby.

"We have been told that the DC had previous knowledge of where the portal was going to open, and they have saturated the area thoroughly with mines."

"That's fucking right," Tank yelled out as he headed to the kitchen. "Hey, any you guys want a beer?" Everyone turned to look at him in disbelief. "What?" Tank said. "War beer."

"Sure," Sam said. And they all sat and watched as the Talc flowed through the portal to be squashed like bugs.

The DC carriers and Separatist horticulture vessels set up a blockade just outside the perimeter of the minefield and laid heavy fire into the portal. The mines, along with the debris created, were taking a heavy toll on the invasion. Any ship that managed to limp through the hell was quickly picked off by a human fighter squad or heavy-weapon fire from a larger vessel. However, they kept coming.

Chapter Twenty-Eight
Hail Mary

"No! Damn it!" Thorbin said, slamming a fist against the console. Omega was heavily engaged and three times he had incurred near misses in order to move the portal into the line of fire, and three times the launch had failed.

"Admiral Durant! This is Omega. The device won't launch I need a contingency," Thorbin yelled into the console as he banked away from his firing position for the fourth time.

As he came about he saw a war bird being set upon by the enemy. Instinctively he tracked it with his eyes and his machine responded. Then with a thought, the Talc fuselage was decimated by his canons, and it snapped in two before shattering apart. As Thorbin soared by he could see the Talc pilot's body, rigid from instantly freezing in the cold vacuum of space.

"Captain Monroe," a voice hailed from the console. "This Is DCI. Hang in there, we're working on it."

Somewhere on Mars

Agent White and Agent Black stood facing a large room in front many rows of desks filled with people the DCI classified as the best in their field. The look on Agent Black's cigar-laden face suggested that he questioned that classification. Behind them was a large projection of operation 'Hail Mary'. It displayed a readout of all the vital statistics of Omega Squad's pilots next to a dynamic schematic of their war birds, and a large map that displayed the entire scene as it unfolded.

"I thought you numbskulls said they wouldn't see us comin'!" Agent Black barked at the entire room while squarely looking one operative in the eye.

"Sir, contingency stated that there was a twenty-three percent chance the Talc would be prepared for a Hail Mary scenario."

"Is that an excuse?" Black said, taking a step towards him.

White intervened; dropping a pile of papers he had been sifting through.

"Omega is heavily engaged but sustaining, the device is negative on launch. We need answers and solutions, people."

One of the operatives from the back spoke up.

"Sir," he said, pointing to the projection as he took control of the screen. The map of the battle shrank and the schematic of Thorbin's war bird replaced it. The schematic spun around until they were looking at the bottom then zoomed in on the missile that had the device. The operative marked the screen at a specific location by the device then continued.

"The primary dock aperture has been hit by enemy fire. The optic bus has been compromised. There is no way to fix it without that fighter returning for repairs."

"OK, now for the solutions?" Black barked.

Another operative spoke up. "A firmware update wouldn't require the craft to return for repairs."

"OK, people, contingencies based on firmware, and I mean now!" White commanded.

The Battle of Mars

Back at Mars, the eternal dark sparkled with steel and blood. As the Muir approached, the Allied blockade was beginning to fail. The deluge of Talc ships had plowed a path through mines and fallen comrades alike and warriors collided. The Muir's war birds swarmed from her deck and her heavy weapons began to scream angrily at the enemy. As she came about to help strengthen the line she too was set upon.

A wounded Talc carrier limped towards her and belched waves of enemy fighters in her direction. She slowly turned her broadside towards them as her fighters went forth to protect her. The enemy carrier continued to approach. As she came about the large Talc vessel was greeted by an increasing line of fire and let free the last of its spawn before it was destroyed. Hundreds of the grayish green Talc vessels came at her – savage fighters and smaller vessels that didn't seem to be armed. Nonetheless, the Muir's warriors and guns hunted them down. From beyond the wreckage of the Talc carrier came another. It too coughed up its vermin at her. It too became the focus of her heavy fire. The small Talc ships began to overwhelm the Muir and her fighters. The Muir wasn't taking much damage, but there were too many targets. The smaller Talc vessels began to approach her, then attach themselves like leaches.

Tank

"Tank! No!" Lili insisted. "You have to stay here," she said to him as he slung Ben's shotgun around his shoulder and rummaged through their room for kill gear. She grabbed his arm and forced him to look at her. "You can't go," she pleaded.

"And let everyone else kill Talc except for me? Negative, dumpling," Tank said.

"Nega... what? Does that mean you're staying to protect us?"

"Would ya rather wait here for the Talc, or would you rather I go kill them before they get here?"

Lili didn't answer, she didn't really want to see any Talc, but she didn't want Tank to go anywhere. She looked away and he continued to rummage.

Sam sat in the living room nervously eating a peanut butter and jelly sandwich and watching the live news feed of the battle unfolding around her.

This is it, she thought. *We're all going to die.* Then she took a healthy bite of her sandwich.

"Man, this is a good sandwich," she said to herself.

Tank burst out of his bedroom with Lili close behind. He was horribly be-weaponed and half-dressed.

"Ben," he yelled out.

"Yeah?" Ben answered.

"I'm off to kill Talc, you got things under control round here."

"Sure."

"Lorilei," Tank continued. "You take care of the girls while I'm gone."

"OK," Lorilei answered.

"Tank," Mika protested in a whine. Before she could formulate a full argument he turned towards her and one of his biceps twitched oddly as if it were hungry.

"Don't worry," he consoled. "You just stay here and try not to overdo it."

"All right," she conceded. "But take Lorilei with you," she said with a smile.

Omega

Thorbin couldn't believe he was still alive. The Talc had definitely seen them coming. There were so many enemy ships he could hardly see his squad mates. There was so much debris from downed Talc fighters that they presented a danger equal to that of the ones that hadn't yet been downed.

"Captain, we're uploading a firmware update to you as we speak."

"What's the problem?"

"The missile dock is FUBAR."

"What's the solution?"

"The firmware will allow you to detonate the device without launching it. If you're close enough to the portal, some of the payload may make it through despite not being launched."

"Won't that tear my bird apart?"

"Yes, but you can delay the charge, set a course, then eject."

"Clear," Thorbin acknowledged.

Tank

Tank exited the elevator and entered the rotunda, where he found himself at an artery of the Muir's defensive line. Wounded marines lay splayed about as medics prioritized their injuries then treated them as best they could. Freshly wounded soldiers poured in from the terrarium as reserve units rushed into it. Tank watched as an officer barked orders like a traffic cop. He approached the man as he instructed a fresh squad as to the location of enemy.

"They made it to the terrarium; our job is to push them back out. Double time it to the first trail head and a Separatist officer will instruct you where to go from there."

"Right," Tank said. The officer and the squad looked at him. "Should I go with these guys then?"

The men didn't say a word. Tank looked liked death chilled over, a monstrous mesh of graying old man. To each one of them the answer seemed obvious.

You are in no condition to fight, they thought. However, Tank still looked formidable enough that none of them wanted to be the man to tell him no. So there they remained in thought until from the flank a melodic voice could be heard.

"It would be our honor."

Tank turned to see Sariel in full kill gear, along with a squad just like him. Tank smiled.

The Battle of Mars

Outside the Muir, things weren't going well. The Talc deluge was persistent. All the mines had successfully found a target, but still the Talc came. Three Separatist horticulture vessels had been destroyed along with the few remaining DC carriers except for one. The line had been breached and broken in two. Humanity's last line was being outflanked and outnumbered. There was only one gleaming sign of hope. The enemy portal had closed. At least there would be no more.

It was a small hope. The human fighter pilots had lost half of their comrades. The DC carrier was the only ship that hadn't been boarded, and they fell back to her. She looked like the eye of the storm, the place of calm in the space around Mars. Her heavy weapons could not be avoided. So it was decided; all large vessels were directed to stay out of her line of fire. Slowly she moved towards distressed Separatists vessels. Where her heavy weapons cut a swath through the enemy large enough for the combined strength of the remaining fighters to sneak in and escort the distressed vessel within range, where it would be safer.

One by one the fighters escorted the remaining Separatist behemoths into the sphere until all were there. The wagons were circled and the enemy surrounded.

Tank

"YEEEE! Motherfuck'in' haw!" Tank bellowed with glee as he dove into an unsuspecting puddle of Talc. He had long since run out of ammunition and settled for a cruder but nonetheless effective means of offing the fury little bastards.

After stomping one into the ground as he landed, he grabbed another and used him to beat his comrades to death. All the while the clatter of the mercenaries ensured that the wretched little monsters never got the upper hand.

The mercs were in awe of Tank's brutality. He wielded lifeless Talc bodies like they were meant for beating each other. Fighting tooth and claw, Tank forged a path through the battlefield leaving behind a trail of broken Talc like bread crumbs to be followed back home when the fighting was done. The tide was turning for the Muir, and the Talc seemed frustrated by their inability to down this one redneck.

News quickly spread that the Muir had entered the defensive sphere and no more Talc landing craft could assault her. Reinforcements from other ships were arriving to clean out the remaining Talc on board. But it didn't seem as if that would be necessary, most of the remaining Talc on board were in the terrarium, and they had given up on taking control of the Muir. They seemed only to care about one thing – killing Tank.

They swarmed on him from every direction until he was waist-deep in a sea of the enemy. He didn't even have to aim his strikes; every blow was guaranteed to send several Talc to their makers. All the while the mercenaries stood at the perimeter of the growing Talc advance picking off as many of them as they could. Soon, Separatist solders and DC marines joined in until they formed one large circle around the remaining Talc, at the center of which was a monster of a man still hanging in there with a great big shit-eating grin on his face.

Tank fought with joy, he knew this was it, the last hurrah. He wasn't going to die a convalescent in some hospital bed. He felt every vicious cut the Talc were able to get in, but it didn't hurt, it felt like penance and vindication. Blood and venom coursed through his veins like fuel. His heart burned and his body demanded that he let it die, but there were still Talc to be squashed.

The circle of enemy grew smaller and smaller as the human warriors fought towards the center where at last stood Tank, alone with a single Talc. He held it up by the neck as it growled, angry and hopeless, the giant squeezed the life out of it, then let if fall atop its kin.

The Earth warriors circled the mighty Tank and stood silently in awe. They wanted to ask if he was OK, but it was clear that he was not. Sariel approached, lowered his mask and their eyes met. And there, beneath the redwood canopy, Tank spoke his last words that day.

"Hell yeah," he said before collapsing to the ground.

Thorbin

Thorbin pulled out of a sharp bank, the debris from the Talc he had just destroyed smashed into the hull of his bird. He closed his eyes and held his breath, praying that it wouldn't tear him apart. His prayer was answered. Omega had been fighting valiantly, and there weren't as many Talc as there used to be. Not a single Omega pilot had been shot down.

"On my six!" a distressed pilot called out from the com then blazed past Thorbin's field of view with two Talc trailing after him.

"Hang tight, pilot," Thorbin commanded as he turned about to assist. "I got them."

"No!" Lieutenant Wice yelled over the com. "The portal is closing. Launch the device."

Thorbin turned and brought the portal into view. It was closing and fast. He gave his bird full throttle as he set the device to detonate.

Then he reached forward and hit the eject button. The bird immediately began to slow down.

"What the hell?" Thorbin said. He looked at the portal closing fast and knew at this speed the bird would never make it.

He throttled back up and the onboard computer responded, "Ejection aborted."

The Battle of Mars

Back at Mars, the defense sphere appeared to be working nicely. Separatist horticulture vessels orbited the remaining DC carrier and held the enemy at bay. The Talc had pulled back and were regrouping, giving the human warriors an opportunity to jump from carrier to carrier in order to clean out the remaining enemy that had boarded. For a moment all was calm. No shots were being fired. The human fleet was collecting itself, and the Talc were pacing back and forth just out of range.

Both sides were sizing what remained of each other up. The Talc still outnumbered the humans grossly. Their numbers, however, had been severely decreased. If the human vessels were at a hundred percent, they could defend against the Talc easily. The human vessels, however, were not at a hundred percent. While still floating there wasn't a single large vessel that was whole, and more than half of the fighters had been lost. At the same time, the remaining Talc vessels weren't doing all that great either. The two fleets looked like tired old dogs squaring off for a decisive final strike – waiting for the other to show greater weakness.

The DC carrier broke from the sphere and led the final charge.

Thorbin

Thorbin sat comfortably as his war bird screamed towards the closing portal. He was either going to make it or he wasn't, and he was fine with that. The device was going to score. That was all that mattered. The sense of purpose that had eluded him set itself securely in his heart. He rested one hand on the throttle while the other held his PJU. He had pulled up a picture of Mika, lying in bed under the covers the morning after their wedding night.

"Here I come," he said to her.

Omega watched as their wing commander tore towards the portal. Each second that passed he flew closer, and it shrunk smaller until it looked like a brilliant blue horizon. So brilliant, they couldn't see him. Then it flashed away, and Thorbin was gone.

Epilogue

Humanity

Humanity was not lost that day. After the Battle of Mars humanity was devastated, but not lost. The Separatist society opened up completely to invite those who had lost their homes until a new world was discovered far away. While the old world was dead, without an atmosphere, a few brave souls stayed to look after her, while humanity was introduced to a large young planet, fertile and welcoming. Three large continents and vast oceans void of life. Swords were beaten into plowshares, and you can be sure the Talc never visited. The people spent their days planting forests and seeding oceans. Humanity Took pleasure as Earth species made a home on a planet that seemed to enjoy the company. You might say that many people lived happily ever after.

Thorbin

What happened to Thorbin remains a mystery. As the decades passed, conjecture turned to legend and his legacy was an example of courage. The example. The spirit of Thorbin's courage was bandied often by politicos and honored by fighting men, and often times was heard in the quiet utterances of those hoping to channel their own boldness.

The legend had a way of growing as humanity spread forth and multiplied. In generations to come humanity's reach discovered other civilizations that had been touched by the Talc, and they heard tales of a lone alien warrior and his army of robots that had liberated star systems.

Tank

Tank was pronounced dead three separate times before he stabilized. As soon as he could walk, he snuck out of the hospital and met up with the rest of Victoria's people. He stayed with Ben and the others and worked for a while, performing as a second in command for Ben. The immense wealth he had amassed quickly dwindled. He gave most of it away to the orphaned children, or to wounded warriors; he only kept what he needed. With that, he set Mika and her son up for life and bought himself a little place to share with Kryst. Lili was welcome but she couldn't bring herself to leave Victoria. The little place was a bed and breakfast, and in true Tank fashion its location was telling. A nice little place he called the Stardust Café, nestled in the last few kilometers of space in the old solar system – last stop before the portal to the new world.

From time to time familiar faces would stop by. Liz would often stop and stay for a while as she passed on from one assignment to the next. Ben and Sam would visit during vacations. It became a popular haunt and the connection between the old system and new. The DC declared it the gateway to the neutral zone – a buffer of space patrolled by DC pilots to ensure that pirates didn't interfere with portal operations. Lastly he bought something nice for Lorilei.

Sam

Sam and Michael became quite the item, adventuring with Ben and the rest of Victoria's people, until they decided to settle down. Sam got a job with the Defense Core as a lead integration engineer. She helped merge the Separatist technology with the rest of humanity's. In recognition for her part in the Battle of Mars, she was granted a large plot of land on the new world where she built a small house and shared it with Michael, and Spot, who found the rocks on the new world to be particularly tasty.

Lorilei

After the Battle of Mars Lorilei made two personal commitments. She would never cease to cherish the memory of Thorbin and what he gave her, and she would personally see to it that every Mosot in the old system was rescued. The first was easy; cherishing the memory of Thorbin was more like a sweet reward. The second was more of a challenge. She spent a few years on Victoria sorting out what seemed an insurmountable task until one day Tank gave her a gift – a pretty little boat she named Cleopatra.

Ben and Vicky

The Separatist well-wishers managed to put Victoria back together again. Which was fortuitous, she was humanity's only remaining tugboat, which meant that Ben had more than enough work to curse at for the rest of his life. So much in fact that his business grew to become a large fleet. An economic staple for the new economy, Victoria Inc. After a year of success Ben was able to take Vicky off the job and fix her proper. A new lower deck, the finest gear, and a candy apple paint job with chrome trim, and captains paid doubled to be towed by her. After decades as Victoria Inc's CEO, Ben eventually turned over operations to his first mate, Lili, who thrived as the first Mosot to run a human corporation of that magnitude, while Ben and Vicky retired happily on the new world. Ben didn't build a house on a plot of land, he simply docked Victoria in a grove of young trees on Sam and Michael's property, near a pond, and continued to live in her.

After Ben's long and happy life, Victoria, the little tug that could was put to work for the Defense Core. She became a classroom where test pilots were taught philosophy – ideas like the nature of change and adaptability, and irony.